HILLS OF HEATHER AND BONE

K.E. ANDREWS

Hills of Heather & Bone

COPYRIGHT

K.E.Andrews has asserted her right to be identified as the author of this work in accordance with the copyright.

Editors:

Copyeditor: Maddy D. https://www.fiverr.com/maddy216?source=order_page_summary_seller_link

Proofreader: Maddy D.

Map Design: Sheridan Falkenberry @ancientmariner115

Cover Art: Jade Mae Yee https://www.artstation.com/jademaeyee/profile

Cover Design: K.E. Andrews

Created with Vellum

Created with Vellum

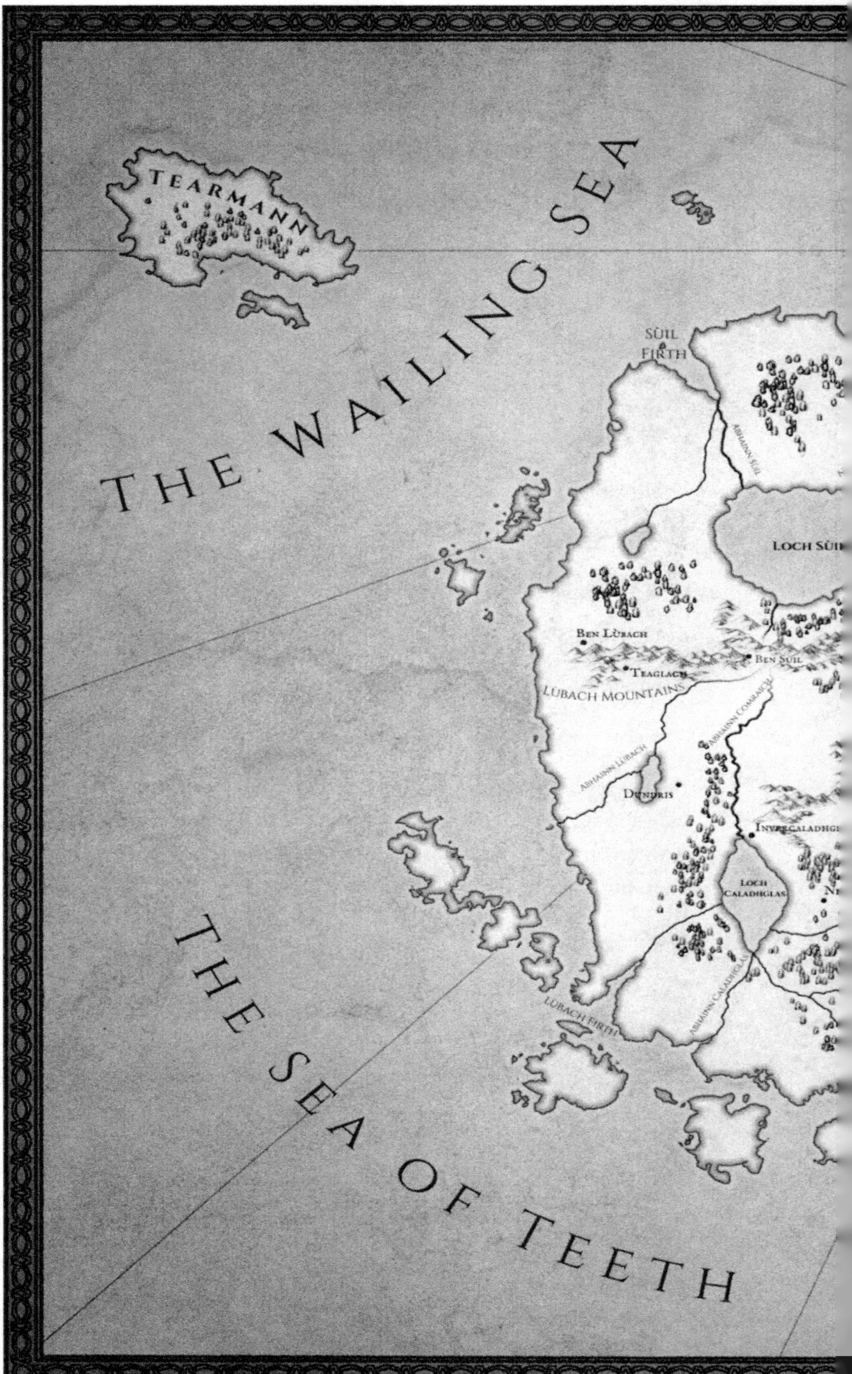

TEARMANN
THE WAILING SEA
SÙIL FIRTH
ABHAINN SÙIL
BEN LÙBACH
TEAGLACH
BEN SÙIL
LÙBACH MOUNTAINS
ABHAINN LÙBACH
DUNDRIS
LOCH CALADHGLAS
ABHAINN CALADHGLAS
LÙBACH FIRTH
THE SEA OF TEETH

Camgallan
Donnalaich Mountains
Cluaran Mountains
Inverauchendrain
Dunathol
Lòchran
Loch Auchendrain
Auchendrain Firth
Auchendrain
Auchendrain Mountains
Cruithneachd
Abhainn Airgead
Sea of Auchendrain
Tir Dhè

Please be aware that this book contains some scenes of violence, death, depression, mentions of miscarriage, birthing scenes, suicidal thoughts, suicide, and cannibalism.

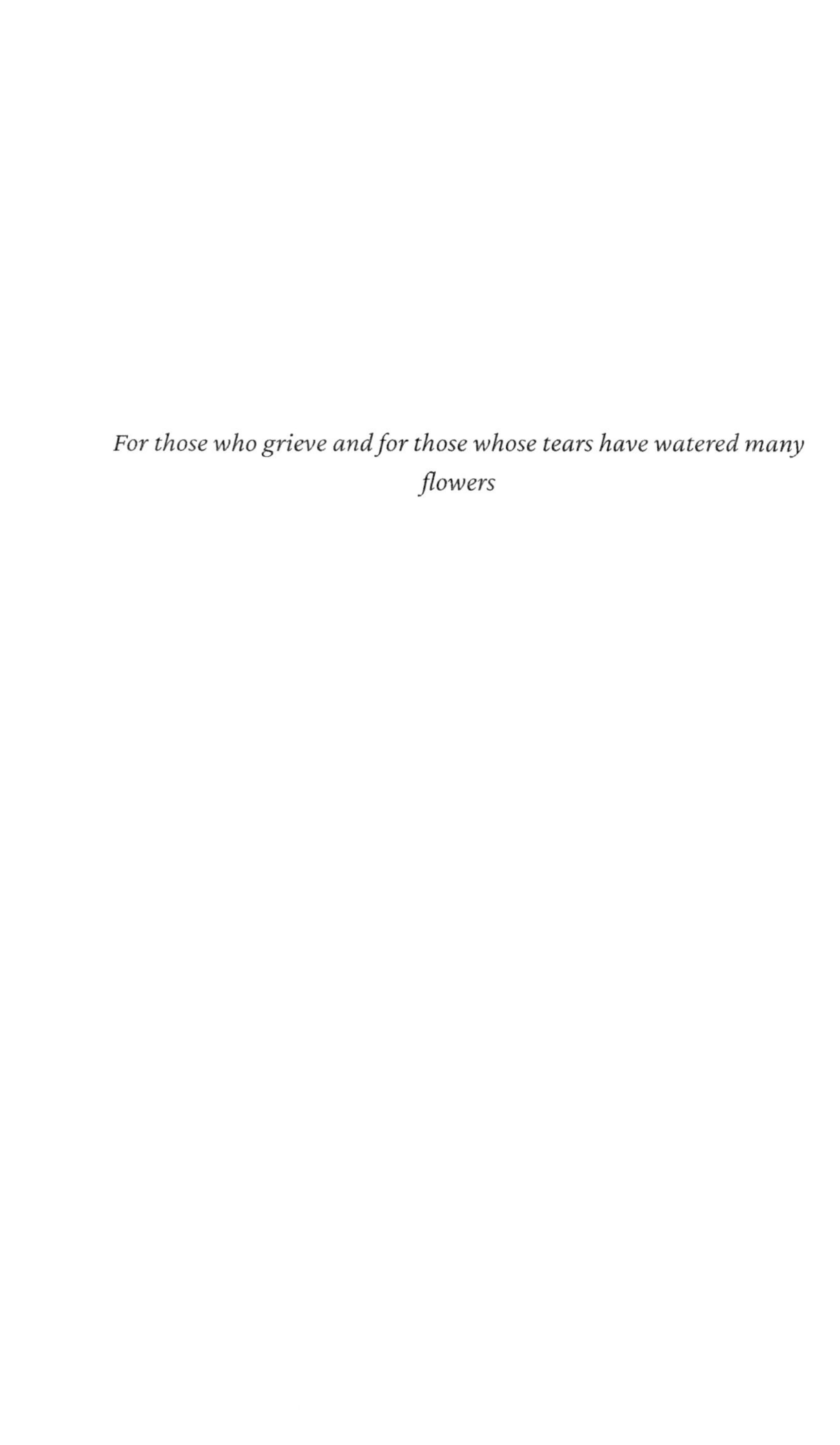

For those who grieve and for those whose tears have watered many flowers

I
Daffodil

Narcissus

New beginnings · Rebirth · Resilience

Death hums beneath the dirt as I tear up a web of ground-ivy from the bed of lettuce. Purple blooms are set like gems against green leaves. Its roots are tangled around a mouse skull. I run my dirty fingers across the yellowed eye sockets. Flashes of scurrying through plants and sunlight trickle out before the fearful image of shadowy wings and pain end the wafer-thin memories. The squeaking, wordless voice of the mouse calls to the power in my blood, tugging at me to collect its bones scattered around the garden and make it whole again.

A peck jabs my left hand by my wedding ring and I wince. The sunlight comes back into focus through the trees as I blink. Morhenna growls, canting her red-combed head to give me a beady stare. I'm not pulling the weeds fast enough for her liking. The old gods would find the black and white speckled chicken an imposing contender to their pantheon. She thinks she walks with the gods, far above us mortals. None of the chickens back home were this spiteful. I thought she would have softened toward me when I saved her from that fox last year, but no. It somehow made her hate me even more.

I pull my hand away, tracing the primroses carved along the smooth heatherwood band. Untangling the roots from the mouse's skull, I slip it into the pocket of my long blue skirt and gather the rest of the weeds. Percy's voice echoes through my head with the names of different plants as I sort them in the basket. Dandelions for salads and tea. Lambsquarter for pain. Chickweeds go well with dandelions. I chew on some lambsquarter, hoping it'll help my knees.

Over the years, Percy's taught me about every seed, sapling, and flower we've encountered since we got married —he even made a book with pictures to help me identify them. He gets this look in his eye that spills past the lenses of his glasses when he touches a leaf or coaxes seedlings to life. As a rootsower, he hears their songs in ways I can't understand, just as he can't understand the voices of bones.

A raven caws from the woods beyond the garden wall. Thin claws dig into my shoulder through my tunic, and a wing brushes my ear. Siobhen, my shadow. The chicken purrs and tugs at a lock of black hair that's escaped from my hair ribbon. I think she prefers me over Percy because when I stand, it's the closest she gets to touching the sky—and is out of Morhenna's reach.

My right knee creaks when I rise from my crouch, the ache moving up my stiff calves. It's only a matter of time before my hands start hurting, too.

"A storm's coming soon," I whisper to the chicken. Percy tells me I sound old when I say that instead of like a thirty-year-old woman.

Siobhen grips my shoulder as I go down the rows of the garden. The basket around my arm is laden with greens, potatoes, carrots, and herbs. The other two chickens, Fergus and Fiona, dart between the tomatoes and the rhubarb. Fergus ruffles his trailing tail feathers before stalking after a sídhe with four pearlescent wings. The sídhe's small, lizard-like body ribbons through the air, tail scales shimmering. Morhenna pecks at the ivy flowers, but I still feel her gaze on me as I head toward the house.

Among the chaos of vegetation, there's an order to the garden's layout—medicinal plants closest to the house. The middle plot is used for growing food. Herbs thrive near the chicken coop. My favorite is the area filled with an assortment of plants near the garden gate—the Random Plot—where Percy grows different plants he's cross-pollinated and seeds he's altered.

I take in the house with its sagging roof and squat chimney, nestled in this garden paradise, and hold the contentment tightly. Flowering vines hug the stone walls encircling our garden. Bees drift between the crimson poppies and the flame flowers. A green butterfly lands on the axe by the stump where I chop wood. I can imagine growing old here, living without fear or always looking over my shoulder.

The curtain in the open bedroom window ripples in the breeze, and a mop of brown hair bobs above the windowsill. Percy hunches over the writing desk inside, his eyeglasses teetering on the edge of his nose. His forehead's a wrinkled canvas as he tries to squeeze out some thought he can't piece together. A streak of dried ink darkens his earlobe where he's been tugging at it.

I set the basket on the sill, my frame taking up almost the whole window. Siobhen repositions herself on my shoulder. I make sure not to knock off the walnut shell halves that had been filled with syrup this morning for the sídhe. My parents said the sídhe bring good luck and might clean your house if you give them gifts, but I've never seen them clean anything. Usually, I find bits of food missing or a nest they've made in the ceiling beams of the healing room because they like the flowers, but it's best not to anger them. A swarm of angry sídhe is an unlucky thing to encounter without a bit of iron to protect you.

"Stuck?" I ask Percy. My gaze darts over the sketches of limbs and organs with his looping handwriting beside them scattered around him.

Percy looks up, blinking away whatever swirls behind his brown eyes. His smile is a crooked crescent. "With Siobhen on your shoulder, you look like one of Arianrhod's messengers," he says and pushes back the sleeves of his cream-colored shirt.

"The Goddess of Death's messengers use ravens instead of chickens as their Eyes," I tell him.

"Who's to say they didn't have other birds when ravens were in short supply?" Percy rests his head in his hand. The metal knotwork pendant of a tree with roots threaded around a hand—the symbols of the gods Beathag and Kester—lays against his chest from a woven cord. "Did you stop your work so that you could stare at me?"

I hold up a dandelion. "Gathered some carrots and potatoes for a pie tonight and pulled weeds. I thought I'd see what you were doing and if you needed anything."

Percy takes the flower and sticks it behind his ear. The yellow petals unfurl more as soft green light pulses from his fingertips. "One might think you have feelings for me, Morana."

I tap his nose, leaving a smear of dirt behind. "I should hope so since we *are* married."

The corners of his eyes crinkle as his grin broadens. "Glad to know that after ten years you haven't grown bored of me. Maybe this will help me get unstuck."

He stretches across the desk to kiss me. Warmth blooms in my chest. We live where our hearts beat, and this is where mine rests—in this walled garden with this man who can stir my soul with a smile.

His fingers brush my jaw before he glances back at his work. "Thought that would work, but it was worth it regardless," he says, pushing up his glasses. "I finished treating my patients for the day and wanted to work on this. These diagrams are from an ancient proposal for regrowing limbs and have me stumped. Very few fleshmenders have the skill to attempt such a thing."

"Are you thinking it's still possible to attempt?" I ask. He's been thinking about this problem for years. I've often woken up to the crinkle of papers left on the bed and him mumbling about bones and muscles in his sleep.

"Knitting different layers of flesh together while rebuilding the delicate parts is the challenge. Fleshmenders can repair organs and sections of flesh, but recreating a whole organ or limb is more complicated and requires much more energy from the patient and the bloodgifted. If done incorrectly, it could harm the patient or create dead limbs," he says, running a finger along the metacarpal bones of a sketched hand. "Still, I think it's possible to determine the correct method of flesh restoration. But there's the matter of experimenting..."

I nod, grasping part of what he says. Bloodgifted can peer

into the fabric of the world and grasp the chaotic threads to bring order to the elements. Percy strives to understand that order, even after he left the Acadamaidh. Even here on the fringes of Errigal, he's always learning something new to improve his fleshmending abilities. As easily as he can make a withered plant healthy again, he can stitch skin back together and ease any pain. He's a rarity, a doublegifted.

While bloodgifted like rootsowers and fleshmenders can create order and bring about life, I wonder what purpose boneweavers serve by moving the dead. People call my magic an affront against life and that it's dangerous. If that's the case, why does it feel soothing when I use it?

A sharp jab at my shin makes me turn to find Morhenna tugging at my skirt, growling. She has a soft spot for Percy and sees me as competition. I'm sure if she could smite me, she would. Morhenna hisses and tries to jump onto the windowsill from the stump. Startled, Siobhen darts through the open window onto the desk in a swirl of speckled feathers and fearful trills, her wing smacking my face.

Percy catches her before she knocks over the ink bottle. "Morhenna is in fine form today," he says, cradling Siobhen. Gray and black feathers drift across the desk and scattered papers.

Morhenna's claws dig into my hand as I shoo her away. "That's one way of putting it. I think Cadhal knew her true nature when she gave her to us. A fine way to repay you for healing her broken leg," I tell him.

Percy hands Siobhen back to me through the window. The chicken stares in the direction of Morhenna's squawks. "She's a good egg layer. Nothing will compare to Grizel, though. I still miss that goat."

Tucking the chicken under my arm and grabbing the basket, I head for the well. Morhenna remains by the window. Percy speaks to her, and she puffs up her feathers. I swear her comb gets redder, as if she's blushing.

I set Siobhen down and pull up a bucket of cold water. Grabbing the soap bar on the stump beside it, I scrub the dirt from my hands. The smell of lavender and honey hits my nose as I wash the suds away. The scratches along my arm crisscross older, pale scars. I draw another bucket of water and start to clean the vegetables.

A door slams in the house. "Healer Bracken! We need you!" someone shouts from inside.

I look up from cleaning the potatoes. That sounds like Athol, the farmer who lives near the rapeseed fields. Percy's the only healer here in Àitesìol, so he sees anyone who comes to our door, no matter the time.

A prickle runs along my neck, like someone is standing too close. The sensation tugs at me, tasting like damp ash, like the mouse skull in my pocket. The faint pulse of death—of something dying.

Leaving the vegetables and my basket, I dry my hands on my handkerchief before heading into the house. No doubt Percy's already gone to see who it is. I grab my dark robe from the hook in the kitchen and throw them on. I gather bowls and fresh water from the kitchen that Percy will need. The prickle of death comes from the next room, and I resist the urge to touch the skull as I head for the healing room.

II
Azalea

Rhododendron

Fragility ❧ Temperance ❧ Death

The smell of burning sage permeates the healing room as I cross the threshold, my blood thrumming. Percy's already dressed in the red robe he wears when he works. The prickling gets stronger as the presence of death seeps from the large, limp figure Athol and his young daughter, Lileas, struggle to carry between them. Aodh, Athol's twenty-three-year-old son.

"Aodh collapsed in the field," Athol gasps. The older man's red hair is damp against his sweaty forehead. "Dinnae ken how long he was there, but he's not wakin' up."

"Lay him on the table," Percy tells them.

Grabbing Aodh's legs from Lileas, Percy and Athol lay him on the large table. Aodh moans, a hollowness pressing on his pale face. Lileas flinches as the body thumps against the dark wood. The smell of sweat and wet earth breaks through the sage, and I shut the door.

"Was Aodh ill before he went to work?" Percy asks, one hand going to Aodh's neck to check his pulse, his other pushing back his eyelids.

Athol hovers near the table, worry bending his whole

frame. He isn't a tall man, but now he looks much smaller. Lileas squeezes his hand, her other clenching the front of her brown skirt.

"He was complain' about stomach pains for a few days and threw up last night, but I thought it was 'cause he was out drinkin'," Athol says. "He seemed fine when he left. Lileas found him when he didnae come up fae the field."

Percy nods. I lay everything on the table by the wall and approach them. "Please hold his head still and tilt his chin back," he says to me while removing Aodh's tunic.

Aodh's clammy skin burns beneath my fingers, his breaths rattling. The yellow light of Percy's magic flickers beneath his fingers while his palms hover over Aodh's broad chest, moving up his neck. Aodh twists with a guttural cry when Percy touches his right side. Athol's face is drawn as Lileas presses closer to him.

"His appendix has burst. He's septic, but I'll do what I can to remove it," Percy tells Athol and Lileas. "His lungs are struggling to take in air."

Percy glances back at me, and I recognize the tension along his brow. I keep the worry from my face as I nod, confirming what he already knows. Death creeps over Aodh like a shroud, his pulse fast and fluttering beneath the skin that's growing colder. An ashen taste hits the back of my tongue. It's moments like these where fleshmenders and boneweavers can sense the same thing—death's approach. While I'm drawn to it, Percy will try to keep it at bay.

Percy slips his wedding ring into his pocket and grabs a bowl of water, a knife, rags, and jars of dried herbs on the shelves. He breaks off leaves from the different plants growing on the walls. He mixes ingredients in a bowl, grinding them up before uncorking one of the vials and pouring the dark liquid into the mixture. There's a spark of green that drifts through the herbs and plants as he infuses a bit of magic to make the draught more potent.

I lift Aodh's head and ignore the ache burning through my knees. Aodh's chest rises to try and grasp what breath he can. Athol is praying to Beathag and Arianrhod as he braces against Lileas. While I've seen death up close my whole life, known its bite and soothing ebb against me, watching someone see their loved one fading never gets easier. I whisper my own prayer to Arianrhod to stay her hand even though my power is hungry for the stories in the bones.

"Aodh, if you can hear me, you need to swallow this," Percy says.

He tilts the contents of the bowl into Aodh's mouth. Some liquid dribbles past the man's lips as he sputters and struggles to swallow. Aodh groans and tries to push him away, but his arms drop back down to his sides like they've been cut. It'd be easier for Percy to use his bloodgift to sedate Aodh, but that'd be one more thing for him to concentrate on.

"Hold him down and keep him as still as possible until the sedative takes hold," Percy tells Athol and me, gesturing for me to stand across from him.

A gray sheen seeps across Aodh's tan skin, and the tug grows stronger. Aodh's quick pulse thrums up my fingers as they rest against his stubbly jaw, intertwining with my heartbeat. Each strained breath clenches at my lungs. His pulse is mine, and I'll share his breath until it ceases or if he continues to remain here with the living.

"How close is he?" Percy whispers to me.

"Close. There's something else, isn't there?" I mumble, wrestling with my bloodgift to keep it from spilling out.

"It's his lungs. There's a bit of fluid and several cysts that are causing pockets of air, which is making it difficult for him to breathe. Those have been there longer, and I can't deal with those until I remove the infection and get him stable. I can only help him breathe while I stop the toxins from killing his tissues and organs."

Athol holds his son down, stroking his brown hair. Aodh groans, and Percy grabs a knife and wipes the younger man's skin with sharp-smelling alcohol. Percy presses a glowing yellow palm against Aodh's side to dull the nerves before he makes a cut.

"Talk to him, Athol, and focus on his face. It'll help keep him calm," Percy tells the father. I suspect he says this to keep Athol calm as well and not looking at the incision he's about to make.

"Hear that, Aodh? Healer Bracken's goin' to make you well again," Athol murmurs and blinks away the sheen of tears in his eyes. "Just hold on a wee bit longer."

Percy cuts Aodh's right side near his hip, and blood seeps onto the table. Yellow ribbons snake from Percy's finger under Aodh's skin, illuminating his veins. The glowing lines Percy grasps remind me of plant roots connecting him to Aodh. Pus and dark globs seep from the wound as Percy draws them out and separates them from Aodh's blood. Beads of sweat catch in the creases of Percy's forehead, fingers straining as he pulls out the infection into the bowl. Fluid follows, and the water turns pink.

"What are you doing?" Lileas asks, her voice cracking behind me.

My eyes dart to her as she sits by the window with carved animal figurines in the windowsill that I made years ago for the younger patients. She watches with an intensity I haven't seen in a child before. Part of me breaks with her, and old buried pain is drawn to the surface.

"I'm trying to draw the infection from his blood before I cut out the source," Percy tells her.

Aodh's breathing grows stronger, and color returns to his lips. My breaths even out as our pulses unravel from each other one strand at a time. While my heart is relieved, my blood longs for the whisper of death to return. It leaves behind a hollow ache I can never get rid of. I keep my hands on Aodh's arms, his skin growing warmer. Percy has to keep a hold on the man's breathing and circulation while healing different areas. I don't know how he can keep track of everything all at once.

Body tensing, Aodh's chest heaves, and a cough spews bloody globs of phlegm onto his father's face. Red splatters Aodh's chest. The quick breaths become ragged as he grows paler. He's sinking, the thread connecting him here slipping away. Whispers seep from Aodh's bones, and my bloodgift is eager to uncover the secrets in the marrow. I bite down harder on the inside of my cheek, trying to keep Aodh's body from jerking around. Percy's face tightens.

"What's happenin'?!" Athol cries, wiping his face and staring at his son's crimson mouth.

Percy releases the infection into the bowl and places his hand on Aodh's chest. "Holes have opened in his lungs. He can't breathe." His words are hurried but steady, and he places his hand on Aodh's chest. "Athol, step back, please."

The farmer backs away to where Lileas sits. The light from

Percy's hands grows brighter, glowing cracks moving across his exposed skin. A golden handprint spreads across Aodh's chest, and I see the faint outline of his ribcage. I try and catch Percy's gaze, but he's too focused. He's a skilled healer, but fleshmending also requires the energy of the bloodgifted and the patient's to speed up the body's natural healing process. I've seen him push himself to exhaustion before, and the more magic he uses, the more it will take from him.

I sense a shift before another wet cough splatters the air. He slumps against the table, and the thread between us snaps. Percy's gift swirls around the man's heart to keep it beating and heal his lungs so he can breathe. Death crashes into me with cold waves. Aodh's memories curl around my fingertips as they call to me from his bones. Sadness and loss come as Aodh's body realizes it's been separated from his spirit. It's a keening wail in my ears, grasping at me to anchor itself.

Fresh deaths are always the strongest—the loudest, the most painful. Memories are more vivid in their final moments. The body remembers what the soul leaves behind. Being this close to someone dead makes my blood rush faster as the pent-up power builds beneath my skin. I long to reach out and bring some semblance of life back to Aodh's body, but I can't bring his soul back.

"Percy..." I say as he continues his compressions.

The glow fades from Percy's palm, and he steps back. A heavy exhale takes the tension from his shoulders, and they slump. Percy's bloodgift flickers out, and his face is drawn, the bulk of his emotions gathering in his eyes. I come around the table and place a steadying hand on his back.

Lileas sits like a statue, her eyes round like a deer's.

"Aodh? Aodh, wake up," Athol says, shaking Aodh's shoulder as he holds the limp hand. He wipes a smear of blood from his son's face. "Please, son...Open your eyes."

Percy looks at Athol. "I'm so sorry, Athol." His voice is a quivering leaf moments away from breaking off a branch.

Lileas takes her father's arm, lips wobbling. "He's gone, Da," she whispers.

Athol crumples, head resting next to his son's face as sobs shake his body. Percy turns away and cleans the blood from his hands with a damp rag. I look at Lileas, who is holding back tears, and wish there were words of comfort I could give her. But everything would sound hollow against the sorrow settling in her heart. When someone's born, people offer gifts and excitement. In death, there is silence and empty words. Sometimes it's better to say nothing at all than to say something trite.

Athol lifts his head, tears staining his ruddy cheeks. "What happened? He was fine. Then he was coughin' up blood," he says in a ragged voice.

Percy clears his throat, pushing up his glasses. "Cysts in his lungs burst. It felt like they had been there long before the infection happened. The stress and the infection most likely caused them to rupture and made holes in his lungs. His weakened state couldn't handle the additional strain. If I can examine him further, I could give you a clearer cause of death tomorrow."

Athol doesn't look away from his son. A heavy silence fills the healing room, the sunlight coming through the window unable to warm the somber air. Lileas' eyes shimmer. I want to go to her and embrace her, but I'm afraid if I move, she'll dissolve into sobs. Witnessing the grief of others feels like I'm intruding on something I shouldn't. I try to focus on something else while Aodh's death fills my head with flashes of his final moments, holding a baby, and a smiling woman with brown hair. The images tickle the back of my throat, trying to coax something out of my chest I don't want to unbury.

"Lileas, go get Caitrìona and the bairns. They need to know what's happened," Athol tells his daughter. His bleary eyes shift to Percy as the girl leaves to return home. The door slamming behind Lileas snaps me out of my trance. "Would you be...cuttin' him up?"

Percy nods. "No marks will be left on him when you take him home," he replies.

"Caitrìona's decision," he says before his words dissolve into sobs again.

I place a hand on Percy's shoulder, and he squeezes my fingers. "I'll make some food and put out some water and whisky," I whisper. That's the only comfort I know how to offer people. I long to tell them the full story of their loved ones, but I can't.

Aodh's death clings to me as I head to the kitchen. It seeps from his body like smoke from a smoldering fire. The whispers of the dead are known to us boneweavers alone. People are woven together with so many layers of memories soaked in emotions that linger long after death. Boneweavers can only reanimate the body, but it's only an empty husk of memories written in the marrow. His soul's beyond my reach in the talons of Arianrhod's winged Eyes. Arianrhod taught the ancient boneweavers how to bring spirits back so they could help her resurrect the fallen gods, but, after some of her boneweavers and bloodgifted betrayed the remaining gods to side with the morrigans, all boneweavers have been hunted through the centuries until our abilities are only a fragment of what they once were.

I hang up the dark robe and start a fire in the oven. In a clay pot on the table are oat and walnut biscuits I made yesterday. Cups clatter as I gather them from the shelf. I fill a pitcher of water and take the bottle of whisky from the cupboard. I pour myself a dram, the smooth heat trickling down my throat. Shifting to my right foot, I try to take as much weight off it as possible as the ache gnaws on my left knee. There's still much to do. Death may be an end, but it leaves too many things to do in its wake.

Looking out the window, I watch the chickens in the garden, the calm coated in the late afternoon sunshine a stark contrast to the sounds of Athol's grief in the other room. My hand slides into my pocket, feeling the curve of the mouse skull. The allure to let Aodh's voice in is almost too much, but I can't answer it. If anyone found out that I'm a boneweaver, Percy and I would have to flee again. The thought of losing the garden, our home, and the life we've built here hurts worse than the ache in my bones. Every time we have to leave a place, it takes a part of me with it, and I don't know how much more of myself I can lose.

The smell of burning wood and the heady peatbrick in the oven tugs me away from the ashen scent hovering around me. The door creaks open in the healing room, and footsteps shuffle across the hard-packed floor. The crackling fire makes it hard to hear Percy's low voice before keening cries rise from the healing room. I gather my shaky breath and steel myself to return to the room filled with grief and death.

When I bring out the drinks and biscuits, Caitrìona,

Aodh's wife, is standing by the table with her three children and Lileas. She holds her baby boy, Tadg, who Percy helped deliver last autumn. Tadg pulls at her windswept brown braid while the other two sons clinging to her skirts, crying. Athol kneels on the floor with his head in his hands. Caitrìona's eyes are moist, her lips trembling. She remains rooted like a tree as she takes in the sight of her husband on the table.

Percy speaks quietly to her as I set the drinks on the cabinet by the door, his composure steady and sympathetic. As a fleshmender, loss feels like something's been severed. For me, it wraps around like a comforting shawl, even though my heart knows the pain of grief. It's a boneweaver's nature to see death not as a loss but as a gain. We're privy to something so intimate, feeling something's final moments.

"You want to examine him more?" Caitrìona asks Percy, cracks of her sorrow breaking through. Her free hand reaches out to touch Aodh's cooling cheek.

"Yes. I'd like to take some samples from his body to study with your permission," Percy replies.

"Will we be able to come for him tomorrow?"

Percy nods. "Of course."

With the plate of biscuits in my hands, I go over to Caitrìona's boys, Bran and Calum. I can see Aodh's features on their round faces and in reddish-brown hair. I try not to grimace as I crouch down. I offer them biscuits, and I wipe the snot from their noses with the corner of my skirt. Lileas crouches beside her father, her face red and streaked with tears. Her mother died before Percy and I arrived in the village. I was a few years younger than her when I first lost someone close to me. My stomach knots as I try not to think about the room that smelled of sickness and Da's coughing that still rattles in my ears years later.

"I'm so sorry," I tell her and hold out a biscuit to her. Aodh's death clutches my arm, begging me to look back at him.

Lileas swipes at her eyes and takes the biscuit. My hand brushes Aodh's hair as I grip the table to stand. A fragment of a memory jolts through me, a baby held in roughened hands. Tears sting my eyes. Percy looks at me, his brow wrinkled with a question I don't want to answer.

"Do what you will, Healer Bracken." Caitrìona's whisper is so quiet I almost don't hear it.

Leaving the plate by the whisky and water, I return to the comfortable warmth of the kitchen. The bones in my knees scrape against each other when I move, tight pain biting into my legs. I clean the rest of the vegetables and form the dough for the pie crust. There's food to be made, both for Percy and me and for Aodh's family. Their family and the village will make sure they have food, but I want to do what I can to ease the physical effects of sorrow. "Grief takes, so we need to feed the grieving," an old woman back home used to say.

I reach up and crumble dried sage and thyme hanging in the window onto the vegetables in the bowl, mixing everything into the gravy I made this morning. Athol's sobs mix with the sounds of children crying. As hard as I try to focus on preparing the food, the power in me keeps wanting to return to Aodh. My throat tightens as I cut up the potatoes and carrots, along with leek and mushrooms from the root cellar. Another voice seeps from the crevices of my mind, older and familiar. Its callused hands lead me through heather fields and nights by a fire, comforting and sad all at once.

The knife nicks my finger and beads of red well up. The crackling of the flames from the oven fills the kitchen. A heavy exhale leaves me as I lick away the blood, pain needling under my skin in time with my breaths. Hoarse voices scratch the walls, saturated with weariness. Percy will let Aodh's family stay as long as they need to, but I know he wants to start examining Aodh's body as soon as possible. For the work that will come next, his family can't be here.

No one can know what we're going to do.

THE SMELL OF BUTTER, HERBS, AND BAKING DOUGH CUTS THROUGH the sage smoke in the air. I clear away the plate, cups, the empty pitcher, and the half-finished bottle of whisky now that Aodh's family has left. Percy draws the curtains closed and locks the door. I return to find him bringing over knives and a few jars, rolling up the sleeves of his red robe. Flames dance on the candlewicks and fill the space with a flickering dimness. Percy opens a journal and begins sketching an outline of Aodh's body. Whether it's a bone, an organ, or the intricate layers of a marigold, he manages to capture every detail.

I stand by Aodh lying on the table. Shadows fill in the hollows of his face, and the color is gone from his skin. The smell of ash changes to a mixture of damp leaves and earth, a scent that settles deep in my nose and reminds me a graveyard and freshly dug soil. It's an oddly relaxing smell. Every time we do this, I fear someone finding out. I've never seen a Failinis patrol near the village since we've lived here, but I've heard they sometimes use spies in towns. Wood, metal, and curtains are the only things keeping someone from discovering the truth.

"Ready?" Percy asks, looking up from his finished drawing.

Nodding, I place a hand on Aodh's cool forehead. I've tried keeping my bloodgift hidden for so long, but eventually, the whispers of the bones become too much to ignore. The prickling sensation travels along my arm to my fingers. I fall forward into the whispering waters. Purple light glows beneath my skin around my bones.

The glow seeps into Aodh's body, traveling along his skeleton as we inhale. His chest rises with empty breaths, limbs twitching, and eyes opening as purple magic swims in his unseeing pupils. A sharp pain in my lungs and side makes me stiffen before it fades. Death hums through the body and floods my veins, vibrating like bees. I sigh as a part of me that's been hidden for so long returns.

I'm pulled from the bothy to yellow fields of rapeseed flowers bending in the wind. *The petals brush my fingertips as the sun beats against the back of my neck. The day stretches into dusk, and my shadow tries to crawl home. This place is beautiful, but I wish I could provide my family with more. I hear my name being called, and I turn—*

Percy's knife makes the cut on Aodh's side larger, the iron smell of blood pulling me back to the present moment. He pushes aside the skin and blood, the yellow light of his bloodgift running through his veins. Percy sticks his hand into the wound and pulls out a dark piece of flesh. Washing it off in the bowl of water, he sets it on the table. It wiggles as he flicks it with a finger, straightening the small organ out.

The quill's nib scratches the page as Percy sketches it. "His appendix must have been inflamed for days before it burst," he says, more to himself than to me. "He would've been in incredible pain and vomiting. Why didn't he come here when the pain first started? Things wouldn't have progressed this far if he had come in...And the cysts in his lungs..."

I didn't know what the pain was. I couldn't stop working. My family needs the money. Aodh's roughened voice echoes as more of his memories press against my skull. His churning emotions make it hard to keep myself separate from what are his and what are mine. My fingers itch to write everything down. To rouse the dead means hearing and recording their stories; that's the cost of using my power.

I feel Aodh's bones part as Percy opens his chest, exposing ribs and wings of muscle. A dog barks in the distance, and my eyes dart to the door. My hands shake as I pull away.

"Are you alright, Mor?" Percy asks, his bloodstained hands resting on the table.

"I forgot how intense the voices of the recently dead are," I say, each breath forcing the lump in my throat back down. My hand rests near the mouse skull in my pocket. Its memories would be manageable to sink into, only images and simple emotions. But I've taken a risk using my power.

He dips the quill in the inkwell and scribbles something down. "I can handle things here. It'll probably take a couple hours, but I'll let you know when I finish so you can put Aodh to rest before bed. There should be an extra ink bottle on the desk if you need it."

"I'll fix a plate for you and leave it on the stove. Try not to stay up too late," I say, shifting to take the pressure off my left knee. "Do you want any tea?"

"I'll have some when I'm done."

Percy turns back to his work, the knot of concentration forming between his brows. He's separating his emotions as he works, focusing only on the problems of the flesh he pulls back and cuts through. I envy his ability to contain his heart when he needs to. Mine bleeds at the slightest prick, trying desperately to shield itself in mossy walls and Percy's smile.

III
Marigold
Tagetes

Grief · Mourning · Remembrance

Ink dries on the page as the last sentence falls into place, and the whisper quiets. I flex my stiff fingers and set the quill down. Several hours have passed since I bathed and started writing. Aodh's story needed to be written, and I couldn't stop until it was recorded.

The candle is a melted pile of wax and struggles to keep the night at bay. In the garden, an owl hoots. A small death tugs at me. A mouse being carried off into the woods. The rodent skull sits in one of the desk's cubbies next to a jar of seeds and a wooden figurine of a badger I carved.

Water splashes from the kitchen in the next room and there's movement in the dim kitchen. I left the tub filled for Percy once he finished his work on Aodh's body, but I must have missed him going in to bathe. I shuffle out of the bedroom in my long night shift, knees stiff. Percy sits in the wooden bathing tub, his back to me. The embers in the oven glow in the ashes. His shoulders slump, and his spine looks like it's trying to escape through his skin. Percy's glasses and clothes are on the table.

I glance at Aodh in the healing room through the ajar

door. My power was released a while ago, and his voice has settled like silt at the bottom of a creek. The thread connecting us is slack but still there.

I rest my hand on Percy's shoulder. "Are you alright?" I ask, standing behind him. "Can I get you anything?"

He shakes his head and glances up, cheeks glistening. "I should've paid more attention to the cysts in his lungs," he says. "But I was so focused on his infection and appendix that I didn't think about the tears in his lungs."

In the years I've watched Percy treat people, he's rarely lost anyone. He knows he can't save everyone, but he still struggles when he comes to the limits of his bloodgift. For all the abilities fleshmenders have, even they can't stop death—no one can. Percy is usually steady and confident, so seeing him broken always hits me hard. Grief swallows any words of comfort I have for him and leaves only bones.

I grab the bar of soap on the lip of the tub and crouch next to him. The musky scent of calendula flowers wafts up as I leave sudsy circles with flecks of orange petals across his back. "What else did you find when you examined him?" I ask.

Percy splashes water on his face. "The cysts were abnormal—cancerous. Some had been there a long time, and others had formed recently. Cancerous cells are difficult to eradicate unless you rewrite the whole cellular structure—which is almost impossible. And his appendix, I still don't know what caused the infection that made it burst."

I often wonder if he wishes he'd stayed at the Acadamaidh to continue his studies with all the resources he could ever want instead of intertwining his life with mine—a life looking over his shoulder and unable to lay down permanent roots. Percy's told me many times that he wouldn't have chosen any other life, but I sometimes hear the longing in his voice when he talks about the past.

"What was his story like?" Percy asks as I grab the wet rag to wipe the suds away.

"We always saw Aodh as a cheerful and personable man, but he was a lot calmer beneath the surface and tended to bury his sadness so that his family wouldn't worry. His story is more melancholic," I reply while fragments of Aodh's life flit through my mind. They settle on my tongue and leave behind an emotional aftertaste. "He wanted to tend to his fields and make sure his family had enough to eat. When he was a child, he swore he saw a cat-sìth in the woods that attacked him and left those scars on the back of his leg."

"That explains why he didn't like cats," Percy mumbles.

"They weren't his favorite." I think about how he was wary of the cats in the village as I dunk the rag back in the cooling water. "I'm going to heat some more water," I tell him.

I grip the tub and stand, pain running through my tight knees and up my hips. A sharp inhale hits my teeth as I grimace. I'll probably have to use my walking stick when I go to the shop tomorrow.

Percy frowns and turns around. "Are your knees bothering you again?"

"They started hurting earlier. The left one, mostly. Might be a storm on the way," I reply as I grab the pitcher. "I took some lambsquarter in the afternoon, but it's not been helping."

He straightens. “Let me look.”

I pull a stool next to the tub. Gathering up the hem of my shift, I dip my legs in the water. Percy pushes back the fabric, wrinkled palms warm against my skin. He massages the swollen area around my knees and presses out the ache with each circular movement, reminding me of when my Ma used to knead my sore joints when I was a child.

My arthritis has been with me since I was five. I felt like an old woman shuffling around when the pain got bad, struggling to keep up with my siblings or walking the hills with the cows. I was tired more frequently and would sometimes get fevers out of the blue. My grandma had the same thing, and her fingers became so bent that they could barely hold a spoon. My fingers aren’t bent yet, but I’ve noticed slight bumps along my knuckles.

Percy’s salves and fleshmending are the only treatments that provide long-lasting relief. He keeps trying to figure out how to heal the inflammation for good; there’s a notebook with sketches of my joints and muscles. He says it’s more difficult than healing a wound since the inflammation is caused by my body attacking itself.

“Have you been feeling pain in your hands or anywhere else?” Percy’s breath brushes my knee as he kneads the muscles.

“There’s some stiffness in my fingers,” I say. It’s been three weeks since he last soothed the arthritis pains. “It grew worse standing in the healing room.”

His eyes are half-lidded beneath his long lashes. I know the look. He’s writing down the information in his head to think through later. Yellow light spreads through his hands and seeps into my knees. Percy unravels the tight knots, the soothing heat of his magic rushing through my muscles and bones. I sigh, and he kisses the mole on my left knee before taking my hands and caressing my knuckles. The cut on my finger vanishes.

"I'll make another salve," Percy says. "I could try something for the inflammation—"

I cup his face. "Rest, Percy. You've done enough for today." He does so much to heal my aches that I feel like a burden sometimes. There are moments I have to remind him to stop trying to fix everything.

Percy's lower lip wobbles, and he sinks into my lap, tears hitting my thighs. I wrap my arm around him and stroke his damp hair. His shoulders heave with quiet sobs. We cling to each other while the world continues to turn.

Sunlight warms my face, tall grasses swaying around me. The smell of damp earth and the sweet scent of flowers from the meadow carries along the breeze. The surface of the pond ripples with broken shards of light. My arms are sore from chopping wood and clearing the garden back at my cottage. The story of the rabbit I raised an hour ago scratches at my mind, eager to be written. The ground cushions my aching hips. Maybe when I'm done writing, I'll nap here, although I worry if I'll be able to get up afterward.

I turn the page of the journal resting on my knee, charcoal smears staining my fingers and leaving faint black fingerprints next to my words. I didn't set out to raise the rabbit. Its death had been fresh after being torn apart by a fox. I didn't dislike the power warming in my veins, the familiar cool ashen smell, and the hum of a story flowing through me. It's a comfort I want to reject, but it's a part of me I can't deny.

A chirp and the flap of wings comes from my left as a sparrow lands on my muscular arm. Tiny claws dig into my arm, and it hops toward my wrist, tilting its black, white, and chestnut-colored head. It's one of the birds I've taken to feeding at the cottage. The bird chirps, and I stop writing, smiling. I'm reminded of when Da used to go down to the moorlands, whistle tunes that carried across the hills, and hold out his arms for all the nearby birds to land on. While I'm no beastcharmer like Da was, he taught me how to be quiet and patient to win the trust of the birds. And that a bit of seed and bread mixture doesn't hurt.

I reach into my trouser pocket for a handful of seeds, and several other birds dart from the nearby trees. They perch on my shoulders and knees, filling my ears with high-pitched notes.

"I see you've brought friends," I tell the first sparrow as the others take turns pecking at the food in my open palm.

Something nudges against me, a rush of warm power that makes my skin prickle. I haven't been around people in a while, but it feels like the presence of another bloodgifted. A figure moves from the trees, and there's a glint of sunlight against something. I stiffen, trying to remain still. A man steps out of the woods across the pond, glasses on his face and wearing green robes.

Someone's found me.

I jump up, grabbing the axe lying next to me. The sparrows scatter and go for the seeds falling from my hand. My sore body protests, but I push through the pain. I hear shouting behind me as I tear through the trees. I have to run. People don't venture into these woods often. That bloodgifted could be a Failinis. And if they've found me, all I can do is pray to the gods that I can escape.

My lungs burn as I clutch the journal close, the axe held tightly in my hand. I stumble through the brush, branches tearing at my clothes. I've left my walking stick behind, the one I carved for myself when I left home five years ago. This is the longest I've stayed in one place without being found or chased away, and the thought of leaving cleaves to my chest like a fresh wound.

WIND SWEEPS OVER THE BARROW, RIPPLING THE GRASSES AND THE blue forget-me-nots covering the hill. Butterflies and the occasional sídhe land on the flowers. The people of Àitesìol cluster around Caitrìona. Aodh's widow is dressed in a brown and white tartan tonnagand, wrapped in her grief. The metal triskele pin holding her dark hair in place glints under the weak sunlight poking through gray clouds. Small Bran lets go of the blades of grass in his hands, his older brother Calum fighting tears while Lileas holds her baby cousin Tadg. Percy and I stand on the edges of the crowd, holding bouquets from our garden to lay on the grave.

I glance over the grief-painted faces and the bright petals contrasting with the somber tones. People weep while the priest in green robes says words over Aodh's grave to help guide him to the Forests of Cadal. The cairn stones are placed on the grave by his family. Athol's face is tear-stained. Countless other stones dot the hill, overtaken by tall grass, nettles, and moss.

Beneath our feet, hundreds of dead voices call to me.

Older bones lie buried beyond in the fields, unmarked and forgotten. I know that Aodh's limbs have been bound in iron to prevent him from moving should a boneweaver raise him, the heavy stones placed to keep the dead in the ground. It's strange to think that many graveyards have become prisons for the dead instead of resting places.

I came to the barrow when we first settled in the village three years ago. Two women were visiting a grave, and I overheard them talking about a patrol of Failinis in one of the larger towns that watched graveyards because boneweavers were drawn to them. I've avoided the barrow since then unless there's a funeral. Being here is soothing and fills me with worry at the same time. I try to make myself smaller anytime someone makes eye contact with me. I always have this niggling fear that people can tell something isn't right about me. It doesn't help that being taller than most of the men here already makes me an oddity.

My gaze drifts to where our bothy lies on the outskirts near the forests. The crescent-shaped cluster of squatty houses that makes up Àitesìol forms a stone-and-wood smile against the golden fields of rapeseed, wheat, and barley around the barrow. Our walkway is lined with yellow forsythia bushes and pink azaleas Percy planted years ago. Beyond that, I'm aware of the tug in the direction where the winding Abhainn Airgead glitters through the trees—to the old willow tree. Days of loss open the wound still trying to heal.

A flash of white at the tree line behind our house catches my eye. A herd of red deer moves near the garden wall, and standing amongst them is a white hart. Its antlers are like a halo over its head. Many believe they're messengers of Kester and Arianrhod, some attributing them as harbingers of death and doom. Many older people back home used to say it was ill luck to come across them.

"Are you alright?" Percy asks, taking my hand. I blink, and the deer are gone.

If anyone should be asking that question, it should be me. Bloodshot veins spider in the corners of Percy's eyes. His sleep lately has been fitful and filled with muttering. He still carries the heavy weight of Aodh's death on himself even though no one blames him for what happened.

"It's nothing," I reply. The purple ribbon in my hair tickles my neck as the wind blows against me.

Athol and a few men set the stone slab with a triquetra etched into it across the freshly turned earth. Arianrhod's Eye sits beneath the threefold symbol to show her messengers where Aodh's soul waits to be taken to the Forests of Cadal. I want to leave Aodh's story with his family, but it's too risky. For now, his words will remain tucked away on the shelf in the bedroom, known only to me.

When the priest finishes blessing the grave, Aodh's family toss their flowers onto the slab. Other villagers follow suit. Percy and I release our bouquets of marigolds and rue as we approach the mound. Even though this is Arianrhod's day, Beathag is honored by the flowers to symbolize death and life being separated by a single breath that binds us to our houses of flesh and bone.

Percy leaves my side to speak with Athol and the rest of Aodh's family. I'm left feeling slightly exposed without him beside me. My eyes drift to Caitrìona, her tears watering the fallen flowers. Her children cling to her while people offer condolences, and my throat tightens. Aodh's memories of her were like drinking honeywine, his love for her evident even though he regretted not showing it enough.

For a moment, I see a hazy image of Ma standing in Caitrìona's place while she holds my hand and my young siblings at a graveside. I remember her face clearly, the sunlight sparkling in her tears while my brothers cried. Their sadness confused me because even though Da wasn't with us, I felt him under the ground and his presence around me. That was the first time I really understood that my bloodgift made me different, caught between the dead and the living.

A long, drawn-out note of Wylie's fiddle cuts through the muttering conversations. The villagers quiet as Ualan begins playing his bagpipe. Osgar, the carpenter, stands in front of them and clears his throat, rubbing his thick red mustache.

"When the sun sinks away,
And the last of the summer flowers fade,
Arianrhod welcomes all souls to her side
Into Cadal's everlasting shade.
Over the hills and glens we wander
To reach the deserv'ed rest.
Sorrow burdens our hearts
But we will be reunited
Beneath eternal boughs."

Percy returns to my side, and I rest my head against his. Osgar's deep voice rises as other mourners join in. The dead seem to harmonize with us as the dirge hums in my throat. Death binds us, scars us, and frees us. It may be the end of things, but it has a way of bringing people together.

• • •

STEAM RISES FROM THE CUPS OF CHAMOMILE AND PEPPERMINT TEA. I drizzle forsythia syrup into the pale liquid. Purple clematis vines and ivy climb walls to the rafters in the kitchen. Percy decided the space needed another plant on the inside, which I don't mind, so long as there are no leaves on the floor I have to clean up. Growing plants is how he copes with heavy things. There have been several instances where our home has had plants bursting from the walls that it was hard to tell if we were inside a house or in a garden. The iron disk hangs from the ceiling to keep the sídhe from nesting in the kitchen, spinning in the slight draft that sweeps in.

Putting the stopper back on the syrup bottle, I look out the window, the glass smudged and with a few cobwebs in the corners. Percy crouches over the bed of carrots and tomatoes in the garden where he's been for the past two hours. His fingers glow green, and the leaves grow larger. Morhenna is nestled beside Percy on his moss-colored tunic folded on the ground. If a chicken could look content, Morhenna would practically be smiling as he strokes her feathers. The other three chickens move through the garden, heads bobbing as they look for things to eat. The setting sun melts into shades of pink and orange while dark clouds gather beyond the treeline.

Liquid bubbles behind me, and I give the hairst bree on the stove a stir. Chunks of leeks and potatoes bob over the peas, onions, and carrots in the soup. The smell of the baking bread in the oven is a warm embrace around the kitchen that helps ease the heaviness of the funeral. I put the lid on the pot and grab the cups of tea to take to the garden. Heat seeps through the thick clay vessels. The wind causes the back door to creak and slam shut behind me as I step outside.

As I approach Percy, Morhenna voices her displeasure with a hiss, black and white speckled feathers puffing up. Percy's spine pushes against his freckled back as he bends over the vegetables. I know each vertebra, and I want to run my fingers along them, but I have the cups in my hands. Morhenna flaps her wings as I crouch beside Percy and hold out the mug to him. Our shoulders touch, and Percy smiles. Siobhen pokes her head out from underneath the wrinkled kale leaves, warbling.

"Thank you," Percy says and blows on the tea. Dirt coats his hands, flower petals and leaves sticking to his arms. The tree and hand pendant rests against his sweaty chest.

I wipe some of the vegetation off him. "You've been muttering in your sleep again," I tell him after a few beats of quiet pass between us.

The corners of his mouth crease. "Was I saying anything good last night?" he asks.

"Nothing I could really understand. I think you were naming different muscles."

"Ah. I was hoping it was something witty." Percy looks at me. "Then, at least when I woke you up, you'd be amused. I suppose I'm not as amusing asleep as I am awake."

"Are you talking about your *ability* to make puns as being amusing?" I reply, raising an eyebrow while sipping my tea. The hot liquid warms my throat while the taste of peppermint follows with a cooling sweetness.

"I'd say it's more of a gift."

Siobhen inches forward, head bobbing as she keeps an eye on Morhenna. She waddles toward me and hops onto my right knee, claws digging into the fabric of my skirt. "Is that another gift of Kester's blood?"

"What better way to honor the God of Growth than telling plant jokes?" I roll my eyes as I pet Siobhen's keel. "I *carrot*-bout making you smile. It's a big *dill* to me." He takes my hand and presses closer, palm warm from his mug. "I know you find it *romaine*-tic."

There are many reasons I love Percy, some known only to me and whatever gods are still living. His puns aren't one of them. When we first met, he told jokes—half of which made me smile because they were so terrible, and I felt bad for him. His patients always laugh when he tells them a riddle or a pun, which only encourages him to come up with new ones.

My lips tighten into a line, fighting the smile trying to wiggle out. "Gods, please stop," I tell him.

Percy clutches his chest with a wounded look on his face. "Unbe-*leaf*-able. My own wife. You've *beet*-en me down by your harsh words," he gasps.

I rest the mug on my other knee. "Percival, mo ghràdh, I beg you to stop before I go gray."

"You'd look so *radishing* with gray hair, though." He leans in and kisses me. "Last one, I promise," he mutters against my lips, peppermint and syrupy sweetness lingering on his mouth.

Morhenna makes her disdain about our closeness apparent through loud squawks and wings beating against my leg. Siobhen flutters away into the safety of the underbrush with Fiona and Fergus. Claws scratch at my arm, and I pull away from Morhenna, cursing. Tsking, Percy picks her up and tucks her under his arm. His tea spills out onto the carrots as he struggles to keep it steady while holding the chicken.

"Henna, jealousy isn't flattering," he scolds her, handing

me his mug before taking the chicken to the henhouse. Fergus, Fiona, and Siobhen follow Percy as he whistles for them.

Blues and purples spill across the sky with dark grays on their heels. A flash of lightning snakes through the clouds, and sídhe in the trees flicker with beads of yellow-green light like fireflies. Sorcha's fighting with her brothers, Muiredach and Erroll, while Deòrsa burrows deeper into the earth to escape her wrath. Her rage continues to crackle even after she was struck down during the Darkening.

I used to be afraid of storms as a child, but now there's something beautiful about the chaos fractured by tongues of lightning and the thunder rattling the air, something only a lightningstriker could understand.

"Is the storm bothering your joints?" Percy comes behind me and throws his tunic over his shoulder. A few sídhe fly from the rows of vegetables, their glowing bodies breaking through the darkened garden.

I hand him back his half-empty cup of tea. "No, thankfully, and nothing else aches. You heal much better than you tell a pun."

Percy's grin parts as he stares up at me, wrapping his arms around my waist. He sways, and I follow his movements. "I'd be more hurt if you were right. We have the rest of our lives for you to appreciate my jokes. Humor is like whisky. It gets better with age," he says.

I let out a breathy laugh as we move to the music of the rumbling thunder. "Let's pray to the gods that it does because if 'you're radishing' is the best you can do, it'll be a long rest of our lives," I tell him and lean my forehead against his. My fingers trail along the base of his neck, over the bumps of his backbone, before moving down to the curve of his ribcage.

"Oh? You think you can do better?" Drops of rain hit my face. Percy glances up as lightning reflects off his glasses. "We should continue this inside before we get drenched."

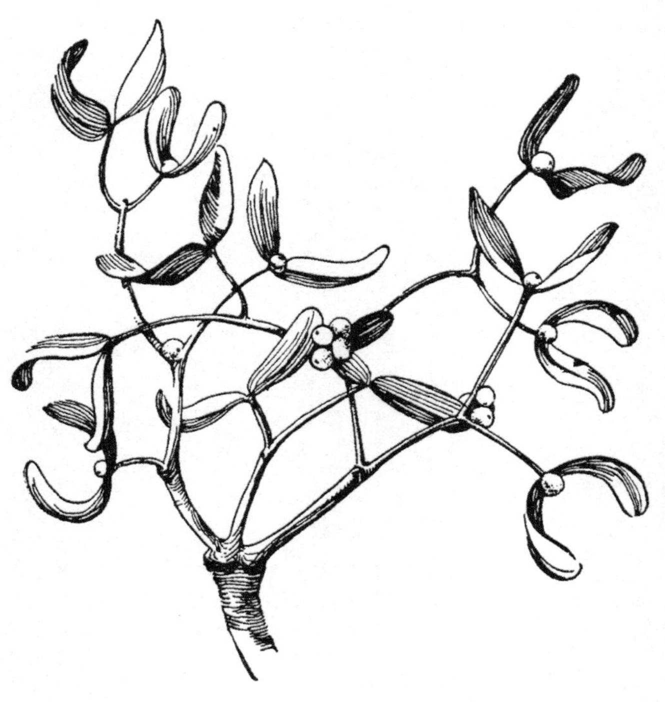

IV
Mistletoe

Viscum

Difficulties ❧ Overcoming Obstacles ❧ Protection

A fist pounds on the door, and I tense, my spoon clattering against the bowl. Rain batters the window as the storm clashes outside in the night. Percy glances up from the journal he's writing in. We wait a moment before the pounding continues.

"Who could that be?" he mutters, rising. He takes one of the candles from the wall sconce.

Sudden late-night visits stoke the embers of my fear. My nightmares often have me being dragged from my home. This could just be someone to see Percy, but my pulse still quickens. My leg bounces beneath the table as Percy heads to the front door, and the hinges creak open.

"How can I help you?" I hear him ask.

There's an edge to his calm voice that makes my heart jump. This is a small village with about eighty people. Percy has a good memory for faces and names, so we know everyone. Whoever's at the door isn't someone he recognizes.

"May we come out of the rain for a bit? My companions and I have been traveling for a while," a voice says with a brogue too polished and pristine for this part of Errigal. It's the accent of someone from the Mainland.

"Do you need directions?" Percy asks. "I can only offer you some whisky and bread. There's a tavern in town that might have a few rooms."

"We won't be staying long."

Boots shuffle across the floor, and I stand, moving to the door of the healing room to peer through the crack. My blood tingles at the presence of other bloodgifted. Four hooded figures in dark green cloaks enter the room, water pooling onto the floor from their clothes. One of them is as tall as me and wide as a tree. The shortest one moves around Percy, lightning illuminating his blue eyes. There's a silver torc around his neck shaped like the jaws of a wolf. Pinned to all their cloaks are metal dog heads. Failinis. My blood congeals to ice, shards stabbing my lungs as I try to inhale.

"You're a healer?" the man asks.

"Yes. I like to know the names of the people in my home," Percy says, standing by the open door. He keeps his voice steady, and posture relaxed.

"Where are my manners? Captain Alistair MacAdoh," the stranger says and throws his hood back.

The candle in Percy's hand dances as the man walks by. His blond hair is pulled back in a knot, and a short beard rims his sharp features. He looks several years older than me, late thirties. Wrinkles soften the edges of his eyes, the smile on his face deepening the lines. He would have looked kind, friendly even, if not for the glint behind his eyes. His gait reminds me of a wolf—a wolf that's now inside our home.

"Why don't you close that door? Wouldn't want to let in a

chill." Percy closes the door as thunder rumbles. "Do you live here alone?"

Percy keeps his gaze fixed on the men. "My wife and I live here," he says.

The captain's eyes flick toward the kitchen door, and I duck away. All bloodgifted can sense each other, but I've heard rumors that the Failinis have secret abilities they use to track down rogue bloodgifted. I stifle my fearful breaths and pray to the gods, both living and dead, that they'll leave and not hear my nervous heartbeat.

"I'd love to meet her," the Failinis tells him. "We haven't met many bloodgifted in these parts. Where did you study?"

"At the Acadamaidh. I have my seal of course completion," Percy tells him.

"I'd very much like to see it," the Captain says.

I step further back into the kitchen, eyes darting to the backdoor. Every part of me wants to run, but it's too late. They know I'm here. I haven't been arrested yet, so there's a chance that they'll leave without discovering I'm a boneweaver. Could we even escape without a fight?

There aren't as many Failinis in Errigal as on the Mainland, but they still have forts and patrols across the island. Percy and I came here because the Failinis rarely come out this far. The first time I saw them was in Auchendrain as they dragged an accused boneweaver and three other bloodgifted toward their garrison in the city while onlookers cheered and spat at the captives. Boneweavers caught by the Failinis are never seen again. I always tried to avoid them, but now my greatest fears have been made real.

The kitchen door opens, and Percy looks at me, worry breaking through his calm. His hand brushes against mine as he heads for the bedroom. My ring gently squeezes my finger from the rootsowing magic moving through it, Percy's way of trying to calm me.

Captain MacAdoh smiles as he steps toward me, the hilt of his broadsword visible beneath his cloak. "Let me guess. Earthcarver?" he asks and looks me over. That's what people assume because I'm taller than most women. My broad shoulders and muscular arms let people believe that I spend my time moving rocks and earth instead of chopping wood and listening to bones.

My tongue sticks to the roof of my mouth. All eyes are boring into me. My heart pounds, trying to betray my mounting fears. Sweat coats my palms. The longer I remain silent, the more suspicious they'll be. I nod, every bone in my neck ready to snap.

"Did you train at the Acadamaidh as well?" he asks.

"I'm self-taught," I reply and dislodge the words, each swallow like a rock lodged in my throat. It's not required for a bloodgifted in Errigal to train at the Acadamaidh, but those who don't are viewed with suspicion by the Regency on the mainland of Tìr Dhè.

"You don't sound like you're from this area. A highlander?" the Failinis goes on, and my stomach twists into tighter knots. I've tried to keep my northern accent hidden as best I can but haven't erased all traces of it. This man is too sharp if he can tell where I'm from.

Percy returns with a black stone tablet. Etched across its surface is his name, bloodgifts, and credentials from finishing his mid-level courses. It allows him to practice healing wherever we go and gives him access to most places with a library. The people here accepted his abilities without much proof, but some cities we've stayed at required him to show it.

The Failinis turns it over in his hand. "Doublegifted. What's someone like you doing out here, Percival Bracken?" he asks.

"I wanted a quieter life with my wife. We can do more good in places like this that don't have access to healers," Percy tells him, standing between me and the Failinis.

The Captain hands Percy the tablet back. "I'm sure Beathag honors your sacrifice," he says. "How long ago did you and your wife come here? Your accent's from the Mainland."

"My parents are from Tìr Dhè, but they travel around a lot. I was born there but raised in Errigal. My wife and I came here a few years ago."

"I can see why you like this place. It's charming. A hidden gem." The Captain's grin hides something. My knees weaken, but if I move, I'll draw attention to myself.

Percy meets MacAdoh's smirk with a polite smile. "I don't mean to be rude, Captain, but it's late. If you head to the tavern and speak with Aileen, she'll give you food and rooms." Percy touches my shoulder. "Why don't you get them some shortbread biscuits to take with them?"

Captain MacAdoh's grin sharpens. "That sounds lovely."

My feet are leaden as I turn back to the kitchen, desperate for air. A sliver of hope worms its way up at the thought of them leaving and that I might go undiscovered. I clench my fists in front of me to stop them from shaking.

"One moment, lass. I don't think I quite caught your name." The Failinis' words grab me, and I freeze. "Before we go, I want to make sure I have your bloodgift correctly. We like to keep records of any bloodgifted we encounter, especially those who didn't go through the Acadamaidh."

I glance back over my shoulder and see the Captain holding a glowing, semi-clear crystal that looks like strands of glass woven together in a chaotic design. Percy told me about such crystals, about the giant one that illuminates the central hall of the Acadamaidh.

It's a God's Tear.

Said to have formed during the Darkening as the dying gods wept, the crystals react to the bloodgifted. This is how initiates at the Acadamaidh are tested, making it impossible to hide the nature of their blood. One drop on its surface shows a person's bloodgift by the color it glows. One drop of blood, and I'll be exposed.

Breathe. Breathe. *BREATHE!* I look away from the stone, the ice in my chest coursing through my whole body. The Failinis' eyes narrow at me, fixated on my face with a look that tells me he sees my fear. His hand moves to the weapon at his side.

He knows what I am.

Percy jerks me back by my arm as thick roots burst from the floor and wooden spears shoot from the ceiling beams toward the Failinis. The plants along the walls come alive and grasp at the four bloodgifted. Pain moves up to my shoulder, and I stop against the counter. A wall of fire and wind crashes into his attack. Captain MacAdoh leaps back with flames dancing around his fingers now glowing orange. He's a flamekindler. His teeth glint in the light. The presence of his bloodgift makes heat bubble in my veins, but there's also a strange coldness there.

Everything moves slowly, the sounds distant in my ears.

So many nights, I thought about how this moment would go, how we'd escape, but now I can't think through the pulse roaring in my ears. All I ever planned to do was run, not fight for my life. Each time we had to leave, it was because the whisper of danger reached us before anyone came to break down the door.

Percy stumbles into me, green light glowing at his fingertips. "Go!" he shouts.

A peal of thunder shakes the bothy, and everything comes into focus. Smoke fills my nose as the floorboards burn. The windows shatter as the vines in the kitchen grow larger and cover the doorway to block the Failinis. Tears sting my eyes, and I bolt for the backdoor. Cold rain needles my skin, and the mud is slippery under my boots. I grab the axe leaning against the bothy wall.

Inside, Percy holds the wall of vines up while the Failinis try to burn and hack through. Just as I prepare to rush in and grab Percy, the kitchen wall smashes outward, knocking him to the floor and sending me staggering into the bed of tomatoes. The earthcarver Failinis emerges from the hole, a tawny light glowing along his hands, and throws chunks of stone at Percy as he tries to crawl away.

Percy scrambles to his feet, and a nest of thorny roots and vegetation erupts through the kitchen and throws the earthcarver against the stove. I grab Percy's arm as he rushes outside. Blood smears across his forehead from small cuts, and I forget how to breathe. Rain soaks us. The chickens screech. Flames glow inside the house, smoke curling out the broken windows. The vines in the kitchen won't hold forever. Percy's hand grips mine as we run for the garden gate.

Pain strikes between my shoulder blades, and I crash into

the mud. Earth twists around my ankles and drags me toward the house. "Morana!" Percy yells and tries to grab my wrist.

I claw at the ground with my free hand, unable to find something to hold onto. My arms and shoulders strain as I twist around and swing the heavy axe down to sever the muddy tentacle. It breaks, and I get onto my knees as the earthcarver lunges for me. I roll away before he aims a punch at my face. The blunt side of the axe head strikes his left side as I bring it around with a yell. He grunts but doesn't stop. I feel the ground beneath me rumbling. Gnarled tree roots come up from the ground and hurl the man against the house, his screams cutting through the thunder.

"Don't let them escape!" a female voice cuts through the air.

Percy hauls me to my feet as the other Failinis fan out around the garden. A thin waterdancer parts the rain with glowing blue hands to create a dome of water overhead, stopping us in our tracks. Crackling flames snake around the walls and burn the plants. Percy shields me as the orange tongues lash out. The winds howl as the windsinger riles them up, pale gray light swirling beneath her skin. Part of the coop is damaged, and the chickens run to escape the flames.

Captain MacAdoh steps out of the smoking bothy, fire wreathing his hands. Flames from the kitchen backlight him and orange light burns through his veins up to his neck. The metal pendant of a twisted, wingless dragon dangles at the end of the necklace he wears. Caorthannach's symbol. The Failinis are bloodgifted honed to be weapons. And they have us outnumbered.

"This could have gone painlessly," the Captain shouts

over the storm. "You can give yourself up and stop this, boneweaver."

When he says that, the sliver of hope that we can escape shrivels. The rain stings my eyes. I never wanted this—to put Percy's life in danger.

"I'm not letting them take you," Percy tells me, his hair plastered to his face and glasses broken.

"I don't want you to get hurt," I say, throat tight. I can't let Percy die. "They want me, not you."

"I'd gladly bleed for you if it means you'd be safe. When I make a move, run," Percy whispers and kisses me. "I'll be right behind you."

"Very moving," Captain MacAdoh says, placing a hand over his heart. "I won't separate you. If you surrender, neither of you has to die here."

Percy stomps his foot, and thick roots break through the earth and slam through the flames to bring down the garden wall. The magic in the now-freed earthcarver's veins burns brighter, and a cord of mud and rocks shoots toward me. I bring the axe around to break the grasping coil, wincing as other clumps slam into my side and legs. Wind cuts my face as I run through the smoldering gap, my vision blurring with tears and smoke.

Two threads snap. I recognize the deaths of Fergus and Fiona as they tug at me with flashes of the garden and my hands reaching to feed them. I stagger over roots and broken stones. Percy holds back the three Failinis bearing down on him. Charred plants struggle to remain upright as fire eats at them, and the winds slice them. Green and yellow glow under his skin as he uses both bloodgifts, and the veins along his neck look ready to burst. A dark thread of blood drips down from his nose. Our blood can only give us so much power before it takes from us. Percy's using too much of his abilities at once, and I don't know how much longer he can keep fighting. There aren't enough bones in the garden for me to attack with.

Overhead the dome of water solidifies into spears of ice before the waterdancer releases them. "Percy!" I scream, the sound ripping from me as thunder shakes the air.

Giant thorny branches envelop Percy as the spears strike the shield of vegetation. The sphere of plants writhes like a monstrous creature, and twisting arms extend from it and whip out at the Failinis. MacAdoh and the waterdancer deflect an oncoming strike. Percy emerges from an opening in the tangle of plants and sprints toward me while the sphere unfurls and grows more thorny tendrils that swing at anything close by. The roof of the bothy groans as it goes up in flames.

Percy takes my hand, and we run for the woods, our clothes soggy and heavy. My lungs burn, and I don't know how long we've been running. Each step threatens to shatter me. I spare a glance over my shoulder, our bothy burning like a faint orange eye through the trees. We slide down a muddy slope before stopping by a familiar gnarled tree.

Panting, Percy parts the wide trunk and roots to reveal two packs covered in waterproof cloaks. He opens one of the packs and slips in the black tablet and the soggy journal he was writing in at supper that I didn't see him grab. Every month, we'd come here to store supplies and restock food for travel if a day like this ever came. Percy hands me the pack, and he slings the other over his shoulder, throwing on one of the cloaks. The bag is a boulder in my cold hands. Everything spins as I gasp for air. A strangled sob escapes me, and I nearly collapse, leaning against the axe to keep myself upright. The adrenaline drains away, leaving me empty and trembling.

Percy catches me. "Morana, look at me. Breathe," he says and places a hand against my chest, the glowing warmth unclenching my lungs. "Breathe, love. I'm here."

I inhale and exhale in time with his voice, eyes darting around as the trees groan. The tightness loosens, but my pulse still pushes against my ribcage. Putting the cloak around me, Percy helps me stand, and we continue down the worn trails coursing with streams of rainwater.

The wind screeches, and the trees in front of us splinter and fall, severed in half. The windsinger rides on the air behind us, readying another invisible scythe in her arcing hands. Green veins pulse along Percy's cheeks, and the trees lash out with their branches at the Failinis. We don't stop as more trees fall and shake the ground.

Wet grass and barley slap my legs as we cut through the fields, leaving the protection of the woods. The barrow and the church are dark outlines against the rain. I find myself moving toward the call of the dead in their graves, Percy struggling to keep up as my long legs overtake his strides. Lights burn in the houses in the village and blur like fireflies. If I can get to the barrow, then I can at least do something—

The ground shakes, and I'm blasted onto my face by a punch of wind against my head. Mud and blood coat my teeth, my ears ringing as I roll onto my back. Pain throbs through my nose. My fingers almost release the axe, but I clutch it until my knuckles hurt. Percy's shouting, but I barely hear him. Specks of light flit across my eyes as I blink.

As my vision focuses, I see the earthcarver standing on a mound of earth several yards away to separate us from the barrow, the windsinger hovering in the sky like a winged creature with her cloak flapping about. The Failinis are keeping me from the barrow graves. But they don't know what lies in this field. The bones of the unmarked and the unknown, both human and animal. The voices of dozens of dead in the ground call out to me, growing louder while the world pulls away.

I hear Aodh's bones from the barrow. All I need to do is tug on the cord connecting us, and he'll answer. They all will. They've longed for me to hear them, and this time, I listen. I reach for the ones in the field, and my bloodgift wells up from some part of me I didn't know existed. Pain, sadness, anger, and longing fill me. All their collective memories bleed across my eyes, threatening to burst out.

The purple outline of my skull is reflected in Percy's glasses as he gets me up. Hundreds of empty breaths are tethered to me, a mass of cracking bones and papery skin coursing together into one entity. Lightning illuminates bodies draped in rotted shrouds and rusted metal restraints as they climb up through the muddy field. Skeletons of horses, sheep, elk, and other animals shamble toward the earthcarver. They neither scream nor growl, just silent wraiths driven by my will binding their bones together. In their empty sockets burns the purple light of my bloodgift. The earthcarver screams as skeletons emerge from the mound of earth he's on and swarm him. The windsinger drops out of the air to help him, hacking at the mass of bones swarming the barrow with her drawn sword.

I'm barely aware of Percy's hand gripping mine or the rain

stinging my face as we run back into the cover of the forest. Warm wetness drips from my nose. Hundreds of voices swim in my head, memories filling every crevice of my consciousness. The forests pull us in, and their boughs weave together to hide us. We cross the bridge over the Abhainn Airgead and leave the outskirts of Àitesìol.

I lose track of how long we've been running until we find a cleft in the forest and collapse against the rocks, gasping for air. Percy draws vines and bushes over the entrance. Everything washes over me, and the last of my strength drains away. My fingers unclench from the axe, and it sinks to the ground. The threads of the dead have snapped, but their whispers follow me.

"Morana?" Soft yellow light flickers along Percy's palms, and the pain in my nose fades. His hair is stuck to his face, a crack running through his right glasses lens. Soot, blood, and dirt are smeared across his cheeks.

The chill sets into my bones, and I can't stop shaking. Salt and iron slide on my lips. All I can see behind my eyelids is fire consuming three years of memories. The journals with Percy's drawings, our garden, the shelves with stories of the dead, the chickens, and hopes for the future all vanish before my eyes. Sobs tear free, and I crumple. Percy holds me, whispering in my ear. The pain in my chest cuts deep, threatening to leave me bleeding out on the ground.

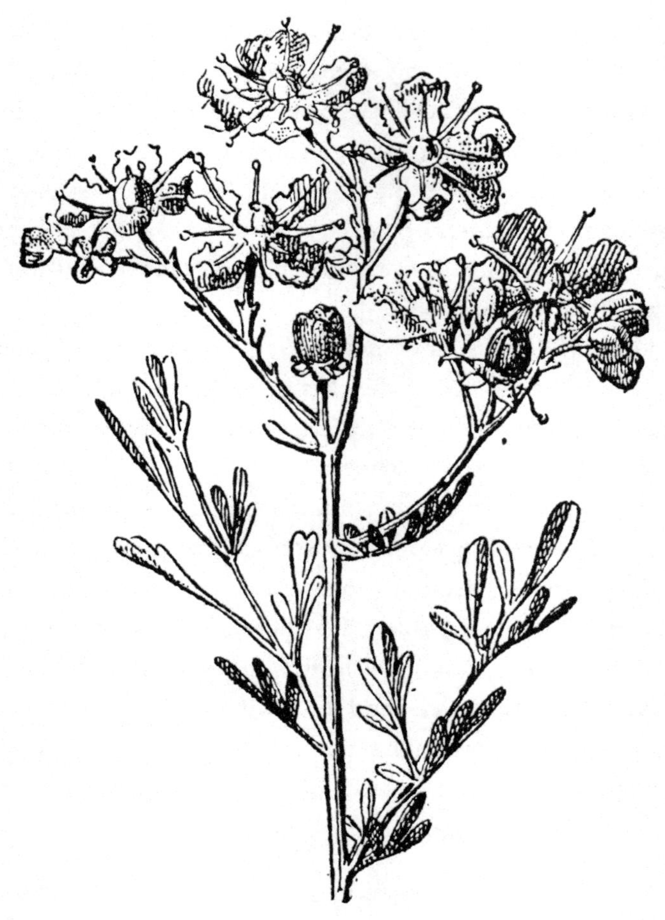

V
Rue
Ruta graveolens

Regret ❧ Endurance ❧ Sorrow

Gray light breaks through the branches covering our hiding place in the rock cleft. My eyes feel like they're full of sand as I blink. For a moment, I don't know where we are. Then the realization of what's happened crashes into me. Splitting pain clamps around my head, and the edges of my nose are crusty with blood. I don't know when I stopped being aware of my body, separated from my heavy limbs.

Percy's head rests on my shoulder as he huddles against me, bundled in his cloak. "Did you sleep at all?" he mumbles and opens his red-rimmed eyes, his cracked glasses perched on the edge of his nose.

"Not much." My voice rasps against my throat. Whenever I closed my eyes, I thought I sensed the Failinis nearby or smelled smoke. The hours passed in tense silence except for the voices crowding my ears, the shifting shadows making my heart race. "Did you?"

"I tried. How are you doing?"

The purple eyes of the dead light up the night. Fire eats through stone walls. Captain MacAdoh's wolf-like grin full of smoke. All the memories leaking through makes me feel disembodied from the present. The question hovers around me, but I know Percy isn't asking about my emotional state. It's too soon to peer into that wound while it's still bleeding.

"I've never raised that many people before..." I tell him. There's a whole barrow talking inside my pounding head, growing more insistent with every passing hour I don't write down their stories.

Percy sits up with a grunt as his joints crack. "How loud are the voices?"

"Deafening. There's three hundred and forty-two of them, not including all the animals."

My wet clothes cling to my skin. Each throbbing ache constricts my muscles as I shift. I overextended myself last night. The bloody nose, my headache, and my hollowed-out veins are reminders that I used too much of my bloodgift. I can only imagine how Percy feels having used both his gifts for so long last night.

"I..." My hands drop into my lap as I chew on my lip. I imagine the horror of the villagers seeing the remains of their loved ones swarming through the fields, lying scattered like vomit from the barrow when my connection to them severed. "They must think I'm a monster. I dragged all their dead from their graves. They'll hate me now that they know I'm a boneweaver."

It's a silly thought, but I can't stop thinking about Aodh's family finding his corpse uprooted from its resting place. Where I grew up, children were told stories about boneweavers who would steal their skeletons and eat their bones if they didn't behave. The stories made me confused about my gift. I longed to tell someone that all I could do was hear the stories in the bones but feared being handed over to the Failinis to be killed since I heard that's what happened to boneweavers that were caught. Now, I'm like a villain in one of those stories...

Percy takes my hand, kissing my dirty knuckles. "Does it matter what they think of you now? You did what you had to do, Morana. People fear what they don't understand, but I like to believe that perhaps they will remember your kindness over the years instead of giving into hatred."

I rub my aching shoulders. My feet hurt, and blisters rub against the wet socks inside my boots. Pops crackle through my fingers as I flex my hands, looking at the axe leaning against my pack. There's a dull pang in my stomach, but the thought of food makes me sick.

"Does anything hurt?" he asks me and reaches his hand out toward my arm. The warm light of his bloodgift springs to life in his palm, deepening the shadows under his eyes. I'm sure Percy can feel every sore limb and swollen joint in my body.

"I'm sore, but I'll be fine," I reply, stopping him. "You used too much of your gift last night."

Doublegifted are powerful, but they can exhaust themselves quicker. If he keeps overusing his power, his magic will take more of him than he can give, devouring him as payment.

He holds my gaze, lips pursed, but the light fades beneath his skin. Percy drags his pack over. He parts the plants, and the light hurts my eyes. I grab his arm, panic swimming up my throat.

"What if they're out there?" I hiss, scrambling for the axe.

I don't know if the Failinis survived the attack at the barrow, but I never felt their deaths, so they might be alive.

They probably had horses with them when they came to the village. The windsinger and the earthcarver could travel quickly with their gifts. They'll catch up with us once they find our trail.

"I asked the trees, and there's no one around for miles. We need to get out of these clothes and eat something." I open my mouth before Percy adds, "And if the windsinger's still flying about, the trees would've sensed it too."

Has he been using his powers all night? To reach all the plants for miles, he must be using a lot of his gift. I let go of his arm. We both look half-drowned, covered in mud and blood. Exhausted, drained, and barely able to stand, I don't know if we could take on a strong breeze, let alone four bloodgifted.

"Don't use any more of your power, Percy. Not until we've rested. Please," I tell him.

"I'll try, but I won't hesitate to heal your injuries if I need to, regardless of the cost," he says, his words loving but firm. He can be so stubborn sometimes. For a healer, he doesn't always take care of himself first.

We leave the cleft in the rocks and go through the packs. Each one has a few sets of clean clothes, socks, a waterskin, a blanket, hardtack, a jar of oil, flour, honey, nuts, and dried vegetables and fruits. The bottle of whisky sloshes around, swaddled in a scarf. There's a pouch of jewelry, and I find the healing ointments and salves wrapped in a long strip of cloth. Percy sniffs the pouches of herbs, checking the seals on the jars. Vials of seeds are tied together with spools of nettle fiber string tucked inside bronze cups.

"Looks like the food's still good," Percy says as he holds up a dark frying pan before trading it with me for the seeds.

He finds an unbroken pair of glasses and slips the cracked ones into one of the pockets. I need to find the map so I can chart our course.

As I dig around, I find two journals and a graphite stick. The dead whisper in anticipation of their stories being put to paper, but I stare at the two journals in my hands. Tears fall on the wooden covers, rolling into the etched lines of flowers I carved years ago. These were Percy's gifts to me when we got married, to write our own memories and dreams down in. I always felt they were too precious to write in, not until I was sure we were truly safe. I decided to move them to our travel packs so we wouldn't leave them behind if anything bad happened.

Two dried flowers slip out between the pages onto the ground. A yellowed daisy tied with blue thread to a sprig of baby's breath. A hole punches through my gut as the memories slide through my insides. I smell blood and feel that string inside myself snap, that hollow loss. It pulls at the gaping wound and unravels me further.

Gone. All gone.

I drop the journal, bile burning my throat. "Morana, what's wrong?" Percy is at my side, searching my face.

Shaking my head, I stuff the journals back in my pack, and find the sgian dubh. I tear off the cloak and slip out of my wet clothes, the wind chilling my skin. My back aches as I bend down. When I remove my socks, the red blisters on my toes are bright against my pale skin. I can't think about the past while I'm already drowning in the present memories.

"Morana." Percy's hand on my back makes me jump.

I dry my face, pulling on dry trousers. "It's nothing."

"Please don't shut me out. Talk to me," he says, but I don't meet his gaze. I don't want to talk about any of it.

Heavy silence hangs between us as I change. The tunic smells like earth and cedar oil, and I breathe it in to clear my head. There's a tin of beeswax salve I rub over the blisters before putting on dry socks and slipping back into my boots. Percy is dressed in fresh clothes, his brown eyes ready to drink up all my grief if I let him, but I can't. We have too much to carry and too far to go, wherever that may be.

I reach for the sgian dubh and run my fingers through my long, tangled hair, removing leaves and muddy grass. I undo the purple ribbon that I wore to the funeral, holding the dirty strip of fabric in my grimy hands. A few tears fall on it before I stuff it into my pocket. Pulling the matted locks straight, I cut through them. By the time I'm finished, I must look like some wild, disheveled creature. I can fix it when we stop again, but for now, this will help disguise me.

Percy tugs at his own dirty hair. "I could dye my hair darker if I find the right plants. Or use my gift to change it. Maybe the mud's enough to hide it."

"You can do that?" I ask, sheathing the knife.

He nods. "When I was still completing my studies, a few patients wanted me to change their hair color, so they didn't seem as old. Not the most glamorous work for a fleshmender."

I readjust the cloak over my shoulders, my head feeling lighter now that it's been freed of most of its hair. "Could you change our appearances?"

He purses his mouth, eyes closing for a moment. "That type of fleshmending was only taught to heal scars and surface-level marks. I *could* attempt to change our skin and eye colors, but it's not a quick process or a comfortable one."

It doesn't sound like it'd be a simple thing, either. And would it help us if the Failinis can sense bloodgifted? I don't want Percy to exhaust himself further.

"Once you're rested, you can use your bloodgift change our hair colors," I say and pull out the cloth map from my pack.

Magic prickles against the back of my neck. I turn as green lines move up Percy's right hand as he touches one of the trees. A long limb grows from it and becomes as thick as the axe handle before it breaks off.

"A new walking stick in case your knees start acting up again," he tells me, holding the stick out to me.

I take it, the grain a bit rough against my palms. The surface of my old one had been worn smooth by the years. "Thank you."

Percy breaks off a piece of hardtack, passing me the other half. Leaning the walking stick against my pack, I nibble on the food as I study the landscape on the map. Maps have always soothed me, giving me a sense of clarity being able to see where to go. But even though I can see the whole expanse, I have no idea where we should go or where we are.

I take a deep, shaky breath. Da used to say that there are times when you have to keep walking, taking things one step at a time before the path becomes clear. Always find north. Despite the cloudy skies and my foggy thoughts, I eventually find my bearings by the shadows and the battered compass. We crossed the Abhainn Airgead in the south last night, past where Àitesìol lies, and are heading southeast. Errigal's covered with sloping moors and hills in the south, the highlands and mountains pushing the land upward in the northern and western parts. I recite the landmarks like a prayer until the map becomes clear again.

Percy glances through the trees. “There’s a creek nearby where we can fill our waterskins. The woods go on for miles, so we will have cover for a day or so,” he says. “We know there are at least four Failinis after us, and if they’re this far out, they most likely don’t have reinforcements.”

“We still don’t know how they found us in the first place,” I reply. “Someone could have turned us in or—”

The bushes rustle, and I lunge for the axe, my shoulders resisting the sudden movement with a sharp pain. How did they find us already? My heartbeat throbs through my fingers, searching for any dead nearby. I barely feel the bones beneath our feet through the sea of chattering. I don’t know if I have the strength to raise them if necessary.

A twig snaps, and a soaked Morhenna struts out. Her speckled feathers are in disarray, but despite the singed spots, she appears unharmed. Percy and I look at each other, my confusion mirrored on his face. I’m seeing things from lack of sleep, or this is a sídhe playing tricks on us.

“Is that...?” I begin.

“It looks like it,” Percy says. “Seems she followed us all the way here.”

My hands remain clenched around the axe handle. “Could it be a trap? What if they have a beastcharmer?” I don’t trust anything at the moment, let alone one of our chickens appearing.

“I don’t think so. No pink glow of beastcharming magic. Besides, what could a chicken do to us?”

"*This* one can do a lot when she puts her mind to it." I lower the weapon as Morhenna runs up to Percy.

I glance around, hoping to see Siobhen following, but minutes pass with no sign of my little shadow. Another part of my heart crumbles as I imagine her falling to the same fate as Fergus and Fiona. It seems silly to pray that she escaped and found a home with one of the villagers, but I hope she did.

"What should we do if they have a beastcharmer?" I ask.

"I can make an ointment to hide our scent and throw off any animals they might be using to track us," Percy says. "We'll have to keep an eye out for any birds or other animals that stare at us too long."

Percy scoops Morhenna up, drying her off with the edge of his cloak. She tilts her head with a soft croon. It's a small relief to see her alive. I reach out to stroke her head, but she pecks at my finger with a hiss. Seems escaping death has done little to change her personality.

"Well, this'll help us with food. Fresh eggs will be nice," Percy says as he sets the chicken down. She sticks close to him, pecking at bugs crawling on the muddy ground.

Percy picks up the flowers and the fallen map. His eyes glisten, but he sticks them back in the journal before closing the pack. He hands the map to me.

"Which way do we go now, Morana?"

VI
Thistle

Cirsium

Harshness · Persistence · Pain

The next four days pass in a blur of long hours, short rests, and constantly looking over our shoulders. Our pace feels too slow, like the Failinis are still breathing down our necks despite the miles we've traveled. My thighs are chafed, and the pack straps dig into my shoulders, the pain matching the aches in my feet and legs. Sometimes I wake and think this is all a dream, that the bothy still stands and that we aren't being hunted. But each night, the hard ground leaves bruises on my back, reminding me that it's all gone. There are moments when it feels like I'm living someone else's life.

The forests thin to the hilly moors blanketed with a sea of grasses and flowers. Morhenna clucks as she follows behind us, making it known when she wants Percy—and Percy only—to carry her when she tires. My cheeks sting from the wind as I slow. I lean on my walking stick as a twinge goes up my left leg from my tight knees. I'll bear with it because it's something to keep my mind off the reality that we're on the run.

Percy glances at me. He's kept pace with me no matter

how slow I've been walking, but he's neglecting to shave the shadowy stubble on his chin. "Are you sure I can't heal anything?" he asks. "I don't like seeing you in pain."

He's asked the same question the last forty miles. "I'll be fine," I tell him. He looks stronger than he has in days, but I'm afraid that even healing minor bruises and pains will take a lot out of Percy and me. I don't want him using more of his gifts to offset the fatigue either.

"I'd still want to heal the blisters at least, Mor. Don't want them to become infected."

Percy's right. I know I'm being too paranoid again. As much as I worry about the Failinis, I shouldn't risk my health. "Tonight, when we make camp," I say and check the map again. "I don't want you overexerting yourself, Percy."

"I'll try not to, but I'm a healer. I can't leave someone alone when I know something's wrong with them that I can fix," he replies. "Overexertion often comes with the territory. I'll make some nettle soup tonight. That should help both of us. Lots of iron."

Morhenna gives an irritated cluck, and we stop. She always knows how to ruin a moment. Percy picks her up, and we stare at the reddish moorlands laid out before us. We have miles to go before we reach the forests and find someplace to settle down for the night. There's a town in the distance, and the thought of a bed tugs at me, but it's dangerous to be near people right now. I'm afraid anyone we meet would be able to see the purple glow of my gift or hear the storm of voices inside my skull.

The voices...I've only been able to write down two stories, my writing small and squished, so I don't use too much paper. I tell Percy a story or two to ease the headache. But the dead demand permanence, to be remembered by something other than a spoken tale lost in the wind. Even if I manage to find enough paper, I don't know how much time it'd take to tell all their stories. Will I be stuck with their words until I, too, join them?

Sunlight comes through the window, catching dustmotes in its beams. Herbs hang from the ceiling rafters in the kitchen. The flowering vines along the walls sway as nature makes its way inside. Chickens run around in the garden, and Percy moves between the rows. Laughter taps against the glass as he reaches for a small hand sticking up between the flowers and kale leaves.

I open the door and step into a stormy night with lightning and thunder battling in the darkness. Our bothy burns, laughter now turning to piercing screams. Pain bites into my stomach, and blood runs down my legs. The garden cracks, and the earth rushes up to swallow me. I claw at the ground as I'm pulled under where the dead wait for me. Blue eyes rimmed with fire peer down at me. A smoke-wreathed smile opens as the burning house crashes on top of me.

I start awake, smoke and ash burning my throat. Tears coat my cheeks. The ground digs into my side, and drizzling rain hits the covering of leaves Percy bent over our heads. The fire embers are low, darkness blanketing the glen. Frogs croak, and the call of a fox nearby cracks the quiet. Morhenna is tucked in close to Percy's head, asleep.

Percy tightens his grip around my waist. "What's wrong?" he mumbles. The weak firelight falls into the hollow of his eyes.

I blink away the tears, wiping my nose. "I fell asleep again," I whisper. It was my turn to keep watch, but I don't remember closing my eyes.

"You need the rest. You haven't been sleeping well."

How can I rest if the nightmares come? The exhaustion and the voices of the dead kept them at bay the past few days, but that isn't enough to stop the dreams from finding me.

"What dream did you have?" Percy asks and moves closer. He's using the tone for his patients to put them at ease, and it rubs my wounds raw.

"I saw our house burning. The Failinis. And..." The words are spilling out, ones I kept buried so I wouldn't be cut by the empty answers. "We've lost everything. Where can we go where we'll be safe again?"

Percy runs his fingers through my short hair. "I don't know what tomorrow holds for us. I *do* know that we made it to today. We're still here, together, which gives me hope about whatever we'll face."

His optimism tries to find purchase on my mounting despair, but it doesn't break through. The burning look in Captain MacAdoh's eyes reminds me of a hunting hound willing to chase its prey to the ends of the earth. The Failinis are named after the god Artair's war hound who hunted down the morrigans during the Darkening. The Captain was ready to burn everything to get me, and I don't believe he'll stop until I'm in chains or dead.

"What if we can't escape them? What if we aren't strong enough?" I whisper.

"Then we'll find each other in the Forest of Cadal, never to be separated again," Percy says, the corners of his eyes creasing.

That thought doesn't calm my fears but makes them worse. How can he sound so calm about death while I, a boneweaver, am afraid of it? Irritation prods me, and I want to snap at him, but I'm too exhausted. It's not the dying that scares me, but losing Percy and being alone again. There's always that chance that someday I'll feel his life snap, sense his, and be left with his ghostly voice clinging to me.

"My head...it's too crowded," I murmur and press the heels of my palms against my eyes. "I can't tell what are my own thoughts anymore or what belongs to the dead. Sometimes I wonder if I'm losing my mind. I find myself thinking about how I should restock the cellar or go feed the chickens like we still have our home, but then I remember. I'm forgetting things, and my head is full of fog."

The fogginess started two years ago, clouding one of those years so much that I barely remember much of it except the heavy pain it couldn't erase. It dissipated last summer, allowing me to see the world clearly again, but that same sensation is creeping in again to steal more of my sanity.

"When I was studying to be a healer at the Acadamaidh, others in my classes were training to work on battlefields on the Mainland. They noticed that a person's mind can try to shield them from traumatic events by blocking out memories. To protect us from pain and stress, the brain forgets," Percy says. "Unfortunately, the mind is more complex. We don't know how to mend it like we do flesh."

I remember Percy telling me this a while ago after the daughter of one of his patients grew concerned when her mother began forgetting that her husband had died. He tried giving me a medical explanation for the grief and fear I've felt over the years. His way of coping, but it did little to help me.

"I'm afraid too," Percy continues, tracing the curve of my ear with his finger. "We can't always help being afraid, but we can work on managing its symptoms until we deal with the source. The body and the mind can't function without rest. I can make a tea or use my magic to help you get to sleep."

I brush the dampness from my eyes. "You've done enough for today."

His lips are set in a way that tells me he wants to say more but decides against it. "Well, let me give you something better to dream about then. Think of the morning. I'll cook eggs, gather some berries and nuts to add to porridge with honey. Eat, drink, sleep, and stay safe. That's what we need to focus on right now."

He makes it sound like it's another morning at home. His words may not always soothe, but sometimes his closeness is enough.

"Why don't you tell me another one of the stories?" he goes on and props his arm under his head.

I sigh, sifting through the crowd until I find an older woman with steel in her voice. "Morag Anstace MacGregor. She was seventy-six when she died. Osgar's great aunt. Born in a winter storm," I begin, flashes of memories swirling behind my eyelids. "Her father taught her to play the bagpipes and how to make them in the workshop they had..." Her words flow off my tongue, following me into sleep.

The smell of dirt hangs around me as I finish digging the hole. Sweat drips from my nose, and I wipe my forehead. Four dead voices hum in my blood, their memories flashing behind my eyes. The corpses I found on the outskirts of Auchendrain's forests shuffle through the graveyard. Three of them are mostly rotted corpses with tattered clothes, the other a skeleton with only a rusted locket around her neck. I knew they were there for weeks, but I tried to resist their calls until they became too painful to ignore.

I stare into their purple eye sockets as my gift breathes empty breaths into them and outlines their skeletons. "This should be better than where I found you," I tell them and unclench my stiff fingers from the shovel.

Something flashes through the trees, and I grab my axe. A dozen sídhe slither through the air. The presence of another bloodgifted hits me, warming my veins as panic hatches in my chest. I didn't sense it before. The dead shift in the direction of my distress.

"Wait! I'm sorry. I didn't mean to startle you." A man steps into view, adjusting his glasses. His green robes look like the kind Acadamaidh students wear. He has a walking stick in his hands but is otherwise unarmed. "I'm not going to hurt you."

Everything moves slowly while my heart is ready to burst from my chest. Panic fills me with heat and cold all at once. I let the dead go, and they topple into the open graves, unmoving. He's the man who found me weeks ago—the one I ran from. I had lain low for a while, afraid to go outside, but when no Failinis came into the forest, I thought it was safe. No one knew I was here the past three years. Now my hiding place has been discovered, and he's seen me using my gift. My pulse feels too thick for my veins to contain.

The man sets his bag down and holds up his hands as he inches closer. I raise the axe higher, and he stops. He looks at the corpses, not with revulsion but curiosity, before his eyes drift over the graves.

"Did you do all this?" he asks. "There are quite a few people buried here."

"I didn't kill them," I say, my breath hitching. "Just leave me alone!"

"I'll leave, but I wanted to return this to you. You left it behind after you ran away. I've been trying to find you again to return it. And I keep getting lost in these woods," the man says and holds out the walking stick.

My gaze snaps to the long honey-colored stick with the familiar animal carvings along it. I'd been too afraid to return to the field to look for my walking stick after I'd been spotted that day. Taking one hand off the axe, I snatch my staff from him.

"The carvings on it are lovely. Did you do them?" he asks, but I don't answer. "Can I help you with anything, at least?"

"Help me?" I repeat. "Why?"

He gestures to the holes. "Seems like you could use some help. I'm sure it's hard work digging four graves."

I keep the axe up as he stands beside the nearest grave. The man's hands glow green, and the ground comes to life. Roots shove the dirt over the bodies, and grass grows over the mounds. A few orange sídhe take to the air, startled by the sudden disturbance. Blue and yellow flowers sprout across the graves where the headstones will go. He's a rootsower.

I stare down at him. My legs are tensed, ready to run at any second. "How did you find me?" I ask. "Why are you following me?"

"I was looking for medicinal herbs when I came across you writing in the field. The plants told me where to find you today," he

replies. "I didn't know anyone lived out here, let alone a boneweaver."

Most utter my bloodgift as a curse, but he says it with a smile. I shouldn't trust him. I survived a bear attack and winter storms, so why am I afraid of one man shorter than me? He doesn't look like a Failinis, but even the kindest faces can hide dark hearts.

"I'm Percy, by the way," he goes on. "Percival Bracken. Peas *to meet you." He holds his hand out to me, but I frown at it. "Get it?* Peas, *instead of pleased?"*

Peas? Maybe he's insane. Should I knock him out and leave him in a field far from here? But what if someone comes looking for him? I don't want to kill anyone, but I can't have anyone else finding this place. Or about me.

His smile doesn't change as he points to my forehead. "You've got dirt on your face."

My cheeks warm, and I look away, rubbing my brow until I realize my hands are covered in dirt. The rootsower takes a white handkerchief from his pocket and offers it to me. Tucking my walking stick under my arm, I clean my face, my trembling fingers fused to the axe handle. The fabric smells like lavender and something else I can't place. It's better than the stench of rot. I must smell like the dead too, but he isn't recoiling.

"You've put a lot of work into this place," the man says, looking at the dozens of headstones around us. "Did all these people die out here?"

I swallow, holding the answer back for several long seconds. "I found them...Thought they deserved better than being eaten by animals or forgotten," I mutter, afraid to look up. I hold the dirtied handkerchief back out to him.

"Keep it. I won't tell anyone about this place." He walks away.

"I don't think the dead could have asked for a better resting place. It's beautiful."

I look up, pulse skipping a beat. The man—Percy—waves his hands, and more flowers grow around the other graves. He picks up his bag and slips into the woods. Regardless of his words, I don't think I can stay here any longer.

THE MAP ON MY LAP THREATENS TO FLY AWAY AS THE WIND PICKS UP. My walking stick lays across it, the top of the stick bearing the engraving of a chicken I started carving. The smell of the flowers in the gully rises along the breeze. A week of traveling puts us roughly sixty miles from Àitesìol. Errigal isn't a huge island, but it feels like there are few places we can hide. The highlands are remote, with forests and unpredictable weather, but they're at least two hundred miles from where we are, which means weeks of traveling and more supplies.

I stare at our island, with its two major lochs that look like eye sockets, the lines of rivers, and its jagged coast in the south that gives it a toothy expression. Waterstains mar the map's edges, some of my notes about safe places and distances smudged but readable. I'd love a newer map, maybe a world map with places I've never heard of. I saw one years ago that Percy showed me in a book. It's childish to want something like a fancy map when I should be focusing on our survival.

Percy's shadow falls across me. Sunlight glints off his glasses. His hair is now red instead of brown, mine a dirty blonde. Percy said the change should fade in a month, so he'll need to use his fleshmending again to keep the current colors. Between his fingers, he twirls a blue cornflower. The flowers in the field seem to turn toward him, red poppies and purple asters swaying. A few yellow sídhe flutter between the blooms, edging out the bees and butterflies to get to the nectar. The wind tugs on the edges of Percy's brown overcoat. Morhenna wades through the field.

"Find our next destination yet?" he asks, grinning.

"We could go to the highlands. Ben Taibhse or Glentaibhse, or the Cluaran Mountains," I reply, pointing to the jagged peaks toward the top of the map. Beyond it is Loch Sùil and the serpentine Abhainn Sùil. It's surrounded by natural barriers and superstitions, a better defense than my axe could provide. Many creatures live there that even the Failinis would want to avoid.

Percy places the flower behind my ear. "A mountain cottage sounds nice. The cold would hurt your joints, though."

I manage a smile. "If it keeps us safe, I'll endure it."

It'd be a hard life, but we could make a home there. It wouldn't be the first time I had to build a home from nothing. Up in the highlands, I'd know the terrain better. Da always said that the mountains recognize their own, and maybe it's time to see if that's true. Percy says the strongest roots that can break through the hardest ground are the ones that survive the longest. He always has some sage wisdom that's both endearing and, at times, annoying. Sage wisdom. It's a blessing he hasn't used that pun yet.

"I'd be more worried about *you*, Percy," I go on. "You don't handle the cold well. The winters in the lowlands are very different than the ones in the highlands."

He sucks on his lower lip. “I suppose I’ll need to get another coat and some more woollen socks. And I’ll have you to keep me warm,” he replies with a wink. “Still, I’ve always wanted to visit the highlands. I read about so many unique plants that grow there. The quiet might allow me to work on my research.”

Despite his smile, the sadness darkens his eyes. Most of his papers were lost in the fire. Only one journal and a few sketches he copied and hid in the packs remained, along with the notebook he grabbed. In the mountains, we wouldn’t be around many people. Percy thrives off human contact. Healing is his gift and passion. Being unable to express that part of himself would be like chopping off a limb, and I don’t want to see him wither away behind a forced smile.

“We’d be heading that way, right?” Percy goes on, pointing in the direction to my right.

“No. That’s southwest. We’ll need to head north,” I tell him and use the walking stick to move his arm to the moorlands in front of us.

“Ah.” He stares northward. “That’s why you’re in charge of the map.”

The gods gave Percy many gifts, but he wasn’t blessed with a sense of direction. I realized this very quickly after he tried to lead me to a field of medicinal flowers that he’d heard of growing in the forest but instead got us lost for hours before I got us there and back. Even with his ability to talk to plants, he still couldn’t find his way.

“The are smaller towns in the foothills that are secluded,” I go on.

“Maybe get ourselves a nice croft with some more chickens and a goat,” he says.

"Morhenna would like other things to terrorize." The hen looks up as if she knows I'm talking about her. Even with singed feathers, she carries an air of superiority.

I take a swig of water and look back at the map where the Lùbach Mountains cut through the western side of Errigal. The longing for home brings to mind the rounded stone backs of mountains, and towering pines and spruces that break the white winters with green. The sound of cows lowing and the taste of Ma's bread with a chunk of salty butter. I can almost smell the crisp, foggy mornings. Only a few hundred miles separates us from the house tucked against the hillside like an exposed tooth.

I worried my gift would bring trouble to my family if people found out about it, so I left when I was fifteen to find a place where I'd be safe. I thought the world beyond the mountains was terrifying and so much larger than any map described. The first few years were hard, and I struggled until I ended up in the forests outside of Auchendrain, where I carved out a place for myself in that abandoned cottage. Where I eventually met Percy.

I glance at the clouds grazing on the blue sky. Would it be safe to go back to Teaghlach now? Or did the Failinis already find my family, which led them to Àitesìol?

Percy whirls around, going still. A pulse of green light flickers under his skin. My heartbeat speeds up at his change in demeanor. "What's wrong?" I ask and put the map away, grabbing the axe that's never far from my side.

"Four riders are coming. We need to move now." His voice remains steady as he gathers up his pack and Morhenna.

The ground seems to drop beneath me. They found us. My lungs can't pull in enough air.

"There's an outcropping and a bush on the other side of the hill," Percy says. "We can hide there."

"We can't stay here! They can sense us," I gasp as we run for the ridge.

"I have a way for them not to notice us."

I don't know what he means by that. The panic in my chest leaves me breathless and unable to ask the questions bouncing through my skull. I glance over my shoulder, waiting for the Failinis to appear or for the ground to swallow us up. Even the wind feels like an enemy. The skies are clear for now, but the waterdancer Failinis could bring a storm with them. Can the windsinger hear our breaths in the air? Can the earthcarver sense our vibrations through the ground? Do they have a beastcharmer with them that caught our scent? The Failinis are highly trained compared to the average bloodgifted, but I don't know how much of that is true or just stories used to instill fear.

My foot slips out from under me, and my right ankle twists. Something tears in my knee, pain shooting through my leg as I skid on rocks. I drop the axe and my walking stick. My hands catch on pointed green leaves hidden in the heather and tall grasses. Fiery needles sting my hands, the sensation prickling up my arms and making my face twitch.

"Morana!" Percy rushes to me as I writhe on the ground. Through the tears, I'm staring at the stinging nettles inches from my face. I know its bite well as the prickling sensation pulses under my skin.

"Nettles," I seethe through my teeth. "Gods' bones! Something's torn in my knee."

Percy drops the chicken and hauls me up, handing me my walking stick and grabbing the axe. We scramble to the top of the brae and spot the rocks surrounded by yellow whin bushes. I clutch my burning hands to my chest. The brush of my clothes against my skin makes the pain worse. We hobble down the slope and through the opening Percy makes in the thorny bush. He leans me against the rocks, and I almost scream as my leg jostles. I can't bend my knee.

Branches fold around us as he regrows the plants. "How close?" I say through gritted teeth.

"Too close. I can't heal you without risking them finding us," Percy whispers as he takes my wrist. I flinch at his touch, biting back a cry. "I'm sorry."

We huddle together as the sound of hooves against the ground grows closer. My heart's ready to explode, my breathing labored. Releasing my walking stick, I clamp my hand over my mouth. I try to remain still and ignore the throbbing pain in my limbs. The thorny points of the whin jab into my arm as I press myself as close to the rocks as I can. Morhenna clucks several yards from where we're hiding. We left her behind in the field. They'll see her and know we're here. We're trapped. No escape.

As my vision narrows and the terror stings my throat, my heartbeat slows, and my body feels heavy. Percy's hand is on my wrist, his breathing even as his eyes dart to every moving shadow filtering through the twist of thick branches and leaves. Panic races through my veins, moving like a water strider over a pond.

Hooves thunder past us, and four dark shapes move about fifty yards away. They slow, and I bite on my fingers. Morhenna squawks and flaps her wings at the Failinis, and one of the riders moves closer. "It's just a chicken," a woman says.

"Must have wandered away from one of the nearby farms," a man replies. "Looks like it's had a rough go of things out here."

There's a pause that stretches on forever before the horse moves away. "There's no sign of them in this area. I can't sense any bloodgifted around."

"Our prey is more evasive than expected." That voice makes my blood run cold. "If they slip past us here, Moray's company is patrolling near Ben Sùil and Sheabhag. We'll send word to him and regroup to get more hunters."

More Failinis are forming a noose around us. The hand clenched around my lungs releases a bit as the Failinis ride away. I stop biting my hand, afraid to move even when the sound of hooves disappears. Morhenna struts around the bushes.

"They're heading away from us in the opposite direction," he whispers, drops of sweat staining his green tunic. He drops the axe to the ground next to me.

I don't trust the quiet. "What if it's a trap, and they know we're here and are waiting for us to run?" I tell him through my trembling fingers.

"I can sense them through the plants to keep track of where they're heading."

"But if you use your gift and they sense us again..."

He takes a deep breath. "I'm going to have to use it to heal you."

We wait for minutes, hours maybe, until my heartbeat returns to normal and remaining still becomes unbearable. Percy touches the grasses as the green light burns in his veins. I don't fully understand how plants can see or hear anything, let alone talk, but he knows their ways better than I do.

"They're gone. The only people around for miles are some farmers," he says.

The yellow arms of the whin bushes open, and Morhenna stares at us with a look that I can only describe as incredulous. Air hisses through my teeth as I move. A bumpy red rash has spread across my hands, and the stinging hasn't abated. I'm afraid to look at my ankle, and the pain in my knee makes it impossible to move my leg without crying.

"What did you do so they couldn't sense us?" I ask.

"If you lower a bloodgifted's blood pressure enough, it temporarily masks their presence, and other bloodgifted can't sense them. I discovered the method during my last year at the Acadamaidh. But it's risky to do. It doesn't work if you're moving, and if your pulse drops too low, you'll go unconscious or worse."

"Could you have done something like that before to the Failinis to make them pass out?"

He tugs at his earlobe. "I can't do it from a distance. Dropping the pulse of two people is challenging. I could only hold it for a few minutes. I don't know if I could render a Failinis unconscious quickly in a fight."

His oath as a healer and his nature as a fleshmender means he doesn't kill. We've never been in a position like this where we've had to fight people. My eyes drop to the axe. I could have killed the earthcarver that night, but I didn't. Maybe it was weakness or fear of what the dead might scream at me if I did. Next time, we might have to make a choice whether to sacrifice our own morals to survive.

"I'll be right back," Percy tells me as he stands and leaves the outcropping.

Sweat coats my back, and nervousness wiggles around in

my throat for the few minutes that Percy's gone. I whisper a prayer and grab the axe despite the pain in my hand. He returns a few minutes later, holding several broad, green leaves. Dock leaf. He rubs them across the stinging areas, leaving a greenish residue on my skin.

"Kester has a sense of irony having dock leaves and nettles growing so close to each other. The cure to the problem a few inches away," Percy says.

"Too bad the god of plants didn't make a plant to fix a broken ankle," I mutter.

"I don't think it's broken." He rolls my trouser leg up past my swollen knee, and I bite my cheek to keep from crying out. The air grows warm as he touches my ankle, his bloodgift seeping from his fingers. "It's a sprain, which is easier to heal, but something's torn in your knee. It'll take me a bit to make sure it's repaired fully. And you'll need to rest."

I chew on my lower lip, the tears coming again. "I'm sorry..." I whisper.

He looks up. "You have nothing to be sorry for."

The soothing warmth spreads over the pain, and I relax. My muscles prickle as Percy mends the injury. The needle-like stinging from the nettles has dulled, the twinges running up my arm subsiding.

"What if something like this happens again and we can't get away?" I ask.

In the back of my mind has always been the whisper that my body will give out one day, and I won't be able to escape. Before I met Percy, my arthritis would get so bad that I couldn't move for a day or so. That cold dread that I'll slow us down to where the Failinis will catch us is clawing itself free, and I can't push it back down.

"Healing you isn't a burden, Morana. You're the strongest person I know," Percy says.

I stare at the crushed white clovers by my leg. At this moment, I'm anything but strong. This is what our lives have become—trying to grow amidst chaotic circumstances until something eventually crushes us. I want to cling to Percy's optimism, but I'm afraid to hope like that again, only to have it ripped away until there's nothing left.

When the fire in the severed tendons is soothed, Percy helps me stand. I know better than to question his skill, but it feels like the slightest step will undo it all. How long with it be until I break, and no amount of fleshmending will be able to fix me?

The sunlight grows brighter, and the voices of the dead become an incoherent sea of noise. I blink as the landscape ripples like waves. My palms grow sweaty, and I lean against my walking stick. The axe slips from my hand as I double over and vomit onto the wildflowers swaying in the breeze.

VII
Snowdrop

Galanthus

Consolation · Hope · Friend in need

I wipe my mouth with the back of my hand and stare at the mess on the ground with tears in my eyes. Percy's hand goes to my wrist. "Your pulse is high, but there's no fever or infection," he says. "Did you eat anything that didn't sit well with you?"

"I don't know," I manage to say.

The voices are growing louder, making it hard to focus. Burning fear slithers up my throat. I can't get sick. The Failinis were too close, and we can't afford to slow down again.

Percy places a hand on my stomach, the other touching my temple. Warmth moves through me, and the nausea retreats, but my heart hasn't settled. "Mor." Percy's change in tone breaks my thoughts, and I look up. Surprise rests on his face. I've seen that look before when he's examining patients.

The fluttering beats harder now. "What? Why do you look like something's wrong?"

"Nothing's wrong...You're pregnant," he whispers, and the words strike me in the chest. His grin is bright against the sunlight.

My breath hitches. That can't be right. "No...why now? Ever since—I haven't been able to..." My voice cracks, and I swallow the fragments as they cut my mouth.

Percy's eyes shimmer as he moves closer, palms resting lower on my stomach. "I'd say you're at least five weeks along. I can't believe I missed this," he says with tightness in his voice. "Your symptoms make sense now. The quickened heartbeat, shortness of breath, exhaustion, and nausea... When I lowered your pulse, I should have caught this. I...I'm sorry I wasn't paying more attention sooner."

The joy wavers in his voice as he begins to slip into a moment of guilt. Would knowing any of this sooner have changed things, or would it have made me more afraid? I think of the last time we were intimate, and I can't remember when I last had my monthly bleeding. We weren't trying, not after losing our first child two years ago. I wasn't ready, the grief still too fresh. Life before the fires is too muddled.

"You're not to blame. After all that's happened...You did the best you could. How could you have known if you weren't looking for it?" I tell him. I know as soon as I say the words that they probably will do little to help Percy feel better about missing this.

I take in Percy's face as he continues to stare at my stomach, the outline of his smile returning in the glow of his magic. While he's pushing aside his guilt to focus on this new life, the memories of all our expectations for the future we tried to grow sting me. All I can think about is when the heartbeat will be snuffed out, and I'll be filled with emptiness again. Another cluster of dried flowers pressed and forgotten between the pages of a story never written or buried under another willow tree.

Percy guides my hand into his where it rests against my stomach. His hand is smaller than mine but stronger and steadier. For a moment, I only feel my heartbeat before a tiny pulse nudges against my palm.

"Do you feel it? It's there. Strong, healthy," he says.

I pull away and stare out at the field. My mouth is dry as I try to breathe. I'm trembling, and my knees threaten to give out. Percy follows and takes me in his arms, his head resting beneath my chin.

"It'll be alright, Morana. It won't be like the last time. I'll make sure nothing happens to you or our child," he says. "I'll be here and help bring our child into the world healthy and whole."

"How can you know that?" My voice sharpens. "Last time," I swallow as tears form, "everything was going fine until...What if I lose this one too? It was so hard for me to conceive before. Something's wrong with me."

Percy takes my face, eyes glistening. "Who told you that? Nothing's wrong with you," he tells me. "I wasn't there last time, but I'm here now."

It wasn't his fault, and I never blamed him for going to see a patient in another village that day. There'd been no reason to worry that anything would go wrong. One moment I was in the garden, and the next, I felt the presence of death in me and the pain. The midwife in the village stayed with me as I bled and cried until Percy returned. It wasn't like all the other times when the familiar sensation brought peace amidst the sadness. This was darkness and the rotting promise of what could have been. Something so small that had barely left a mark on my body managed to leave such a gaping hole within me. It was a story I dared not awaken. I pushed those wounds down deep, buried them with the bundle beneath the willow tree.

"How can we bring a child into this world when we're being hunted? We're not safe here," I whisper as Percy wipes away a teardrop rolling down my cheek. "I'm afraid to hope for this again." If I lose anything else, I don't know if I'll be able to come back again.

"The world's rarely safe, but should that stop us from trying to hold onto some happiness?" Percy asks. "I'm afraid too, but I don't want hope to be another thing the Failinis take from me."

When I was trapped in the dark days, Percy didn't let me sink. He held on, even if it was in silence, his hand around mine to tether me. Eventually, I came back. The sun continued to rise each day, even after seeing all the broken things in the world, and so would I. Exhaustion hits me, my racing thoughts trying to stay above the surface.

I break away from Percy as Morhenna struts toward us. "What do we do now?" I ask and take a drink from the waterskin. Even though the past week has pushed me to my physical limits, I feel like any sudden movements will disturb the small life now growing inside me.

"I know it's a risk, but maybe we should stop in a nearby town," Percy says, adjusting the strap of his pack. "Sleeping inside might be good for us both. We still have money. Now more than ever, you'll need the rest. And it'll be a chance for you to write down the stories of the dead."

It seems impossible that we'll be able to find rest for long. Things were already dangerous, and now...Despite Percy's magic keeping the nausea down, the worry of what could go wrong makes me want to throw up again. Still, the thought of a bed and hiding in a house instead of in the woods sounds nice. I only nod, swishing more water in my mouth to remove the vile of worry taste clinging to my tongue.

"I'll make a tonic to help with morning sickness," Percy says and takes my hand. "Let's try and find a place to get some rest before the sun goes down. The plants say there's no sign of the Failinis nearby."

I manage a weak smile. Percy has always been able to shift his emotions from sadness to happiness with ease, while I seem to struggle to be optimistic. He's already focusing on this new life as if we weren't just hiding and holding our breaths with the Failinis so close to us, and I hate how I can't move past what's happened to us. The past has its claws in me, and I'm not able to let go of the life we had in Àitesìol. Percy's excitement is glowing on his face, but even as we walk through the field, I can't feel anything but the weight of dread.

THE TONIC STICKS TO THE INSIDE OF MY THROAT, THE CHAMOMILE, peppermint, and ginger concoction settling in my knotted stomach. The vomiting from yesterday has subsided while nausea creeps up each time I swallow. Exhaustion hunches my shoulders and pushes against my spine.

"How are you feeling?" Percy asks. The question wears grooves across the air with the number of times he's asked it.

I shoot him a sharp look and hand the glass vial back to him, pulling my cloak closer. "Better. The tonic's working." It eases my symptoms but does little to unknot my insides or change the fact that I'm pregnant.

A worn road cuts through the meadows and moors where farmlands stretch across the landscape. Clusters of houses appear over the rise. I can sense their dead and the scattered bones of animals in the fields. To sleep in a bed and not in the rain or the middle of a forest is a long-forgotten dream. I can't get rid of the sense of danger the closer we get to people.

"Do you still think it'd be worth the risk?" I ask.

Percy rubs the back of his neck. "I think a chance to get a decent night's sleep is worth it."

I'm sure I sound calloused, not wanting to put ourselves in more danger even though we're not looking out for ourselves anymore. Some moments it's easy to forget yesterday's revelations.

Morhenna glances at the fields as a herd of sheep amble toward us. Black faces peek out beneath white wool, the baaing growing louder. Ewes with lambs walk past, much to Morhenna's annoyance. A man with a blue bunnet follows behind them, whistling and encouraging stragglers to move with a tap of a stick. His blue and brown feileadh mòr is tied across his chest and wrapped around his waist, held in place with a leather belt and silver pin.

He glances at us before I can tell Percy that we should head in the opposite direction. A wide grin appears. "Greetings, lads," he says before giving me a second glance. "Oh, my apologies, lass. Dinnae see many women your height. My eyes must be failing me. Where you folks heading?"

Percy smiles as he holds Morhenna under his arm. "We

got turned around in the woods after our chicken got loose, and we're in need of some directions."

"Best be careful of the woods. There have been some cu-sìth seen recently. I heard the ones close to Glencnàmhan dhè have some sídhe swarms and will-o'-wisps near the peat bogs," the farmer says, grimacing.

"We're looking for a place to stay for the night," Percy says.

The farmer points in the direction we're heading. "Neòinean is just over the brae."

"We'll keep our eyes open. Any decent lodgings there?"

"Aye. The Green Goose, Meadow Springs, and Kester's Grove. There's one called the Dripping Bucket, but it's not the best. It's best if you don't wander by yourselves at night. People go missing, although no one's disappeared in a while, thank the gods. When the gloaming comes, things get strange. There's news about boneweavers terrorizing villages by raising the dead. Gods' bones, thought the Failinis got rid of that lot ages ago."

The man shakes his head and spits on the ground. My stomach drops, the spiteful way he says boneweavers hitting the air like a slap. Has word of what I did in Àitesìol spread that quickly? If people are afraid of boneweavers in the area, any nearby towns may already have Failinis looking for me.

Percy doesn't react to the farmer's words. "We'll heed your warning."

"Try the Meadowsweet Bakery while you're visiting. Best shortbread and scones around," the man adds with a tip of his hat before he follows his sheep, whistling.

My grip tightens around my walking stick. "Do you think

the Failinis are in that town looking for us?" I whisper. "It doesn't seem safe to go there."

The draw of the dead calls to me again, and I catch a tinge of sadness and fear coming from the direction of the town, but it's hard to tell with the hundreds of others clinging to me.

"The plants haven't seen any others come by recently. That farmer didn't mention a man and a woman specifically, so the rumors could have changed into something else by now," Percy replies. "The man *did* say there was good shortbread there. I'd risk being abducted for that."

I sigh through my nose. Gods' bones, this man is telling jokes when we're faced with a serious decision. His humorous attempts to lighten the situation aren't helpful. Sometimes he can be so irritating.

"Do you think I should disguise myself as a man?" I ask and look ahead down the road.

I've been wearing trousers instead of a skirt because they're easier to travel in, preferring my roughspun tunic over the blouse. I'm sure my appearance and the dirt from the road makes me look the furthest thing from womanly.

Because of my height and build, it's not the first time I've been mistaken for a man. There were boys back home who made fun of me, but they stopped laughing when I grew taller than them and could cut wood without much effort. Da used to tell me that Beathag didn't make me a willowy lass because she wanted there to be more of me to love. I think it's because she knew I'd need broad shoulders to carry the weight of life.

"Are you thinking about making a beard? You'd look cute with one," Percy tells me.

"I'm being serious," I say.

"I am too. Beards are a serious thing, especially since I can't grow one well, so at least one of us should have one."

THE TOWN OF NEÒINEAN IS A COLLECTION OF HOUSES AND STONE buildings growing out of a hill. There are more shops and markets than there were in Àitesìol, so many more bloodgifted. We get a few glances from people passing us, and I keep my head down for fear of being recognized. We haven't seen any Failinis yet, but it feels like there are eyes on me. Percy smiles at anyone who walks by, using his friendliness to shield us from suspicion.

We find a green sign with a goose on it. Laughter drifts out through the open windows. A dog lounges outside the tavern, lifting its black and white head as it yawns. It eyes Morhenna, but once it realizes that we're not going to give her up, it puts its head down.

"Guess this must be the Green Goose," Percy says, rubbing Morhenna's head. "Looks cozy. Hopefully, they're chicken friendly."

His words are distant as I look up the road, drawn by the familiar tug of new spectral whispers. There's something else that makes its way through the swirl of the dead pressing against my senses. There's a deep anger rooted here, tinged with fear. I leave Percy and follow.

"Morana?" The dead toss my name around as they try to get my attention. "I guess we could look at the others. I think I overheard some people saying that the Dripping Bucket has good handpies."

When I blink, I'm standing outside a two-level building.

The smell of baking bread surrounds it, making my stomach twist. The sign above the door says "Meadowsweet Bakery" in bold lettering, with loaves of bread and flower bundles painted beneath it. A woman and two children step out, a basket of wrapped bread balanced on her hip. She casts us a look before she pulls her children along down the street.

"Found the bakery, I see." Percy follows me as I step inside the shop.

Shelves of bread, pastries, jams, honey, and preserves line the walls. Pies are displayed on stands with trailing lace across the counter. Sunlight comes through embroidered curtains. But despite the tantalizing smells, my palms are clammy, and a numbing chill creeps up my legs.

"Are you alright?" Percy asks me, readjusting his grip on Morhenna.

"I—"

"Oh! I didn't know I had customers," a lilting voice says. "Sorry. Was putting some pies in the oven. What can I get you?"

Percy matches her grin. "We're passing through and were told to come here," he tells her.

Flour-covered hands tousle the blue apron around the woman's waist, leaving dusty handprints on the fabric. Her dark hair is pulled into a bun, and a yellow cloth that matches her skirt and blouse covers her head. She looks a bit older than us, mid to late thirties. A smudge of white streaks her brown cheeks. The gap between her front teeth is visible as she smiles, doing little to put me at ease with the loud yells clamoring over the other voices here.

The woman turns her dark eyes on me. Gods' bones, my blood's alive with energy. She's a bloodgifted—a strong one.

It's overwhelming, but familiar somehow. Cool like water pushing against me.

My knees give out, and I vomit onto the floor, feeling cold and hot at the same time. All the voices crash into me and pin me to the floor.

Flashes of lightning cut across the sky. The cold air hits my teeth. Mud and rocks scrape my knees. Fear is a raging river in my chest. A figure swings a blade that catches the fading light—

I jolt upright, a scream working its way out. A sour taste coats my mouth, and I gag. My hands search for the axe, but it's not at my side. Panic tightens around me until my heartbeat pulses through my whole body.

"Mor, it's alright!" Percy appears, gripping my shoulder. "Breathe."

Blinking, I look at the room with unfamiliar walls and a musty smell. This isn't the bakery. Morhenna sits on a stool in the corner by a small desk.

"What? Where are we?" I rasp.

"You passed out after you threw up. You've been asleep for a few hours. The baby's fine, but I'm worried about what happened. Anstice helped me get you into bed." I raise an eyebrow at him. "The baker. Her name's Anstice."

He hands me a cup of water, and it slides a cool path down my throat. Slowly, things come back. The intense weight bearing down on me. The memories—whose? I don't recognize the whispers crawling up from the floorboards. The presence of death is strong here. Too strong for any place outside a barrow or a battlefield. It's painful and angry.

"What's wrong?" Percy asks and sits on the edge of the bed.

I shake my head, a throbbing ache building under my skull. "Something's not right here. We need to leave," I tell him. "There are bodies under the bakery. The dead here didn't die naturally. I think they were killed and buried here."

His brown eyes widen behind his glasses, his gaze darting to the half-open door. "We can make an excuse to leave," he whispers. "We'll leave this town and go somewhere else."

"We need to leave now—"

The room spins as I stand, nausea reaching up my throat. "Careful," Percy murmurs as he steadies me. "If you think she's dangerous, I'll knock her out, and we can get out of here—"

The door creaks open as I grab the axe. The woman, Anstice, stands there with a confused look on her face. "Oh, you're up. I wasn't sure you'd be moving so quickly after the fall you took," she says.

"Yes. Thank you for letting us rest here, but we should be on our way," Percy replies, keeping his voice light as he gathers our packs and the chicken.

"There's no need to rush. I've made supper, and it looks like you both could use a good meal. There's cock-a-leekie soup and pies." Anstice opens the door more and steps into the room. A knife slick with red is in her left hand, her smile never faltering. "I insist."

My eyes don't leave the blade. She's only one woman, not a group of Failinis, but her bloodgift is strong, and I can't tell what abilities she has. No doubt she knows we're bloodgifted too. If we try fighting her here, it could alert someone.

Everything inside me screams to leave this place, but

there's something else that's refusing to let me go. The dead voices gather here and urge me to stay. Blood and bones, have I gone insane? I lower the axe, sweat coating my palms. Or do the dead know something I don't?

I meet Percy's gaze as his hand tightens on my shoulder. "Supper sounds lovely," he tells her.

VIII
Witch Hazel

Hamamelis

Protection ❧ Light in the darkness ❧ Joy

Anstice moves around the kitchen, placing food on the table while humming a tune. She's cleaned the knife and set it on the counter. I glance at the hanging chandelier made of stag bones. This place is a disorienting contradiction—sweetness masking something darker. The anguish of the dead beneath me is overwhelming. I don't know how many are here. Ten? Fifteen? The other voices still talking to me make it hard to concentrate.

Silent questions pass between Percy and me when our gazes meet across the table. I nibble on a piece of thick bannock bread slathered with butter. Morhenna struts around the table, pecking at crumbs that have fallen. Nausea and hunger battle in my stomach, and I'm afraid to eat the soup. Everything smells delicious, but I know most of it has meat in it. I didn't eat a lot of it growing up because it was strange to have death inside me and feel the creature's memories sitting in my stomach. Flesh isn't like bones I can connect with, and the memories it gives off are like decaying flashes, warped and rotting.

While Anstice is turned away from us, I see Percy rise, and

I think he's going to make a move, but she turns around, so he reaches for the teapot instead. If he can surprise her and wrap her up in vines, I can try holding her down long enough for him to make her pass out so we can leave without drawing attention to ourselves. Or...The dead beneath the floorboards would be my last resort. I want to avoid a fight if possible.

"So, where did you two say you were from?" Anstice asks as she sits across from me. Around her neck is a pendant carved into the shape of three interlocking hearts. A love knot made of a piece of skull bone—human bone. My blood goes cold. Why does she have that?

"Cruithneachd, but we've traveled to different towns for years," Percy tells her, hand around the cup of steaming floral-smelling tea.

Anstice leans forward. "Why did you travel?" she asks.

"Just doing odd jobs for people."

"Oh, so secretive." Her smile appears as she pours herself some tea. "Let me guess, you're a healer of some sort?" Did he let something slip when I fainted earlier? "You have the look of someone smart, and I could tell by how you tended to your wife after she collapsed."

I resist the urge to cover my ring. She's too observant. Or we've been too careless.

Percy gives a dry laugh. "I'm not much of a healer. Just doing what I can. It's mostly herbal remedies," he replies.

"Still. Could you check out this rash on my back?"

Percy pushes his glasses up with his knuckle. "I suppose I could...How long have you had it? Has it been itchy or oozing?"

Anstice laughs and waves her hand. "I'm only joking. I bet

a lot of people ask you to look at their ailments and wounds once they find out you're a healer."

"It keeps life interesting." He stirs the chunks of chicken and leek in the dark broth.

"I used to travel around a lot too before I came here. I took over this bakery when the owner went missing three years ago," Anstice tells him.

My hand knocks against my cup, and I steady it before it falls over. The dead react to Anstice's words with anger and sorrow, and coldness creeps up my skin. That shepherd mentioned people have gone missing in the past. Could they be connected to her? The bones here know the secret, but I can't risk using my bloodgift to find the truth.

"A farmer mentioned disappearances. Does that still happen?" Percy asks.

Anstice sips her tea, a shadow passing over her smile. "Not often. Rumor is that a hunter was responsible for the disappearances. They lured travelers to their house and kill them. It was only one or two a year, but then they began taking people from the town. Soon people began vanishing every month. No one knew what happened to those people, and everyone grew so afraid they stopped going out at night alone."

Her words take the warmth out of the air. There's a glint in her eyes that reminds me of Captain MacAdoh. It's the look of something cunning that's trapped its prey.

"Since no bodies were ever found, people whispered about what happened to those who were taken. One person even suspected they might have been eaten. Still, no one knows what happened to the hunter and their victims. It could be that they left or are waiting to strike again."

Percy's eyes go to the pie and soup, jaw tightening as he lets go of the spoon. "Could I have some water, please?" he asks.

"Of course!" Her face brightens as she stands, going for the pitcher by the cupboards.

I look at Percy, grabbing a knife from the meat pie. Its handle is made of smooth bone. It's not human, but the sickening feeling grows. Percy nods to the ceiling before looking at the door. Anstice's back is to us as she fills a cup. We have to catch her by surprise now.

My hands tremble as my magic wraps around the skulls and different bones of the chandelier, the memories of the stags flooding me with images of forests, lakes, and blood. The buzzing sensation warms my veins, and I stand. They clack, and the purple light fills the empty sockets and courses like cracks along the yellowed skeletons. Gripping the knife, I lunge for Anstice, bringing a storm of rib and leg bones shooting toward her.

Vines slither out and wrap around Anstice's legs. Morhenna squawks, but I barely hear her over the raging voices of the dead filling my ears. Anstice whirls around, and the bones stop before they reach her, held in the air between us. I freeze as the purple outline of Anstice's skull appears underneath her skin. The cool prickling sensation floods me, resonating with my bloodgift. It feels like my gift, that familiar ashen taste hitting the back of my tongue.

"You're...a boneweaver?" I say, blinking. My power wavers for a moment.

"Just like you," she responds with a grin. There's no surprise in her voice, only excitement.

I often wondered if all the other boneweavers had been

found and killed or fled and that I was the only one left in Errigal since I'd never met another one. Despite the fear and adrenaline still rushing through me, I'm elated. Even if she's a killer, I'm not the only boneweaver left.

"Morana." The floorboards rattle beneath my feet as long wooden arms reach around us, sharp ends pointed at Anstice. The vines continue to crawl up her body.

"I think there's been a misunderstanding," Anstice says.

She brushes aside some of the bones with a wave of her unrestrained hand. The stag skulls turn to face me, toothy grins waiting. She's much stronger than me. Trying to keep my grasp on the bones is like pushing against a wall.

"The people under this house," I start, unable to move the deer skeletons, "did you kill them?"

"Ah. I suppose that's what drew you to this place," she says. "No, I didn't kill them. I *did* kill the one who murdered them and buried him in the yard, though."

"Why should we trust you?" Percy asks, the green glow becoming brighter in his palms as he steps toward her.

Anstice faces him. "Your wife can ask the dead for the truth."

I shift my attention to the bodies many feet below. They're waiting to tell me their side of the story. There's a young girl's voice that spreads through my consciousness as I fall into the cool stream, letting go of the stag bones. Her life flits by, the ending a patchwork of cutting emotions as a man's face comes into focus, a cleaver in his hand. The girl, Adamina, cries out, and her mother's name is on my lips. I stagger back as the blade cuts my throat, and I choke on the blood. The bones clatter to the floor, and tears streak down my cheeks as I release Adamina.

"She didn't kill the people here," I whisper.

"You spoke with Adamina," Anstice says, sadness creasing her face. "She was one of his youngest victims."

I grip the table as Percy helps me into a chair. My hands go to my throat, but there's no slice. Violent deaths leave a different mark on me, the bones remembering that pain much longer even though the spirit has gone on to find peace. My body's heavier with the added presence of the little girl.

The floorboards settle back, and the vines snake away from Anstice. Waving her hand, the bones lift, coated in the purple light of her bloodgift, to reform the chandelier. Anstice goes and grabs a dark bottle from a shelf. She uncorks it and pours me a cup of something that smells floral and honey-sweet.

"I'm sure you have a lot of questions," she says.

THE CANDLE ON THE TABLE HAS MELTED DOWN TO A NUB, THE shadows along the walls thick in the low light. We've been sitting and listening to her for the better part of an hour. Adamina clings to me as she begs me to write down her story, but I have questions that I want answered. Percy drinks and listens, head resting in his hand. Morhenna sits under his chair, preening herself.

"I came to Neòinean because I was drawn to its dead. I knew it was dangerous for a boneweaver to linger where the dead are, but no one seemed to know what was here," Anstice says, sipping her cup of lilac mead. "Then I found what was buried here and the man responsible. He owned this bakery, and I befriended him to learn how many he killed. The Failinis came to the town to see if a bloodgifted was responsible. He wasn't a bloodgifted, just a sick man. I killed him before he hurt anyone else. I convinced the townsfolk I was his niece and that he'd gone to the highlands to visit family, but died on the journey there and left this place to me.

"If they knew the truth about the monster that stalked their streets and served them foods made with their loved ones, they would've burned this place to the ground. Selfishly, I've grown fond of this bakery despite its history."

I felt fifteen bodies resting in the earth. How many more did this man kill and dispose of that aren't here? "If you killed him, why not return the bodies to their loved ones?" I ask, my cup of mead untouched.

"It'd draw too much suspicion. The Failinis left after a year when the disappearances stopped. If the bodies started turning up, it'd make people panic," Anstice tells me as she stares into her cup. "Someday, I want to bring them home, so their families can have closure. Sometimes their relatives and friends come in here, so the best I can do is bake the favorite foods of those who died."

When I lived on my own in the forests outside of Auchendrain, I sometimes came across the bodies of people who perished in the woods. I didn't want to leave them scattered and alone, so I made a graveyard in a glen—far from my house. No one tells tales about boneweavers being collectors of stories or us saving people.

"How did they not find out that you're a boneweaver?" I ask. The God's Tear glinting in Captain MacAdoh's hand appears in the back of my crowded mind.

"You'd be surprised how well a smile and some pastries can disarm people. They were here for a local investigation. While the theory about a boneweaver stealing people for some sort of dark ritual"—she rolls her eyes—"was mentioned, the Failinis couldn't find any evidence of that. The gods were looking out for me. That and I had a little bit of help from this."

She takes a faded red and tan pouch out of her pocket and sets it in the middle of the table. Percy reaches for it, eyes widening as he opens the small bag. "What kind of plant is this?" he asks, pulling out a pinch of dark dried leaves. Percy's rarely been stumped by a plant. His magic sparks at his fingertips, and his brow scrunches. A few pieces shift, but the flakes remain mostly still in his hand. "This plant isn't from Errigal or even the Mainland. It's strange that I can't use my abilities on it."

"It isn't," Anstice tells him. "It's called bloodleaf, and it grows in a land far from here. When ingested, can suppress a bloodgifted's ability for several hours. Once you take it, you're unable to use your abilities until it passes through you, but no one can sense you, either. It's a trade, but it's saved my life many times over the years. It even tricked a God's Tear into thinking I was ungifted."

My eyes remain glued to the pouch. A plant that can hide a bloodgifted's nature? A thrill runs through me at the thought of not having to hide, yet some part of me wonders how life would be without being able to hear the bones that whisper to me.

"How do you have this? I've never heard of a plant doing such a thing," Percy says.

"Do you think the Failinis know about this?" I ask.

"I doubt they know about it," Anstice tells us. "I got this long ago from someone I knew. The plant had been passed down through their family for generations long before they came to Errigal. It doesn't like to grow here and resists most rootsowers. I was told that the bloodleaf was believed to have been created by the morrigans to fight the gods and their bloodgifted, which is why it affects us the way it does."

Percy looks up as he dusts the powder back into the bag. "Do you have more of this?"

Anstice takes the pouch back and holds it in her hand. "This is the last of what I have. I use it sparingly, but the Failinis rarely come here much these days."

"Were you on the run from the Failinis before you came here?" Percy asks as he tears off a chunk of bannock bread.

She touches the inside of her wrist. There are blue ink lines, but I can't see the design. "Someone close to me was killed by the Failinis many years ago." Anstice's voice is wistful as something from the past draws her away from the kitchen. "I fled before they found me."

"Are there more boneweavers still alive?" I ask.

Anstice looks back at me. "I take it you haven't met many."

My head swims with new things. Other lands. Herbs to hide a bloodgift. Another boneweaver. "You're the first. Everything I know I taught myself or heard from stories."

"Arianrhod's blood still lives, despite how much the dogs have tried to destroy us. The gods still have a purpose for us even though most people can't understand why we exist." She takes a sip from her cup.

"When we were fleeing, Morana raised an entire barrow full of dead, and the surrounding field," Percy tells her.

"That's impressive." Anstice's eyebrows raise, and my cheeks warm. "Reminds me of the boneweavers that used to fight on the battlefields and raise armies of the dead."

"I can't imagine doing that more than once. It took so much out of me, and it felt like my veins had been sucked dry afterward," I say. "All those voices at once would be distracting. When would they have the time to write down all their stories?"

"Is writing the stories of the dead your price for raising them?"

"I didn't know the requirement was different for every boneweaver. I write down what the dead tell me as a story. It's the only way to satisfy them."

"Mine's making the foods they liked the most in life, which has helped me run this place.

It's my way of reminding the people who come in that the memories of their loved ones live on," Anstice says and slathers a thick smear of butter on a piece of bread. "I'm guessing that you haven't had a chance to write down everything since you left your village?"

Can she hear all the dead around me with how loud they are? I've never gone this long without completing the price requirements. "I haven't."

"I think I have some paper lying about you can have. It's best not to keep the dead from their payment."

"The dishes with meat in them...Do you normally eat foods like that? Doesn't that bother you?" I ask.

Meat and other parts of dead creatures that aren't bones, like vellum and leather, make me sick when I'm near them. Our boots are made of plant fibers Percy wove and layered together that were treated with wax and shaped by the cobbler in the village, and our clothes are a mixture of nettle fibers and wool.

"Not really, but some of us are more sensitive to it than

others. I'll make some meals without meat for you." Anstice looks out the darkened window. "You can stay in the backroom as long as you wish. Your chicken will be fine in the yard."

"Are you sure? The Failinis are after us. What if we led them to you?" The thought of the bakery going up in flames and Anstice being swallowed into the earth chills me to my core. Trouble followed us to Àitesìol, and I don't want to bring it here.

"If the Failinis come, I'll introduce them to all my friends," she says with a wink. "I'll let you both get some rest. I'm sure you're eager for a decent bath and to sleep in a real bed. I'll make Adamina's favorite in the morning—honey scones with clotted cream and blueberries."

As she gets up to start clearing the table, I realize how tired I am. But for the first time in a while, my mind's buzzing with something other than the voices of the dead. What could I learn from Anstice? Does she know any stories about boneweaver lore? To have found someone who understands the pull in my blood uncovers the desire for kinship I've wanted for so long.

Percy snores in my arms, the sheets wrapped around us. With the warmth of his back against my chest, the smell of pungent herbs and calendula soap wafting from his hair, and the soft mattress beneath me, I should be able to sleep, but I'm wide awake. The whispers are quieter after the hours I spent writing down some of their stories. Even though we're not in the woods, I can't relax. I'm still afraid of the nightmares that will visit me once I close my eyes. MacAdoh's face and the flames continue to follow me. But now I fear that lost babies and death will find me again.

My stomach knots up, and I grit my teeth. My pulse quickens as I untangle from Percy, rushing to the washtub in the corner. My body clenches as I vomit. My legs shake, and I brace myself against the wall until the nausea stops. Every whisper presses down on me, and I feel all at once too small and too big for my body.

Percy stirs. "What's wrong?" he mumbles.

"Feeling sick again," I tell him and wipe the sweat from my upper lip. The bed frame creaks as Percy gets up, and his bleary eyes are illuminated as the yellow light from his bloodgift. The magic helps to ease the nausea that clings to my insides. "I didn't get this sick the last time I was pregnant."

"Each time is different. Stress could be adding to it, along with the fact that you haven't written out all the stories for the dead yet," Percy says, crouching beside me.

I lean against the wall, spitting out saliva. "I'll do that tomorrow." I can scarcely think about the next day with all that's happened recently. "How long can we really stay here, Percy?"

"Are you worried about Anstice or the Failinis finding us?"

"Both." As much as I want to trust Anstice, it's hard to know who to trust. I still don't know how to feel about being pregnant, but I don't want to endanger our lives more by lingering in one place too long.

"I think we can trust her. She's also hiding from the Failinis like we are." His hand moves in slow circles across my back. "But if you don't feel comfortable here, we can leave."

I chew on my lip. This could be my only chance to learn

from another boneweaver. I try to stand against each wave of worry threatening to wash me away. Today we may be safe, but what about tomorrow? My injury on the hill and this child remind me of my fragility, and that terrifies me.

"It's not that Anstice makes me uncomfortable...It's being in one place too long," I reply. "No place seems safe."

"They didn't find us in the field. We can keep a low profile here. The Failinis don't know where we are yet, and they didn't have a beastcharmer with them. And now, there's the bloodleaf to help us hide."

I wonder if it'll all be enough. Percy rises and gets me a cup of water. My mind continues to race, but the exhaustion leads me back to bed. Percy and I sink back under the covers, his forehead pressing against mine. I pray to the gods for dreamless sleep.

IX
Whin

Ulex europaeus

Vibrancy ❦ Endearing love ❦ Light

The dough slaps the counter, and Anstice kneads it with flour-covered hands. It's been a week, and she hasn't mentioned us leaving. Every morning before the sun rises, I've been helping her prepare foods for the bakery. The rhythmic mornings help keep my mind focused on something other than burning houses, Failinis, and being pregnant. I needed something else besides writing down the stories of the dead. Writing has been a relief, but I'm aware of the danger the stack of papers pose. Evidence of my bloodgift is spelled out in ink, yet it's hard to let the stories go.

Percy's made himself at home in Anstice's garden as has Morhenna. His usual cheeriness seems brighter as he studies the bloodleaf and tends Anstice's plants. He keeps a close eye on me, checking my pulse and the baby's while reminding me that I shouldn't be staying up late writing. Each morning I hold my breath, expecting the worst, yet the tiny heartbeat continues. Percy would prefer us to stay here for as long as possible, but I can't shake the feeling that we need to leave soon. The Failinis could show up without warning.

A puff of white explodes across my vision. I jerk back,

sputtering. Anstice continues pulling off handfuls of the dough and rolling them out to set on a tray.

"Was that necessary?" I ask and blow flour dust from my lips. I wipe off my face, giving her an offended look.

Anstice brings over a tray of risen loaves that have been sitting in the morning sunlight. "You can't be focusing that hard on the dough, so what's with the troubled look?" she says, looking at me out of the corner of her eye while cutting flower and leaf designs onto the dough. Her dark eyebrows are raised, a question folded between them.

I blink more flour from my eyelashes. Even though we've only been here a short time, there's a kinship with Anstice. It's not that I don't trust Anstice, but if I utter the words to another person, it becomes real and more vulnerable.

My fingers dig into the squishy dough, aches running through my hands. "I'm pregnant," I whisper, not sure for a moment if I actually spoke. "I found out last week."

Anstice regards me with a look I can't figure out. Putting the small razor down, she pulls me into a hug. She's not tall, but her arms hold me tightly. Something tickles my throat.

"This must be hard for you," she says. "The fear and worry probably overshadow any joy you have."

"I don't want to lose this one," I tell her. "It took years to conceive, and when I finally did...it was a miracle."

Anstice steps away and grabs a stool, placing it next to me. I sit and wipe my wet eyes, streaks of white coming away from my fingers. She brings me a plate of oat biscuits with raspberry jam. She says nothing for a minute and leans against the counter.

"It can be hard for us who know death intimately to keep our focus on the living. We spend our lives preparing for death that we forget to hold onto the happy moments of life," Anstice finally says. "How does your husband feel?"

"He's excited. Percy sees what this child will become, whereas I only see the ending. His optimism is overwhelming and frustrating at times." The biscuit crumbles on my lips, and swallowing is hard with tears running down my face.

"Even though we're drawn to death, we're still affected by the pain of loss," she says, wiping her hands across her apron. "Sometimes we have to remember that it was better to have those moments than to never have had them at all."

The sadness darkens the color of Anstice's brown eyes. She turns the carved bone pendant between her fingers, and I hear a worn, mellow voice emanating from it. I see a flickering memory of a woman standing on a hill—a younger Anstice—with her hand in another's. I block it out. It's too personal to peer into, and there are still dozens of voices swirling around in my head.

"Whose bone is that?" I ask.

Her finger stops over the center of the carved knots. "It belonged to another boneweaver. Airlie," she replies. The words deepen the lines in her face, and she seems much older. "They gave themselves up to the Failinis so I could get away. This was the only part of them I could salvage after they were killed."

Anstice flips the pendant over. On the other side is a four-eyed raven with four wings. In its claws is an eye. Arianrhod's symbol. Worshipping Arianrhod isn't forbidden, but for a boneweaver to wear her symbol openly is risky. Yet it fills me with excitement to see it.

"We're Arianrhod's children. What we know that death doesn't mean the end. Stories live on in the bones even if the soul has found rest beyond our reach," Anstice goes on. "'Though the parting may be sorrowful, our reunion will be eternal joy.' It may not lessen the present pain, but we have a hope that we'll see those we've lost again."

The eye on the pendant stares at me. "Is there any place for us in this world?" I ask. "People only see us as the bloodgifted that betrayed the gods. No matter where I go, the Failinis will always be searching for me. They think our kind doesn't deserve to exist."

"People like to forget that those few boneweavers weren't the only bloodgifted that sided with the morrigans. There were others. Our kind was the easiest to blame because our power already made people afraid. The chaos was brought by the morrigans and the angry souls of the fallen gods," she tells me as she takes a biscuit. "I believe Arianrhod has a plan for us and wants to bring her siblings back to life someday."

"You have a peaceful life here. Don't you fear being found out?"

"Yes, but after a while, I decided that the fear was keeping me from living my life. I chose to settle here and make the best of it, even if it willnae last forever. I've seen the cruelty of the Failinis, but not every person is like them."

My hand drifts toward my stomach, but I stop. For a moment, I see myself holding a baby in my arms, and Percy and I stand inside a house. It's too soon to think such thoughts. I don't want to be afraid, but escaping it is like trying to pull myself from a bog.

"I heard rumors of a place bloodgifted can go that's hidden from the Failinis. A hidden island in the north called Tearmann. I was told that if I wanted to gain passage to the island, I needed to seek out the Forests of Claigeann and wait for the will-o'-wisps to show me the path."

No maps I've seen have any island called Tearmann. Following will-o'-wisps to a secret island sounds like a story for bairns. The Claigeann Forests are beyond the Cluaran Mountains, a treacherous stretch of the highlands with thick snow and unpredictable weather. Not to mention the jagged terrain and strange things haunting the land.

"What happens after you find the path?" I ask.

"No idea. It was a story passed to boneweavers and any other bloodgifted who needed sanctuary," Anstice says with a shrug. "People I talked with believed it was real."

"If such a place is real, why have you stayed here instead of trying to find it?"

She brushes crumbs off her blouse. "I planned to, but these people needed a protector, even if they didnae realize it. I grew fond of them because they treated me well. This was where Arianrhod needed me to be."

I think of something like bloodleaf existing beyond the reaches of the Failinis or the Regency. Errigal feels so removed from the rest of the world. Maybe there are places where boneweavers can live in peace. Would it be worth it to search for such a sanctuary based on a tale?

Anstice takes my flour-caked hand and squeezes it. "I know you carry much sorrow in your heart, Morana," she says, "but don't mourn what isn't dead yet."

I STARE AT THE WHITE FLOWER ON THE TABLE, TRYING TO IDENTIFY IT. I can see the drawing in my mind, but its name is out of focus. My heavy sigh sends it tumbling onto the pile of other flowers laid out around the cups of tea.

"Daisy?" I say, sinking back in my chair. It's not right.

Sitting next to me, Percy moves the flower back and opens his book. "Close. It's greater stitchwort," he replies and points to the slender petals sprouting from the yellow center. "Daisy petals that are wider, and their florets are circular. Stitchwort usually has five pairs of petals with a thicker stem and leaves higher up."

Stitchwort. They're used to treat bug bites and skin conditions, and I can't remember the rest. Out of the hundreds of plants Percy's been teaching me about the past six months, I only know a handful by name. I know a lot of the common edible ones, crops, and some herbs Ma told me helped with pain and other ailments, but it's hard to keep them all in my head. Guess it's good that I'm not a rootsower because I'd be a terrible one.

"Want to know an interesting fact about stitchwort?" Percy asks, putting the flower on the page with a sketch of the plant next to his notes. "It's believed to summon lightning storms because of the popping sound the seed pods make when you crush them."

"If it storms, then you can add that fact to the book," I tell him.

His smile almost tips off his face as he presses a glowing green finger against the flower. Roots grow from it and attach to the page, holding it in place before he flips the page. He's been putting this book together to help me identify as many plants as possible.

"You'll learn them eventually. Lots of plants look alike, and it's difficult to tell them apart," Percy says.

Every day he's studying at the Acadamaidh, learning things I can only dream about. He practically oozes knowledge, and I'm often unable to understand half of it. I couldn't attend a place like the Acadamaidh with my gift.

I look out the opaque window of my cottage. "The school in my village never taught me anything like this. I'll never know as much as you, no matter how much I study," I mutter.

Percy turns to me. "Morana, just because you can't name plants doesn't mean you're less intelligent. Knowledge is knowledge, whether it comes from a book or experience. Remember that time you found the rabbit skeleton and put all the bones together in order from memory? I couldn't do that without years of training. Even then, I'd probably mess it up without my gift. That's amazing." My cheeks flush, and I look at my callused hands. "You're amazing."

My head snaps up, and I forget how to breathe. No one besides my family has called me amazing before. Our knees touch beneath the table, and I know he can feel my racing heart. My reflections swims in his glasses. When he's not looking, I study the subtle lines of his face like it's a map I'm trying to find my way across.

I don't know when I started noticing him. Was it when he started bringing me pastries? Or when he asked about all the dead in the graveyard? It could have been when I showed him places in the forest where he could find healing herbs, and he asked if I wanted to learn about them. Maybe it was when I realized that my height didn't intimidate him. Or the way his smile makes my heart race. Could be how the sunlight changes his eyes from the color of tea to almost chestnut. When I wasn't paying attention, the fear gave way to curiosity, and I noticed his absence keenly.

I've been staring too long. My hands are sweaty. I need to do something before I pass out. I lean in quickly and kiss him, tasting the sweet traces of the rosehip tea on his lips. I pull away before I can fully comprehend what I've done. Percy's eyes are wide behind his glasses. The silence is too loud, and I'm afraid the next words he says will be ones of revulsion.

"I-I'm sorry! I shouldn't have..." I stammer and nearly knock over my chair as I jump up. Oh, gods. I've messed up. He doesn't feel the same way. How could he? I'm probably still some wild-looking boneweaver to him, and he's just been kind to me out of pity. It's too hot in here. I want to bury myself in one of the graves.

Percy grabs my hand before I can run. "Well," he breathes, "I guess I learned something new. I just learned that I could have kissed you months ago instead of waiting this long."

I freeze, unsure what I heard. "What?"

"I've been wanting to kiss you, but I wasn't sure how you felt." He stands, taking both my hands. "You continue to surprise me, Morana."

My name wrapped in his soft voice fills my chest with warm cotton. Ma used to tell me about how she and Da fell in love, and I put that dream away long ago. There are no stories about boneweavers finding love. I don't know if this is it, but I don't pull away as Percy stands on his toes to reach my lips.

SUNLIGHT BREAKS THROUGH THE CLOUDS HANGING OVER NEÒINEAN as Percy, Anstice, and I walk toward the market. My walking stick clacks against the cobblestones. All the winding alleyways and houses remind me of Auchendrain, only without the towering walls and fewer buildings. Every time I pass someone, I want to lower my head and make myself smaller. I make sure the dark kerchief on my head covers my still blonde hair. Leaving the bakery feels like a risk even though there's been no sign of the Failinis.

I adjust the basket of preserves, the handle digging into the crook of my arm. This is the first time since arriving in Neòinean that I've left the bakery. Despite the worries still weighing heavily in my stomach, I'm curious to explore this town after being here almost two weeks and looking at the map Percy found. The old houses and buildings carry a refinement that makes me miss Àitesìol's simpler homes that reminded me of my childhood house. The darker stones have flower boxes in the windows and lines of clothing strung about. I feel the scattered bones underfoot and the presence of the barrow outside the town, the noise of the dead humming through the air.

Percy has gone ahead, looking into the window of an apothecary next to the Dripping Bucket Tavern. The red of his hair is bright in the sunlight. He greets people passing by and chats with every shop owner we visit, which makes running errands take longer. His friendliness worries me that we'll be recognized somehow and that he's drawing unneeded attention to us. I know he enjoys being around people, but I wish he'd keep a lower profile.

Anstice bumps against me, meeting my gaze with a questioning look. My face must have given away something again. Percy says I'm easy to read. "Everything alright?" she asks. "Still a voice or two hanging around?"

"It's not that. Large towns make me uneasy," I reply, the hem of my brown skirt brushing the tops of my shoes. "I grew up in a town in the mountains with maybe sixty people—and most of them were related to me. When I visited Auchendrain, it was a whole other world."

A few women wave to Anstice when they see her. She smiles back at them as they turn a corner. Curls escape from her yellow kerchief. "Oh? A highlander. I thought I could tell by your accent. Whereabouts are you from?"

"Teaghlach near the Lùbach Mountains. Are you also from the highlands?"

"Camgallan by the Abhainn Dannalaich in the north. It's about the size of your town."

"Oh! Some of my ma's relatives were from there," I say. I'd seen it on the map, and it seemed remote enough, but I was young and unsure if it was safe, so I headed south instead of further into the highlands. The kinship I've been feeling with Anstice only deepens.

At the end of the street, the crowded market comes into view. It sits in the middle of the square filled with stalls and carts. Walking on the hard cobbles hasn't helped my joints, and my pace has been slowing as the ache in my hips moves downward. I wince as I step on an uneven stone and a twinge of pain tears up the sides of my knees. Percy has helped with some recent aches, but new ones still manage to set in.

Percy turns around and notices me slowing. "Do you need to stop, Mor?" he asks, coming back over to us.

"I need to sit for a moment," I tell him as my eyes drift over to a bench next to a statue of a rearing kelpie. There's blue glass woven into its mane and along its white stone body like ripples of water, making it shine in the sunlight. "You can go on ahead, Anstice. I don't want to slow you down."

"I can stay with you," she says. "Percy, would you be able to finish the errands in the market while we wait here?"

"Of course," he replies as she hands him her basket with flour and herbs. I sit down on the bench with a sigh.

Anstice holds out a note to him with the rest of the supplies. "I usually get a good deal from the sellers there, but if you tell them that you know me, they might be willing to knock their prices down for you. Don't let Lyle overcharge you for his teas. See if Annag has any purple powder too."

"I can say with certain-*tea* that I'm good at bargaining," Percy says with a wink. He kisses my forehead before heading down the street.

Anstice sits beside me. "Does he always tell jokes?"

"Every chance he gets." I grip the walking stick and rub my left knee.

Her eyes go to my staff. The carving of Siobhen is finished, and I started working on some crocus flowers around it. "I like what you've carved. You're very talented."

I feel my face warm. "Thank you."

"Do you have an old injury that makes it hard to walk?" Anstice asks.

I give my ring a twist, my finger swollen and the knuckle stiff again. "Arthritis. Percy helps when he can, but the pain always comes back after a few weeks. Traveling has been hard, and I'm worried my knees will lock up or that I won't be able to run if we need to. And with this child on the way..."

I rest the walking stick across my lap. I remember the aches in my back, hips, and legs with the last pregnancy. It was different when we had a safe place to rest, but how many miles will we go before my body can't go any further?

"Percy's a skilled healer," Anstice says. "How did you two meet?"

"I was living outside of Auchendrain in the forest, and he found me after getting lost. I ran away and hid, but a few weeks later, he came across me while I was..." I look around and lower my voice, "digging graves for people who had died in the woods. I didn't trust him for a while, but he kept showing up. I hadn't met anyone that cheery before. He grew on me."

Anstice raises an eyebrow. "Was that a joke? Because he's a rootsower?"

"After being together ten years, guess he's rubbing off on me," I say, glancing at the market.

"Your husband often loses his head in the clouds, but I think you have also learned that from him, Morana," she tells me.

"That's probably true." Through the crowd, I see Percy talking to an older woman, and a smile creases my lips. "I thought I was fine, surviving on my own. But when I met Percy, I realized I didn't want to merely survive but to have a life. It's easier with him...but it's still hard, knowing that I could lose him."

Anstice glances at the sky, hands resting in her lap. She closes her eyes, and there's a tightness in her jaw. "Such is the nature of loving someone," she says.

"Was Airlie someone you loved?"

She touches the bone pendant. "Aye. We grew up together. Airlie and I were eleven when we found out we were boneweavers." She says the name like a prayer, tracing over the carved lines of the knots. "The town didnae want us to stay, so my father took us away. We never found out he was taking us. He died suddenly once we passed the Cluaran Mountains. Airlie and I moved from town to town for years to survive until we got to Auchendrain."

"Why did you go there when there are so many Failinis?" I ask as a pair of birds land on the kelpie statue. Even though

I've faced the world's hatred for boneweavers, I wasn't rejected from my family. I chose to leave before that could happen. I didn't want to find out what happened when the ties of kinship weren't enough to accept what was in my blood.

"Same reason you were probably drawn there. I'm sure you sensed it," Anstice says and lowers her voice, "all the dead there. Even though that city burns their dead, you can still feel the bones. And there's something else there that isn't like anything I've felt before. Something old and powerful."

The capital city holds many wonders, from the towering buildings to every house and street reflecting the best bloodgifted powers can accomplish, but there was a presence there I sensed when I first arrived. The inexplicable draw to it thrilled and frightened me. Percy had no explanation, only able to feel a slight tug. But if it's something only boneweavers could sense, then it must be something dead.

"Airlie and I never found out what it was. We lived in the city for years before the Failinis found us," Anstice says, fingers clenched around the pendant. "I often wondered if the whole city was built to lure and trap boneweavers after Airlie died."

"I'm sorry...I can't imagine how hard that was for you," I whisper.

She pats my hand with the hint of a smile returning to her face. "It's a strange thing to feel someone you love die. To hear their voice still in their bones while their spirit leaves. It's comforting and painful in a way that I can't explain. I have Airlie's story with me, but my heart knows it's not the same as them being here."

"Our heart aches with the loss while our blood is drawn to it," I say under my breath.

Anstice scoots closer, her arm looping around mine. "I think that's why people fear boneweavers. They mistake our way of mourning and understanding death as being excited for it. That and they're afraid we'll raise the morrigans to destroy the world, or that we're out to steal bodies for dark purposes. We feel that grief as much as any other person while also knowing we can keep a part of our loved ones with us. I met an older boneweaver who told me that we're meant to be the comforters to those who have lost by keeping the stories of their loved alive."

If only more people saw us that way. How many stories were lost because the boneweavers were gone? Who will tell our stories if there's no one left to hear the bones? How will it be when Percy dies? I don't know how I would ever be able to find comfort in his death. Would I be able to raise him, knowing it won't bring him back but that I'd be able to hear his memories again?

"If you're up for it, I have another errand we can do before we head back to the bakery," Anstice says, shifting the topic.

"Are you going to tell me what kind of errand this will be?" I ask.

"I don't think I will." She winks at me. "It's more fun if it's a surprise."

I grip the walking stick. My hips pop as I stand, stretching out my spine. The aches have turned to stiffness, which while uncomfortable, isn't unbearable.

Percy leaves the market, holding up the now full basket as he lopes toward us. His grin must mean he successfully got everything on Anstice's list. "It was difficult, but I managed to get a good deal from Lyle," he says and holds up a jar of tea. "I told him that two of his teas had started to mold, and fixed that while also giving him a few herbal recipes he could try."

Anstice inspects the basket's contents. "Guess it's handy to have a rootsower do the shopping. These are some of the best-looking vegetables I've seen in a while," she tells him and turns over a bundle of carrots.

"Miss MacNally did all the hard work. She's a gifted rootsower who knows how to focus on taste and quality."

"Don't let her hear you say that, otherwise, she may invite you over and keep you for hours in her garden so she can show you everything."

Percy pushes his glasses up. "That doesn't sound like a bad thing," he says.

Anstice stands. "Percy, would you do me one more favor and take these back to the bakery? I want to show Morana one more place before we head back," she tells him and slips my basket over his other arm.

"Are you stealing my wife?" Percy asks, gaze darting from me to Anstice.

"I'm sure Morhenna would be happy if I disappeared. She's the one I'd keep an eye on," I say and lean against my walking stick.

"Will your knees be alright?" Readjusting both baskets in his arms, Percy looks up at me. "Do you need me to heal anything? How's your nausea?"

I nudge one of the jars of tea back into the basket before it topples out. I know he's trying to be helpful, but his collection of questions is like unwanted prods. "I'll be fine, mo ghràdh." I bend down and kiss his forehead. "I'm sure this won't take long. And if I don't come back, I hope you and Morhenna have a wonderful life together."

"The chicken doesn't kiss nearly as good as you do," Percy says.

"We'll be back when we're back," Anstice tells him as she slips her arm through mine and pulls me along. My ring gently squeezes around my finger, a flicker of Percy's magic moving through the carved primroses.

Anstice hums as we head in the opposite direction of the bakery. There are more people in the streets. I recognize this lane from the map and the others intersecting it as I go through the layout of the town in my head. Without the voices of the dead weighing on me, I can focus and take everything in. It's comforting how a map can bring such clarity to the world. Unless you're Percy, in which it's confusing and unreadable. I'm suddenly worried that he won't find his way back to the bakery. It's amazing he got anywhere in Auchendrain before he met me.

We walk for several minutes, and Anstice still hasn't given any hints as to where we're going. "So, where *are* we going?" I finally ask, looking around at the rows of shops. Smells of cooking meat, herbs, and something sugary mix together through the scent of woodsmoke. This area is more crowded, and my hand tightens around the walking stick.

"You'll see," is her reply as she waves to a man selling flowers across the way.

A flash of green and white out of the corner of my eye makes me turn. A dress the color of summer grass sits in the window of a dress shop next to a pale yellow one with a red velvet cloak. There's a white blouse with blue and yellow flowers embroidered along the collar. There was a dressmaker in Àitesìol who made lovely pieces, but I never could justify buying new dresses. I don't know much about stitchwork, but the quality of these pieces on display is beautiful.

"See something you like?" Anstice asks, and I realize that I've moved away from her.

My breath fogs the glass, obscuring the clothes inside. "I haven't seen dresses this beautiful in a while," I say and step back from the window. "The green one is pretty."

My reflection, draped in the worn brown dress I've had for years, stares back at me. I didn't pack many clothes besides what I'm wearing, an extra tunic, and a pair of trousers. The blue and white dress I wore on my wedding day was left behind in the bothy. I only have the purple ribbon I had in my hair the day we fled and a few pieces of jewelry.

"Mairead's the best seamstress in Neòinean," she goes on, and I turn to look at her. "The Festival of Kester is coming up in a few weeks, and I thought you could use something more festive to wear."

"I don't have any money for a new dress." The thought of something new like that feels as if I'd be staying in this place awhile. Knowing what pursues me, lingering here too long is dangerous. It'd be another thing to weigh down my pack and remind me of what I'm leaving behind.

"As your friend, I can't let you go to a festival wearing *this.*" Anstice tugs at my skirts with the faded hem.

"I know it's not the prettiest thing, but it's practical," I tell her.

"Nothing wrong with practical, but you should have something that also makes you smile and that you're excited to wear."

She grabs my arm and pulls me inside before I can protest.

The smell of fresh linens wraps me up like a blanket. A woman in a pink dress organizes shelves filled with bolts of different colored fabrics behind the counter. She turns as the door closes.

"Can I help ye?" she asks, red hair curling past her shoulders. "Oh, Anstice. Looking for another dress?"

"Not for me, Mairead. For my friend," Anstice replies and gives me a nudge forward.

"What are you looking for? Anything caught yer eye?" Mairead asks me.

"The green and white one in the window," I say. "And the blouse. But I'm only looking at them."

The red-haired woman looks me over, and I want to shrink away as she pulls out a measuring string. "The blouse in the window might be too small, so I'll have to make a larger one. The green frock's been popular this year. I have the dress in a larger size that was ordered months ago but never picked up," the dressmaker says. "Let me get my things while ye change. Rodina,"—a brown-haired woman in a blue dress appears from the back—"grab some buttons and pins, please."

Mairead waves for Anstice and me to follow her to one of the back rooms with a curtain. Anstice smiles at me as the dressmaker disappears into the back of the shop. I suppose I could try on the dress to appease Anstice, even though I won't get it.

I step into the small changing room, leaning my walking stick against the wall. "Do you need help with your dress?" Anstice asks and draws the curtain close.

"You can loosen the laces," I say. It's strange to have someone other than Percy help me with my clothes. A wriggle of nervousness twists in my stomach as my bodice loosens, and I shrug the dress off until I'm standing in my underclothes. "You know you don't have to do this. I really don't need another dress."

Silence fills the room, and I feel Anstice's stare on my back. Her warm finger touches the raised scar tissue of one of the slashes between my shoulder blades, and I jump. The claw marks. Only Percy has seen them.

"How did you get these?" Anstice asks in a quiet voice.

"It was from a bear attack years ago—before I met Percy," I tell her under my breath, looking over my shoulder. "A bear came out of nowhere, and I fought it off. I had to raise two of the people I was preparing to bury to stitch up the wounds on my back. One held a mirror, and I guided the other with the needle. It wasn't great stitchwork, but it kept me from dying." Percy cringed when he saw the scars, disapproving of my crude work. Given the circumstances and using a corpse to thread a needle through flesh, I thought I did a decent job, considering I survived.

"Survived a bear attack and raised a barrow," Anstice mutters with a grin. "Someone should write a story about you, Morana."

I hug myself as I face her, pushing my dress aside with my shoe. "I don't think my life would be very interesting to talk about. Your's seems like a better story to write."

Anstice brushes a dark lock of hair behind her ear. "If I die, then you're welcome to the story my bones tell, but you shouldn't discredit your own. Not many boneweavers can make a life like you have. There are too few stories where we get happy endings."

How can someone with so much sunshine in their

expression say something so bittersweet? I open my mouth to speak, but Mairead and her assistant, Rodina, pull aside the curtain, arms full of fabric and a dress. Anstice presses against the side of the changing room.

"Anstice, you'll have to wait outside," Mairead tells her and begins unspooling her measuring string. "There are some new dresses in the corner by the threads from the Mainland. Arms up, lassie," she adds to me.

"Don't tempt me like that," Anstice says and leaves.

My pulse taps nervously against my chest as Mairead and Rodina measure and drape fabrics off me. If they notice me jumping at every touch, they don't say anything and take down my measurements. They aren't bloodgifted, but I can't quiet the worried thought that somehow, they can tell that I'm a boneweaver, that they'll find some evidence of it etched across my skin. Neither woman looks too long at my scars either.

I put on the green and white frock, the fabric crisp compared to the worn material of my other one. The lace collar tickles my clavicle, and the skirts stop at my shins. Whoever this was originally made for was large but not very tall. My fingers graze the pale embroidered leaves sewn along the side pleats. Even though I won't buy it, it *was* nice to wear it, even for a little bit.

Mairead pins up part of the bodice and measures from the hem to my ankles. "I can add some more lace to the sleeves and some ribbons in the back. Alterations should take about five days, especially if we bring Agnes in," she says, and Rodina nods. I'm not sure if she's speaking to me or voicing her own thoughts.

Anstice pokes her head around the curtain, grinning.

"More lace! Also, maybe pearl buttons instead of those front clasps," she says with a wink before I can stop her. "But first, I think you should see how you look in the dress, Morana."

"I-I'm fine," I reply, but she takes my arm and pulls me out of the changing room.

There's a mirror leaning against the wall. I don't recognize my reflection for a moment. I worry that I look like a giant stuffed into a costume, but now I can see how short my hair is now and how the green dress softens my frame. Even with pins and the ill-fitting sections, I can see it conforming to my wide hips and broad shoulders. A smile creeps along my lips.

Anstice stands next to me, her grin revealing the gap between her teeth. "Much better than the brown dress," she says.

"It is, but I can't afford this. Maybe something simpler," I reply. "Or a blouse."

"Who said you were buying this? This is my gift to you," Anstice tells me, and one of the pins in the shoulder of the dress falls out as I whirl around.

"I can't accept this, Anstice. Not after all you've done for us. This is too much."

She sticks the fallen pin back in the fabric. "I told you that everyone deserves to have something that's not just practical. This will remind you to enjoy life a little bit more," she says. "Besides, green looks much better on you than brown."

X
Primrose

Primula vulgaris

Happiness · Contentment · Safety

The sugary smell of jams surrounds me as I pull a tray of pastries from the oven. With the festival drawing closer, Anstice has been getting busier with orders. I'm making a fruit tart I learned was a favorite of an old man Anstice raised named Piran. Heat blasts against my face, sweat gathering on my upper lip.

The glowing coals hold my gaze, and crackling fills my ears. Our bothy stands trapped in flames, orange tongues pulling apart its wooden bones and tearing down the stone walls. The pain clenches my heart again. I blink it away, inhaling the steam from the baked goods until the smoke and ash are replaced by butter and sweet berries.

"Everything alright?" Anstice asks from the front of the bakery, her voice sounding far away.

I unwind the towel around my hands and run my finger along the grooves of my ring. "Aye," I reply and set the tray of pastries on the counter. I push the yellow kerchief around my head back, focusing on my breathing.

Moments like that creep up on me, blurring the lines between memory and the present. They bleed out from my dreams into the waking hours, and it makes it difficult to know if I'm truly sane. Thankfully, this moment passes quickly. Others strike me in the stomach and bring me to my knees in a teary pile.

The door to the bakery opens, and Rodina steps inside with a bundle in her arms. There are several other people in the shop. "Afternoon, Rodina," Anstice says and leans against the counter with a smile in her voice. I peer through the doorway as the sunlight hits the glass dome over a cake next to her. "Here for some custard tartlets?"

"Yes, and some of those apple butter scones," the seamstress replies, stopping by the shelves of bread and teas. "I'm also here to drop off your order."

My heart skips a beat, and my eyes go to the bundle wrapped in purple thread Rodina sets on the counter. I never told Percy where Anstice and I went on our errand, doing my best to keep myself from smiling whenever he asked, but I think he can tell that I'm hiding something.

I walk out of the bakery's kitchen, wiping my hands on my apron before picking up the wrapped dress. "If anything needs to be adjusted, let us know," Rodina tells me.

Anstice moves to gather some tartlets, scones, and some shortbread biscuits and wraps them up in a waxy cloth for Rodina. "Go try it on, but make sure Percy doesn't see. It'll be good to surprise him," she says.

I hold the bundle closer. "I don't want to leave you here to do all the work," I finally say.

Anstice puts her hands on her wide hips. "I've been running this place long before you started helping. The world isn't going to fall apart if you're gone for a bit."

I untie my apron and head for the bedroom. Odd how

something like a new dress can make me feel like I'm a child again getting a birthday gift. It's a giddiness I haven't felt in a long time. The back door to the garden is open, and Percy looks up as I pass. Morhenna growls at me as she struts by him. Most of her feathers have grown back, and so has her ego.

"Where are you going in such a hurry?" he asks, sitting on the bench with papers suspended by vines around him. His notebook lays across his lap. I see part of a leaf drawn next to paragraphs of notes.

I angle the bundle so he can't tell what it is. He's been studying the bloodleaf again and rebuilding his research findings from memory, asking Anstice all she knows and trying to study samples of her blood after she's taken it. Percy hasn't been able to regrow it or connect with the plant enough to understand it, so until he determines the plant's effects on a bloodgifted and the baby, he thinks it's best for me not to try it yet.

"A gift from Anstice," I reply and fight off the smile tugging at my mouth.

He leans his elbow across his knee, staring at me. "A secret one, it seems. Will you show it to me?" I shake my head. "Can I guess what it is? You know the not knowing will bother me."

"You'll have to wait until the Festival of Kester."

Percy groans and straightens. "That's a whole week," he says and begins writing again. "I *suppose* I can curtail my curiosity until the festival."

I head for the bedroom before my growing smile has a chance to give me away. Once the door shuts, I set the bundle on the bed. My pack sits against the wall by the desk, only a few items unpacked since I didn't know how long we'd be staying here or if we'd need to leave suddenly. Percy has put more of his things in the chest by the bed, so I can't hide the dress in there. He's not prone to snooping, but he's done it before when his curiosity gets the better of him.

I untie the coarse string, looping it around my fingers while I push back the wrapping. Green fabric brightens the room, and the sight of it brings tears to my eyes. How can this make me so happy and sad at the same time? Seeing it stirs up a swirl of emotions I can't quite pin down. It nudges the seed of hope that perhaps the worst has passed. As I hold the new dress in my hands, tracing over the embroidery, the bright green color pulls me away from the heavy thoughts of the Failinis and worry about this pregnancy.

Anstice was right. Sometimes it's nice to have something that's not just practical but also brings me a bit of happiness, even if it's for a little while.

THE STREETS ARE ALIVE WITH COLORFUL CROWDS. OVER THIS PAST month, the townspeople of Neòinean have been gathering their first harvests of summer for the Festival of Kester. Green, yellow, and orange ribbons flutter from every window and tree. Music dances through the air as people move between the stalls in the market square. Men and women wear elaborate crowns made of woven grasses, flowers, and slender antlers to represent the god of plants. Bright murals paint the houses, and statues made of plants and flowers grow in the streets. Adamina's memories overlap with the present festival, her excitement and happiness bright.

My knees and ankles ache as I move around Anstice's covered stall with a small crate of bread and pies in my arms. We've been helping Anstice since the sun rose, selling breads and confections with sugared flowers. She's been taking orders nonstop while Percy and I keep track of the stock and help draw people in. I set down the crate by a table of other confections, dusting my hands on my green skirt. The dress fits even better than I imagined it would, the lace on the cuffs and the pearl buttons beautiful touches. Percy's broad smile when he saw me in it made the thrill of wearing the dress even more worthwhile.

I glance over at a group of laughing children while Percy grows daisies and buttercups from his fingertips for them. With a flick of his wrist, the blooms in their crowns extend to tickle their faces. Percy made crowns and grew living flower sculptures for Àitesìol's summer festival. The children see me staring from inside the stall, and they whisper to each other. Drawing so much attention to ourselves knots my insides, but seeing Percy so full of joy calms me.

Percy follows their glances back to me, his smile widening. "I always knew having a pocket full of seeds would come in handy," he says.

The crown of pink poppies and yellow forsythia blossoms growing around a pair of small deer antlers on his head reminds me of when we exchanged our wedding vows ten years ago with only the gods as our witnesses. With the green tunic paired with a cloak made of leaves, the antlers of his crown adorned with colorful flowers, he looks like Kester himself. It's funny how quickly I've gotten used to him having red hair, but I still miss the brown. It's a small reminder that this town is a hiding place.

"Your crown's crooked," Percy says, coming over to adjust the wreath of lilacs and elderflowers on my head. "The children were asking if you were a giantess."

"What did you tell them?" I ask, trying not to feel uneasy by the stares lingering on me.

"I told them that you were the gentlest giantess of all, and if they asked you nicely, you would sneak them a bit of tablet."

I glance at the tray of caramel-colored candies behind a stack of scones on the table. "Those are some bold promises you're making to children."

"What can I say? I'm helpless before their smiles." As Percy withdraws his hands from my head, something tickles my ear. "There. Perfect." I pluck the dandelion from behind my ear to look at it before putting it back.

"You're both adorable, but there's a line of people, and I need to get the strawberry rhubarb tarts you're blocking," Anstice says, squeezing between us to get to other baked goods. Her hair is braided with raspberry blossoms and yellow ribbons. She balances a tray of tarts in her arms, and I step back. "Save it for the ceilidh," she adds with a wink.

"Way to be a distraction, Mor," Percy whispers as he helps Anstice with another basket of decorated pastries. "You got me in trouble."

I laugh and smack his backside as he passes by. I'd almost forgotten the sound of my own laughter, the way it vibrates my chest and shakes loose the cobwebs. As Percy stands in the street, growing more flowers, I can see a life here. My hand rests on my stomach for a moment before I return to my work.

The music continues as the late afternoon sun stretches the shadows. I hum the familiar melody and let the words dissolve on my tongue like honey.

"Come shake off winter's breath
And bask in the summer sun.
See the Lord of the Forest.
Flowers spring up from his hoofprints,
His shadow sheltering the grasses.
His breath stirs the seeds to sprout.
His antlers shake the leaves.
Kester has come now
To make the land green again."

THE LAST BIT OF CRANACHAN LINGERS ON MY TONGUE, THE raspberries and whisky cream warming my throat. Night is illuminated by the torches in the square, and sparks try to latch onto the stars. In the middle stands the giant straw sculpture of Kester other rootsowers in town built, flowers adorning the six-legged elk. His antlers are decked with garlands that people have thrown onto them for good luck. Rootsowers make petals dance through the air while windsingers keep them aloft.

A shadowcatcher and a lightcaster put on a show against one of the murals, creating shadowy shapes as they tell the story of Kester. It fills me with envy and sadness to see other bloodgifted using their gifts so freely while boneweavers have to hide.

The summer air cups my cheeks, and I lean back against the wall. Straw from the hay bale pokes against my legs. Percy's sitting beside me, his shoulder warm against mine. The evening stretches on, but content exhaustion rests on me despite my stiff hands and knees. I flex my hands, the joints popping. I should apply more of the peppermint salve when I have a chance otherwise, it's going to be a very sore walk back to the bakery tonight.

Percy nudges my shoulder. "Tired already? Don't you owe me a dance?" he asks.

"I don't recall you asking me to dance," I say and set my empty bowl down.

"You haven't learned how to read my mind yet? Guess we'll have to work on that."

I laugh and look back at the square as people gather around the statue. Anstice is surrounded by a few men, her mouth curved into a smile. Percy takes my hand, thumb caressing my knuckles.

"I've missed your laugh," he tells me.

"It feels like there hasn't been much to laugh about lately," I tell him, kissing his temple. The scent of the flowers mixes with the smell of his soap and a little bit of sweat.

"This might not be a bad place to blend in. I could set up another practice here. Build a life for us. I think I'm starting to understand the bloodleaf better, and I should be able to try recreating it soon."

This is like when we first came to Àitesìol three years ago. The little bothy had held so much promise after years of constantly moving around, and the garden walls shielded us from the world beyond. We sowed our hopes and dreams in the earth and watched our future grow, the tears and heartaches watering our resolve to keep going. My heart wants to lay down roots again, but the smell of ash creeps into the edges of my thoughts.

"We can't stay in Anstice's backroom forever," I say, my smile drooping.

"I was thinking of looking for a house in town," he replies. "She wouldn't be opposed to us staying longer. You've been a huge help to her in the bakery. It's been good for you to have someone to talk to who isn't me or a chicken."

With the music and joy around me, it's easy to forget that we're being hunted by the Failinis. There haven't been any sightings of the green cloaks and talk about what happened in Àitesìol has quieted. I find myself slipping into a rhythm of normalcy that is sometimes interrupted by cold panic that we're being too careless. If Anstice can live here without fear of being found out, could Percy and I do the same?

"What about this Tearmann Island?" We've talked about it, trying to get all the information we can from Anstice. The thought of it not being on any known map almost makes me worried that it's not real, but Anstice is sure that it is. "A place where there might be other boneweavers...It seems almost impossible."

He nods. "The world's a vast place. There are many places beyond Errigal and the Mainland where boneweavers aren't hunted—maybe even other bloodgifted we don't know about. My parents used to talk about the trips they'd take to foreign lands and some of the things they saw."

I imagine the maps at the Acadamaidh are painted in colors and have beautifully detailed images. I hope someday I can see something like that. There was a hand-drawn one in a book Da used to read to my younger siblings and me. It was just a story, but the thought of there being something beyond our island excited me.

"But the journey across the highlands will be treacherous, especially with winter coming," Percy goes on. "I don't want anything to happen to you or our child. If this town is safe, then I want to stay as long as we can."

Before I can reply, fiddles and clapping fill the air. Anstice runs over and grabs our hands. "The ceilidh is starting," she says, pulling us to our feet.

A deep ache runs from my tailbone up my spine. "It doesn't seem like you're short on dance partners," I tell her as she leads us to the square.

She flashes a smile. "Oh, them? They're nothing but flirts who hope I'll give them a free meat pie or a sweet roll if they pay the right compliment."

Percy and I stand across from each other with the line of dance partners. "Still have a little energy left for a dance?" Percy asks me.

"I guess I do."

The man facing Anstice blushes as she winks at him. The music changes, and the couple on the end of the line skips to the middle and circles each other, hands touching. They spin around before heading to the next person across from them. My foot taps in time with the rhythm in anticipation for our turn. Warmth flows from Percy's hands and through my arms, the magic seeking out the aches and pains in my body. He gives me his usual crooked smile.

"To help you dance better," he says as the music moves through the crowd of dancers.

Anstice and her partner circle each other before breaking off and moving to Percy and me. She clasps my hand with a grin as we twirl around in a storm of flying skirts. The soreness in my knees is forgotten as lightness overtakes me, and I lose myself in the dance.

"You're not a bad dancer," Anstice tells me.

Sweat runs down the back of my neck as I spin around. "It's been a while since I've been to a cèilidh, but I'm good at dancing, despite my joints," I reply, matching her smile.

"The night's young. There's plenty of time for you to show off your skills," she says, and we switch partners again.

Percy's hand finds mine as we come together. Flower petals swirl in the air. Outlined by the flames and surrounded by so much joy, the moment makes my heart swell to the point where I don't know if my rib cage can contain everything. This is the kind of moment I want to write in my journal, to press it into the pages like flowers to preserve forever.

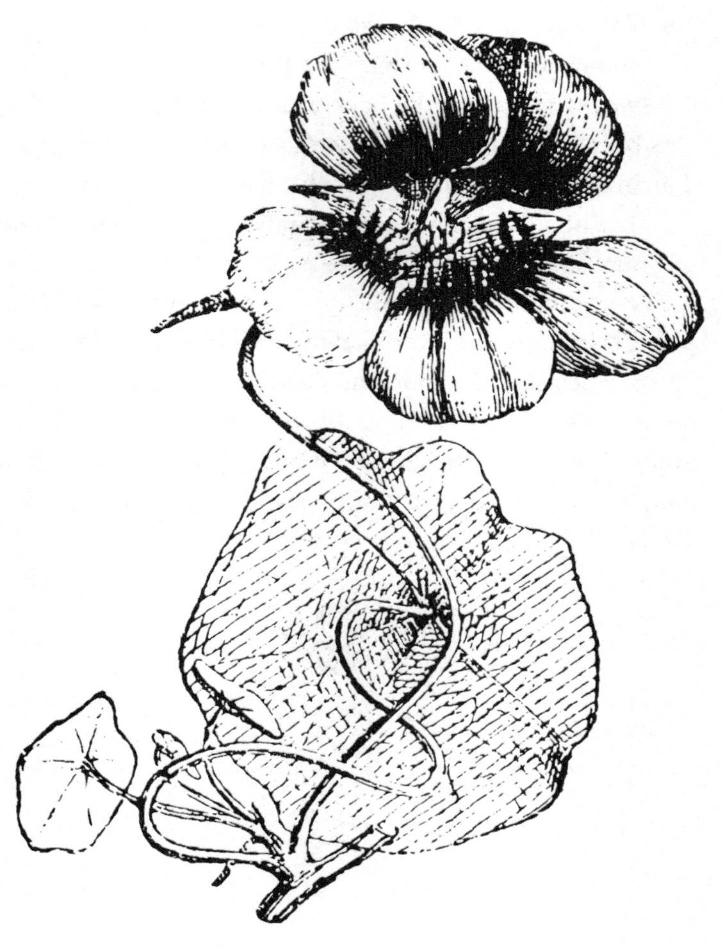

XI
Nasturtium

Tropaeolum

Protection · Strong emotions · Strength

My knife slices the light-colored piece of oak wood, and I brush the skelfs from the elk's antlers. Kester's shape takes form in my hand as I sit in Anstice's garden. The God of Growth's face is the last thing to detail. I hear Da reminding me not to rush and go with the grain. He taught me how to carve wood from a young age, and I continued it after he died because I found it comforting. I started making wooden toys when I first got pregnant, but I never finished them. Instead, I made little figurines for Percy's younger patients when they came to the house.

Morhenna pecks at the shavings, giving me an annoyed cluck when she discovers that they're not edible. She struts off to chase a few sídhe by the lavender and yarrow. The chicken likes it over there, probably because it reminds her a little of home.

I haven't spent much time in the garden like Percy has. I sense the bones of a man buried in the ground—the man who used to own the bakery. His rage claws at the earth that entombs him, and, unlike the other dead beneath the bakery, his voice makes me uneasy. I asked Anstice why she kept his bones so close when they give off such strong emotions, and she said she liked the idea of his body giving life after he'd been responsible for so much death.

It's strange at times to think of a murderer here in the garden, but that was who he was. Now he's bones held together by memories. Whatever punishment his soul is due awaits him in the dark mists of the Forests of Cadal—an eternity of maddening wandering.

A shadow falls over me, and I find Percy standing next to me. Clouds move through the overcast sky. "You're carving again," he says, dimples creasing his cheeks. "Are you going to make one for each of the festivals?"

I brush wood shavings off my brown skirt. "I don't know. That'd be a lot of carving," I tell him. Today my hands don't hurt, so I could make another one after this. The brief thought of making another toy crossed my mind, but I fear it may become like the other ones I never finished.

Morhenna darts out of the bushes toward Percy. She has the gall to give me a look of irritation that *I'm* still here now that Percy has come outside. Percy sits on the stone bench beside me, weaving a chain of daisies and red clovers into a circle. When he's working on a problem, he finds ways to keep his hands busy. He took to making flower chains and crowns when I was first pregnant. I used to find his creations all over the bothy.

"I'm sure there will be time between all the baking you've been helping with. You'll have to rest eventually. Healer's orders," Percy says.

When he talks like that, it makes it seem like we'll be here to see all these festivals. The dread still hovers in my stomach, but I don't shut out the image of a small face peering back at me with a gummy smile and tiny fingers. The bubbling warmth pads around my chest, kneading the space as it prepares to curl up and stay there.

Percy sets the finished crown on my head. "How are you today?" he asks.

"No nausea today or dreams that I can remember," I say, etching one of Kester's eyes on his face. "I'm still worried, but it's not overwhelming me. Some days it's easier to forget that we didn't lose everything."

My knife stops as a tightness grips my throat. I blink and try to steady my breath. A cold lump of sadness leaks through the calm I'd let settle on me. I try to swallow it back down, breathing in the lavender and grass to keep myself centered.

Percy scoots closer. "I think the worry will always be there, but hopefully, it'll get better each day."

He plucks a daisy growing beneath the bench. Another one springs up from the broken stem, white petals unfurling like an old man stretching out his limbs. The chicken comes around to his side in hopes of receiving a pet or a treat from him.

The backdoor slams open, startling Morhenna. Percy and I turn to see Anstice leaning against the doorframe, panting, and her dark hair in disarray. Her eyes are wide as she stumbles outside with sweat on her ruddy face. My breath hitches seeing her usual calm broken. Coldness slithers into my stomach while my chest grows hot with each quickening heartbeat. I clutch the knife tightly and stand.

Percy moves to steady Anstice. "What's wrong?" he asks, fingers at her pulse on her wrist.

"I saw them," Anstice gasps, her gaze going to me, "in the

market. Ten Failinis led by a flamekindler. He looked like the one you told me about. You must leave now."

THE WORLD RUSHES BY WHILE I STAND FROZEN IN THE BEDROOM LIKE I'm caught in a dream. Anstice's description of Captain MacAdoh turned my bones to stone. I try to think through the fog clouding my mind while I pack, but my shaking hands can't seem to grasp anything real. He's found us and has brought more Failinis with him. How did they find us? Did someone at the festival discover that I'm a boneweaver? Or did they track us here?

"Mor." Percy touches my shoulder. When I look at him, words fail me. He helps me with my pack, squeezing my hand. When he puts the green dress I wore a few days ago into the bag, I swallow a sob.

Anstice comes back into the room with bundles of food and supplies. Morhenna clucks loudly and darts around. My knuckles turn white as I clutch the axe, as if doing so will allow me to hold onto the last shred of safety we have left. The roots we started putting down are being yanked up again.

"Do you have everything?" Anstice asks us, but the question sounds so distant as if she's asking someone else.

"Yes," I hear Percy respond.

Grunting, Anstice moves the bed aside and pulls back the rug beneath it. She removes a few boards until a gaping hole is staring back at us with a wooden ladder leading downward.

"The previous owner used these to get in and out unseen," Anstice tells us. "Despite their former uses, I knew one day they'd come in handy. They extend all the way out of town with hidden entrances around the hills."

There's a banging sound from the front of the bakery, and my blood curdles. "Open up!" a muffled voice carries through the house.

The presence of ten bloodgifted burns in my veins. Dogs bark and growl. They must have a beastcharmer. Every pounding fist on the door hits me with a memory of the Failinis, the wolfish smile, the kitchen wall crumbling, and flames going up around us.

Anstice glances over her shoulder. "Keep going straight down the tunnel. It'll bring you to the western side of the town to the barley field," she whispers and points at the hole in the floor. "From there, keep going until you reach the woods."

Anstice pushes something soft into my palm. I look down at the red and tan pouch in my hand. The bloodleaf. "Anstice...No! I...Why are you giving this to me?" I ask. "I can't take this. This is all you have."

She stops as I try to give it back to her. "You need it more than I do," she says.

"But what about you?" The answer constricts my voice, breaking my words into pieces. The pounding on the front door grows louder. "Come with us. Please."

The corners of her eyes crinkle as she touches my face. "Sweet Morana. My place is here. I've been running for too long."

I grasp her arm, throat tight. I don't want to lose her, the only other boneweaver I've met—my friend. "But the flamekindler will kill you."

"I willnae leave this place without a fight." Her brown

eyes are like steel despite tears. "If it's my time to join Arianrhod, then so be it. You and Percy still have a chance. Take the bloodleaf. Just a pinch will be enough, and the effects will start in a few minutes."

I glance at Percy, hoping he'll say something to convince Anstice to come with us. His face is grim as he looks at the pouch of bloodleaf. "I don't like you taking it without knowing how it might affect the baby," he mutters, brows creased as his voice cracks, "but if it keeps you hidden, we don't have another choice."

I stare at the pouch. No choice. Percy never says that. Risk losing our lives or lose another child. Regret rakes its thorns through my insides. My fear continues to fracture, pulsing in time with my heartbeat. The pounding on the door turns into the sound of cracking wood.

"You have to go. Now," Anstice tells me.

I slip the axe through my belt and take a pinch of the dried leaves with trembling fingers. The room around me blurs as I swallow, bitterness and salt slipping down my throat. The sensation of something being leached away from my blood is immediate, even though I can still feel the power in my veins. I don't know what it'll be like to not have my bloodgift.

Anstice leans up and kisses my forehead. "Live well, and may the gods bring you safety," she says and gives my hands one last squeeze.

Percy takes the bloodleaf pouch and climbs into the hole. Morhenna squawks in protest. I don't want to leave Anstice, but she pries herself from my grasp. "I won't forget you," I whisper.

"That's all anyone can hope for. Be sure to tell your little one the stories behind the recipes I taught you. And if it's a boneweaver like you, don't let it be ashamed of its gift."

Pulling myself from the room to descend into the hole tears something from inside myself. My cheeks are wet, the wooden rungs of the ladder rough against my skin. Percy's hand moves along my back as I reach the bottom. Morhenna flies down into the hole after us, refusing to be left behind. Anstice doesn't wipe her tears and replaces the boards and the rug. I take in the last glimpses of her face until the darkness moves in around us.

Percy's hand finds mine, the green glow in his veins guiding our path. Along the walls, fungi appear and create a lighted trail down the tunnel. I have to hunch down, almost crouching to fit. I feel the bones of animals scattered through the ground, but their voices are slipping out of reach.

"Do you feel anything yet?" Percy whispers.

"The bones are distant," I tell him, and the words stick to my dry tongue. "Like the power is being drained from me."

He squeezes my fingers, and a pulse of his fleshmending magic wiggles beneath my skin. "Tell me if your breathing changes, if you're lightheaded, or feel sick."

Our pace is slow, and I don't know how long we've been moving through this tunnel. My hand digs into the damp walls. The musty air's too thick. Each step causes the axe handle to hit my legs. The weight of the earth above threatens to crush us, and thoughts of the dirt collapsing on top of us come unbidden. At any moment, the earthcarver could rip us from the tunnel, or the flamekindler fill it with fire. Or the waterdancer could flood it. I think I hear dogs barking. This place might become our tomb, and no one would hear our screams.

A cold prickle moves up the back of my neck. I can't hear the bones or feel the presence of the Failinis and Anstice anymore. For the first time in my life, the world is silent. I want to turn back or claw my way out. My lungs try to take in as many breaths as they can, unable to get enough in the dusty air. Panic chokes me. I don't know how much further I can go.

I chew on the inside of my lip until I taste blood. Bile stings my throat. "Percy," I gasp and tug on his hand.

A pinprick of light cracks the darkness. "We're almost there, Morana," Percy tells me as he looks back at me, the glow of his magic catching in his glasses. "Just a little further."

We draw closer to the light, but the opening is blocked by a boulder. Percy tries to move it, but it won't budge. Sweat glues my shirt to my skin as my fear reaches a tipping point. Green light brightens as Percy grows thick roots that coil around the boulder and shift it outward. Fresh air hits my face, and I let out a ragged breath, squinting against the gray light. Green fields of barley ripple below. Percy pulls himself out, glancing around before he waves for me to follow.

I stumble out, drinking in the air. "Morana, are you alright?" Percy asks, his face streaked with dirt and cobwebs clinging to his clothes.

I'm not. Everything's been torn from us again, and Anstice is facing the Failinis alone. And it's not just us anymore. How can I take care of a child if we're struggling to stay alive? I look at Percy, not sure if I want to scream or cry. Morhenna stops and looks at us.

Percy takes my wrist, my pounding pulse struggling to fall in time with his. "I can't sense your bloodgift," he tells me.

"We left her," I whisper, my chest heavy under the crushing weight that hasn't lifted.

I look back at Neòinean and see a column of smoke rising up. Is that the bakery burning? Did Anstice make it out, or did the Failinis kill her? My knees hit the ground, and the chicken escapes from my grasp. My mind tells me I have no time for tears, but I can't make my body move.

Percy grips my shoulders. "If anyone can take care of herself, it's Anstice," he tells me.

His words don't erase the thoughts of flames eating away everything and Captain MacAdoh and his burning eyes standing over Anstice. It doesn't ease the barbed guilt growing. We didn't try hard enough to get her to come with us. Because of me, the Failinis found Anstice. I broke her peaceful life with the selfish thought that a boneweaver like me could have a peaceful life.

"Morana." Percy takes my face in his hands.

"The baby?" Another bolt of panic shoots through me.

"It's hard to use my powers on you because of the bloodleaf, but the heartbeat is still there," he says. "We still need to run. Can you stand?"

I haul myself up, knees cracking. He picks up Morhenna. The outline of the town burns behind my eyelids as we run west toward some unknown that might shelter us for the night. The gray clouds fill the sky and grow darker the longer we run. When the storm finds us, I can't tell if the wetness on my cheeks is from the rain or my tears.

I STARE INTO THE FLAMES, MY CLOAK PULLED TIGHT AROUND MY shivering body. A dull ache fills my stomach, but I can't think of eating. I gnaw on my growing worries instead. The fire crackles and hisses as raindrops seep through the cracks in the ceiling of the ruined church. After hours of running, we stumbled upon this place. I don't know how far we managed to get from Neòinean, but it doesn't feel like we're far enough. The effects of the bloodleaf are still in my blood, keeping me cut off from any nearby bones. Every time a twig snaps or an animal cries out, I tense, my hand never leaving the axe. Percy told me that the surrounding plants would alert him if anything approaches, but I'm afraid that the rain won't be enough to hide our trail.

Rain pours through the broken roof in the middle of the church, filling the hole in the broken floor. Vines hang from the ruined arches, and flashes of lightning illuminate the pillars. Blankets of green nasturtiums cover the ground dotted with orange, pink, and red blossoms. Percy plucks their round leaves and the flowers. Morhenna's torn between following him and staying by the fire to dry off.

Percy comes over with two wrapped bundles and sits next to me on a stone slab. "You need to eat something," he says, holding out one of the bundles to me.

The thought of food doesn't interest me, but I take it and unwrap it. A pie sits in my lap, its crust broken in places and the gravy congealed on the sides. On top, a small carrot made of cooked dough remains intact. Anstice did this with leftover crust to differentiate which pie was which. I can hear her voice listing off the ingredients and baking instructions.

Her last gift to me is a vegetable pie. All I brought to her was danger.

The first bite sticks to the inside of my mouth, the crust soggy and buttery. I only manage to get halfway through it before my tears force me to stop, my throat too tight to swallow.

Percy takes something from under his arm. "This was also in the pack for you."

He places a wrapped stack of papers tied up with twine. I undo the knots, and Anstice's curling handwriting fills pages of recipes. The foods she learned from the dead. If she gave these to me, then she wasn't planning on making it out of the bakery alive. Teardrops fall on the papers, and I can't eat anymore.

Percy presses against me, rubbing my back. "It'll be alright, Morana," he says.

Something inside me breaks. Everything I've been pushing down for weeks, years, bubbles over. "It's not alright! Why do you keep saying that? Every time you do, something bad happens!" I snap, his face blurry.

Percy reaches for my hand. "We're still here. We'll get through this as we have before. I don't know when we'll get to a place where we're safe, but each day we still breathe gives me hope that the next might be better..." He falls quiet for a moment. "We can talk about if the worst happens."

My stomach tightens. I don't want to think of my life without him. That's a pain I'm not ready for yet. And I certainly don't want to think about losing a child again.

"What's the point of planning anything if we have nowhere to go?" I mutter and yank my hand from his. "We'll keep running until the Failinis catch us and kill us. Our 'problem' isn't going to be fixed by *talking* about it."

"Mor, I didn't mean that—"

He reaches for my arm, but I pull away. "I don't want to pretend that we can ever have a normal life or that we'll find another place like Àitesìol. This can't be fixed by being positive, so stop trying."

The pie tumbles to the ground in a broken mess as I stand. The recipes scatter and cling to the damp stones. Morhenna goes for the crumbs. Thunder rumbles overhead. The rage in Sorcha's storm outside stirs up every hurt and grief until they're tearing at my insides.

Percy stares at me with a sad expression, shoulders slumped. He sets aside his pie, and his fingers clench in his lap. "I'm not trying to be positive because I'm naïve. Things have looked bad before, but we always pull through. Don't you remember how devastated we were when we had to leave the cottage that we lived in outside of Auchendrain? We had nowhere to go, but then we found the house near Taibhse."

"This isn't like any of the times before!" I yell. "We haven't watched our house burn or lost anyone like this. I haven't been pregnant and had to run for my life. Every time we find a place that's safe, it gets taken from us, and we lose even more. How long before the Failinis catch us? Anstice was living in peace before we arrived, and now..." I suck in a breath, forcing the words out. "She's most likely dead. *Because of me*!"

Percy sets the rest of his food down and stands, jaw set. "Don't put that guilt on yourself. Anstice didn't regret taking us in."

"That didn't save her from them. Maybe everyone's right. Boneweavers bring death and despair with them." My hands shake as fire pumps through me. "Your life would be easier without me. I can't find happiness, and everyone around me gets dragged down with me."

"You know that's not true. Why do you insist on blaming

yourself? That's so self-centered. Don't you think I'm also frustrated and angry?" There's an edge in his voice as it goes up. Percy rarely gets mad, but his composure is breaking. "You've blamed yourself for years. We've had this conversation before where you beat yourself up because of your gift, but your gift isn't the problem, Morana. I don't understand why you try to hurt yourself more. Do you like being in pain, or because you've been hurting for so long that you don't know how to be any other way?"

"Because there's no one else to blame but myself!" My shout echoes off the walls and hurts my ears. A voice whispers for me to stop, but every painful thing I've pushed down is flooding out. I can't hold it in any longer. "I can't stand the way you look at me like I'm not the reason we're here—that my powers aren't the reason we've lost so much. I don't want false hope. There's no getting through this if the only thing that waits for us is misery and death!"

My words explode in the air, leaving hot scratches across my mouth. As I blink away the tears, I take in Percy's expression. No crooked smile or warmth in his wide eyes, only hurt and thinly veiled anger. My anger drains away and leaves cold regret in its place.

Unable to bear the silence, I leave. Rain hits my face through a hole in the ceiling as I go into a side room. Lightning illuminates cracked murals on the walls. All eleven gods watch with faded eyes. Sorcha with her four-winged serpentine body cloaked in lightning. Ciardha's four slitted eyes stare from the shadows of her feline body. I find Arianrhod with her two pairs of wings, one of which has been destroyed by time. Her corvid form hovers over the others, a skull in one claw and flowers that look like foxgloves in the other.

Is it a boneweaver's lot to suffer in this life, only finding peace after death? At this moment, unable to sense my bloodgift or any bones, I feel truly abandoned by the gods. I want to laugh at the irony of missing the very thing that's brought me so much misery. Despair turns what's supposed to be beautiful and wonderful into agonizing reminders of my inadequacies.

My knees hit the wet ground, and I pound my fist against the stone. The broken pieces slice my hand while the rain soaks me. My anger left cracks that leak with fresh grief. Shame is woven along my spine like ivy, too deeply rooted to be pulled free. I want to scream, but it comes out as a sob. I weep for everything—our home, Anstice, my baby, and now the pain I've caused Percy. My knuckles pound the wall with each reminder of my loss. I press my head against the stones, my split lips stinging as I vomit.

No matter how much I try, I keep finding myself back in this pit. Everything I shouted at Percy was what I scream at myself. The frustration of not being strong enough, of constantly being crushed by this weight I can't bear. When I think I've healed from something, a fresh wound appears, or the scars are ripped open all over again.

Warmth brushes my aching hands, and I flinch. Percy crouches beside me. His wet hair hangs in his eyes and rain droplets cling to his glasses. The yellow glow of his magic builds in his fingertips and catches the tears in his eyes. I look away, ashamed to meet his gaze, and wipe the saliva from my mouth. The cuts on my knuckles heal as the blood washes away in the rain.

Percy doesn't say anything as the skin regrows. Apologies build in my throat, but I can't get them out. What words will repair the damage I've done?

"I can't fix tomorrow," he finally whispers as thunder rumbles, the words empty of any emotion. "All I can do is try to fix what's in front of me today."

XII
Bluebell

Hyacinthoides

Humility ❧ Sorrowful regret ❧ Faithfulness

Gray skies have been following us for days. Dampness seeps into everything as the drizzle persists. The blisters on my feet return, and the skin between my toes splits again. The map's wet corners flop in the wind as I hold it as I lead us westward around Loch Caladhglas, "the nose of Errigal," north.

Each day puts us further from the Failinis, but no town feels safe, and I only focus on getting as far from Neòinean as we can. Percy's made an ointment that helps mask our scent, but every animal we watch with wariness and keep an ear out for the sound of dogs. Sleep hasn't come easily since we fled, and I'm once again anxious about every moving shadow and unknown sound in the woods.

Leaning against my walking stick, I stop at the crest of the hill overlooking a valley blanketed in purple heather. Small burns trickle down the brae like silver veins. Rust-colored, long-haired cows graze in the distance. The outline of mountains rises along the horizon through the haze. A flock of brown ptarmigans take flight and scatter. Animal bones chatter beneath the flowers, pulsing like beacons. There weren't many heather fields in Àitesìol, but I could see the purple hills in the distance beyond the forests in the summer. The flowers are a sign of good luck, something we sorely need.

Percy trudges through the heather with Morhenna on his shoulder under his hood. Tense silence has hung over us since leaving the church three days ago, filling the spaces between short conversations. I've snapped several times at him since our fight, and Percy hardly responds, which makes me despise myself even more. The words I shouted at him echo in my head and weigh me down more than the voices of the dead ever did. What he said still stings because deep down, I know it's true. With everything slipping through my fingers, I can't lose him too.

Realizing that I haven't followed, Percy stops to look back at me. His face is haggard, and stubble shadows his chin. "Is something wrong?" he asks.

My breath hitches as I muster the breath to speak. "I'm sorry. I shouldn't have shouted at you the other night," I tell him, my voice cracking. "I...all that's happening...I didn't mean to hurt you."

He remains silent, lips pursed. "This isn't easy for either of us, Mor," he finally says in a tired voice. "I'm not unaware of how hard this is or blinded by optimism."

"I know...I'm sorry for saying that. I'm sorry I've been in this dark mood. I want to be happy and see things the way you do, but it's hard."

Percy comes over, each slow step careful to avoid crushing the plants underfoot. "You were angry and upset. I don't want you to feel that you can't ever be those things. I also said things I wish I could take back. You're not self-centered. I...I don't like seeing you suffering. I know you get stuck in those heavy emotions, and it's hard for you to get out of it. You feel deeply, and I love that about you. I want to fix it, but a broken heart aren't something I can fix with fleshmending. I don't know what to do with things I can't heal. If I don't try, then I feel like I've failed us."

My lips quiver, and my eyes sting. "We seem to be failing," I mutter, sniffling as I worry the edges of my cloak with anxious fingers. "It just feels like I'll never be good enough to be the person you deserve."

"*I* don't feel like I'll be good enough to deserve *you.* Do you know how many times I've wondered why you would ever need someone like me who can't even read a map correctly? There's no one I'd rather be failing together with than you," Percy says. My heart clenches as he takes my hand. "It's not easy all the time, but that doesn't make it any less worthwhile."

Tears tremble on the edges of my eyelids. I blink and stare past Percy to look out over the heather fields. "I want to go back to how things were before, to how I was before. I know I can't...but I don't know what to do with who I'm becoming because of all that's happened. It's frustrating when I can't shake off the sadness and move on."

"I don't blame you or your bloodgift for any of this. I don't want you to blame *yourself.* Even though it may take longer to recover, I'm not expecting you to deal with everything immediately. You don't have to pretend to be strong all the time, Mor. When it's too much, tell me. If I try to fix you instead of hearing you out, I need you to tell me. I'm not one of those fleshmenders that can sense emotions. Just let me know what you need."

I look back at him and press my forehead against his. "A pair of socks that aren't wet and for the rain to stop." They seem like superficial things, but the things I truly need aren't obtainable right now.

His laugh vibrates through me. "I'd give you my socks if they were any drier."

"Your socks wouldn't fit me unfortunately," I tell him.

He leans up, lips seeking mine. Forgiveness tastes like mint and peppery nasturtium flowers. Morhenna hisses, and her wing hits the side of my face. I jerk back as she pecks at me, spitting away a downy feather sticking to the corner of my mouth.

"Henna! Please. I'm trying to have a moment with my wife," Percy says as he puts a hand in front of her beak. She clucks in protest. "Chickens these days have no respect."

"For that, she should walk," I tell him, rubbing my stinging cheek. She's becoming more trouble than she's worth, but Percy will never leave her behind.

"She won't get any of the berries I was going to give her." He stoops down and plucks a green sprig with lavender-colored flowers and a cluster of heather. "I think it's *thyme* we find someplace to set up camp and a place to bathe."

He tickles my nose with the end of the thyme, and I smile. The distance begins to mend even if it hasn't fully healed yet. It feels like there's still more we should say, but I worry that will start another fight I don't have the energy for. He's always been quick to forgive and move on, but the memory of his words still linger in my mind. I bury them away and try not to linger in the past.

Percy places the heather flowers inside the pocket of my cloak before he makes a path through the underbrush. The coarse grasses and shrubs ripple as they part before him. Morhenna shoots me a glare as she readjusts herself on Percy's shoulder. Mist rolls down the braes in the distance. With his hand in mine, I don't feel as untethered.

The gray drizzle stops, and the clouds crack apart to reveal a blue sky. I squint at the sunlight spilling through and warming my face. It turns raindrops on the flowers and leaves into a glittering blanket across the heathland.

"Seems like our luck is changing already," Percy says and throws back his hood. Morhenna puffs out her speckled feathers. "Where are we heading today?"

"Still west until we make it around the loch. Then we'll head north. We should be able to reach the forests before nightfall," I tell him, my walking stick sinking into the squishy ground.

"Is there a town or village we can spend the night in?"

Anstice's smile digs into the still-fresh wound, and I rub my eyes. "There are, but it's probably best to avoid them for now. Failinis could be there. The Captain might have patrols near Sheabhag or the other towns. They could be anywhere."

Ahead, a fox looks at us, its orange fur bright against the purple flowers before it darts away. A strong tug pulls me in its direction. Probably whatever it caught and was eating. As I approach the rock where the fox had been, I see the yellow curve of a human skull nestled in the boughs of heather. Blooms have grown around it and through one of the eye sockets. Rotted remains of a dark dress lie in strips, the rest of the body scattered beneath the vegetation. Sadness seeps from the soil. Percy stops, muttering a soft prayer.

I crouch down and touch the skull. A woman's voice reaches for me, crying. A deep ache saturated in grief cuts me as the memory of wandering the hills overtakes me. A love that's been stripped away, the glint of a knife in her hands. Alone until the end as she fades with a name on her lips. Her eyes glow as my power finds her. The rest of her bones in the field call to me, and I draw them to this spot until all her bones are in a pile.

"I'm so sorry, Edmé Ardrey," I whisper. "I hope you found Aindrea again in the next life."

I let the woman go, her sadness settling on my shoulders and finding companionship with my own. Her family probably never knew what happened to her. I think of what would happen if Percy died before me. I want to believe I'd be alright in the end, but grief is a devious monster that takes more from us than we realize, even our belief that we'll survive it.

"We should bury her. She deserves that much," I tell Percy and set Edmé's skull on top of her bones.

Percy sets Morhenna down, and we collect stones. The sun warms the back of my neck as we set up the cairn. He grows a wooden marker at the base of the grave, and we place flowers on the rocks. I carve Edmé's name onto the marker. Maybe someone will find her again and bring her home. For now, I'll carry her story, so she's not forgotten.

Golden light breaks through the trees as I grab the shovel from the fresh grave. The grasses ripple around me as I move

between the headstones. The dead are whispering their stories to me. The newest voice, a man named Grannus, tells me about his life raising sheep and his dream of being a piper. I'll write everything down once I have a bath back at the cottage.

Percy steps out of the trees in his green scholar robes. His brown hair is unruly, as always, and his smile crooked. I can barely keep my heart in my chest, and I try to clean myself off, knowing how sweaty and dirty I am, not to mention that I smell like the dead.

"All done for the day?" he asks.

"I just finished up," I say, and he stands on his toes to kiss me.

"Come with me. I have something to show you."

"Are you going to tell me what it is?"

"It's a surprise," Percy says with a wink.

"You know I don't like surprises," I mutter, sighing.

We leave and head back to my cottage. I'm not sure what he wants to show me. All I want is a bath and write out the new stories swirling in my head. As the trees part, Percy leads me through a field with blooming flowers and petals swirling through the air. Vines have grown into arches with dangling blossoms. This doesn't look like the same field I crossed through hours ago.

Percy faces me as we stand under the arches. "I have something to ask you." He pulls two rings from his pocket made of smooth, dark wood. "Will you marry me?"

My breath catches, and my knees turn to water. "What?" I manage to say as my heart jumps into my throat.

"The first time I met you, I thought I knew a lot about the world, but then you showed me how little I actually knew. Your bravery doesn't overshadow your kindness. When I found you again that day in the graveyard, I thought I'd wandered into a story—at least up until the point you threatened me with the axe. When I came back days later, you helped me find the herbs I'd been

searching for and made sure I was fed and left the forest in one piece even though you still didn't trust me.

"I never thought there could be anything beautiful about death, but you taught me to see the beauty in the stories of the dead. I want to wake up to your smile and hold your hand until we're old and wrinkled."

"Percy, I..."

My thoughts blur together as my hot pulse climbs into my throat. His words feel like they're directed at someone else, but this isn't a dream, and I'm more awake than I've ever been before. This is something I've secretly wanted. Yet, I'm fearful about what happens next. I look at the rings. He's carved my favorite flower into them—primroses. Is it selfish to want this even with the risk being close to me could inflict on him?

"Is this really what you want? It's not safe being around me. I... I don't know what I can offer you or that the Failinis won't ever come after me," I ask.

"I know you're worried about the Failinis finding you, but I'm not afraid. My love isn't easily scared," Percy says, his cheeks reddening but he doesn't look away from me. "I can't see my life with anyone but you, Morana. I want to be with you for whatever comes."

There was a time when I couldn't think of a life with others. I always thought I'd grow old alone, maybe in the cottage, and live out my days unknown. But perhaps the gods have a different future for me. My worries about putting him in danger remain, but at this moment, he's all I want, come joy or tears.

"I'll marry you." The words are warm wine on my tongue as I kiss him, unable to stop smiling.

Percy slips the ring on my dirt-covered finger, and it pulses like a heartbeat. "No matter how far apart we are, when you wear this ring, you'll always know where I am."

WATER RUNS DOWN MY FACE AS I SURFACE FROM THE RIVER. THE current pulls at me, the dirt of the road swirling away. Sunlight glitters across the waters, and I shiver as a breeze touches my bare skin. Morhenna's on the bank, ruffling her feathers as she guards our packs. Our clothes dry on the rocks. My socks are almost dry, finally, after two days of dampness.

I look down at the yellowing bruises on my legs and the scabbed blisters on my feet. My body continues to ache in new ways, and despite the nausea, I'm always hungry. Itchy red bug bites prickle along my arms, and a few new darker marks have appeared on my thighs from sleeping on the ground again. Another pang pricks my heart as I think of Anstice's house. With everything we've had to leave behind, I miss beds the most. There are still many miles to go before we reach the highlands.

Percy floats on his back a few feet away, plants resting on his stomach. The red has begun to fade from his hair, and mine is almost brown again. We'll have to change the color again. He holds one of the plants up and squints at it. The metal knotwork tree and hand pendant lie against his chest. His eyes shift to me as I wade over to him, and he holds out a leafy stem with little pink flowers.

"*Mentha aquatica*. Water mint," Percy tells me. "It's growing all along the shore. It'll be good to use in balms and to keep the insects at bay. I have some mint oil and lavender left I can mix with it. I'd rather not be eaten alive by midges." I bend down and smell the mint before biting off a few leaves, the cooling sweetness hitting my tongue. "Or you could eat it."

"Seems like a more practical use," I say, running my fingers through his hair before kissing him. Percy's mouth smiles beneath mine, and his hand moves to my thigh along the stretch marks. His wet palm against my skin sends goosebumps up my leg, and the itchy bites and soreness vanish.

"You *do* smell better," he says, and I pull away.

"Careful, or I might push you down the river," I tell him.

"I wouldn't want that. Although I wonder if I can find some brooklime and woundwort further downriver. Maybe some marshmallow root."

"Why bother collecting them if you can grow them?"

"Sometimes it's more fun to gather them. Plus growing something without a seed or plant material uses more energy," he says. "How much traveling do we need to do today?"

"Another forty miles. If we follow the western side of the Abhainn Comraich, it'll take us to the Lùbach Mountains in about five days. Then we can follow the spine toward the Claigeann Forests in the Cluaran Mountains. Anstice said that there would be willow-o'-wisps to guide us to where this sanctuary of bloodgifted is."

It's been almost fifteen years since I was back in the highlands, so I'm sure the landscape has changed. The mountains and forests have always given me a sense of security—of being home. I passed by the Cluaran

Mountains when I was younger and was searching for a place to stay, not knowing there could have been a safe place. Even though worry and doubt whisper against it, I cling to the sliver of hope that things will work out this time.

Percy gathers up the plants in one hand and stands, blinking water droplets out of his eyes. I flick a lock of hair off his brow. His other hand slides along my hip as he steps closer.

"How about the name Teasle for a baby?" he asks, tracing the thin scars near my waist.

"That's a terrible name," I reply with a frown.

"But it's a practical plant, and it's nice. Maybe Marigold? Or Ramson for a boy?"

"Are all your names plant ones?" I ask, raising an eyebrow.

Percy's hand drifts to my navel, tracing the dark hairs there. A knot of heat expands, and my pulse warms. "Not all of them, but most are."

"You are a gifted man, Percival Bracken, but I don't think naming children is one of those gifts," I say and kiss his brow.

"What would *you* name our child?" His voice is huskier, the heat of his skin pressing against me.

"I don't know yet." I haven't let myself think of a name. The one I chose for our first was buried with it. Naming makes it more real.

"I suppose we have time to think of one." His mouth finds mine, and I twine my fingers through his wet hair.

Morhenna squawks from the riverbank. I shoot her a look. If she liked the water, she'd probably swim over and attack me. There's no fury quite like a chicken scorned.

“Seems we’ve upset Morhenna,” Percy mutters against my neck.

“If she could wield the axe, she would’ve done away with me already,” I say.

Percy’s lips trail along my collarbone. “It’s a good thing she doesn’t have hands then.”

As Percy reaches up to touch my face, the sound of splashing and unnatural whinnying rings through the trees. We freeze as the sound draws closer on the thundering of hooves. Morhenna continues to screech, and we rush for the banks, grabbing our clothes and packs. My tunic and trousers stick to my wet skin. I find the axe, feet squelching in my boots. Percy picks Morhenna up, and we duck into the trees as the wailing grows louder.

Through the bushes, translucent creatures run across the river. Their manes and tails are like churned foam, eyes dark stones that have a predatory glint in them. Sunlight passes through their shimmering bodies, throwing shards of rainbows across the waters.

Five kelpies stop where we had been and sniff the plants Percy left behind. Their lithe, equine forms make them look like normal horses, except for the curve of pointed teeth along their muzzles and their predatory movements. Looking at their crystalline bodies, I’m filled with fear and awe.

I haven’t seen one this close before. When I first left home, I saw one by the banks of a loch from a distance. Da told my siblings and me stories about the creatures waiting to devour us at the water’s edge and never to touch one or we’d be dragged away. They’re supposedly the manifestation of Muiredach’s rage when he was killed during the Darkening, taking his form as they search for his scattered body in the waters of the world. I can see how people might be drawn in looking at such beautiful creatures and lured into their jaws.

Percy's eyes widen as he fumbles to put his glasses on. "Kelpies weren't on the list of things I thought would hurt us on our journey," he whispers.

One looks in our direction, nostrils flaring. Its eyes send chills through me. It rears up with a cry, exposing the rows of sharp teeth. Thunder rumbles as its hooves slam into the water. We're far enough away not to be dragged in, but we shouldn't linger here.

XIII
Heather

Calluna

Luck · Protection from danger · Solitude

The gloaming creeps in with the evening mist as another long summer day ends. Fireflies dance in the field around us, green stars pulsing through the grasses. Loch Caladhglas is a silver eye in the valley below as the moonlight melts across it. Percy walks ahead with a trail of glowing mushrooms lighting the way, Morhenna perched on the back of his pack. There's a town in the next glen we'll risk stopping in to get supplies before we continue. The outlines of the mountains are visible in the distance before the sun sinks behind them, and my heart aches at the sight of them. Crows caw in the trees.

My pace slows as exhaustion makes each step harder, and I rely more on my walking stick with each passing hour. There's a strange presence in the air, making it hard to sense Percy's bloodgift or the bones I normally feel in the ground. Perhaps my exhaustion is causing that. The nightmares flooded my sleep last night with burning houses, Anstice being sucked into the underground tunnels, and a kelpie that dragged me into a river. Grief still catches me by surprise throughout the day, knocking the air from my lungs.

Percy turns around, noticing my slowed pace. "Do you want to stop and rest?" he asks.

I flex my stiff fingers around the axe and shake my head as my eyelids begin to close. On the winds, I think I hear barking. "My body wants to, but I want to get into the woods before the sun sets," I tell him as a chill hits my sweaty skin. We can't afford to stop.

"Stopping sooner than we planned is probably for the best. I can tell you're trying to push through the pain again."

"I know...I'm sorry." I stare into the trees ahead, the mist thickening and obscuring the light of Percy's mushrooms. I haven't taken this path into the highlands before, and the strangeness in the air seems to be growing. "Do you feel something weird here?"

He nods. "I noticed it too. It's almost like the bloo—"

A wall of fire cuts in front of us, orange and yellow exploding in the darkness. Morhenna screeches, and I stumble back, the ground cracking between Percy and me. Flames encircle us, and jagged fragments of earth rise like a maw about to swallow us. For a moment, I can't comprehend what's happening until fiery tongues lash out and burn my arm. I cry out and drop my walking stick, the smell of burning skin and clothes erasing the scent of the grass. Percy screams my name.

Now I sense them—ten bloodgifted—and my blood turns to ice as I clutch my wounded arm. Through the swirling flames, riders in green cloaks appear. One has pink veins glowing around their eyes. Large gray dogs circle, snarling and barking with the same pink light in their eyes. How did the beastcharmer track us when we've been hiding our trail and using the bloodleaf? And why couldn't I sense them?

The lead Failinis brings his horse closer, the firelight glinting off the torq and the dog-head pin. The orange light in his veins glows brighter as the flames grow hotter. "You gave the hounds quite a challenge, Morana, but now there's nowhere left to hide," Captain MacAdoh yells over the crackling. Hearing him say my name rips away the last bit of safety I'd wrapped around myself. He knows my name, and someone gave it to him.

His smile's a knife in the dark that cuts my legs from under me. Smoke stings my eyes, and I cough, but there's no escape from the fiery cage. Percy's hands glow as writhing roots split the ground, wrapping around the spikes of earth. I reach out for any nearby dead, but there's nothing of substantial size. The flicker of hope snuffs out.

"There's no barrow for you to raise out here," Alistair says. "I do want to thank you for leading me to your friend. Who knew such a quaint town was hiding such a dangerous bloodgifted."

My body tenses as sparks singe my sleeves and cheeks. The air is knocked from my lungs. Tears roll down my cheek, Anstice's face rising before it's turned to ash. The hope I held onto that maybe she'd escaped crumbles.

"What did you do to her?!" I shout, clutching the axe. Grief and anger swirl together, my fear urging me to find a way to escape while the heat in my veins screams to make this man bleed.

"Do you want to know how she died? It was a shame to burn the bakery, but she refused to come quietly," MacAdoh goes on. My thoughts are melting, each breath growing thinner.

"She wasn't hurting anyone!" Anger and pain bubble up

beneath each word. "We just want to live our lives like everyone else!"

"You can't deny what you are," MacAdoh replies. "You showed that when you raised all of Àitesìol's dead. You left behind destruction and despair in your wake. And your friend? Just a murderer with skeletons under her house. No matter how hard you try, you can't resist seeking out the dead."

The Captain's words cut into me. My heart's wrapped in brambles, the ounce of courage I had to stand and fight burning away. My arms are heavy as they lower the axe.

"Morana! Don't listen to him!" Percy yells at me.

He keeps the roots up while holding a thrashing Morhenna, but the flames move closer, and the plants smolder. A tongue of flame lashes at his ankle. Percy yells through gritted teeth, and I grip his arm to hold him upright. We're back in the garden with everything burning around us.

The other Failinis circle around the flames. "I only want you, boneweaver. Surrender, and you won't have to watch me kill your husband."

Percy's eyes meet mine, his jaw set as pain strains his features. "Whatever you're thinking, Mor, put it out of your mind," he tells me, coughing. "I'm not losing either of you."

"Percy," I rasp through a lungful of burning air. "Let me—"

A bellowing scream tears through the night, rattling my teeth. I clamp my hands over my ears as the sound pierces my eardrums. Blackness oozes from the ground and spreads over the flames, sizzling as it devours them. The Failinis' horses rear and whinny while the dogs scatter. Captain MacAdoh's mouth moves, but I can't hear anything over the horrid scream.

The darkness surges toward them and grows taller than the trees. Six legs crash into the ground, and a deer skull with a broken antler emerges from the roiling body. Its jaw cracks in place, and the screaming stops. The misshapen creature looms over us, eyes empty pits as the strange presence fills the air with a sickening wrongness.

"Gods," Percy breathes. "Is that...?"

Only one word makes it through the chaos of thoughts. *Brollachan.* Some of the elders back home told stories about them—my grandfather especially liked those stories and often told ones to me and my cousins that had boneweavers as the ones responsible for creating them. When the morrigans were killed, their spirits wandered the earth and became the brollachans, something of rage and hunger that searches for their bodies. This thing reeks of death, yet it's not made entirely of bone. I can hear its ancient, reverberating voice, but I can't understand anything but its fury. And it gives off the same power-deadening sensation the bloodleaf does.

Shouts break through the ringing in my ears. Captain MacAdoh unleashes bouts of fire and earth at the brollachan while gusts of wind twist the flames into a fiery whirlwind, but the brollachan's oozing hide absorbs the attacks with a roar that makes my skull shake.

Its body bulges as it charges at the Failinis, batting aside the dogs trying to attack it. Spikes of ice impale it. Earthen restraints clamp around the brollachan and hold it in place for a moment before it turns into a dark liquid and squeezes out. The Captain's horse throws him off, and the brollachan surges forward.

"Come on!" Percy shakes my shoulder, his voice muted beneath the ringing in my ears.

The flames have died down, and the Failinis are busy with the brollachan. Percy's roots break the rocks away. I blink, refocusing my blurring vision as I inhale fresh air. I support him, and we sprint toward the forest, Percy limping as he heals his injured ankle. Morhenna has shot off ahead of us into the forest. The brollachan's head snaps in our direction. I'm overwhelmed by the dread that melts my bones as it howls. One of its legs shoots toward us as Percy stumbles and goes down.

"Percy!"

I swing the axe at one of the inky protrusions nearing him. The axehead squelches in the ooze, and I hack at it, the ichor burning my skin as it splatters on me. I pull my weapon back in time to see more snaking toward me, but I can't raise my arms quick enough to stop them. Large trees sprout from the ground to form a wall, taking the blow in a shatter of wood shards. The arm pounds at the trees and claws at the trunks. Percy's arms shake as he struggles to push the attack back, the green light in his veins flickering.

The brollachan rises over the treetops, its shadow swallowing us. Blackness spreads around it and writhes across the ground. I try to call the bones underground, but my power fails. A blast of fire consumes its skull, and it twists around like an oily snake before crashing down on Captain MacAdoh.

I tear my eyes away, hauling Percy to his feet. We continue stumbling over the uneven ground, branches cutting my face.

The brollachan's roars don't fade the farther we run. I glance over my shoulder, but nothing's following us. Fire has taken hold of the nearby trees and grass, illuminating the creature's twisted features. I pray to the gods, both living and dead, that the night hides us. If this creature took down gods, all we can do is try to outrun it.

WEAK SUNLIGHT COMES THROUGH THE BROKEN ROOF OF THE RUINED byre we're camping in, its walls tangled up in blankets of ivy. Percy crouches over the fire as eggs cook with mushrooms, dandelion leaves, and cattail roots in the pan. He'd tried heating up some garlic, but the smell made me want to vomit. I shift on the ground to get comfortable, arms sore from cutting firewood.

Since the run-in with the Failinis and the brollachan three days ago, no place feels safe. We avoided the town we originally planned to stop in, making do with the supplies we have. Percy can grow most of what we need, and foraging has been decent. Despite the harrowing experience, Morhenna continues to lay her eggs.

Every day the sun rises, I worry that I'll see flames or the broken, oozing skull of a brollachan, MacAdoh standing over me, or the silence of a still heart inside me. Every animal I regard with suspicion, all the birds that fly too close or the deer that bound through the forests. Morhenna is her usual spiteful self, but there's no pink glow of beastcharmer magic in her eyes. For now, we're safe, with no sight of our pursuers or the creature and its magic-dampening presence. I'm trying to hold onto the moments of peace to keep me going, but they're becoming scarcer.

I roll the sprig of heather between my fingers, still fresh because of Percy's rootsowing magic. The burns along my skin are healed, except for the red marks left from the brollachan's ichor. Those wounds have been harder for Percy to fix. Like the bloodleaf, that monster had some ability to suppress a bloodgifted's abilities. Maybe that's how the morrigans were able to kill some of the gods, but I can't recall that ever being mentioned in any story. If we were powerless against the brollachan, maybe the Failinis were too.

"Are you thinking about something, or are you hearing voices of the dead?" Percy asks over the popping oil, and I glance up.

"Thinking. Is it wrong to pray for the brollachan to have gotten the Failinis? Or that it took down some of them or at least stopped them from following us?" I reply, sitting up. A handful of sídhe flitter through the broken holes in the byre's roof.

"Who's to say the gods won't use a method like that so we can continue on our journey," he says. "Are you still set on going to the Cluaran Mountains?"

The jagged peaks of the mountains are a faint outline in the distance beyond Ben Sùil. "I don't know what other options we have. There might be bloodgifted there who can take us to this Tearmann Island." Anstice believed in it so strongly, and that makes me also want to believe.

A crease forms between his brow. "I'm worried about being in the wilderness if something happens, especially with winter not too far off. The weather is already unpredictable here. Your pulse and blood pressure are higher than I'd like.

You've been getting more tired than usual. The Cluaran Mountains are still almost a two-week journey from here, and there could be more brollachan in the mountains."

My hand goes to my stomach. I'm getting closer to the time when I lost my first child—fourteen weeks. That number looms in my mind like a dark cloud I'm marching toward. I understand Percy's apprehension to lengthen our journey. There's no way we could defeat a brollachan or any of the other creatures that could be lurking in the highlands. But if we can't get somewhere safe, what's the point of all this? Always being on the run is no life for a child. Tearmann sounds like the only safe place for us.

"What about going to Teaghlach?" Percy asks. My heart skips a beat at the mention of home.

I put the sprig of heather back in my pocket. "Teaghlach's not in the direction we're heading. It's northwest," I tell him, grabbing my map from my pack.

"True, but it's only five or six days away. I could tell that much from the map."

I smooth out the map on my lap. "But it's not safe to go there with the Failinis after us. They tracked us to Neòinean, and I don't want to bring any danger to them," I tell him a little harsher than I should. Losing Anstice was hard enough. I don't want to see my home go up in flames too.

"It's remote. If we can get to Teaghlach before winter, maybe that will keep us safe from the Failinis—if they survived the brollachan."

I chew on the inside of my lip and stare at the orange yolk in the pan. "I left so they'd be safe from those trying to find me. What if returning undoes everything?"

"I know you're worried, but I also know how much you've

missed your family. I think you need to see them again, especially your mother, and tell her everything that's going on," he says and comes over to kneel in front of me.

There's sadness in his voice. He's probably thinking about his own parents, who had been traveling for years before he started at the Acadamaidh. He's an only child to a waterdancer and an earthcarver. While he grew up in a loving family, their research on bloodgifted for the Regency kept them always moving to other places across the world. Percy got occasional letters from them in the past, but he hasn't seen them in almost ten years. I doubt they'd approve of me, and I know Percy hasn't told them that I'm a boneweaver or much about our lives.

"There will always be what-ifs, but life's too short to stay apart from family." Percy places his hand over mine, rubbing one of the faded scars on my knuckles. "And I'm not saying that because I want to hear all the embarrassing stories about you. But if you think it's too risky, we can keep going on to find Tearmann."

"I don't want to put my family in danger."

"I know, but please, just consider it," he says, squeezing my hand. "I think this will be good for you."

I don't want to fight with him again. The draw to return home grows stronger the closer we get to the familiar mountains. Ma only knew I got married in a letter I sent years ago, and I don't want to write and tell her that I've left Errigal or that she has a grandchild.

"If you think it's best to go to Teaghlach, then we'll go," I begin. "But we need to be careful. They can't follow us to the mountains."

"I'll make sure our tracks are covered and make the ointment stronger so the dogs can't track us," Percy tells me.

I kiss his left palm. "I think breakfast is burning," I say and point to the smoke rising from the pan.

Percy turns around, muttering as he moves the food onto the tin plates. Morhenna cocks her head, her comb shaking as she clucks and scratches at the ground. "I'll grow you some berries to eat soon, Henna. I'll repay you for the eggs," Percy tells her.

A dark shape moves outside the byre beyond Percy's shoulder, and my body clenches. Morhenna flaps her wings and clucks louder with a warning cry. My hand goes for the axe, the joints in my shoulder popping with the sudden movement. Percy's head snaps up, and, noticing my worried look, follows my gaze. Between the trees slinks a black form the size of a dog. Out of the woods stalks a cat larger than anything I've seen before. It seems to melt into the shadows, its black pelt rippling with dappled light and the white spot on its chest staring at me like a third eye. Prickles run along my skin under its gaze.

I recognize the creature from Aodh's blurry memories. It's a cat-sìth.

Percy grabs Morhenna as the cat-sìth comes closer to the byre. I've only heard stories about these elusive creatures. They're said to eat souls and be attracted to warmth, but I don't get the same feeling from it as I did with the brollachan. Shadowcatchers consider them to be good luck since they are kin to the Shadow Goddess Ciardha. For a moment, I wonder if it's a spy for the Failinis, but its gem-like eyes flash amber in the sunlight as it looks at the pan of eggs.

"I think it's hungry," I whisper to Percy as I stand, keeping the axe in front of me. I don't think Percy would appreciate it if I suggested we give it the chicken.

I wrap the edge of my cloak around the handle of the pan and flip two of the eggs out onto the ground outside the byre, a few of the cattail roots and dandelion leaves flopping out as well. Percy takes some of the hardtack and tosses it toward the cat-sìth. "I don't know what else to give it," he says, his fingertips glowing green. Morhenna is pressed close to his chest.

The creature slinks toward the food, sniffs it, and licks the orange yolk oozing across the grass. Its ears are angled toward us as it eats. The cat-sìth's tail twitches before it melts into the woods as if it was never here. I lower the axe and try not to spill the rest of our meager breakfast onto the ground.

"Well, that was certainly something to get the blood pumping," Percy says and sets the chicken on the ground. "Are things like that common up here? We've already seen kelpies and the brollachan. What's next? A pack of cu-sìth? Maybe an oilliphéist or some selkies?"

"I've never seen one, but there are a lot of creatures up here that you don't find in the lowlands," I tell him, setting the pan down. "Doubt we'll see a selkie since they live by the sea."

He glances back at the woods before brushing stray feathers from his coat. "You were thinking of throwing Henna to the cat-sìth, weren't you?"

Guess I didn't hide that thought well. "I didn't think about it for long," I tell him.

"It'd be a shame if we lost Morhenna. Eggs make mornings better." Percy reaches into one of his pockets and pulls out a seed the size of a flea before dropping it on the ground. With a flick of his glowing fingers, a black currant bush springs to life from the ground, dark berries appearing as branches and leaves unfurl. "I suppose we'll be eating mostly berries and vegetables today. Unless something else wants to join us for breakfast."

XIV
Daisy

Bellis perennis

Childhood ❦ Decisions ❦ Gentleness

The rains, hilly landscape, and exhaustion have made the last week of traveling slow, but we managed to get through it. My ankles grow puffy and stiff with each passing day. Thoughts of Failinis, kelpies, and brollachans still lurk in my mind as I worry about what we might bring with us. With the Lùbach Mountains rising like a knobby spine draped in trees, its uppermost peaks coated in snow, there's a calm I haven't felt in a while. For the first time in a long time, there's actually a road to follow. One I'm familiar with. Morhenna darts ahead and often stops to look back at us when we don't keep pace with her.

I glance at Percy as he stares ahead, gaze unfocused on anything. "You look distracted," I tell him and pull the tonnag around my shoulders closer as a chill cuts through the sunny afternoon.

"Just taking in the mountains," he replies with his usual lopsided grin rimmed with a few days' worth of stubble. He grips his walking stick, bundled in his cloak. "I've already spotted quite a few useful plants along the hills."

"While I don't doubt that you're thinking about plants most of the time—"

"That's not what I think about most of the time. I think about you, our child, what foods I could make if we had butter."

"—I think there's something else," I finish, frowning.

Percy scratches his chin. "Well...I was thinking about meeting your family for the first time. Do you think your mother will like me?"

I stop. It's odd to hear Percy be anxious about anything. "Why wouldn't she? I've yet to meet a person who doesn't like you. I spoke very highly of you in my letters to her. She always mentioned wanting to meet you."

"How highly did you speak of me? What do I have to live up to? I hope you mentioned how handsome I am," Percy says, and his grin widens as he nudges my side. "I only want to make a good impression."

"Meeting my ma shouldn't be more terrifying than what we've faced already. She can be stern, but she's a warm person. It's my brothers, especially Ross, you might have to watch," I tell him. "Be yourself, and they'll love you. Just don't tell any of your puns."

He loops his arm through mine. "But you said to be myself. The puns are a part of me. You knew that when you married me. I want to show your family what a *fungi* I am."

Rolling my eyes, I keep walking. The road dips downhill, and I'm staring into the familiar valley nestled between the mountains. Crofts dot the hills, and farmland stretches out in fields of yellow and green. Red poppies spill along the main road. Cows graze on the hillside, their russet coats standing out against the grass and heather. Drovers in the distance call out to bring their herds toward the pastures. Tendrils of smoke rise from the chimneys, the familiar smells settling deep in my lungs. The crisp breath of the mountain winds singing down the slopes tells me that I'm home.

It's amazing how after being gone for fifteen years, my body remembers the way home to the squat white croft by gnarled cherry and elder trees. My throat tightens. Years running around the yard, finding summer berries, helping Da with the cows while Ma bounced little Glenna on her hip, Leith and Ross bringing home some injured animal they found wandering around. The house was always full of life with my family around. Being alone was the hardest thing I had to deal with when I left.

I sense the graves where we buried pets and the family barrow where Da and my relatives are. The lowing of cows grows louder the closer we get. A black bull stands like a dark spot among the cows. We used to only have ten, but it seems that number has doubled. Chickens dart across the path, and Morhenna clucks at them until they scatter. Dried herbs and shards of glass hangs from the wooden gate, ivy and purple clematis climbing over the stone wall.

A cow plods over to the fence covered in shaggy hair. One of the horns is curled toward its head, and I smile. Ceart. Morhenna struts over and cocks her head at the cow. Ceart licks her pink nose, pressing against the slates of the fence. Even after all this time, she still wants me to sneak her a carrot. I'm glad she's still around, a reminder of my childhood that hasn't disappeared.

I scratch her coarse hair. "I don't have anything for you," I say as she licks my hand. “I’m glad you still remember me.”

I brush aside her dossan to see her large eyes staring back at me. She was one of my favorite cows in the herd, always calm and unique with her bent horn. Ceart and Da always had a special bond, and she was my link to him after he died.

Percy leans against the fence, staring at the rest of the russet-colored herd scattered through the field. “They’re quite cute,” Percy says. “I think I want one.”

“They’re also very useful. Good for milk, and we use their hair for clothing and yarn,” I tell him.

In the distance, an echoing call carries through the pasture, rising and falling in a familiar rhythm. Someone stands at the top of the hill. Ma. Ceart turns and follows the herd up the brae. A black and white dog streaks across the field after them, keeping the stragglers with the group. Da was a beastcharmer and didn’t need to do much to get the cows to listen to him, but he always used that call to gather them. Ma uses it so effortlessly, and the cows listen to her like she’s a bloodgifted. She always did put the other drovers in the town to shame.

“Who are you?” a voice behind us says.

We turn to find a little girl wrapped in a blue plaid tonnag. Her red hair is braided, and a gray goose waddles behind her. She can’t be older than six. Her hazel eyes are wide as she looks me up and down, crossing her small arms over her chest. I sense power in her that has a wildness to it that reminds me of Da, and I focus on it like Anstice told me to. She’s a bloodgifted. A beastcharmer, possibly?

“Hello. I’m Percy, and this is Morana,” Percy tells her with a smile. “What’s your name?”

She looks back at the house. “Da! Strangers!” she shouts.

"What is it, Saoirse?"

A man with a thick beard and matching red hair steps out the front door. I didn't see it before—the hazel eyes and red hair. She's Ross' daughter. Ma wrote to me about her six years ago when she was born. He wipes his hand on a rag as the girl runs to him. It's an odd sensation to stare at a sibling I've not seen in fifteen years yet recognizing their face.

I hold my breath, heart hammering. Will he recognize me? Does he hate me for leaving Ma and them on their own? I'm practically a stranger now.

"Morana?" he asks, stopping when he sees us. His hazel eyes widen.

"It's good to see you, Ross," I say, trying to manage a smile and stop my voice from shaking.

My brother sprints over and wraps me in a tight embrace. "By the gods!" he exclaims with a laugh. "I cannae believe you're here!"

There's no accusation or coldness in his voice, only warmth and acceptance. Ross stands as tall as me, smelling of grass and peat. My little brother looks so much like Da now—even has the same rumbling laugh. It's so different than the reedy voice he had as a boy—another reminder of how much time I've missed. My tears land on his tunic, but Ross doesn't notice.

"I cannae hardly believe it either," I reply. My accent slides across my tongue so easily once my heart recognizes that it's home.

Ross steps back, glancing at Percy. "This must be your husband. Skinny fellow."

Percy extends a hand. "Percival Bracken—" Ross pulls him

into a hug, knocking his glasses askew. "Oh, you're a hugging family, I see," he manages to say and fixes his glasses.

"Dinnae break him, Ross," I say.

Ross slaps him on the back and laughs. "But he's a fleshmender, right? He can put himself back together. Although dinnae how good of a fleshmender he is if he hasn't fixed his eyes and has to wear glasses," he says.

"Ross!" Some things never change. Always turning a blunt fact into a joke.

"I didn't want people to think I was too perfect. A few imperfections keep me humble," Percy tells him without missing a beat. "Besides, Morana likes the glasses."

Ross nods before looking to me. "What are you doing here? Ma didnae mention you were comin'."

I dry my eyes, my elation sagging. "She doesn't ken. I didnae have a chance to write."

"Well, this'll be a nice surprise for her." Ross waves his daughter over. "Saoirse, this is your Aunt Morana. Say hello. Dinnae be blate."

Saoirse puts her hand on the goose following beside her. "Hello," she mumbles.

I crouch down, my knees popping as I lean against my walking stick. "It's nice to meet you. I've heard so much about you."

Growling, Morhenna charges at the goose, and it hisses. Saoirse steps between them and holds a hand out as the veins around her eyes glow pink. She's a beastcharmer like Ross and Da.

"Be nice," Saoirse says, and Morhenna stops, wings folding at her sides. She pets the chicken before picking her up. "She's scared, but she's fine now."

"Well, that's impressive," Percy says. "I've never seen Henna so relaxed. You're a very talented girl, Saoirse."

"I know," the girl replies.

"Saoirse, why dinnae you take their chicken to the coop?" Ross says, wheeling us toward the house. "Let's get you inside. Leith willnae be home until tonight after he finishes up at the smithy. Glenna's with Tréasa, my wife, out in the fields. I cannae wait for you to meet Tréasa."

As I'm whisked through the threshold, it's like stepping back in time. The same woven rug lays by the hearth where a peatbrick fire is going, and a tabby with one missing ear lounges, different than the black and white one we had when I left. Blankets are thrown across rocking chairs in the inner room. Strings of sliced apples dry over the stove. Pots and pans hang from the rafters over the counter next to cords of garlic and dried herbs. The smell of the farm hits me with a thousand memories.

"Sit. I'll get you somethin'," Ross says.

I run my hand along the wooden beam in the center of the room. Da put it in one spring after I was born when the roof started to sag. I note the various notches under my fingertips, tracing the worn names. Da wanted to mark our heights over the years. I was always the tallest of my siblings. Glenna never did get taller than Ma, it seems. There are fresher marks dated after I left—Ross surpassing my last height check, with Leith catching up but still not as tall as him. Glenna's a few feet shorter than Ross. The freshest marks have two names—Saoirse and Coinín, Ross' children.

I sit at the long table by the window and stare at the garden and the rolling hills unraveling into the mountains. On the sill, there are walnut shell halves filled with milk and honey, and berries for the sídhe. Beyond the brae, behind the pastures and fields, is a valley where we take the cows to the stream. A stocky gray horse grazes near the byre. Saoirse puts Morhenna down by the coop, pointing to all the chickens as if introducing them. A black dog pads over to her.

Even though this place is home, I'm a stranger here. Ross and Glenna are married and have their own families, Leith has his work, and each of them with lives I only know pieces of from Ma's letters. I know leaving hurt them, and I don't blame them for resenting me. Us showing up here suddenly is bound to stir up things. I don't know how the rest of my family will react.

"This table's been here a while," Percy says, running a hand across the dark surface full of nicks and ruts.

I look at him. "That's the first thing you notice?" I ask.

"It's wood. It says a lot compared to most plants."

The bench beneath me groans. "My granda made the table eighty years ago. The tree it was carved from was growing right here, and he built the table first, then the house around it."

Percy looks underneath the table. "My, my, Morana. Looks like you left your mark on this poor table. You carved your name and did so many drawings that I don't think there's an unmarked surface left," he says with a *tsk*.

I used to take Da's whittling knife and practice writing my name under the table. When there were bad storms, I'd write prayers to Sorcha to make them stop. Eventually, Da caught me and taught me to whittle chunks of wood because he was worried that I'd carve the whole table away. I run my thumb along the newest carvings on my staff. He'd be proud of how much I've improved.

The back door creaks, and my heartbeat quickens. Ma shuffles in with her walking stick and stamps the mud off her boots. Silver streaks run through her dark hair, her back bent a little more. But despite the new lines across her face, Ma's blue eyes remain as bright as I remember. There wasn't a year that went by when I didn't long to be held in her strong arms and hear her throaty laughter.

"Ross, I—" The stick clatters to the ground as she stares at me, her mouth frozen open. "Morana?"

"I'm home, Ma," I rasp, the words getting stuck in my throat.

She comes and cups my face, callused fingers moving across my cheeks as her eyes shine. "You've grown so tall, mo chridhe. You're so much like your da," she says through her smile before wrapping her arms around me, her head coming up to my chest. "What's brought you home?"

My tears fall into her hair. I smell the fields on her clothes, along with smoke and lavender. There's so much I wanted to tell her over the years but didn't. About my lost baby, my own doubts, missing her comfort but not feeling like I could stay. The last time I wrote her was at the beginning of the year. Now, I worry I won't have enough time to tell her everything.

"We can talk about it when you're ready." Ma grips my arms and turns her attention to Percy. "This must be your husband. He's handsomer than you mentioned in your letters," she says. "Fàilte, Percy. I'm Carlin."

Percy takes Ma's hand. "Pleasure to finally meet you. I've heard many good things about you," he tells her. "I want to thank you for raising such a wonderful woman."

"You didnae mention he was charmin', Morana." Ma squeezes one of his arms. "Or how skinny he is. Like a twig.

Who's been feedin' you, lad? Morana's cookin' cannae be that bad."

My face grows warm. "Ma!"

"I'm only jokin', Morana. But he *is* so skinny. Ross, get him some scran before he blows away. Do you eat meat?" Ma asks Percy.

"I don't mind it, but Morana doesn't like to eat it, so we're mostly vegetarians," Percy replies.

"I can make up a fresh batch of tattie drottle and some leek and carrot pies. Sit, sit. I'll go get your sister and the children. She'll be excited to know that you're home."

Saoirse and Coinín play with the cat by the fire, the little girl coaxing it to stand on its back legs while her dark-haired brother giggles. Three dogs lounge around them. I lean against Percy as my eyelids droop, full of good food and fifteen years' worth of stories. My jaws ache from crying, smiling, and laughing. My fears of being viewed as a stranger or the resentment I thought my siblings held toward me were assuaged over the last few hours. Their embraces brought out apologies for years of guilt, and their forgiveness felt warmer than any fire.

After Da died, it was a long time before joy sat at the table again. Ma withered, held together by her shawl and the walking stick Da used in the fields. Now, she's still thin, but there's a strength in her that's as strong as yew. I like to believe that the wrinkles creasing her skin are from laughter rather than sorrow. Loud conversations and stories press against the walls, and I wonder if the house can hold it all.

Leith, my youngest brother, slams his cup down as he tries not to choke on his drink after laughing too hard. Ross claps him on the back, beard parting as he smiles. They're only a year apart, but they look like twins—Leith's hair is more blond than red. My younger sister, Glenna bounces her baby, Craig, on her knee and brushes back his brown hair while Tréasa, Ross' wife, wiggles her fingers at him. The baby coos and reaches for one of her golden tresses.

"C'mon, Leith. You're a flamekindler and breathe in smoke all day. Little whisky heat shouldnae be nothin' to you," Ross says.

"You made me laugh while I was drinkin'," Leith coughs, face red. "Gods."

"You look good with short hair," Glenna says and touches my short locks. "Ma said you always had long, pretty hair."

"It was time to cut it," I tell her.

I left when she was almost eight, so all she probably remembers about me is what Ma or my brothers told her. I still don't know what to say to her since we've spent more time apart than we did as sisters, but she's been asking questions since I arrived, which has helped to bridge the awkwardness.

Ma looks around at the empty plates and bowls, ready to refill them. "Morana, you look ready to fall over," she tells me.

I sit up and fight back a yawn. "I'm fine."

"We should get sleep. We've had a long day," Percy says, squeezing my hand.

"Come. You can have my room," Ma says as she stands.

"Ma, no. That's too much," I tell her, shaking my head.

She puts a hand up. "I willnae hear it. There's room with

the bairns—who should be gettin' to bed now." Her gaze goes to Saoirse and Coinín, and my niece and nephew quiet.

Saoirse and Coinín look up with dejected faces. "Why? I'm not tired," Saoirse protests as she yawns.

Ross stands and scoops Saoirse up before hoisting a giggling Coinín under his arm. "Gran's spoken. Off to bed with you," he says.

"But I want to stay with Auntie Mor and Uncle Percy," his daughter replies.

"Tomorrow. They'll be here for a while."

He takes them down the hall where more rooms are. That explains why the house is bigger. More rooms have been added on to accommodate Ross and Glenna's families.

Percy helps me stand as Leith picks up our packs. There are faded burns on his hands and a permanent ruddiness to his face from working in a forge. Leith's grown into a quiet young man, the opposite of Ross, whose voice carries like Da's did. I know he's a flamekindler, but I try to keep thoughts of Captain MacAdoh from creeping up. I don't want the Failinis to make me afraid of my own brother just because they have the same bloodgift.

My parents' room looks the same as I remember, with the solid wood bed I hid in when storms came, and the giant chest I pretended had treasure in it. The russet cowhide rug is worn, but still where it's always been. Da's voice bleeds through the walls. I blink and see his outline in the bed with a faint smile before he starts coughing, and then he's gone.

Ma comes in behind us to gather up a few clothes lying on the chair. She lights the candle on the nightstand. "The sheets are clean. I can bring you some extra blankets if you need them," she tells us.

"You dinnae need to give us your room," I reply.

Leith sets our bags down. "Best not to argue with her, Mor. You ken how she gets," my brother whispers with a smile as Ma slaps his shoulder. "It's good to have you back."

His boots shuffle against the worn floor as he leaves. Ma lays out a pile of blankets and pillows on the bed. "Do you want to take a bath? I can heat some water for you."

Percy smiles. "Thank you, Carlin. A bath sounds lovely," he says. "Let me know if there's anything I can do to help."

"Dinnae fash about that tonight." Ma waves her hand at him. "We'll have plenty of work for you to do tomorrow. Crops to look at and such since you're a rootsower. Maybe look at a few of the cows that have some scrapes."

"I'm not much of a healer of animals, but I can look at them."

"Do you need me to heat a flaxseed bag for your joints?" she asks me.

"I'm fine, Ma."

"You let me know if you need anythin' else." Ma pats my cheek. "Get some sleep, daughter. You've had a long journey, but you're home now."

The door closes behind her. The bed creaks as I sit. I'm aware now of my aching feet and back and how puffy my fingers are. I pick up the green and yellow patchwork quilt with embroidered knots and flowers my parents always had on their bed. Pressing it against my nose, I smell a hint of woodfire and pine. Da's smell.

Percy crouches down and unties my boots, running his hands over my swollen ankles and feet as he removes my socks to check for blisters and cuts. His fingers start to work the top and sole of my left foot, but I put a hand on his shoulder to stop him.

"You're doing it again," I say. He looks up with candlelight dancing across his glasses. "My feet are fine. You dinnae—don't need to do anything else tonight."

"Sorry. I'm nervous. This keeps my mind busy." He gets up and sits next to me, slipping out of his coat and laying it across the chest.

The muted silence fills the room, broken only by the sound of my family moving down the hall and plates clattering together in the kitchen. I tear up, thinking about how much I've missed the sound of a busy house.

"You didn't tell your mother why we're really here yet," he says. "Or about the baby."

I drop the quilt in my lap. "I dinnae want to worry her today." Telling Ma would mean she'd get hopeful for something that might not be. Seeing her heartbroken again would crush me. I don't want to spoil today's joy.

"You'll have to tell her eventually," Percy says.

"I know. But I'm not sure I have the right words that willnae make her worry."

"She'll worry regardless of what you say. You're her daughter. You'll always be her concern."

My hands tighten around the soft sheets. Our home hasn't been without its sorrows and hard times, but to bring the possibility of fresh sadness here makes me sick. I want to keep the sunshine shining here for as long as I can before the clouds roll in. For tonight, I'll pretend that there are no monsters following us and that nothing can find us beyond these walls.

Percy leans against me, head resting on my shoulder. "I

noticed your accent's back," he adds. "I'd forgotten how cute you sound with it."

I roll my eyes and give him a light slap on the leg. "It's going to be hard to hide it again," I mutter.

"For now, you don't need to," he says and kisses my jaw. "At least for a little bit, be yourself."

XV
Forget-me-not

Myosotis sylvatica

Faithfulness · Memories · Remembrance

My walking stick sinks into a muddy patch as Ma and I lead the cows up the hillside to the grazing pastures near where the sheep are. These hills are covered in memories, and I sense the scattered bones of animals buried beneath my feet. To be back in the mountains doesn't seem real. I still feel that I'll blink and be in some forest, hungry, on edge, and my body aching. The crisp air sweeps out the clouds fogging up my mind, and for the first time in weeks, I can breathe easier.

My gaze finds the house again, my family's bones calling to me. Percy's settled in like he's been here for years instead of a few days. He's even had time to work on recreating and studying the bloodleaf's effects. Seeing the children playing with him, eager for the giant flowers he grows for them, makes my heart clench. No doubt he's thinking about when we have ours, but those thoughts are still painful.

Behind the house, the town is nestled in the valley, the cottages tethered together by smoke rising from the chimneys. Only a few houses are new, but little has changed. Fishermen walk through town toward the smokehouse with baskets of silver caught in the rivers since the salmon run is happening. I find the old schoolhouse and the healer's hut I frequented when my arthritis got bad. I wonder if Aregwydd is still alive since she seemed ancient when I was a child. I know the familiar shapes of my aunts' and uncles' houses, and where the alehouse stands in the middle of town. So many memories floating through the hills and roads.

The lowing of the cows makes me turn as they head down to the stream. Ma's a few feet ahead, and one of the black and white collies keeps the herd together. A few of the younger calves stick close to Ma and nose her pockets for treats.

"You seem distracted, Morana," Ma says. Strands of hair escape from her bun, her cheeks red from the wind. Another calf bounds past her as it follows its mother.

"Just a wee bit tired," I tell her. "I havenae had to walk hills in a while. Àitesìol was mostly flat."

I still haven't told her why we're here, but she gives me that knowing look of hers. There's a small voice that makes me wonder if she'll tell us to leave to keep the peace that's here. My family never made me feel bad about being a boneweaver, but the rest of our extended family and the other townsfolk won't be as understanding if they find out. I grew up letting others believe that I was an earthcarver who couldn't use her gift, putting up with the mocking from the other bloodgifted children because that was easier than the truth being known.

"Are your joints botherin' you?" Ma asks.

"They're fine. Percy's been taking care of the pain." There's a tin of numbing balm in my skirt pocket in case some new ache appears.

"You found a great man, mo chridhe. There are plenty of good ones, but it's the great ones that are harder to find."

I smile. I didn't find him. He found me.

Ma waves me over as she sits down on a flat boulder. I sit next to her, and she pulls out a tin flask from the pouch at her waist. "A bit of whisky should put some fire back in your veins," she says.

"I cannae drink," I tell her, gathering the strength to say the words. "I'm pregnant."

I'm left breathless, more aware of the new weight growing in me. It's been sitting heavily on me for so long and having it out in the world leaves behind an odd weightlessness.

"Oh, that's wonderful! The gods have truly blessed you!" Ma breathes and kisses my cheeks. "Why didnae you tell me sooner?"

"I didnae know how to," I whisper.

Ma pulls away, squeezing my hands. "This is such joyous news, but you dinnae look happy. Why?"

The dried baby's breath sinks into the mud of my memories, the branches of the willow waving in the wind. "I...I dinnae ken how I should feel. This isnae...the first time I've been with child. I'm worried that I'll lose this one like I did my first."

Her fingers tighten as her smile crumbles. "When did this happen?"

Salty needles prick my eyes. "About two years ago. I didnae write you because I was ashamed. And...I didnae want to remember."

I tell her everything—the lost baby, the fires, our burning garden, Anstice, and my fears. Ma's arms wrap around my neck, holding me close. I'm a little girl again, held together by threads while fissures crack me apart. When there are no more words left to say, I'm hollowed out and clinging to Ma. She runs her hands through my hair and kisses my forehead.

"I'm afraid that if something happens...if I...lose this one... Percy will realize that this is too much," I tell her before my voice dissolves into sobs.

She grips my shoulders. "I've seen how he is around you, and that's not the character of a man who leaves when things get hard."

"I dinnae want to bring any danger here. The Failinis keep finding us. There's more of them now, and I'm afraid it winnae be long before the whole island is searching for us."

"You're safe here," Ma tells me and pulls me closer. "You can stay as long as you want. If the Failinis come, I'll show them what happens when they try to take my daughter from me."

I touch my stomach. All these breakable moments litter the ground, leaving me no room to move without crushing them. I look at the softening lines across Ma's face. Her eyes drift far away from here, her sadness reflecting something deeper.

"Losin' a child is never easy," Ma says and wipes the damp trails from her cheeks. "That'll always be a part of you, but you'll find enough room in your heart for another. Grief doesn't shrink, but we grow around it."

Moist pressure clamps on my arm, and I see Ceart chewing on my forearm. My sleeve becomes slick with saliva as she sucks on my arm. Bits of grass stick to my clothes as she lets go. I brush the hair off Ceart's face, taking her large head in my hands. I smile as I kiss her nose, her tongue licking my neck before I can pull away.

Ma stands and pats the cow's flank. "She's missed you."

THE CRY OF A FOX WAKES ME FROM A DREAM SPUN TOGETHER WITH smoke, ash, and silver wolf jaws closing around me. Sweat soaks my nightgown, and tears wet my cheeks. Percy mutters about patellas and tibias next to me. I breathe in the smokeless air of the room, my eyes adjusting to the darkness. I slide out of bed and shuffle to the door. The dreams have been visiting me for the past week since we arrived here, grief catching me off guard when I'm not looking.

Grabbing my coat and boots, I head outside. Moonlight covers the garden and byre in a silvery sheen, the house glowing against the night. The dark shapes of the cows litter the fields as they sleep. Clusters of flickering sídhe light up the hillside.

I follow the path to the barrow beyond the fruit trees. The voices beneath the ground stir and rise to greet me. Grandparents. Cousins. Aunts and uncles. I sift through them until I find Da's deep voice. I thumb through my memories to recall the fuzzy details of his face. It's been years, but that grief is still tender.

The wind chills the tear trails on my skin. "I'm sorry I haven't been home in a while, Da. There's a lot to tell you," I mutter, my words falling on the flowers growing around his rain-stained stone marker. The triquetra on the slab is covered in lichen, and I pull the soft patina away. "I'm pregnant, but I dinnae ken if I can do this...I miss you and wish you could tell me what to do."

"Morana, what are you doin' out here?"

I turn to see Ma cradling Craig under her shawl. Her hair flows down her shoulders, ribbons of silver shining against the dark tresses.

I clear my throat. "I didnae mean to wake you. I couldnae sleep."

"I was up already. This little one was fussy, and I didnae want Glenna to wake," she says. "You used to come out here when you had bad dreams. Is that what's happened?"

I nod. After Da died, I spent many nights out here. I wanted to be close to him, to hear his voice again. I clung to the pieces of his memories like a blanket. The bones in the barrow gave me comfort. My family was always with me even if they weren't living anymore.

She takes my hand and leads me back to the house. "Let's get you somethin' other than mountain air to fortify you."

A low fire burns in the fireplace as we step inside, and she hands Craig to me. He fusses, his face scrunched up as he fights sleep. I swallow the twinge of panic. He's so small in my arms as I sit in one of the chairs and rock him.

Ma returns from the kitchen with two cups of warm milk and a rag. She hands them to me, setting the second cup on the table between the rocking chairs. When my brothers and Glenna were little and got fussy, she'd let them suck on a milk-soaked cloth until they calmed down.

I dip the rag and let Craig take it, his cries quieting. He smells like soap and milk and something soft I can't quite place. Tiny fingers grasp mine, and my heart's pressed beneath a warm fluttering.

Ma sinks into the other chair. "What dreams are keepin' you awake?" she asks.

"I keep seeing our house burning. Percy dying. Anstice being captured," I whisper and stare at the baby's face. "So much death, and I cannae do anything but watch."

"Does Percy know about your dreams?"

"Yes...but it's hard to talk about some of it with him. I know he struggles like I do, but I feel everything so much more. It's like a wound, and those memories that aren't mine live in me. My friend, Anstice, was the only one who could truly relate. She is...was a boneweaver too."

Ma nods, the fire crackling. The sadness shadowing her face makes my eyes sting.

"Did you and Da..." I lick my dry lips. "Did you regret that I was born a boneweaver?"

Ma sits up, the chair creaking. "No. We were never afraid of your gift, Morana," she says and shakes her head. "We knew when you were a wee bairn. You could always sense when one of the animals was close to death, and you'd go out to comfort it. You were always findin' animal bones and tellin' these stories about them we thought you'd made up, but we soon learned you were tellin' us stories about our relatives in the barrow. You also stopped eatin' meat once you turned five, said it didnae feel right."

She leans forward, touching the metal pendant of a bear with antlers around her neck. The symbol of Artair, the God of Beasts. Da's pendant. There were so many nights I wished that I'd been born a beastcharmer like him or something other than what I was. Percy's told me before that bloodgifts aren't necessarily passed down through blood but that we're given our abilities however the gods see fit. I still don't know why Arianrhod decided to make me a boneweaver. I probably never will.

"When you were three, you asked about the baby buried beneath the willow tree by the barrow," Ma goes on. "No one told you about the child I lost. About Moina. But you found out when there was no way you could have."

She lost a child? How did I forget that? The sorrow I'd seen on the hill the other day had been deeper because she knew what it was like to lose a child. I look at my feet and take a sip of milk, the buttery taste sliding down my throat.

"When...when did you have Moina?" I ask.

"She was born years before you and only lived a few days. When I lost her, I didnae think I'd have love again for another. When I was pregnant with you, I was so scared I'd lose you too. But Beathag watched over you and brought you into this world healthy and strong."

"I'm sorry I didnae ken."

She clenches her hand around the pendant. "Children aren't meant to ken everythin' about their parents. But maybe if I'd told you sooner, you could have felt less alone when you lost yours."

Regret cracks Ma's voice as she goes to a shelf next to the fireplace mantle and opens a dark chest. A tattered journal rests in her hand, and she runs a hand across the cover. She takes Craig from me and sets the book in my lap. She sits again with a sad smile on her face.

"The day after Valan died, I found you at his bedside talkin' with him. You'd reanimated him. I was startled, but I told you to let him sleep. I dinnae think you knew what you were doin', but he was still again. Then the next day, you gave me this."

I leaf through the journal's yellowed pages filled with childish scrawl. Da's story rests on the paper, and my eyes sting. I flip to a section of the journal where I wrote about Da and Ma meeting. I'd forgotten about doing this, forgotten the night I reanimated him. I was young I didn't understand that he was gone. I only wanted to see him smile again, and he did, eyes glowing purple in the dark room. Now, the memories rise from the silt of my mind.

"I'm so sorry, Ma. I didnae mean to." My words are too big for my mouth, getting stuck behind my teeth.

Ma pats Craig's back as he sucks on the cloth. "You dinnae need to apologize, Morana. You gave me one of the greatest gifts," she says, taking my hand. Her callused fingers are warm and strong, smaller versions of Da's—as if the years they spent intertwined shaped them into matching pairs. "Your da's story helped me through my grief. I learned so much about him I didnae ken. It's filled with all his love for us, for you. He never despised your gift. We only told you to hide it so you'd be safe from those who wouldnae understand, not because we hated that part of you."

I hear the familiar voice, deep and rumbling like laughter in my chest. Da speaks in the memories of wandering fields, hands holding mine as I whittle a cow out of wood, embraces when my body hurt too much to stand. That's why his voice has always been so clear, why I remember certain things about him. They weren't my memories but his. He's been with me this whole time, and I didn't realize it.

"Your gift isnae a curse. You hear what so many cannae and give back somethin' precious—the stories of our loved ones that we wouldnae have otherwise," Ma tells me.

A fresh wave of sadness rises in me, bringing to the

surface old shame and guilt. "Are you upset with me for leaving all those years ago? I didnae explain why I left, and I'm sorry. I didnae mean to hurt you and leave you to take care of my siblings alone."

She straightens, facing me. "When you left, I was upset. Not at you for leavin' but because I couldnae create a place where you felt safe enough to be yourself. It took a while to get your brothers and sister to understand because they were hurt. I know why you had to leave, and now I see that it was good. You found Percy and created a life for yourself. But I still worried, even when I got your letters. I prayed for years for you to come home, even though I knew you might be too afraid to."

The words run together until I can't read them anymore. Layer by layer, I'm being pulled apart until I'm a pile of frayed nerves. Through it all, the sense of pride wraps around me like Da's strong arms holding me.

"I've never loved you any less because of your gift. No one in this family thinks of you differently because you're a boneweaver. I cannae make the nightmares go away or stop the Failinis, but you have a place here, Morana," Ma says. "Always."

I squeeze her hand, unable to get any words out. The knot in my chest loosens.

"Everything alright here?" Percy's quiet voice comes up behind me. He walks over and crouches beside me. "Was my snoring that bad?"

"I'm fine, Percy," I say, drying my eyes and holding the journal closer. I take his hand and kiss his knuckles. "Just bad dreams."

Percy presses his forehead against mine. "*Lettuce* see if we can do something about that. I don't know if *thistle* help, but I can sing you the song my mother sang to me when I couldn't sleep. It might give you *peas* of mind."

Ma smiles at us as she continues to rock Craig. My cheeks warm as I get up from the chair. "I think your puns are going to give me more nightmares."

XVI Dandelion

Taraxacum

Wishes ❦ Hope for the future ❦ Happiness

Summer leaves its mark with sun-soaked fields and green hillsides. Several calves were born, which has kept us busy. Saoirse's already named all of them, and they follow her around like she's their mother. Morhenna's gotten prouder since she's assumed the role of overseer of the byre and has been following Percy around as he tends to the garden. Ma insists that I stay in the house and have nettle soup, but walking helps keep my mind off the nervousness growing in me. I want to believe this calm will last, but even as the weeks turn into three months with no whisper of Failinis, Captain MacAdoh's shadow looms over me.

Teaghlach hasn't changed much except for a few younger faces I spot as Glenna, Tréasa, and I walk through the village. The first week I was here, I was overwhelmed by all the people coming up to me, asking where I've been and what I've been doing. I'd spent so many years in places where people hardly knew me that it was jarring to return to a place where everyone knows everything about me. Percy enjoys hearing the stories about me as a child from my aunts, uncles, and cousins, much to my embarrassment. Somedays this feels like living in a dream—having a normal life.

As the warmer days grow shorter, I notice my body changing. My hair, which is back to its usual brown, now tickles my chin and freckles run across my arms and face. Everything's expanding and leaving me with new aches while my skirts shrink against my swelling stomach. The stretch marks run like dark rivers across my thighs and breasts. My navel sticks out now, which shouldn't be as strange to me as the fact that there's a child pushing on my organs. An ache spreads up my lower back, and I knead the area through my yellow blouse. I have to adjust my skirt as the waistband digs into my tight sides.

"It's amazing how something so small can make our bodies hurt so much," Glenna tells me, holding Craig against her chest.

An older couple, the MacDonalds, wave at us. I remember they used to mend our clothes for Ma after Da died. "It's nothing I'm not used to," I reply and tighten my grip on the bundle of peatbricks in my free hand, "but it seems the aches in my knees have merely moved to the rest of my body."

"Luckily, you have a fleshmender husband who can take care of those things," my sister says with a wink. "Are you hoping for a boy or a girl?"

"I havenae thought much about it. I just want a healthy child." I glance at Craig as he chews on his fingers.

Glenna smooths out Craig's brown curls. "Seumas wanted a girl. He had no boy names thought out, so Craig didnae have a name for the first month he was born. He didnae like my suggestions because he was still in denial I think."

"When's he supposed to get back from Auchendrain?" Tréasa asks, adjusting the basket of candles and fabric resting against her hip. She carries an empty bucket in her other hand.

"He should be back before the snows come. You'll like him, Mor. He's like Percy, always talking and making friends. I swear he knows half of Errigal," Glenna tells me.

"I'm sure they'll get along. I havenae met a person Percy doesn't get along with." We stop by the well in the center of town, and I put down the bundle of peatbricks. I rub my lower back with a sigh. "How often is he gone?"

"Spring to autumn usually. It depends on what he's selling and the season. But I have him home for most of the winter." A smile crosses Glenna's face, making her look a lot like Ma.

Ma spoke highly about Seumas in her letters when Glenna got married two years ago. He was a merchant passing through in the spring and met her, then returned in the autumn to stay until she agreed to marry him. It sounded like one of those stories about princes and princesses meeting by chance. He's also a lightcaster. I can't imagine how hard it must be for Glenna to have her husband gone so much. I know how hard it's been for me when Percy had to be gone for days to see patients.

"Whether it's a boy or a girl, are you hoping your child's bloodgifted?" Tréasa asks, brushing her blonde hair over her shoulder.

Another thing I hadn't thought about. I wanted to get to the point where I could hold my baby instead of dreaming about what bloodgift it might have. We just wanted a child that was healthy.

"Seumas and I hope Craig will be an earthcarver or a rootsower. That'd be helpful around the farm, but it'd be nice to have a non-gifted child like me," Glenna says.

Setting the bucket down, glowing blue veins run along Tréasa's arms. She raises her hand, and a stream of water rises from the well. "Ross wants Coinín to be a beastcharmer like Saoirse, but I'd be fine if he's a different kind of bloodgifted—maybe a waterdancer or a lightcaster. I'd like to wake up without strange animals in the bed," she says and guides the water into the bucket. "I cannae imagine how it was growing up with your brothers."

"There was always something crazy going on," I reply. "Ross would always bring home injured animals while Leith set things on fire accidentally. Leith almost burned my hair off when he was seven because I didnae share some tablet with him."

Tréasa sighs. "Ross *still* brings things home. He and Saoirse always find animals they want to keep or something that needs to be nursed back to health, but ends up staying with us permanently. That's how we ended up with three dogs."

I look down the street at the white and gray houses with mossy roofs. Two children run between them, chasing a cat. I see a child with shaggy hair and Percy's brown eyes running after them. Here the years will pass nestled in between mountains and streams, winter giving way to rainy spring. Home would be something etched into the mountain wind and hills.

Glenna nudges me. I turn to see Percy approaching with a blanket in his arms, half-concealing a basket. A few gray feathers cling to his trousers, and there's a streak of dirt along the collar of his tunic. He must have been in the garden with Morhenna. I'm surprised she's not trailing after him.

"What are you doing here?" I ask.

"Do I need a reason to find my wife and have lunch with her? I thought you might be hungry by now," he replies, shrugging. "I want to take you someplace special."

"What's the occasion?"

"I'll tell you once we get to the secret location." His grin refuses to hang straight as he winks. "It'll all become ap-*pear*-ent soon."

Glenna chuckles and I resist rolling my eyes. I don't know of any special places in Teaghlach that I'm unaware of. I showed Percy all the places I enjoyed spending time at as a child, but he's making it sound like we're going to a magical place. He always does this, planning surprises when he knows I don't like them. I've told him that for years, but he thinks it's funny to keep me in suspense.

He looks at Glenna and Tréasa. "May I steal her away for a bit?"

"Aye. We've finished our errands," Glenna tells him and takes the peatbricks from me. "Just be back for tea. Ma's making haggis and potato pie with clapshot."

"I'll have her home before the sun sets," Percy says and takes my hand.

My fingers brush the golden heads of wild oats as we walk up the hill toward the woods. Green and brown sídhe startle and whip away in a hum of wings and glittering scales. The incline makes my legs burn, and my back ache more. Sweat glues my blouse to my back and rolls down the side of my neck.

"How much further is this *secret* place?" I ask Percy, sucking in a breath. "Because if it's much further, you're going to have to carry me."

"Not much further," Percy replies with a smile. Yellow light snakes from his fingers through my palm, the tiredness melting away.

The brae flattens and rolls into the woods. When we stop, Percy lays out the green blanket and unpacks the basket. Oatcakes with honey, bannock bread with flax seeds and blue cornflower petals, and a small log of cheese. There's a dark bottle I uncork as I sit, my skirts gathered around me. A syrupy floral smell hits my nose. Elderflower and blackberry cordial. I'm glad I don't find it unpleasant like I have with the smell of citrus, meat, and ginger now, unfortunately. Thank the gods that Percy packed cheese with the bread.

"So, this is the *special* place you wanted to take me to?" I say and look out over the fields.

His lips part as he grins. "I liked the plants in the area. Also, you being here makes it special. Who knows, this could be our own secret place someday."

"You're being especially romantic today," I say, taking a sip of cordial as I sit and struggle to remove my boots from my swollen feet. I want to lie down, but I'm not sure if I'll want to get up again. "You still haven't told me what this is all for. Our anniversary isn't until next week."

"I know," Percy tells me and sits beside me. "This is to celebrate something different."

My brow scrunches as I slice the cheese. What else is there to celebrate? The fact that we've been here almost three months without any sign of the Failinis? Was there another anniversary *I* missed?

He adjusts his glasses and smiles, setting his shoes next to mine in the grass. "Before I tell you why, I have something for you."

From the bottom of the basket, Percy pulls out a rolled-up piece of tan nettle cloth. He hands it to me, and I open it to reveal a detailed map of Errigal. The Mainland and the surrounding seas are stitched across it. Mountains and rivers are outlined with different colored threads, and the landscape is dyed green and brown. The Wailing Sea in the north seems to go on forever, but maybe there's an island out there—one Percy and I might eventually get to. The fabric shimmers as I lay it across my lap.

"Percy, this is…I don't know what to say." I can't take my eyes off it as I run my hand across the stitchwork and names of the towns and villages, tears welling up. "Thank you."

"You've always wanted a better map of Errigal, so I asked your mother and some others to help me with this. One day, I'll get you one of the whole world," Percy says. "I wanted something to celebrate you being twenty-six weeks pregnant. The risk is less now that you're over halfway there."

I stop, the taste of the cordial sticking to my tongue. When fourteen weeks had passed, I didn't allow myself to celebrate, afraid that my joy would turn to sorrow. I've been clutching that fear so tightly that I didn't realize how deep the barbs were embedded in my flesh until I unclenched my stiff fingers. Over halfway there.

"Are you sure…there's less risk?" I whisper.

His hand rests on top of mine. "There's always risk, but

you're both healthy, so I'm confident that we'll get to meet our child soon."

The barbed knot of worry loosens, and excitement expands around it. Laughter spills out, and the tears slide down my cheeks. "It doesn't seem real," I tell him as I roll up the map.

"With all that's happened, we deserve to celebrate this." He wipes the wet trails from my face, his own eyes shimmering. "It's real, Morana."

I stare out at the swaying boughs of the trees as the warm sunlight breaks hits the back of my neck. For the first time in a long time, I feel fully awake. "Do you want to stay here?" I ask him and put the map down.

"Here in this field? As long as you want to. Here in Teaghlach? The answer's the same. You're happy here, and I think I found the perfect spot for us to build a house," he replies and takes a bite out of the pie before reaching for the cordial.

"Ma would want us to stay at the house with everyone."

Percy lies down on his side, fingers resting on my thigh. "Not that your mother's room or the house isn't lovely, but I was thinking of a croft of our own. We'd live close, so it'd be like we're living with them without having to hear your brothers snoring in the other room."

Taking an oatcake, I lie next to him, the weight on my stomach shifting as I roll onto my right side. "What did you have in mind?" I ask, honey sticking to my lips as I snap off a piece.

"There's a plot beyond the stream that'd be perfect. You'd still be able to see your house. We can start a garden again, and I can set up my practice again, help the midwife in town.

I think I might have finally figured out how to regrow the bloodleaf and would like to see if I can get it to take root here. There'd be a room with a bookshelf and a nursery for our child—or children." His smile widens.

"We haven't even had this one, and you're already thinking of having another?"

"What can I say? I'm the dreamer. I just want our lives to be full."

"And is Morhenna in this dream home of yours?" I ask and finish the oatcake.

His hand moves to my side. "As much as she loves Saoirse, do you think she won't follow us wherever we go?"

"I suppose we can't get rid of her that easily."

"One of your aunts tried to give me a chicken after I fixed her abscessed tooth. I almost took it."

"Another chicken is the last thing we need."

Percy moves closer, his nose brushing mine. His finger traces the exposed skin between my blouse and the waistband of my skirt. The warmth in my chest grows hotter. Percy's lips move along my jaw before he kisses the hollow of my neck. My skin flushes where he touches me, and I grip his waist. The grass tickles my cheek while his thumb caresses the spot behind my ear. The sunlight turns the brown depths of his eyes into chestnut-colored pools. I take his glasses off, setting them by our boots.

"The first time I saw you in the woods, birds sitting on your shoulders as you wrote, I thought I'd stumbled into a dream," he says. "Then you threatened me with an axe when I found you again in the graveyard weeks later, and I thought you were going to kill me."

I was shaking so badly when he found me that day that I

wouldn't have been able to use the axe against a log. For weeks I was afraid he'd find me again, that the Failinis would come for me. And then Percy saw me burying bodies, and I thought my life was over until he helped fill the graves. When he grew flowers by the headstones, I felt less afraid.

"You're no dream, Morana. You're flesh, bone, and smiles, and that's more beautiful to me than anything I could imagine."

My heart flutters, and I roll on top of him. His eyes widen as he smiles up at me. "Sometimes you talk too much, Percy," I say as our quickening breaths mingle.

Percy's hands move under my blouse and rest on the bump of my stomach, cradling it. "True, but I do it because I want you to shut me up."

"Gladly."

I kiss Percy and undo his tunic, my tongue sliding past his teeth. I drink in the syrupy taste of the cordial in his mouth. He pulls the strings of my shirt loose. Heat follows his fingertips as they move over the raised scars across my back. My lips trace the edge of his jaw down his neck, and his pulse quickens against my mouth. I run my hands along the planes of his chest and down his sides, feeling the curve of his ribcage. Every ridge and angle is a map I've read many times before, but one I want to reread until he's tattooed on me forever.

PERCY'S HAND TRAILS ALONG MY RIBS LIKE HE'S STRUMMING AN instrument, kissing the spot above my heart as he presses in closer. The wind cools the sweat along my skin as we lie in the field, the smell of crushed grass clinging to my nose. I pull the blanket around my shoulders and pluck a leaf from Percy's hair. My arms are wrapped around him, our legs tangled together. Even though there's new soreness, breathlessness, and the burn in my throat I get after I eat now, I'm content.

The blue sky turns yellow and orange, the shadows of the oat stalks dancing across us. "I think we should be getting back to the house," I murmur against his forehead. Moving is the last thing I want to do, but if we're not back, Ma will come looking for us.

Percy opens his eyes and reaches for his glasses. "It does seem to be a lot later than I remember. Wouldn't want them to send out a search party," he says.

He props himself up on one arm and brushes out his hair. The sunlight hits the pendant resting against his bare chest. A painful twinge runs down my backside to my feet as I reach for my clothes. As I move to sit up, something flutters in my stomach, and I stop. Seconds pass before it happens again, a nudge against my side.

"Everything alright, Mor?" Percy asks.

"Something's moving. I think...I think it's the baby." I have felt it move inside me before, but nothing this strong.

Putting on his glasses, Percy puts his hands on my stomach. The flutter twists inside again near my navel now, and his mouth curls into a grin. "Seems she's excited," he says.

My breath hitches, and my eyes moisten. "She? We're having a girl?"

He nods, his own eyes filling with tears. "We're having a girl," he says, voice cracking.

I didn't ask Percy whether our first baby was a boy or a

girl because it was too painful. The realization makes our child—our daughter—no longer a far-off dream but something kicking against my palms.

Percy kisses my stomach. "I know she's excited," I say and grab my clothes, "but I need her to stop because now I need to pee."

Rain patters against the leaves, the branches shaped into a covering over our heads. Glowing flowers hang from the arches of living wood like pulsing hearts. White waterlilies drift along the surface of the pond. Each droplet hitting the water mirrors the anxious fluttering in my heart as I stare down at Percy. As far as wedding days go, I think ours puts the ones in fairy tales to shame.

A crown of purple heather, blue forget-me-nots, and white anemones rests on his head, a cloak made of drooping bluebells and thistle flowers draped across his shoulders. A similar one hangs off me, its weight helping to keep me from floating away. Pinned to the front of his green vest is a thistle pin that matches the one I wear. I take in the depths of his brown eyes and the soft lines of his jaw to calm myself.

The purple silk ribbon tied in my hair tickles my neck. I resist the urge to fix the braids pinned against my head, afraid to damage the primroses Percy wove through my dark tresses. I tried to do the braids like my cousin Ilka had when she got married, but I doubt my shaky fingers got it right. Had life been different, Ma would have helped me. Instead, I have tattered memories of her fingers in my hair, weaving the locks together. When I write to her about this, I expect her response will be full of excitement tinged with sadness.

I touch the lace cuffs of my sleeves, the back of the blue and white dress sticking to my sweaty skin. It's no wedding dress like the princesses in Da's stories wore, but it's the nicest thing I own, and Percy's staring at me like I'm made of gold. Even though it's the two of us out here and the eleven carved figures of the gods spread in a half circle around us, I can't calm my nervous excitement.

"Ready?" Percy asks, taking my hand.

I squeeze his fingers. "Yes," I reply and match his grin.

We hold up the strips of cloth in our other hands—his a dark emerald color and mine the leftover purple ribbon from my hair. Percy's veins fill with green light as vines shaped like fingers grow upward. The leafy hands tie the cloths around ours as Percy clears his throat. My voice weaves around his as we recite our vows.

"You're blood of my blood, and bone of my bone.
I give you my body that we two might be one.
I give you my spirit until our life is done.
You cannot possess me, for I belong to myself,
But while we both wish it, I give you that which is mine to give.
You cannot command me, for I am a free person,
But I shall serve you in ways that honor you.
We swear by peace and love to stand,
Heart to heart, and hand to hand.
Beneath the eyes of the gods, both living and dead,
I vow to be at your side through this life and into the next."

The cloths are tied around our hands, our fingers interlaced together. The words fill the air between us. I bend down and kiss him while my lips tingle with our promise. Petals brush against my cheeks as they fall from flowers blooming in branches. White, pink, and orange dance around us. Raindrops hit the leaves harder, but none fall through the twisted boughs.

"I know it's not much," Percy says as he picks up the pewter quaich filled with whisky from the stump next to us, "but know that none of these flowers compare to you, Morana."

"It's perfect, Percy," I tell him, taking the cup's handles. I never dreamed that the simple things would fill me up to the point of overflowing.

The whisky burns before unfurling its warmth down my throat. A petal falls in as I pass it to Percy. He finishes the drink, sucking in a quick inhale. The blossoms have stopped falling, blanketing the ground.

"I also have these," Percy says and picks up the wrapped bundle that had been sitting beneath the quaich. He pulls back the white cloth to reveal two journals with wood covers. Dark whorls flow along the amber grain, and my throat tightens. "You're always writing the stories of others, so now you can write our story in these. And as they get filled, I can make more."

I open the one on top. It has today's date in Percy's looping script. Each blank page holds a promise of a life I couldn't have dreamed for myself. "Thank you," I say and set the journals back on the stump.

"You're truly the best gift the gods could have given me, Morana."

Laughter bubbles up, and I scoop Percy up by the waist, spinning him around. I set him down before the petals settle, kissing his whisky-coated grin.

"I was going to say something else very poignant and

romantic, but you've made me forget what I prepared," Percy breathes, setting the quaich down and adjusting his glasses.

I press my forehead against his. "Tell me tonight. I'm sure you'll remember then," I say.

"I have a feeling I'm going to forget it all again until the morning."

XVII
Cornflower

Centaurea cyanus

Hope in love ❦ Freedom ❦ Courage

Liath, the horse, shakes his head with a huff, tugging on my sleeve until the groove I'm making in the chunk of wood goes off to the left. Gray light streams in through the byre's walls and makes the horse's icy blue eyes brighter. He's upset because I'm not paying attention to him. Percy's tending to Ceart, who's been lame with a split hoof and an abscess. I've been watching him work most of the afternoon while I try to finish this carving of a cow Saoirse has been begging me for.

I shift on the hay bale by Liath's stall, trying to loosen the knot between my shoulders. The tightness runs along my neck and digs into my spine. "I'm not going to get anything done because of you," I tell the horse as he tilts his head.

Percy stands up from behind Ceart. "Am I that distracting?" he asks, pushing his glasses up with his knuckle. "That's why you're here instead of working in the house, right?"

I scoot away from Liath as he tries to nibble on my shoulder again. "You know I'm talking to the horse," I reply, arching an eyebrow.

"And I'm talking about how you've been staring at me when you think I'm not looking," Percy says.

I roll my eyes, fighting a smile. He pats the cow's side and wipes his arm across his brow. Ceart licks Percy's empty hand before settling down on the hay-lined ground and starts eating.

I brush skelfs of wood off my skirt. "I like watching you work. Ma and Ross are with the cows today, and the byre seemed like it'd be quiet."

Percy wipes his hand on his trousers, the front of his tan tunic streaked with mud. He saunters over. "I wish I'd done something more impressive than healing cuts and hooves for you to watch. I don't want to be boring," he says.

"I haven't grown tired of you yet," I reply with a wink. "No matter how bad you stink."

Percy sniffs his tunic and wrinkles his nose. "That's a comforting thought now that we've been married eleven years."

"Let's see how I feel next year after our twelve-year anniversary." I stop whittling. It's been a while since I've looked that far ahead at our lives. The last several months have been about making it to the next day, bracing myself for the next bad thing to happen.

"Hopefully, next year will be anything but boring with little...Teasle keeping us busy," Percy says.

"We're still not naming our child that." Percy comes around behind me, rubbing my sore shoulders. I close my eyes. "Are you doing this so that I'll say yes in to the name you picked?"

His lips graze my ear, a smile hanging on his breath. "No,

but if this helps change your mind, then it'll be an added bonus," he says. "Was I wrong to assume that you wanted a shoulder rub?"

"No. But you can always ask," I tell him.

A warm kiss presses on my neck, and the tangled mess of nerves in my back smooth and unclench their thorny barbs. He can be such a persuasive man. I had thought about naming the baby Valan after Da if it's a boy, but since we're having a girl, I haven't decided on a name I liked. The only thing I *do* know is that I don't like the name Teasle. Maybe as a middle name, but there's still time to decide.

Morhenna and a few other chickens run into the byre, followed by Saoirse as she races toward us, red hair flying behind her. "Saoirse, what's wrong?" I ask.

"Ferlie's calf's not coming!" she gasps, cheeks flushed. "She needs help. Da and Gran found her by the river."

Percy stops rubbing my shoulders. "We'll follow you," he tells her. "Do you want me to walk with you, Mor?"

I stand up without too much difficulty and grab my walking stick lying against the hay. "Go on ahead. I'll catch up," I tell him and put the carving into the pocket of my skirt. Ferlie is one of the best milk cows, and her calf is long overdue.

He kisses my cheek and follows Saoirse and her flock of chickens. I give Liath a scratch on his nose before I leave the byre after them.

WHEN I GET TO THE RIVER ON THE OTHER SIDE OF THE GRAZING fields, the cool prickling sensation runs through my veins, and the faint taste of damp ash fills my mouth. Death is approaching. Percy's couched by one of the cows, sleeves rolled up and arms streaked with red fluids. Ma and Saoirse stand around Ferlie laying on her side while Ross holds her head and one of her horns. Her strained breath snorts out of flaring nostrils, her coat damp with mud and sweat. A few other cows are grazing near the river, watching.

Ma's brows are furrowed. "We only found her an hour ago. Dinnae know how long she's been in labor, but Ross noticed she was missin' this mornin'. The calf's backwards," she tells me and looks at my face. "Can you tell if it's dead?" she adds in a whisper.

"Its pulse is weak," I say and lean against my walking stick, feet aching and my breath ragged.

"Ferlie's scared and in pain," Saoirse whispers and takes my hand.

The veins around Ross' eyes are pink as he keeps Ferlie calm with his beastcharmer abilities. Percy grasps the small hooves of the calf, straining to keep his grip on its slick hind legs. The cow lows, and her sides heave. Watery red and yellow fluids ooze out with each push.

"Ross, I need your help," Percy grunts, and my brother comes around to help him pull.

I stood in the fields with dying cows many times growing up, the presence of death rolling over them as their breaths grew shorter. The slow heartbeat of the calf intertwines with mine, and the ashen taste grows stronger. Percy's hands burn with yellow light as his gift courses through the calf and the cow. We're both tangled together at this crossroads of life and death like we were with Aodh. I grip my walking stick, hoping Saoirse can't sense my bloodgift as it's stirred up in my veins.

The minutes tighten around the flickering thread tethering the calf to this world. With one last yank, Percy and Ross haul it onto the grass. The cow shudders and puts her head on the ground, sides heaving. Percy pulls away the bloody membrane of the afterbirth and holds a hand to the calf's nose. The fluttering brush of its pulse is a ripple on the ashen waters rolling against me.

Percy moves the newborn upright and straightens its legs, opening its mouth to let the fluids spill out. Ross crouches down and shakes the calf along its torso while Percy squeezes its nose. The calf coughs, and its eyes blink open. They continue to jostle it until it tries to stumble up on weak legs. Ma sighs as Saoirse goes to Ferlie and her newborn. The prickle of death fades, and my blood quiets. I smile despite the hollowness it leaves behind. Ferlie heaves herself up, licking her wobbly baby.

"For my first time with a non-human delivery, I think that went well," Percy says.

Ross claps Percy on the back. "Maybe you should become an animal healer, Percy," he says and rolls his shoulders.

I walk over to Percy and straighten his glasses. "Do you have a handkerchief on you? I think it's going to take a little more to clean me up," he says, staring at his blood-caked arms and dirty clothes.

I wrinkle my nose at the smell of damp dung, sweat, and blood but wipe a sticky smudge from Percy's cheek. "The river's over there."

Percy's eyes widen, mirth disappearing. "Morana, you know very well I'll freeze to death before I can wash any of this off in that water. It's the end of summer, and it's already too chilly for me to bathe outside."

"We used to bathe in the river to get clean when we were younger. The cold's not so bad once you get used to it," I say. Ross is already waist-deep in the water, dunking his shirt in the churning current. "See? Ross is fine."

He grimaces. "I wasn't built to handle the cold. I'd have to use my bloodgift just to keep myself from turning to ice."

"No need to put him through that," Ma says. "Saoirse, run and tell your mother to heat up some water."

Saoirse looks up from petting the cows. "But I want to stay with Ferlie and the baby," she tells us.

Ma waves her hand. "She'll still be here when you get back. Let her rest after havin' such a rough welcome into the world." Grumbling, Saoirse takes off down the hill toward the house. "Thank you, Percy. It would've been a shame to lose either of them."

"Glad I was able to help," he tells her.

Ma turns back to Ferlie as the calf nurses. Percy and I begin down the hill, my arm looped through his. Our pace is slow, and every creak and ache in my body is more noticeable now. The walk took a lot out of me. I don't think I'll finish Saoirse's carving until I've had a chance to lie down.

Percy stops. "So, there by the elder tree," he says, drawing my attention past the fruit trees beyond the barrow with his grimy hand, "is where our house will go."

A tree with white blossoms stands in the empty field. I know it's one Percy's grown, the blooms out of season as it stands as a marker. It's past the stream and close enough to be within eyeshot of Ma's house. And near enough that I can hear Da and the rest of the dead.

His finger traces a roof and the outline of a house in the air. "We'll have a kitchen, a healing room, maybe a study near the bedroom. Nursery and kitchen over there. Then the garden, of course," he says.

The house takes shape stone by stone. I see the vines and plants growing along the walls. A kitchen with sunlight and the smell of baking bread. Small feet running across the floor. Laughter sprinkled over the garden filled with bees and chickens. Rain, sun, wind, and snow would come, but we'd be safe inside.

"It's perfect," I say. The words overshadow thoughts of going to Tearmann, the distant island replaced with a house nestled between the mountains.

Orange and yellow leaves crunch under my boot while my breath curls in the autumn air. The landscape's changed so much in only a few weeks. On the hills, the raised rings of sídhe nests can be found where they hibernate for the winter, their bodies huddled together to form twisted shapes beneath the layers of grass, and moss they pull over themselves to keep warm.

My bones creak while my joints pop—the usual signals of colder weather approaching. The new blue and white dress Ma made hugs my body, the thick skirts comfortable across my expanding belly. Percy wears his green tunic and usual brown overcoat and an additional woollen layer underneath, my hand intertwined with his.

The town's lit up with torches, and orange and white linen streamers stretch between the houses. Saoirse and Coinín run through the square, each clutching the four-winged serpentine figurines of Erroll I carved and wearing flower crowns Percy made for them. Morhenna races after them with an orange ribbon tied around her neck. Saoirse said she needed to come with us because she was lonely.

In the field outside of town, torches burn in a circle around a bonfire. Everyone's dressed in their nicest plaid fèilidhean mòra and dresses. Covered hay bales ring the area, and long tables are decorated with carved gourds and woven straw ornaments. People gather around barrels of whisky and honeywine. The laughter almost covers the echoes of animal bones beneath our feet, and the ashen taste of death I can't help but notice. Meat roasts on spits near food stands, and the smokiness of salmon being cured hangs over everything. I try not to gag and focus on the woody smell of the heather pinned to my tonnag. This pregnancy has made me strongly dislike those scents.

Beyond the axe-throwing targets and the larch caber beams is the straw statue of Erroll. His four wings are unfurled, and his eight tails curl around him. The smell of wood smoke and the dancing sound of a fiddle sends me back to when I was a child, excited to win prizes at the festival games. I only ever managed to win a thistle-shaped brooch—the one I have pinned to my blue tonnag—from the wood-splitting contest. Percy and I went to all the festivals in Àitesìol, but they always made me miss the ones in Teaghlach.

"Takes you back, doesn't it?" Ross says as he and Tréasa pass me.

"Aye. Does Finnigan still make his mulled cider?" I ask.

"He shows no signs of stopping. He might even give you

some extra apple slices in yours," Glenna tells me as she turns around. Craig chews on the end of her scarf.

"I take it you'd like me to get you some?" Percy says, and I nod. "I'll be happy to oblige."

"I also want some caboc. There's a woman named Isla who makes hers with a bit of honey. I havenae stopped thinking about it since we came here," I tell him, my mouth watering.

"Then we'll also find you some cheese."

The children run over to Uncle Boduoc and Aunt Aoifee sitting at one of the tables. Most of my cousins have already claimed seats. The rest of the family hugs me and kiss my face, touching my stomach as conversations come from all sides. My cheeks hurt from smiling. Once they found out I was back home, it's been nonstop visits, numerous blessings for an easy birth, and years' worth of stories.

Music swells as people dance around the bonfire. The wind runs its hands through the long streamers as if Erroll himself hovers over the field. The festival seems much smaller than I remember as a child but no less exciting. I walk with Percy to get cider and food as the baby kicks me again.

Finnigan's stirring a pot of sweet-smelling liquid over a low fire. "Good to see ye again, Morana! You've sure grown tall. Not a wee lassie anymore," he says, his mouth crinkling into a smile. "Care for a cup?"

I inhale the steam scented with apples, cherries, cloveroot, rosehip, and sweet flag. "That's why I came all this way," I reply with a grin. "Even after all these years, I havenae met anyone who makes cider like you do."

He ladles two mugs for us, the warmth seeping through

the clay into my cold hands. Three apple rings bob in the drink. Percy clutches his closely, letting the steam wrap around his face. When I find the logs of caboc, I almost drag Percy over. The first bite doesn't disappoint, the buttery creaminess and the sweet, nutty aftertaste almost making me cry. I'm determined not to dissolve into tears over some cheese.

"Do you want some oatcakes or bread to go with that?" Percy asks.

I peel more of the cloth wrapper back. "I'm fine eating it like this."

I look up and stop. Two men laugh around one of the spits, foam from their drinks clinging to their brown beards. I recognize Coran Forson and Timan Conway even though they're older now. It's been years, but I can still hear their jeers. They clap each other on the back and leave to join a group of women.

"What's wrong?" Percy asks.

I keep my head down. It's only by some miracle of the gods that I haven't run into them the past four months I've been home. "I saw some people who used to make fun of me when I was a child, and I'd rather not run into them," I reply as I pull him toward where my family is.

He stops and looks back at the spit. "Those two walking away from the fire?"

"It's fine, Percy."

His veins fill with green light, and with a flick of his finger, roots grow around Coran's foot before he takes a step. His drink flies as he falls, tripping into Timan, who doesn't catch himself in time. The men hit the ground, and everything under their fèilidhean mòra is visible for people to see, which, frankly, is nothing impressive. The roots vanish into the ground as if they were never there.

"Percy!" I gasp, blood draining from my face as heat flushes through me. No one's looking at us, but it's only a matter of time before someone realizes what's happened.

Percy pushes his glasses up. "What? It's not my fault they can't walk correctly."

I'm mortified as we return to the table. Leith and Ross look up at us. "What's going on over there?" Leith asks.

"Just a couple of drunks who tripped over themselves," Percy says as we sit.

Ross jabs Leith in the side with his elbow. "I see Cait over there. Maybe you should go talk to her instead of starin'," my brother tells Leith.

Leith shrinks into himself next to me. "She's too busy," he says into his drink.

"You always say that and then become a pure greetin' mess when you get blootered. Are you waitin' for her to talk to you? You might have better luck findin' a girl in the woods. Ewart mentioned some lovely loireag in the forests you could look for. Worked for Percy, right? He found Morana in the woods."

I give Ross a sharp look. While Percy and I *did* meet in a forest, I'd hardly compare myself to a loireag in the woods. Not unless the loireags also raise the dead to help with their clothmaking. Percy grins as he sips his cider, half of his face buried in his scarf.

Ma shoots Ross a look as she feeds Craig mashed turnips. "Leave him be," she says. "If I remember, you were too daft to talk to Tréasa for years."

Ross says nothing and takes a drink from his tankard. "If

you have that figurine, you've been working on for weeks, you could give that to Cait. I think she'd like it," I tell Leith as I lean over to him.

His ears redden, but I see his hand go to his trouser pocket. I don't remember much of Cait from my days in the schoolhouse, but Leith's taken with her and talks about her more often than I think he realizes.

Children stand around Arth, the weaver, as he juggles balls of woven straw, creating different breezes to keep them spinning above his head. He takes turns letting the children hover in the air. Saoirse's swept up at least ten feet off the ground by a strong gust. Tréasa grips Ross' arm so tightly that he grimaces, her knuckles white until their daughter is returned gently to the ground.

"I hate it when he does that," Tréasa says through her teeth.

"It's fine. Arth willnae let anythin' happen to the bairns," Ross tells her. "It's better than when she tries to ride the cows through the pasture."

Tréasa scowls at him. "And who taught her *that*?"

Saoirse and Coinín run over with a few other children, Morhenna strutting after them.

"Arth willnae send us up again since we've already had our turn," Saoirse says, frowning. "We wanna do something else."

"The games willnae be starting for a bit. Why dinnae we get some food?" Tréasa tells her as she smooths her daughter's red curls.

Saoirse sighs. "I'm bored." She runs around to our side of the table, touching my knee. "Do you have any stories?"

Percy leans back. "Stories, huh? That's Morana's specialty,

but I could try. Why don't I tell you about when we fought a brollachan?" Percy says, and the children grow quiet.

"Brollachan aren't real," one boy says.

"Then how did we fight one? The world is a vast place, and we're living in such a small part of it, so there are many things we don't know about," Percy tells him with a wink. "Morana? Maybe a story about the gods and the titans?"

All the stories I know belong to others, both the living and the dead. It's easier to write down stories than to tell them. My life hasn't been very exciting up until these past few months, but I don't know if those stories would be suitable to tell. It'd bring up too many questions I don't want to answer. As for myths and stories about the Darkening, it's hard to find one where boneweavers aren't villains.

"I was attacked by a bear once," I say, drawing the attention of the rest of my family.

"When did this happen?" Ma asks, eyes wide.

"Twelve years ago, I think? I dinnae remember much, but I'm fine. I chased the bear off. It's not a very exciting story, though."

The children look back at Percy as they settle onto the ground. "I wanna hear about the brollachan," Saoirse says. Morhenna comes over and sits on her lap.

Green tendrils of magic glow along Percy's hands as he creates two people made of grass and roots—me and him. They move around the children with pulsing lights in their chests from luminescent fungi. He grows miniature trees around his dirt stage and moss campions mountains.

"I'll tell you about when Morana and I saw a brollachan and lived to tell the tale," Percy says.

• • •

THE MOON SMILES BETWEEN THE STARS. PERCY HUDDLES AGAINST ME beneath my shawl against the cold, head resting on my shoulder. Dancers follow the rhythm of the bagpipes and fiddles. My foot taps along while the soreness in my body keeps me sitting. The taste of the cider leaves a warm, fiery sweetness in my stomach. Ma dances with Leith in a swirl of skirts illuminated by the bonfire. The pang of sadness tightens around my heart as I think of the last cèilidh we attended.

"You don't have to sit with me if you want to dance some more," I tell Percy. "I'm sure Ma said she wanted to dance with you again."

He sits up. "It's not as much fun if you're not dancing with me," he replies.

I rub the spot around my finger where my ring cuts into the puffy joint. With each thing Percy heals, something new appears the next day. "I wish I had the energy and that my legs didn't ache. I'm lucky I got one dance in tonight."

"You're creating life. As much as I help, it's still going to be an exhausting process for your body. I wish I could do more."

"I don't suppose you could speed this all up?"

Percy rubs my back, easing the aches. "You're going to have to soak up and enjoy the miracle of life for the next four months, mo ghràdh," he tells me. He takes my hand and touches the wooden ring. A spark of green moves along the band, and it expands to not be so tight.

The music fades, and the cèilidh ends with it. Everyone moves toward the statue of Erroll. Percy helps me stand, and we join the crowd. Leith stands next to Cait, her blonde hair pinned up in two braids. Her cheeks redden as he says something, and hands her a metal object. When she says something back to him, he freezes, nodding while she laughs. Leith was never as boisterous as Ross, although he had the same temper, but it seems the years have brought out a shyer side of him.

A young man with a torch approaches the statue. I swallow the panic as smoke and orange tongues consume the God of Wind's straw form. Cheers and claps become a thunderous wall of noise as people shout, "Lang may yer lum reek," to bring in prosperity before the approaching winter. Pieces of paper drift through the air on currents Arth stirs up. They fall like snow as people fan out to grab them. I remember sitting on Da's shoulders to catch the fluttering fortunes.

Saoirse and Coinín come up and tug at my hands. "Pick me up, Aunt Mor!" Saoirse says as she jumps to try and grab the papers. "I wanna catch the most!"

"Leave her be, Saoirse," Ross tells her. "I'll help you."

"No! Aunt Mor's taller," Coinín shouts and Ross frowns.

"I dinnae mind," I say, stooping down and hoisting them both onto my shoulders. The added weight puts pressure on my back, but I don't struggle as I grip their legs.

Saoirse and Coinín grasp at the papers drifting close. Ma told me that you should wait until you feel a tug to grab one that the gods meant for you to have in order for the fortune to come true. Percy reaches up and grabs a piece of paper, opening it for a moment before sticking it into his pocket. He smiles at me with a look that sees this present moment and into something beyond.

"What does your fortune say?" I ask him.

"If I tell you now, it might not come true," Percy tells me.

As the papers fall to the ground, clusters of lights float

through the air like fireflies. The children shout excitedly, and people hold out their hands to catch the lights. Glowing spheres break off and dance around Glenna. She cups one with knitted brows before breaking into a smile.

"Glenna!"

My sister's face lights up as she turns toward the shout. A man with packs on his back rushes through the crowd and scoops her in his arms, dipping her back to kiss her. White light radiates beneath his skin as the orbs swirl around them. As he rights her, the firelight throwing shadows on his face, my heart freezes in my chest. His blond hair is pulled back in a knot, and a beard covers his chin. Captain MacAdoh's features overlap with his, and breathing becomes difficult, numbness moving through me. The weight of the children is too heavy, and the air too thin. My throat burns as acid tries to come up.

"Mor, what's wrong?" Percy steps in front of me as I stagger. "Maybe you should put the children down."

I blink. Glenna's husband, Seumas, is stockier, his face rounder and ruddy. MacAdoh's shadow fades, and the panic releases my lungs. He's not a Failinis. They haven't found us here.

I set Saoirse and Coinín down, and they run to their uncle. "It's nothing," I tell him and straighten. My pulse settles in my fingertips and my stomach feels too full. "Just heartburn."

The look in his eyes tells me that he doesn't believe me. "Might be because you had a log of cheese and two mugs of cider," Percy says.

Ma and the rest of the family pull Seumas into embraces. I watch as Glenna and Seumas hold each other and laugh. The highlands are vast and treacherous, even for bloodgifted.

Months have gone by without any sign of the Failinis. I pray to the gods that the brollachan defeated them or that they're too wounded to pursue. We're safe here, hidden between the folds of the mountains.

I turn this thought over in my mind, letting it seep into every part of me until I force myself to believe it.

XVIII
Nettle

Urtica

Cruelty ❧ Doorway between life and death ❧ Growth

The weak sunlight breaks through autumn's chill. The weight of my stomach slows my pace as I walk uphill through town. Percy's arm is looped around mine, his glasses fogging as his breath hits the lenses. He's bundled up against the wind, and I almost feel bad letting him accompany me on my errands today.

"I still don't see what's so bad about the name Teasle," Percy goes on. "I think it'd be cute."

"I dinnae—don't like the way it sounds," I reply, frowning. "The more you say it, the less I like it."

"I think it sounds nice. You haven't suggested any names yet," he says.

"Nothing feels right. We have months to decide on a name."

"It doesn't hurt to think of something now," Percy says, adjusting his scarf before stuffing his hand back into his pocket. "Blood and bones, I knew it got cold up here, but not *this* cold. And it's not even winter. I can only imagine how this must have been on your joints as a child."

"There were days when it was unbearable, but Da and Ma made sure the house was always warm enough."

Growing up, I was always bundled by the fire with bags of heated flax seeds on my legs when the pain and fevers got bad, snow piling up higher outside the house. Winter was a harsh time, but it was also a season wrapped in warmth.

A girl runs past us with one of the leftover orange streamers from the Festival of Erroll a week ago. "You seemed sad the night of the festival," Percy says.

I hadn't told him what happened when Seumas appeared. "When I saw Seumas, I thought he looked like Captain MacAdoh," I mutter. "It was a silly thing to think, but for a moment, all I saw was the Failinis' face. It made me think about Anstice again..." The tears prick my eyes.

"I miss her too." He squeezes my hand. "And I don't think it was silly that you thought Seumas looked like the Captain. He bears a striking resemblance from a certain angle. It's difficult to completely relax even after so many months, but I hope someday you'll feel at home again."

Grief and I are old friends. If it's not my own, it's the sorrow of the dead I carry. There are days when I'm drowning in it and others when I can hold it in my hand. It creeps up when I'm not thinking about it, roused by a smell or some memory. But this grief is both fresh and distant all at the same time. So much is tangled together that I can't see where to unknot one hurt from the next.

"I was thinking about starting on the house soon before the snow comes," Percy goes on. "I can begin growing the frame and dry it out. I spoke with your brothers and Seumas about helping. We could have it done before the Festival of Arianrhod at the end of the year. It was going to be your birthday present, but I got too excited. Also, it's difficult to hide a whole house from someone."

I wipe the wetness from my eyelashes and gesture to my stomach. "You could have waited another month when I'll be too heavy to get out of bed, let alone leave the house," I say, drawing a laugh from him.

Ahead, Fergus Macleod tugs on the lead of a large calf that wants to go in a different direction. He grunts as the bull pulls him back. "C'mon, ye bampot!" Fergus snaps, face red as his beard.

"Everything alright, Fergus?" Percy calls and walks over.

The older man looks up. "Och, aye. Just cannae get this daft creature to move. He wandered into Miss Elspet's garden. She's pure crabbit now. Got to get him back before she decides to serve him for tea. He's getting more stubborn each day."

"Just be careful not to throw your back out again."

Fergus laughs. "I'll try not to. What ye did the other day makes me feel like a young lad again. I heard ye helped one of Carlin's cows that had a backwards calf. If yer that good with animals, maybe I could ask ye to check on my herd."

Percy smiles. "If you need me to, I'm sure I could spare some time."

The yearling comes over to me and lows, bumping against my waist. His russet hair is curly and thick. I scratch his ears, losing my fingers in his long hair.

"Saw that Seumas is back," Fergus goes on, looking at me.

"Aye. Glenna's happy to have him home," I say.

"Bet she is. Heard he came from Dundris. Said there were Failinis there looking for boneweavers. A good number of them. I thought he was joking. Boneweavers havenae been in these parts for years. Failinis usually dinnae cross the Abhainn Comraich. One was spotted down in some place called Àitesìol and raised all the dead there. A horrifying sight I've heard. Hope they find them and lock them away."

Cold burrows into my skin, and the blood drains from my face. Dundris is only three days from here. News of what happened in Àitesìol has spread here—maybe across all of Errigal by now. The cow licks my hand, but I barely notice. Percy looks at me, his worry hidden from Fergus.

"Don't do that, ye dafty!" Fergus exclaims and pulls the cow back. "Best be getting this one back to the fields. Take care, Healer Bracken, Morana." He tips his bunnet and leads the cow away.

The world shifts around me, but Percy takes my arm. "Seumas was there five days ago. They could have already moved on," he whispers. "The news from Àitesìol could just have spread up here. No names were mentioned."

"In Dundris? This close to us?" I reply, my tongue working again, but my thoughts are churning. "It has to be them. Failinis dinnae normally come this way. The Captain already got others to hunt us. All the Failinis in Errigal are probably looking for us. We cannae stay here." The words cut my mouth.

I pull away and walk as fast as I can to the house, my heart wriggling up into my throat. My worries push on my belly, writhing and cutting my insides. It was too much to hope we could be safe here. Now, we have to leave everything behind again. I burst through the front door, only focused on taking what we can and leaving as quickly as possible.

"Morana. Wait!" Percy calls after me.

I rush into our room and grab our packs, out of breath and on the verge of tears. Even in such a short time, we'd begun to leave our marks here. Percy's papers are scattered on the small desk next to the pouch of dried bloodleaf. New clothes for me fill the chest. A vase of cornflowers sits on the nightstand on my side of the bed. A sketch of the house he was planning to build. I reach for the blue and white dress I wore to the festival. My tears dot the fabric. All these things we can't take with us.

"Morana, stop," Percy says as he stands in the doorway. "We can't keep running forever. Winter's coming and traveling through the mountains isn't safe."

"But it's not safe to stay here," I choke out. "We've tried that, and look where it's gotten us. We dinnae ken what animals they're using to track us or if someone found out I'm a boneweaver and told the Failinis."

"That's what I'm trying to say. We run, and they find us. But what if we fought back? I want us to have a permanent home that we won't have to leave."

Grief claws its way out of the healing wound, showing me Anstice's sad face. To lose our daughter when I've gotten used to the thought of meeting her cuts deep. I couldn't bear it if anything happened to Ma or my siblings—or their families.

My hands tighten around the dress as I look at him. "Dinnae you think I want that too? But we can't. Not here. I willnae bring my family into any danger."

"You know they'd do anything to keep you safe, Mor," Percy tells me.

"I ke—know. That's why we have to leave before the Failinis come here."

"Let's at least talk to your family about this and the Failinis—"

"This isnae negotiable!" I snap, throwing the dress on the

bed. "No one else can get hurt protecting me! Anstice did, and she's dead!"

"Morana." Percy grips my shoulders, his voice sharp. "Just listen to me. I'm scared too, but I'm also tired of running and being unable to do anything against them. I know this is how you have lived—how *we* have lived for so long, but how far can we run before there's nowhere else left to go?"

"How could we fight them? They're stronger than us, and there willnae be some creature to save us this time."

Running has been what's kept me alive, always trying to stay ahead of any danger before it finds me. Percy has voiced my greatest fear, but staying and fighting where there are too many people who could get hurt if we fail frightens me more.

"I don't know, but we must try something. For us, for our child."

I sink onto the bed, unable to bear the weight pressing down on me. Percy picks up the dress, and I can sense the disappointment in his silence. The rift begins forming again, and the cruel voice in my head whispers that this might be the thing that rips us apart. Will his patience and his optimism finally run out? Am I too much of a coward in his eyes now?

"What's goin' on?" Ma stands in the doorway with Glenna and Ross. The worried look on her face is the last thing that breaks me, and I dissolve into sobs. "Morana, mo chridhe, what's wrong?"

I can't look at her as she sits beside me, stroking my hair. I can't get the words out. I clutch my stomach, gasping for air.

"Fergus said that Seumas saw Failinis in Dundris," Percy says, keeping his voice steady.

"Are you sure it's the same ones who are lookin' for you?" Ma asks, her hand clenched around mine.

"It doesn't matter," I croak. "They're looking for boneweavers. If they're in Dundris, it's only a matter of time before they come here or tell the ones chasing us where we are."

"There's no one here outside this family who knows your gift," Ross says.

I wipe my eyes and stand. "No matter how well we cover our tracks, they keep finding us. If they find out you've been hiding me, they'll burn the farm or worse." The last word sticks in my throat. I continue grabbing clothes, burying the thought of this house going up in flames at the bottom of the pack.

"You're not leavin' today," Ma says.

I meet her gaze as she tries to yank the pack out of my hand. Tears swim in her blue eyes, but her jaw is set. Any protest I have, she'll refuse. She has the will to stare down angry bulls; I've seen her do it.

"Isnae there any way they can stay? Cannae we hide them or do something to protect them from the Failinis?" Glenna asks, coming into the room. "We just got you back."

Ross' face is pained. I know he's weighing the cost of fighting and protecting his family like I am. He has to choose *which* of his family he can protect.

"We dinnae know if they're already headin' this way. It only took Seumas a few days to get here, and he was in Dundris almost a week ago," Ross says.

"So, there's a chance they dinnae know about Morana being here." Glenna looks at me and Percy, who hasn't said anything in a while. His jaw is clenched, hands balled into fists at his side.

"I know you'll never forgive yourself if anythin' happens to us," Ma says as she straightens. "If leavin' is the best way to keep you safe, then so be it. But if this is to be the last time I see you—and I pray to the gods it isn't—then I'll have one more day with you. I dinnae care if there are morrigans at the door. You're not leavin' without a proper goodbye."

My grip on the strap loosens, and Ma takes the pack from me. Glenna and Ross come over, keeping me upright as they pull me close. Numbness weighs me down, and I keep praying that none of this is happening, but I can taste salt, and my pulse pools into my fingertips. My family is the only thing keeping me from crumbling to pieces on the floor.

THE NEXT DAY COMES, AND I STRUGGLE TO ROUSE MYSELF. FEAR SITS on my chest like a stone. The hours were sluggish, and I struggled to do anything besides packing. Percy held me all night while I cried, and I felt his tears mixing with mine until the pillows were damp. I know he wants to stay more than anything, and we've avoided talking about that, focusing on packing what we can carry. I kept expecting the front door to be kicked down at any moment and for my home and family to be ripped from me again.

Percy left when the sun rose, kissing my brow with promises to gather breakfast, but the thought of food doesn't interest me. The pressure of the baby on my stomach, coupled with the anxiousness already swirling there, fills the space.

When I clean my face and dress, I find my family moving around the house. Glenna, with Craig bundled across her back, Tréasa, and Ma stand over pots and stoke the fire in the stove while Ross, Leith, and Seumas gather the chairs and firewood to take outside. Percy's nowhere to be seen, and I swallow the jolt of panic.

"Ah, you're up, mo chridhe," Ma says, stepping away from a pot of soup to cup my face. Red veins crack the corners of her eyes, but her wrinkled smile hides her sadness. "I'll get you some tea and scones."

"Where's Percy?" I ask, my voice scraping against my throat.

"He's outside with the bairns showin' them the best way to check when the vegetables are ready and preparin' the winter crops."

I stare out the window as Percy walks between the rows of plants with Coinín and Saoirse. He taps the green leaves of the kale, making them grow larger. Percy hands them seeds to plant, pointing to the ground. The smile on his face doesn't seem forced. I don't understand how he can have any happiness left when I'm drained.

Ma hands me a hot cup of tea mixed with honey. A plate of tattie scones with eggs rests on the table. "Once you're done with breakfast, we'll go check on the cows," she says.

"How can you be so calm, as if everything is normal?" I ask, looking away from the window. "I cannae pretend like tomorrow isnae going to happen."

Ma sits on the bench, back bending as something is cut inside her. I sink beside her and take her hand. Glenna watches us, wiping her eyes. Tréasa rubs her shoulder as Craig babbles.

"I'm not pretendin' like this isn't happenin'. If you want to spend today greetin', then I'll sit with you—we all will. But I want to wring out every last moment I can," she says. "When your da was dyin', I didnae want to accept it, but I spent so much time upset with somethin' I couldnae change instead of spendin' what remained with Valan. My sadness didnae go away, but I learned I could be sad and still be with him. What mattered was each day he remained with us."

Anstice's words that day in the bakery find me: *Don't mourn what isn't dead yet.* I don't know how to keep walking toward the inevitable without being crushed.

"I've missed fifteen years of your smile, so I'm selfish for wantin' to see it as much as I can." Ma touches my cheek. "That doesn't mean you have to pretend to be happy for me. Sad or happy, I want you here as long as possible. We cannae get back the time lost, but we can make the most of what we've been given now."

Ma's smile threatens to push her tears over the edges of her eyelashes. She's been through deep sorrow too. Losing Da, raising a family on her own, burying a child, and running the farm. How long will it be before the loss doesn't cut me when I touch it? Grief and pain are monsters I haven't learned how to coexist with yet.

I look back to the garden where Percy's grown a towering sunflower over the children. He's making the most of this, planting for the future instead of watering the ground with tears. I wipe my eyes as teardrops fall into my tea. Even if these hours are stained with sadness, I'll hold them close. I may not have a say in what's happening to us, but I can move through it or remain at the bottom of this dark pool. I fish that reminder from the murky depths and clutch it with the fragile strength I can muster.

"What can I help with?" I ask, standing.

Ma touches the pendant around her neck as she rises. "We can start on the pies for tonight. I'm also makin' a black bun since you love it so much."

THE FIRE DANCES AS THE FLAMES CLIMB UP THE TENT OF LOGS WHILE the sun sinks behind the hills. Leith and Ross refill their plates from the table of food set up on hay bales. Cows graze in the field beyond the stream. Morhenna and one of the geese are looking around for crumbs. She and Coinín stare at Seumas as his hands weave through the air, lights shimmering from his fingertips. His story about encountering a cu-sìth one night in the highlands takes the form of a luminous hound bounding around the fire. Saoirse and Coinín sit on the ground, eyes wide. Two real dogs lay at my niece's side.

I balance the empty plate on my stomach as I sink back in the chair, unable to eat another bite. The shiny rocks and bundles of flowers the children gave me rest in my pocket. My cheeks are still warm from the windy afternoon when Ma, Glenna, Tréasa, and I walked the fields with the cattle. The pastures and the quiet town surrounded by the orange and yellow trees sit in the back of my mind. Ma's stories and the rolling hills made yesterday feel like a dream.

The dog made of light leaps over the fire, and the children laugh. It pads over to Craig on Glenna's knee and licks his face. The baby giggles, chubby fingers passing through the hound's face. He shows off his toothy smile now. Tréasa refills Ross' mug with honeywine and runs her fingers through his hair before sitting next to Ma on the bench beside us. Seumas brings the hound back to him, and it explodes in the air, sprinkling clusters of light down on all of us. Coinín jumps up to try and catch one of the glowing petals.

Percy leans in close. "He's almost as good of a storyteller as you," he says, bundled up in a blanket. It's the first thing he's said to me almost all day.

"It's a shame I cannae make animals out of light or plants to liven up a story," I mumble. "I doubt little skeletons would be very popular."

The firelight reflects off his glasses. "I'm sure a bone rabbit or chicken would be fun. Dress them in clothes or cover them in flowers, and they'd look adorable," he replies. Percy stands and takes my plate, the blanket hanging off him like the cloak of a king. "I want to show you something, Morana."

I grunt as he helps me stand. Ma gives me a look and smiles as Percy and I leave the warmth of the fire. I'm hesitant to pull myself away from my family, but my husband's hand tightens around mine, and the cold reality prickles down the back of my neck. Tomorrow is coming, and there are still unspoken things between us to resolve.

The elder tree comes into view, whispers from the barrow gliding on the breeze. Clusters of white blossoms glow in the blue gloaming. Percy stops by one of the stone markers for the house. A simple thing that held so much potential and dreams that'll never be. We stand silently for a while, Percy staring out at the town. He's not silent often, and when he is for long stretches, it's unsettling.

"What are you thinking about?" I ask him.

A sigh leaves him as he turns to me, blinking. "A lot of

things, probably too much for one day," he replies, his voice heavy.

Releasing my hand, Percy crouches down, and his veins glow. A patch of ground moves, and a sapling pokes up from the earth. It unfurls its branches, sprouting thick needles. Percy coaxes it to grow until it's at my waist.

"I know that our lives have taken a vastly different turn than what we planned, and that tomorrow isn't going to be what we expect, but I'm not going to give up on this dream," Percy says and touches the yew tree's branches. "I'm planting this tree in the hopes that when we return, it'll be big enough to make a table out of right here."

I bite my lower lip. "Do you really think we'll be able to come back here?" I whisper. "The Failinis dinnae seem like they'll ever stop looking for me."

"I don't know, but stranger things have happened. Like finding someone in the woods and then marrying them." A breathy laugh knocks a few of the tears loose despite my efforts. "One of my professors used to say, 'Plant the seed of hope today to reap tomorrow's dream.' No surprise that you'd hear something like that from a rootsower, but as a student, I didn't fully understand it. Now, with all we've been through, I think I understand the words a bit better."

Night air pinches my cheeks. It's a strange thing being caught between hopefulness and despair. It's like falling from a great height, stomach knotted as the ground rushes closer, but the weightlessness makes you think you can fly at any moment. Somewhere out there lies either our salvation or our end. There's something else besides the elements and Failinis that unsettles me but whispers for me to go to it.

"I ken you want to stay and fight. I wish we had better

options than heading out to find some hidden place of refuge," I say. "I'm sorry for yesterday. I panicked and didnae listen to you. At some point, we willnae be able to run anymore, and we'll have to fight, but I want to do all we can before it comes to that."

My baby kicks my side, and I look down. This future we're fighting for will be her inheritance, even if we have no house or gold. A place where she can plant her own trees and live smiling is all we can give her.

"I'm terrified," I say.

Percy comes closer to me, placing a hand on my stomach. "I am, too," he whispers. "And I didn't react well either. It's so hard to keep pulling up our roots once we find a place to settle down. But...whether we fight or run, I want it to be with you."

The ring around my finger gives a small squeeze, saying more than words could. Tired, scared, happy, or angry, it'll be together. Back by the fire, I hear my family singing and clapping. My ears perk at the pieces of the song I catch, one I haven't heard since Da was alive.

"...Where the road goes through the woods,
Over hill, valley, and glen,
Remember from whence your footsteps came,
Of home and hearth where memories are made."

I reach for Percy's hand, bending down until our noses brush against each other. His lips open against mine, and I want to stay on this hill with him and dream of a home here. My breath hitches, and the pain jabs beneath my ribs.

Percy frowns as I pull away. "Did you have to stop? Your

face was so warm," he says, wrapping his arms around my waist.

"Why dinnae we do something else to warm you up?" I say and rub his arms. Ross and Tréasa circle each other while the clapping grows louder. "I feel up for a dance or two."

MORNING COMES TOO SOON. I FEEL THAT I'M WATCHING MYSELF gather the last of my things and walk out of the bedroom. Percy's remained quiet since we awoke, and I'm afraid if he speaks, I'll start crying again. The memories from yesterday are a bittersweet draught I sip, savoring every drop. The firelight dances and the laughter of my family feel like a distant memory except for the smell of woodsmoke in my hair and the aches in my legs and back.

Now, my family speaks in hushed voices at the table. Outside, it's still dark, the wind rattling the windowpane. Snowflakes brush against the glass. Ma rises, eyes red and hair flowing free as she manages a smile. She holds out a cloth bundle of jars and wrapped foods.

"I made you some tattie scones and packed the leftover pies. There's also cheese, pickled carrots, toasted oats, and dried fruit. Oh, and some blackcurrant jam to go with the black bun. And some damsons in syrup," she says in a hoarse voice as Percy takes the bundle from me and puts it in his pack. "This should keep you goin' for a while. I'd send you with the whole larder, but that'd slow you down."

Ma picks up a small, quilted blanket with russet cows stitched on it and hands it to me. Under the folds of the blanket, there's a tiny nightgown, a knitted hat, socks, and a blue and green plaid dress. On top of them is a woollen cow with one curled horn.

"I hope there's still room in your pack. I was goin' to give you this when you had your baby," she says. "The dress was made from an old one of yours. Should keep her warm."

I hold the bundle close, lips wobbling. "Thank you, Ma."

Saoirse comes over, still dressed in her nightgown, with Morhenna in her arms. "She doesn't want you to leave her," the girl tells us, setting the chicken down. "She'll be lonely."

Morhenna cocks her head and warbles, walking to Percy. We decided she'd be better off here, but it seems she will follow us wherever we go.

"You've taken such good care of her. She'll miss you," Percy tells Saoirse.

"Why do Aunt Mor and Uncle Percy have to go?" Saoirse asks. "I want them to stay."

Ross gets up and pats her head. "There are bad people after them. They're goin' somewhere safe."

"Come back?" Coinín asks, rubbing his eyes.

The answer looms over me as I etch the faces around me into my mind. Hope creates expectations that sustain, but when it crumbles away, we're cut by the jagged pieces. This may be the last time I see them, that thought driving barbs through my heart. I want to promise that we'll return, but the future's a twisted briar forest I can't see through.

"We will someday," I say, offering it up as a prayer to the gods.

I look at the central post in the middle of the room. Ma insisted Percy and I record our heights on the wood, pointing to the spot where we'd be adding our child's name. I want to believe we'll be back, but that's a small flickering light in a forest of looming darkness.

My eyes shift back to Ma. I've dreaded this goodbye. It's taking everything in me not to break apart. Her callused hands are warm against my face. My resolve to leave dissolves with each passing second.

"Mo chridhe, you've grown into a strong woman. I couldn't be prouder, and I know you'll be a great mother. Someday I hope to meet your daughter. I'm sure she'll be a bonnie lass," she says and hands me my walking stick. Saoirse and Coinín have carved their names along the wood. "Wherever you end up, I pray you're safe and that you'll write to me again."

"I will," I whisper. She takes off Da's necklace and slips it over my head. "Ma, I cannae take this."

"I have other things to remember him by. May it remind you how much he loved you," she tells me and kisses my cheeks. Ma pulls Percy and me close. "Take care of each other. May the gods watch over you. Go with our love, and know that this goodbye isnae the last. You'll always have a home to come back to here. Haste ye back."

I bury my face in her hair, unable to hold back tears. Ross and Leith wrap their arms around us, Glenna, Seumas, and Tréasa joining them. Small arms hold onto my legs. Quiet sobs shake me as my family surrounds me. I cling to the smell of home and the embraces, drinking them in like the last gulps of air I can get before I drown.

XIX
Wormwood

Artemisia absinthium

Bitterness ❦ Separation ❦ Don't be discouraged

The cold bites into me despite the layers of clothing I have on. Morhenna stares at me from Percy's pack without sympathy, partly bundled in a scarf. The bridge we're on creaks, the planks icy from the frigid waters. I grip the damp railing and try not to think of slipping or the wood giving way. The Abhainn Comraich slashes the valley between the ridges of the Cluaran Mountains, a churning gray serpent with foamy white scales. Dark clouds obscure the peaks as snowflakes swirl in the wind, erasing the memory of the soft mattress and warm fire we left three days ago.

"This bridge has seen better days," Percy says behind me, his teeth chattering.

I scan the waters, half-expecting kelpies to appear, but I see only frothy currants and taste the cold droplets in the air. We need to keep moving if we're going to cover all the miles ahead of us. I just hope my body can make it. Each day I grow heavier, and even with Percy's magic to help me, I tire quickly. I take small comfort in knowing that the bloodleaf is keeping my gift hidden for the next few hours.

Once my feet are on solid ground, the knot in my stomach untangles. There is still evidence of a road ahead with faded stone town markers pointing in different directions. I wish there was a place to sit while I check the map. Percy walks past me, staring out at the hazy landscape before us.

As I pull out the map, something moves behind the shrubs by the shore. I see a skelf of a woman hunched over a pile of clothes at the river's edge. Dark hair drips down from her head like wet reeds. Her dress seems to be made of murky water, clinging to her frame and flowing into the river.

She scrubs a green tunic, and water drips from her skin. Red seeps from the fabric. Blood stains the other clothes next to her—a brown overcoat and a blue dress like the one I'm wearing. My heart shudders, and I stop. That *is* the dress I'm wearing. The tunic is the one Percy has on beneath his thick coat. The cold grips my insides and squeezes with icy fingers.

The woman looks up, her face sunken and eyes empty pits. I see her for what she is—a bean nighe. Her gaze chills me, and the same feeling I had with the brollachan squeezes the air from my lungs. Even with the bloodleaf dampening my abilities, the damp taste of ashen death finds me now, and a prickle runs through my veins. Ma told me stories that the bean nighe are Arianrhod's darker messengers who appear to those approaching misfortune. The blood seeping from the clothes grows darker until the river runs red.

The bean nighe stands and screams, the sound cleaving to my bones. Her boney finger is pointed at me. Images flash behind my eyes—Percy's sightless pupils, red snow, me screaming and covered in blood, our child unmoving. I shut my eyes to erase them, but they keep clawing at my mind, changing but always the same outcome—death. I stagger back, my hands clamped over my ears.

"Morana, what's wrong?" Percy's gripping my arms, his voice full of worry.

I blink, and the bean nighe is gone, the waters gray again. No sign of blood, no clothes left on the shore. The sound of her scream still rings in my ears.

"The bean nighe," I gasp, and I point to the water's edge. "She was over there. She screamed."

Percy follows my gaze, brow creased. "I didn't see or hear anything, only you covering your ears," he says.

Did I imagine her? Is it because I'm a boneweaver and can sense dead creatures? "She had our clothes, Percy. She showed me our deaths," I say, legs shaking.

"I believe you." He squeezes my hand, but the look in his eyes tells me that he doesn't fully believe me. "We shouldn't linger here in case something else shows up. We need to find shelter, though, before the snow worsens."

I clutch Da's pendant as the mountains loom closer. Percy moves ahead and I can't get the images the bean nighe showed me out of my head. If death awaits us, how can we go forward? It stalks us from every side. My resolve is melting away as I think about what will kill us—the elements, some creature, the Failinis? The howling winds don't answer me as the snow falls faster, melting on my cheeks.

My knees pop as Percy and I crest over the hill. The village of Àitesìol sits nestled by the golden fields of rapeseed, wheat, and

barley. Sheep dot the farms, and forests bump against the houses. Even this far away, I'm pulled toward the barrow by a stone church, a swirl of voices calling to me from the graves and the surrounding fields. Weeks of traveling from Cruithneachd have brought us here to the edges of Errigal. We've brought only the packs that hold all our possessions on our backs and the hopes of finding a new home.

Percy turns to me. "Do you want to rest before we head into the village?" he asks.

I wipe sweat from my eyes, leaning on my walking stick. "No. I'm just..." I chew on my lower lip and look over the houses and the people there. This place is small enough to be forgotten by the Failinis, but that means we'll be noticed easier. In seven years, we've had to move to four different places. "I'm worried that this place won't be safe for us either."

I know it's the exhaustion and sadness stirring up these thoughts. I hadn't realized how much moving around and looking over my shoulder would wear on me until I had Percy in my life. He shares the burden, but now I worry about how it affects him. Our plans for starting a family haven't happened yet, and when we start to settle, something rips us away. This last time had been because a Failinis fort had gone up near the town and seeing them every day in the shops made it too dangerous to stay.

Percy takes my hand, the wind ruffling his hair. "We won't know until we go down there. The man on the road said there's a tavern here we could try staying at until we figure out other lodgings," he tells me.

We head down the hill toward a bothy on the outskirts of the town. Long grasses brush against my legs, buried bones whispering memories. Vines grow over the stone walls surrounding the little house. A place like this is far enough from people not to be bothered but close enough not to draw suspicion.

A fox darts in front of us with a hare in its mouth. There's a snap, and the ashen taste of death seeps across my tongue. I look around, worried someone is watching us, but no one is nearby.

Percy's hand trails along the tangled plants. Green magic lights his veins, and the plants shift closer to his fingers. "This place is abandoned," he says, grinning. "And it has a garden."

I smile. Of course, he'd find a place with a garden. Even if it didn't have one, he'd grow one. There's a gate on the side with rusted hinges. I pull on the handle, and it doesn't budge. I yank it back, hearing the latch break away from the wood.

"I didn't mean to break it," I mutter.

"I thought you were going to break the gate down with your axe. Arthritis or not, you're pretty strong, Mor," Percy replies and peers into the garden.

In the yard, it's a tangle of high grasses, unkempt bushes, and dead plants long forgotten. "I thought you said this was a garden. It looks barren and too overgrown to me."

Percy steps over a rotted sack of rocks. "It may not look like one, but it can become one. All it needs is a little love and a tender hand to make it flourish again."

He bends down and touches a brittle leaf hanging from a dead rosebush. Vibrancy spreads through it, and new ones grow until the plant is restored to life. Pink flowers bud and open their petals. The smile on his face tilts to the point where I worry it may fall off his face. With Percy, nothing is too far gone that it can't be brought back to life.

"It needs a little work, but we could start some herbs over there," he says, pointing to a corner where dark beams lay. "Maybe

some tomatoes and kale in the middle. The possibilities are endless. Kale *me crazy, but I think we could even have some fruit trees."*

I roll my eyes and walk toward the bothy. The windows are gone and broken glass litters the ground. There are holes in the roof and soot marks from a fire. The inside has pieces of broken furniture, a table, and scattered animal bones on the floor. A cluster of sídhe flit around the ceiling beams and have built a tangled nest of grass and leaves up there. That'll take a bit to remove, and they won't be happy about it. It's not the worst home I've stayed in, but it'll need a lot of work.

"What do you think? Think we could make it into a home?" Percy asks behind me.

"We need to find out if this village would even let us buy a place like this," I say.

"I'm sure someone will be eager for us to take it off their hands. We still have a good amount of money, and I'm sure I can offer my services as a healer." He sticks his head through the window. "This could be a bedroom, and I see a stove over there. The other area could be a healing room. With a little bit of paint and fixing the roof, it could become a decent home.

I look at the garden where the revived rose bush blooms, unsure if I can release the tension I've been carrying for miles. Percy's words stir up memories of our old cottage in the woods outside of Auchendrain, which tugs on the still-healing wound from when people found our home and we had to leave. I pray to the gods that we can stay here for a while and not have to leave anytime soon.

I GRIP THE WALKING STICK AND STRUGGLE TO MOVE FORWARD AS MY boots sink into the snowdrifts blanketing the ground. The snowfall has gotten heavier the past several days. We tried to wait it out in the hut Percy grew from the side of a tree, but we couldn't remain where we were any longer or risk getting snowed in.

Percy's beside me with Morhenna still tucked inside his coat, watching in case I fall. My pack and the added weight of my stomach continually throw me off balance. The axe handle hits against my thigh with each plodding step. The cold slips in whenever it can, and the aches turn into burning sensations throughout my body as the inflammation in my joints worsens. I can feel my bones scraping together.

Look for the will-o'-wisps, Anstice said. We were told as children not to follow the glowing lights, or we'd be spirited away. Percy says it's gas being released from bogs and marshes, but I've heard people swear they've seen the lights do unnatural things. I don't know if we're looking for literal will-o'-wisps or something else, but our only chance of getting to safety is somewhere in these woods.

Sounds are muffled by the snowfall and the wool lining my hood, the wind swaying the towering trees of the Claigeann Forests. Ever since we crossed the river almost a week ago, there's been a strangeness in the air, an overpowering presence that I can't describe that hovers over the usual ashen taste of death. The bean nighe and the brollachan had a similar feeling, but this is something else—older and more overpowering. It's pulling me deeper into the woods and confusing my senses. I feel the pouch of bloodleaf inside my coat pocket. It's been many hours since I've taken a dose, and it's starting to wear off, but I want to conserve what little we have until Percy can grow more.

"Percy, do you feel something?" I ask, slowing. "The strange presence again?"

He looks back at me, half of his face hidden beneath his scarf. "Yes. It's hard to sense your bloodgift. Do you think it's another brollachan?"

"No...it's different. Not as sinister, and this feels like actual bones, but I've never encountered anything like this." There are stories that say the bones of the gods, titans, and morrigans are spread across the world. I've heard of people claiming to have pieces of the gods' skeletons to use as amulets, but I haven't come across any. Whatever this is isn't too far away and floods my veins with a buzzing power that moves up to my skull.

A strong wind blasts against us. I grab Percy's arm as white swirls across my vision. Through the cold howls, I hear dead whispers. A clacking sound echoes through the forests while crows caw. Bones dangle from the branches above us with feathers, pieces of glass, and braided cords affixed to them. Most are animal skulls and carved remains, but human skulls smile at us with yellow teeth and rain-stained eye sockets.

"Well, those are some unique decorations," Percy mutters, his breath clouding upward. "I'm guessing the birds didn't put them up there."

The voices prickle along the back of my neck as we pass beneath them. These bones are old and go on at least a mile ahead. This whole forest is filled with so many flashes of stories breaking through the strange presence surrounding everything. I can't tell if these were left as a ritual or as a warning, but they don't give off anger or pain like the bones under Anstice's bakery did.

When the trees thin, the ground levels out to a slight incline on the next snowy ridge. The expanse of the forests covers the mountainside, disappearing into the valleys below. Through the gray and white haze, the other backs of the mountain are visible. I want to call out into the vastness, but I don't know what will answer. The tug of the strange bones is stronger, and my body is buzzing under the weight of the power emanating from the air.

"There are only a few hours of daylight left," Percy says as his voice is tossed on the winds. "We should find a place where I can make us a shelter before it gets too dark. This storm's only going to get worse."

The baby kicks, and a tightness coils across my stomach. I inhale sharply and stop, leaning against the stick. Her kicks haven't hurt before. This is different. Are these contractions? No, they can't be. It's too soon. A ripple of panic worms its way up and the cawing of crows grows closer.

"Morana, what's wrong?" Percy asks.

"There's this tightness," I reply, touching my belly as I breathe in the frigid air. "I-I don't know what's happening. Is it a contraction?"

Percy rests his hands over mine, snowflakes frosting the lenses of his glasses. "They're false contractions. You'll feel them every so often at this stage of your pregnancy, but it doesn't mean anything's wrong. They should go away soon. Drinking water will help."

I focus on my breathing until the discomfort eases. My baby continues moving, unbothered by the changes happening around her.

"What's that?" Percy asks.

I follow his pointing finger to the dark outline of the rest of the forests and see a flickering purple-blue orb in the distance. It dances in circles, holding my gaze. I've never seen a will-o'-wisp before, but this light sends a wave of calm over me. I wonder if that's why travelers were so willing to follow them in the stories and be led away, never to be seen again. The bean nighe's screams in my head have quieted.

"I think that's our guide," I tell him. For a moment, I don't move. The whisper of caution urges me not to follow it.

Percy watches the will-o'-wisp. "Didn't Anstice say we needed to follow it?" he asks.

The light dances and seems to wait for me to follow it. Snow crunches beneath me as I move toward it. My dwindling hope is stoked, and the exhaustion is lighter now. The light darts into the woods, and we follow it. The ghostly glow flickers through the trees and is obscured by the swirling white. As I follow it, able to sense the bones more clearly now.

The winds shift, and Percy and I are slammed onto the ground. Spots dance across my eyes, and my brain rattles inside my skull. Pain shoots through my back as the pack digs into my spine. Morhenna screeches as she's thrown from Percy. Percy shouts and stumbles toward me. The ground shakes as earth and stone claws rise and close in. The will-o'-wisp is gone, and I taste blood from my split lip.

A figure hovers in the sky, their dark cloak spread like wings. People emerge from the snowy forests—twenty in total, but I can't tell with the overwhelming presence covering everything. Glowing blue and brown veins are visible as the bloodgifted close in, the green of their cloaks cutting through the swirling white. Crows circle in the sky, eyes flashing with pink light.

Percy grips my arm to help me stand, and I go for the axe. Panic is a rushing torrent through my veins. The Failinis have found us, and there are more of them now. They used the birds to find us. My bones have turned to water as I whirl around and find no escape. Tightness encircles my heart, squeezing it with every breath.

"It's been a while, Morana." Orange light crackles, and Captain MacAdoh steps forward, snow hissing and melting into steam around him.

"Run when you have an opening," Percy tells me as his bloodgift springs to life in his hands, and green light moves through the veins along his face.

I search for any nearby bones, but my power still feels sluggish from the bloodleaf. "I'm not leaving you!" I snap.

Over the roar of the winds, I hear wood splitting as green threads illuminate the hazy white. The forests move, and spiked branches shoot out at the Failinis, their roots clawing at the ground. A few of the Failinis are knocked back before they can raise walls of stone and ice to block Percy's attacks.

"None of that, Healer Bracken," the Captain says and waves his orange-veined hand at one of the trees twisting in his direction.

The forests erupt in flames, and Percy flinches. Ash mixes with the snow, and I can almost hear the trees screaming as they groan and crack. I reach for the bones in the treetops before they are consumed and gather dozens of skeletal bodies to me, but it doesn't feel like enough. Their voices swirl through me as purple burns in their empty sockets, weaving the bones together with glowing tendons.

The windsinger in the sky turns the air into cutting blades that slice my clothing and open wounds across my body. I see the Failinis' face, recognizing her from Àitesìol so many months ago. I gather the dead and fling out sharp rib bones like arrows at the Failinis.

Percy brings up thick roots that pierce the ground toward the woman while another comes at Captain MacAdoh from behind. The windsinger dodges and blasts Percy back, but the flamekindler yells as the root stabs through his side before he sets it ablaze. Blood splatters across the snow from a long gash opening across Percy's face. His glasses lie broken in the snow.

The premonition from the bean nighe plays out before my eyes. "Percy!" I scream and run to him. Tightness slithers around my insides, and I stagger, icy tears clinging to my lashes.

My shoulder locks as I twist around to bring the bones down at an approaching Failinis. I hurtle another human skeleton and a collection of animal bones at the windsinger, but my attacks are blasted aside. Shouts bounce across the wind, orders to close in and surround us. The roots around Percy are severed by a scythe of wind, and I'm knocked back as the blast of air slams down in front of me.

An arrow strikes me in the shoulder, pain ripping through like teeth until I drop the axe. Waterdancers ready lances of ice, and Percy gets to his feet and throws up a wall of roots as they fly at us. I can't hear him calling my name as my ears ring, my teeth rattling in my head when I hit the ground. I reach for Percy's hand as the ground comes alive and rips him from my grasp.

"No!" The sound rips from my hoarse voice. I try to scramble to my feet, but I can't get up without doubling over in pain. My blood leaves the warm tang of iron in my mouth.

Percy struggles as rocks wrap around him and pin his arms to his sides. The Captain staggers forward, pressing a red-hot hand to his bleeding side and stifling a scream. The crows cackle and screech. The Failinis grabs Percy by his hair and yanks his head up. His flaming palm nears my husband's bloody face. Percy's face is twisted in pain.

"You chose this, boneweaver. Now, you get to suffer the consequences," Captain MacAdoh snarls, his blue eyes glowing orange.

A scream tears my throat, and I grasp anything I can find to stop this. Something answers, something ancient and massive beneath our feet. The same presence that seeped through the mountains rumbles with my gift and fills my veins with icy fire. Purple light burns my vision. A voice I can't understand crashes over me, consuming all the others. The pain of my wounds becomes numb as my body trembles with a power that's broken free.

I haul myself up, feeling split from my body as my consciousness floats somewhere outside of myself. The ground breaks, and finger joints the size of trees rise around me. They're cracked and blackened in places, but overflowing with power. What I've awakened longs to be free, and I use every ounce of rage to call it to me.

From the mountain slope, the snow slides off as a lupine skull emerges, followed by the rest of the titan's massive skeletal form. Two arms reform, but I can't sense where its other pair are. MacAdoh doesn't release his hold on Percy, shouting orders I can't hear over the all-consuming noise in my head.

Memories drown me. Stars are tossed into the unraveling sky while the molten world below cools and forms. Oceans are poured out, and life is drawn into being by the breath of the gods. I tower over the mountains and traverse in the shadow of mighty beings. Creatures twisted by chaos and rage break apart the earth and spill immortal blood. I'm undone and scattered, all at once small and intricately woven into something beyond my understanding.

What I do understand is its rage, a millennium of wrath stored where marrow should be. It's a rage that echoes mine and is layered with a sense of loss I know all too well. I let it flood my veins until my blood is boiling with the ancient emotions.

The bloodgifted throw their attacks at me, but the ancient hand is cupped around me, deflecting them. Its bones creak like trees, and the ground continues to shake. The crows scatter like soot blown on the wind as the skeleton swings its arm out and slams its other hand down, scattering the bloodgifted and tearing through the forest. I taste ashen death and hear their panicked voices knocking against me.

I lash out at any bloodgifted moving toward me, their attacks melting against the ancient bones. Through the churning snow, I find the flamekindler. Captain MacAdoh is a flame flickering with fear. I won't let him take Percy. He's done taking things from me. All I need to do is snuff him out and end this. It's his turn to know what fear is.

As I move to charge forward, my legs give out. Warm liquid runs down my face from my nose and eyes, dotting the snow red. There's a lance of ice in my leg, but I can't comprehend the pain that should be there. The world's muffled by the creaking bones and the roaring gale.

The snow wraps me in its wintery embrace, and it's hard

to keep my eyelids open. Blackness closes around my vision as Percy's dragged away, my name broken on his lips. I reach out to him before I fall into nothingness.

XX
Water Lily

Nymphaea alba

Birth ❧ Life ❧ Grief

Mountains erupt as we fall. Fire splits from the earth's broken shell. From the magma, we emerge, stars burning in our eyes. We push the land up from the seas and watch over the small vessels of flesh and blood. Out of the darkened corners of the world, chaos comes, twisted forms of the gods that howl for their thrones. They rip and pull apart the tapestry. The gods scream, and the skies crash down on us—

The light crawling beneath my eyelids dissolves the images, the resounding voice drowning out everything. When I try to discern its words, an overwhelming pain threatens to crush me. Its name is something I don't have words for, but it carries the essence of mountain stone and molten roots. A ceiling comes into focus. Dried herbs hang from rafters. The air smells like Percy's healing room. A gray owl peers down at me with dark pupils reflecting the fire in the large hearth. Voices rush around me, and shadows move along the walls. The scent of smoke sends a wash of memories cascading over me.

"Percy!" I cry out, groaning as stiffness cracks across my

body. I'm propped up on a cot, but I can't sit myself up. A thick blanket covers me, and the air's warm, with only a sliver of winter tracing across my face. Everything hurts, and the false contractions are tight across my belly and back.

Morhenna's head pops up next to me, watching me with a beady stare. Have I died? I thought we lost her during the fight. Morhenna's never laid next to me and only gets close when she wants to peck or scratch me.

"She's awake, Brennus," a woman's voice says, and a round face framed by blonde hair hovers over me. I try to jerk away, but my body refuses to move.

A hulking figure crosses the room draped in a fur cloak. The firelight turns his red beard and hair coppery. I can't sense if he's bloodgifted through the roar of the titan's voice in my head. These people don't look like Failinis, but I can't trust them. I realize I'm not in my clothes but dressed in a long, roughspun nightgown. I search for the axe, but it's not here, and neither is my pack.

"Calm yourself, lass. I'm not going to hurt you. We went through the trouble to bring you and your chicken back here," he says in a rumbling voice.

"Who are you? Where am I?" I ask. "Where's Percy?" I can't sense him nearby or feel anything from my ring.

Flashes come to me, and my head aches. The snow, the Failinis, the titan, Percy being dragged away. I killed people, felt their deaths. Even if they were Failinis, to end another's life...I wasn't even aware of what I was doing beyond the desire to bring them down. I could have killed Percy.

"Dinnae ken who Percy is. We found you alone and brought you here to Lòchran. Save for the dead Failinis and this...chicken," the man says, shrugging off his cloak and putting it on the back of a chair by a table. The man goes to a row of jars and bowls. "I'm Brennus, and this is Rowenna and Ula, my assistants." He gestures to the other two women. "You're in Lòchran village. This is a healing house."

My heart squeezes. It wasn't a nightmare. The Failinis took him. I don't recognize the village's name. Am I still in the mountains? I try to roll onto my side, but my bones threaten to snap. On my hands, dark red veins crack my skin. The tang of blood lingers in my mouth, and my pulse pounds under my tongue.

"Rowenna, get towels, a bucket, and a basin for hot water. Have Ula get Selma." Nodding, the blonde woman heads to another room out of sight. "I wouldn't try to move. You were injured and used too much of your gift."

Another painful cramp takes my breath away. Something's wrong. My hands inch to my bulging stomach. I feel no movement, and the blood drains from me. "My baby... How long was I...?" The rest of the question sticks to my dry mouth.

"You've been unconscious for two days," the man tells me, mixing something together in a cup. "Your gift almost consumed you and your child, boneweaver."

My fear spills out like an icy torrent, making it harder to breathe. Nausea comes up. He knows what I am. I need to get out of here and find Percy. I'm not safe here.

"Your baby's fine. But her heartbeat dropped for a while, but it's still there," the man goes on. "And you dinnae have to fear us. We're not enemies of boneweavers."

The blonde-haired woman in a gray dress reappears with another woman with shorter brown hair, carrying a large metal basin and towels. They set the basin on a stand in the hearth over the flames. There are five other empty cots in this room.

"Selma's on her way," the woman says.

The man crouches beside me, holding out a cup. "Drink this. It'll help with the pain," he says.

"I can't stay here," I tell him. "I have to find my husband."

He sighs through his nose, sharp blue eyes like chips of stone. "If you leave now, you'll die, as will your child. I dinnae ken where your husband is, but if he's alive, you're no good to him dead. Do you understand?"

I bite my lip to stop the tears from falling, but I can't stop hearing Percy screaming my name. "What's in this?"

"Herbs to help with the pain and strengthen your blood. Honey to help with the taste."

My arm shakes as I reach for the cup. I see part of a pendant resting between the furs he wears. It's like Percy's, but Artair's antlered bear symbol sits above Beathag's hand. He's a fleshmender and a beastcharmer. The warm liquid is bitter, with spices and honey mixed in. I wince as another false contraction comes, waiting for it to pass. But they seem more frequent.

"What is your name?" the man asks. I bite my lip, unable to settle my apprehension. "You dinnae have to tell me. You *do* need to do is to listen to me. Your water broke a few hours ago while you were unconscious, and you're in labor."

I drop the cup, spilling what liquid remains. "No. These are just false contractions. It's too early," I gasp. Nausea burns the back of my throat. I'm aware of the wetness between my legs, and I hold onto the blanket as the brown-haired woman, Ula, comes to move it aside. Shame and fear rise up.

"Bucket," Brennus says.

As I double over to vomit, a bucket is held out in front of me to catch the watery bile. I hear a curtain being drawn nearby, and footsteps moving around me. My back feels like it's going to break, the sudden movement jarring every bone. I can't be going into labor. My baby isn't ready. I'm not ready. I can't do this without Percy. He talked about delivering early babies, and that not everything is developed yet, especially the lungs. Will she be able to breathe on her own? Is she going to be in pain?

Further down the hall, a door opens. Another woman with red hair steps in, shaking snow off her coat. Dim gray light comes in from outside, and the sudden gust of wind makes my skin prickle.

"Selma, could you get the water ready?" Rowenna says, ushering her forward.

Tears sting my eyes as I spit into the bucket. "We're going to make sure your child is delivered safely," Brennus tells me and lowers the bucket. "This is early, but you have to trust me. Rowenna and I will do our best to dull as much pain as we can, but you're going to feel discomfort. Do you understand?"

His voice is like stone, the opposite of Percy's, which is like a gentle breeze. Everything is moving too fast, like I'm on the outside, watching all this happen. Is it because of what I did on the mountain slope?

"Ula, get some snow and put the chicken in the closet for a bit," Brennus says, washing his hands in a bowl. Selma fills the basin over the fire, blue veins glowing along her fingers conjuring water from the air.

I want to stop Ula as she picks up a clucking Morhenna and takes her away, but another contraction takes my breath away. The chicken's all I have left right now, even if she is a spiteful bird. Rowenna removes the blanket and gives me a warm smile, faint lines creasing in the corners of her eyes. Her hands glow yellow with the familiar light of a fleshmender. Some warmth soothes the aches, but moving still makes me groan. Sweat coats my skin, and I try to focus on my breathing.

"I know you're scared, but it'll be alright. We've delivered many babies. My own was an early one, and he's ten now. A healthy lad," Rowenna tells me and takes my arm. "We'll lay you on your side until the contractions speed up. Then we can try some other positions."

I don't know how many hours pass as the contractions grows quicker. Anytime Rowenna shifts me, I clench up, knees digging into the pillow between my legs. The fleshmending magic soothes some of the pain, but it doesn't seep down far enough. I'm fed spoonfuls of snow that cool my mouth while my skin feels like it's on fire. I try to focus on Rowenna and Brennus, but the titan's voice crashes through my head like falling boulders.

Beings of darkness come, made of bones and shadows. They strike at the living. Blood that burns the gods—

"We're going to have to move you again, lassie." Rowenna's voice breaks through the memories, and I focus on her face through my blurry tears. "Your baby's shifting."

"I can't do this without Percy," I manage to say as she and Brennus grip my arms, helping me to my feet.

Every time I've imagined this moment, Percy is here, talking me through how to breathe and not to worry. Is he still alive? Did I hurt him with the titan? A sob catches in my throat. All I want is his hand to hold, not be surrounded by strangers in a place I don't know.

"Is Percy your husband?" Rowenna asks as they lead me to a low wooden chair with a sloped back and handholds on the sides. I nod. "I know this is scary, but you're almost there."

Standing knocks the breath from me and pulls on the vertebrae in my spine downward. I shuffle forward, my legs shaking. I groan as I sit. I feel my baby's head move lower. Her bones are so tiny, and I can sense them all, even the ones not fully formed together. She's become such a part of me that I'm afraid of losing her.

"I'm going to check and see how close the baby's head is," Brennus tells me, meeting my gaze. I nod and let out a shaky breath.

Brennus crouches and lifts my nightgown over my knees. I stare at the ceiling where the owl is still perched. Modesty was left behind two days ago, but to be touched by someone who isn't Percy is uncomfortable. I grip the handholds until the wood digs into my palms.

"You're ready to start pushing," Brennus says. "Push when your body tells you to. Breathe in between."

The waterdancer brings over a bucket of hot water and sets it beside him with an array of tools and towels on a stool. Everything's happening too fast, but there's nothing I can do to stop it. Rowenna rubs my back as I push.

The ground shatters and breaks when the first god dies. The world mourns, blood coursing through rivers. Our bones are being broken. Death has come, and its goddess weeps enough to fill the seas—

"You're almost there. One more push," Rowenna tells me,

brushing matted locks of hair off my forehead while she dabs my face with a cool towel.

My muscles strain, and teardrops hit my knees. Part of me is pulled away from the present into the titan's memories. I grip the birthing chair and push down. Remaining upright is exhausting, and my bones are like jelly. The last one takes all my energy, my cry digging into my ears. Wetness slides down my legs as my baby does into the towel Brennus has waiting for her. I slump back in the chair, lightheaded and my body shaking. My insides feel hollowed out.

For a moment, I can't hear anything besides the roaring of my pulse, the crackling fire, and the titan's voice. Worry forces my eyes back open to see Ula cutting the gray cord connecting us. Brennus holds a small figure in the towel, and I catch a glimpse of a ruddy face streaked with blood and fluids.

"Is she...? Why isn't she crying?" I begin to say as he goes to the table.

The chair creaks as I try to rise, but my body won't move. I can't sense death—I can't feel anything. I don't know which of the two is worse.

After an eternity, a cry comes from the table. Rowenna smiles, hazel eyes sparkling. "You did well," she tells me, drying my cheeks.

Brennus returns and places the bundle in my hands. The infant in the towel seems strange to me, too tiny in my hands. She weighs so little. Blue veins run beneath her almost translucent skin, still coated in a waxy substance and blood. A fine layer of dark hair covers her. Her tiny breaths expand in her chest as I hold her close. My daughter—*our* daughter. The ache in my heart battles with this elation.

"Do you have a name for her?" Rowenna asks.

"No," I say. We hadn't decided on one yet, and even now, I can't think of one. I can almost hear Percy telling me what the name should be, and my throat tightens. He's not here to meet our daughter. I'm all she has, and I don't know what to do. I can't tell if she looks like Percy, but she has that same scrunched-up look on her face he gets when he's upset.

"Some names take time to come," she tells me. "She may not be strong enough to latch, but you can try feeding her."

I bring my baby close to my chest. Her eyes remain shut, and tiny feet kick against the top of my stomach. Seeing her lying in my arms sends a rush of emotions through me that I can't fully sort through. Tiny fingers wrap around my pinky as I run it along her hand.

"I'm so sorry, wee one," I whisper through the lump in my throat. "This isn't how I wanted you to come into the world." My baby wiggles in the towel as a tear falls on her chin. I brush it away with shaking hands.

Rowenna begins to take her from me, and panic sets in again. She meets my gaze when I resist. "'Tis alright. She's not going far. We need to clean her up and keep her warm since she's come into the world early. And you need to rest. Your body's been under a lot of strain."

Even though her words make sense, I don't want her to take my baby. I can't lose another part of me. I fear if I let her go, I won't get her back. My heart's beating too quickly, the room too hot again. "Please, I just want to hold her a bit longer."

Brennus' shadow falls over me. He places a hand on my shoulder, and the warm magic floods my tired limbs, making them heavier until my grip on my baby loosens. I try to fight it, eyeing Rowenna as she takes my baby to Ula and moves toward the hearth. Their silhouettes are backlit and move along the curtain separating us. I strain to get up again. An orange glow moves through Ula, her bloodgift crackling in the air.

"No!" I cry out. She's a flamekindler, like MacAdoh. All I can see are flames and feel smoke choking my lungs, Percy's cry ringing in my ears.

Brennus touches my forehead, his bloodgift sparking in my blood as yellow light fills my vision. My pulse slows, and exhaustion presses down on me like a heavy blanket.

"What are you doing...?" The words are heavy in my mouth as he carries me to the cot.

"Sleep. Your child will be fine," Brennus says, laying me down on the straw mattress. The owl lands on his shoulder. "When you wake, Guennéan will want to talk with you."

I struggle to keep my eyes open, clinging to consciousness, but it slips from my grasp, and I fall into the depths of blackness.

I JOLT AWAKE, GROANING AS PAIN SHOOTS THROUGH MY BACK AND MY lower half. I'm in the same room, the fire still going in the hearth, but I don't know how much time has passed. Morhenna sits in my lap, pressed against my stomach. Something's different, like I'm empty. The titan's voice is louder, demanding to be written along with the other bones I raised that day. I grasp for the pieces of my memory before sleep, and a soft cry makes me turn. A few feet away by the fire is a crib.

My baby. I have a daughter.

I sit up and smell sharp witch hazel and grassy comfrey wafts. There's a thick pad between my legs that soothes the ache there. The weight of my stomach shifts easier now as I try to sit up and move out of the cot. Morhenna gives me an irritated cluck, and, for a moment, I worry she's going to peck me, but she settles down by my feet.

Rowenna appears from another room and goes to the crib. "Don't get up yet. I'll bring her to you," she says.

"What did you do to me?" I ask.

"Brennus might have been a bit hasty using magic on you. He felt you were too overwhelmed by everything and didnae want you to become too stressed so soon after giving birth."

I watch her as she picks up my baby, wrapping her in the blanket my ma gave me when we left. "Where did you get that blanket?"

"From one of your packs. Some of the food was damaged and got on some of your things. We went through the bags when we brought you here to see if there was anything to help us learn about who you were." She lays my baby in my arms and points to the stained packs lying against the wall beside my cot. My heart jumps at the sight of our things. "Ula and Selma washed the clothes and cleaned what could be salvaged."

I stare at my baby as she settles against my chest. My veins still feel brittle and empty, but the pain's now a dull ache. "How long have I been asleep?"

"Many hours. 'Tis nearly morning now."

My baby must be hungry. As I go to undo the front of my nightgown, Rowenna stops me.

"You dinnae need to do that. She was fed a wee bit ago by a wet nurse. She's got a healthy appetite. It's a bit hard for her to latch, but I'll show you how to feed her."

A strong wave of protectiveness comes over me, and I hold my child closer. Even if they saved me and my baby, the thought of my daughter being alone with people I don't know doesn't sit well with me. I remember the flash of yellow light and Brennus' face before darkness came. He's not here, and neither is the flamekindler. They may not be Failinis, but I can't dislodge the mistrust.

"You must be starving. Ula's making breakfast, and we've been waiting for you to wake up," Rowenna says and heads toward the other room behind the hearth.

While she's gone, I reach over and haul my pack over, searching through its contents while keeping my baby nestled in the crook of my arm. The food Ma gave me is gone, leaving a sweet and vinegary smell inside the pack—probably from the broken jars of jam and the pickled vegetables. I find my journals undamaged, save for a few waterstains on the pages. I can't find the charcoal sticks, but maybe there's one in Percy's pack. My map is wrapped in a waxy fabric, Da's pendant lying at the bottom of the pack.

I can't find the bloodleaf pouch, and panic wiggles in my chest. As I continue digging through the bag, the sprig of heather from many months ago falls out, now dried without Percy's rootsowing magic to keep it vibrant. It lays in my lap, and it undoes a part of me, a reminder that Percy's not here. My ring gives off a weak pulse of his power, and I know he's not dead, but something's not right.

I clutch my left hand to my chest, tears trailing to my lips as I hold my baby as close as I can without hurting her. This is all my fault. I thought I was keeping us safe, but all I did was put us in danger. The bean nighe screamed our deaths, and Percy's blood is on my hands. I don't know where he is or how to get him back, but he's in danger the longer I stay here. But my baby is too young and fragile to leave here. If I lose them both, I'll be left alone with only their ghostly voices to haunt me.

Panic grabs my lungs and squeezes. I try to find my breath again, but I'm left gasping. The Failinis attacking us, the dead, the arrow piercing my shoulder, Percy's pained yell, and his blood in the snow, my scream as the bones crack open the earth, called by my rage. The thunderous voice is a mountain crushing me. The titan's memories begin to overtake me again, trying to take more from me. Black spots eat at my vision as I claw at anything to keep me from collapsing. My baby begins to cry.

The curtain next to me swishes, and someone rushes over, taking my wrist. Morhenna leaps up and ruffles her feathers. "Lassie, breathe," Brennus says with a finger on my pulse. I didn't know he was here. "Breathe. You're not in danger."

I can't stop the blood-soaked snow from falling. I can't reach Percy. I can't do this without him. Each breath is an icy spike, my sobs stealing what little air I have left in my chest. I feel him trying to take my baby, and I jerk away.

His grip remains on me, yellow light moving in his veins. "Rowenna! I need you!" My head snaps up to meet his gaze. Even in my drained state, I search for any nearby bones. "You have to calm down, or you're going to hurt your child."

"For a fleshmender, your bedside manner's as comforting

as being dunked in ice water, Brennus," comes a gravelly voice.

An older woman stands in the doorway behind Brennus. A dark cloak hangs off her, thick brown skirts brushing against the ground as she enters. Her gray hair streams down like melted silver. A necklace with carved bone pendants hangs around her neck. The symbol of Arianrhod dangles at the end, very similar to Anstice's. There's a pouch at her side with dozens of voices emanating from it. The power radiating off her calls to my own that lays quiet in my veins. It's so different from Anstice's, like a river whose strong current churns underneath the surface—a river that's sucked me in and dragged me down deep. The hairs along my arms rise.

A boneweaver.

The older woman pulls up a stool and sits down beside my cot with a soft grunt. "Take a deep breath and hold it for a couple seconds and then release it until you need to inhale again," she says, green eyes staring into me.

I follow her instructions, unable to look away. I continue until the blackness recedes and the crushing weight lifts from my chest. The baby's cries quiet until she's gulping in breaths.

"I'm sorry," I tell her.

"Better?" the woman asks, and I nod. Her accent carries the refinement of the Mainland. "Looks like I'm a better healer than you, Brennus. And the people I work with don't even breathe."

The fleshmender lets go of my wrist with a sigh, standing. Rowenna hurries over with a tray of food, Ula at her side. The owl hiding in the rafters eyes Morhenna. "Leave her, Comhachag," Brennus says as pink light flashes through the veins around his eyes. The owl swoops down and lands on his shoulder as he walks over to the worktable with heavy footsteps.

"Congratulations are in order," the woman says, smiling at my child. "She's a bonnie wee thing. After your ordeal, I'm sure this has all been overwhelming. Why don't you let Rowenna and Ula tend to your bairn while you eat? I'm sure you're famished."

I eye Ula, swallowing my fear. She's not MacAdoh. I know this. I'm not afraid of Leith even though he's a flamekindler, so I shouldn't fear her. But worry is a creature with raised hackles that prowls around, growling.

"Ula, bring the crib over. You can keep the bairn warmer than the fire can. That way, this woman can eat with her child close."

After a long moment of hesitation, I let Ula take my baby after she brings the crib closer. The flamekindler holds a glowing orange hand above my daughter as she puts her down on her back. Instead of flames, I only feel heat. The last of my daughter's cries fade away, and she settles into sleep.

Rowenna sets the tray of food on my lap. There's a bowl of porridge with honey and rowan berry jam, green nettle soup, tattie scones covered in butter, and a steaming cup of tea. My stomach lets out a painful gurgle, and I realize how famished I am.

"Who are you?" I ask the woman as I tear into the tattie scones. Morhenna warbles, and I give her a few pieces of bread. "Who are these people?"

"I thought you would've guessed by now, considering you followed the lights," she says. "People don't find us otherwise."

Find them? The glowing wisp in the forest rises from the back of my memories. “You’re the wisps?”

“In a manner of speaking. Most people call me Guennéan. I’m one of the council members of this village. The ones you saw were created by lightcasters here. But instead of leading people to their deaths, we lead them to a new life here in Lòchran.”

A new life Percy and I were so close to reaching before the Failinis found us.

“I’d very much like to know your name, child,” Guennéan tells me, her hands resting in her lap.

Like Anstice, there’s this pull toward her—the power in her blood calling to my own. Is it like this with all boneweavers? Or because I’ve found another person who is like me, one who has survived into her graying years.

“Morana Bracken,” I reply and sip the raspberry leaf and fennel tea sweetened with a floral-tasting syrup I can’t place. “Are there more boneweavers here?”

She nods. “Yes. There are a lot more of us than you think, a good number of them finding their way here. Some choose to remain or leave Errigal to escape the Failinis.” Her sharp eyes seem to cut through me. “Judging by the look on your face, you haven’t met many before.”

I move my spoon around in the porridge. “You’re the second one I’ve met.”

“I’m sure you must have felt alone in the world. Our bloodgift is far from spent. You’re the first who’s awakened the titan on this mountain. Raising one of the ancients is something no boneweaver has done since the Darkening,” Guennéan says, her expression soft. “It destroyed part of the forest and caused an avalanche when it was awakened.

Almost destroyed you too. The Council will be eager to know more about you when you're well enough to talk, especially since the Failinis were after you."

I look at the veins still visible like red riverbeds across my hands. "I didn't mean to. I've never been able to do anything like this before. The Failinis were after me long before that," I tell her. "We were living quiet lives, and then they found us. I didn't want to hurt anyone, but... I was only trying to protect myself and my husband."

"The fact that your gift exists is a threat to them. After what you did, I'm sure they're more scared of boneweavers than ever," the old boneweaver says, the bones of her necklace clacking together as she shifts.

My shoulders slump, and I want to melt into the ground. I've ruined this too. I've brought the enemy to this place and the people trying to live in peace. How soon will my daughter and I be safe here until we have to flee again? The porridge sits as a heavy lump in my stomach while worry paces around restlessly.

"I'm sorry...I—"

Guennéan lets out a cawing laugh. "You misunderstand me. Their fear doesn't worry me. In fact, you brought us something valuable. The bones of the gods, titans, and morrigans have a unique quality to them that hides bloodgifted from each other. They had been scattered across Errigal and the rest of the world since the Darkening, so finding a whole skeleton of an ancient is a rare thing. We knew the titan was here but weren't able to dig it up. Its presence has hidden us from the Failinis for years. I'm sure you noticed how it was disorienting in the mountains and made it hard to sense other bloodgifted. Now, those bones have been brought to the surface, and we can use them to our advantage."

"What do you mean?" I ask her, my brow scrunched.

"The bones are valuable to us boneweavers, even if we can't raise it. We're more powerful near them. And since this one's been raised, its power is stronger. The bones of the ancients are also impervious to the magic of the bloodgifted —except to boneweavers. We now have better means to protect ourselves and hide than we did before."

Now that I've had time to rest, I feel the presence of the titan's bones hanging in the air here. I recognize it now as the same thing I felt whenever I would go to Auchendrain. Do they have a titan skeleton there? Or perhaps the bones of a god? That explains why my bloodgift felt harder to use, and my senses were confused when I passed through its gates.

I scrape the last bits of porridge from the bowl. I look back over at Ula, the glow still pulsing through her palm. Rowenna moves around the room, cleaning and straightening jars of herbs and vials on the shelves. Brennus is busy grinding something up in a bowl, and the owl's head swivels to look at me and Morhenna. I give the chicken another piece of bread.

"How many people are here? Is everyone a bloodgifted?" I say and finish off the last tattie scone.

"Two hundred or so. Not everyone is bloodgifted, but many are. Some stay here instead of going to Tearmann Island, but we help any who are searching for a safe place to live," Guennéan tells me. "This village has been around longer than the Failinis know and longer than I've been alive."

My ears perk at the mention of Tearmann. This *is* the place Anstice told me about. All our months of searching brought us here, and we had been so close to reaching it together. I think of all the things I could have done differently. If we had moved faster or left sooner, would Percy and I have found this place? Would my baby have been fine and born at the expected time? The what ifs slice my already frayed heart, and tears blur my vision.

Guennéan's bony hand rests on mine, callused and warm. "You and your daughter are safe here. Even your chicken." She smiles as Morhenna side-eyes her and hops off the cot.

"I need to find Percy, my husband. The Failinis have him," I say and swipe at my eyes.

"His fate is in the gods' hands now. You can't change that, especially not in your state. If you want to help your husband, you need to rest and regain your strength. You also have a price to pay that's long overdue and a child to take care of. I'm sure it's no easy thing to have a titan's voice in your mind," she says, the corners of her mouth softening.

My eyes go to my journals by my legs, knowing the truth of her words and loathing them. Percy would tell me to heal, but the longer I stay here, the more the thoughts about what Captain MacAdoh is doing to him grow.

Guennéan lets go of my hand, her joints popping as she stands. "If you need anything, let Brennus know. He may have the face of an angry bear, but he's a gifted fleshmender," she says, and Brennus glances over his shoulder with what looks like a scowl.

"Could I have a quill and something to write with?" I ask. "I have to write for my price."

The big fleshmender turns and comes over with a charcoal stick. "I look forward to reading what you write about the titan if you'll share it with me," the boneweaver says. "I'll be back tomorrow to check on you, Morana."

Guennéan heads toward the door, and a shiver runs down my spine. She said I did something no boneweaver has done since the Darkening. What does that mean? First, the barrow and now the titan. What's happening to me?

Bright light reflects off the snow outside, stinging my eyes as Guennéan opens the door. Crisp mountain air coated in the frost of winter sweeps in. A man peers in and grins as his gaze lands on me. Snow catches in his chestnut-colored hair, and I sense bones near him.

"Is she awake?" he asks Guennéan. "Can I talk with her?"

"Not now, Louarn," Brennus replies, blocking the door as the old boneweaver leaves. "You'll talk her to death after I went through the trouble of saving her."

The man strains to look past Brennus' shoulder. "But I just have one question—"

Brennus steps outside and closes the door behind him. "It's never just one question with you. You're practically made of them."

"Would you like some more tea?" Rowenna asks and sets a stack of clothes next to the cot. They're mine and Percy's. I pick up one of Percy's tunics off the top, laying it in my lap.

"Yes," I say, and she takes the empty mug. "Thank you."

"It's good that you have an appetite. Best eat the soup while it's warm."

I set my empty porridge bowl down for Morhenna to pick over and continue to root through Percy's pack, unable to find his journal among his undamaged things. He'll be saddened to learn that more of his research is gone. I stop my search and run my hand across the carved flowers on my journal's cover. A crumpled piece of paper falls out, and I open it. The words are slightly blurred from water damage but I can make out "love will be your tether in the storm." It's one of the fortunes from the Festival of Erroll. He's kept it all this time.

I clutch all these pieces of Percy in my lap as if their closeness will ease the pain of him not being here. My sobs seep into Percy's shirt as I hold it to my face, the pungent herbs and his calendula soap still clinging to the fabric through the smell of lye and woodsmoke.

Percy never left me, and I won't leave him either. I'll find him, no matter how long it takes.

XXI
Yarrow

Achillea

Healing ❧ Renewal ❧ Strength

Stiff aches run through my body as I walk around the healing house with my baby. The next week passes with strange quickness. My daughter's almost able to successfully suckle. Innogen, the wet nurse, helps when I can't breastfeed. I've gotten more comfortable around the flamekindler and can tamp down the spark of panic I get when Ula nears my child. She, Rowenna, and Brennus tend to the other patients that come in and make sure I'm healing and that my baby is healthy.

Guennéan has visited a few times, asking questions about the titan's memories while I wrote. My head is clearer without the titan crowding it, the pages of the journal bursting with sentences I can't fully comprehend. Still, my restlessness hasn't abated, and I wonder how long it'll be before I can leave this place to search for Percy.

Snow falls outside as villagers move between the houses. "What about Sláine?" I ask my daughter, touching the downy hair on her head. She's wearing a nightgown Rowenna gave to her that's too big. "Your Da wants to name you Teasle." She squirms, tiny fingers grasping at my neck. "That's how I felt about it. Not a name that suits you, mo chridhe. Heather, possibly. It's a plant name like he'd want."

Her smell reminds me of Glenna's baby, and I'm homesick for my family. A heavy sadness presses on me that I can't shake some mornings. Rowenna and Innogen say it's normal after giving birth, but I'm still frustrated with myself. My child's here, but Percy isn't, and the two thoughts pull me in different directions. I brush away my tears before they wet my cheeks, and leave the kitchen.

As I pass Brennus' worktable, my eyes drift over the bundles of herbs, jars of liquids, and stacks of notes. Seeing the familiar herbs and healer's tools makes me miss our bothy. Beneath the papers next to a small box, I see what looks like Percy's handwriting. I push the notes aside to reveal Percy's notebook. Its pages are stained but intact. Brennus has had it this whole time, and it's flipped to Percy's notes on the bloodleaf.

I scoop up the notebook, and the door opens. Brennus comes in with his owl on his shoulder. The cold chills me, and I hold Heather closer. He sees the journal in my hand, his expression unchanging as he shakes the snow from his cloak.

"Your husband was a talented fleshmender. And a rootsower. He kept very detailed notes. I did my best to salvage them," Brennus says, going to the fire where Morhenna rests. The owl, Comhachag, ruffles his wings and flies into the rafters. The chicken puffs herself up as Comhachag passes by.

"Is. He *is* a talented fleshmender and rootsower," I snap, heat building in my chest. "Why do you have his notes? What else did you take from our bags?"

"Would you have preferred I left it covered in whatever

was broken in the bag? You showed up near our village, chased by Failinis, and raised a titan to bring down half the mountain, all the while carrying notes on a plant no one's seen before that can quell bloodgifts." Brennus turns to me, holding my glare. "This is a place of safety, and we didnae ken if you were an enemy or not."

His footsteps shuffle across the floor, and I take a step back. My body tenses as he brushes past me and opens the box, taking out the pouch of bloodleaf. He's had this too.

Anger builds behind my teeth, but he drops the pouch on top of Percy's journal. "I dinnae ken how you got this or but remember that you're going to be here until winter passes and your daughter is strong enough to travel," he says, his voice low and steady. "If you want any help finding your husband again, it's best if you're honest with us. You're not the only one who came here because of terrible circumstances."

Brennus returns to the fire, his words hanging around me. The anger drains away, and my baby squirms against my shoulder. "Did you show this to anyone else?" I ask.

"Only Rowenna. We felt it in your blood when we first found you, and didnae know if it contributed to your early labor," Brennus replies. "We want your permission to bring it to the Council so a rootsower can try to try to make sense of it."

I stare at my ring. Percy's power is still alive in the wood like a taut string, I fear it'll snap. Percy's voice whispers to trust, for his sake, my sake, and the sake of our child. I do owe these people my life for saving us, but trusting them is another matter. If this plant could keep people safe from the Failinis, then Percy would want to do all he could to help.

I put the journal and the bloodleaf pouch back on the workbench. "Percy was starting to figure out how to regrow it in the hopes he could get seeds to plant," I say. "Maybe some other rootsower can figure it out."

Cold air sweeps around me again as the door opens, and Guennéan enters bundled in so many furs that she resembles a furry creature rather than a woman. "Good to see you up and moving, Morana," she says and shuts the door. "If you're up for it, I want to show you around the village. Brennus can keep your baby company."

This will be the first time I've been separated from my baby, and even though I probably won't be far from the healing house, worry fills me. She's sleeping, but what if she wakes up hungry? I want to see the rest of the village, but I don't want to let my child out of my sight for too long.

"I know leaving her for the first time is scary, but she'll be well looked after by Brennus and Comhachag." The boneweaver's green eyes find the owl before she looks at my baby.

My restlessness is stronger than my apprehensions. My daughter doesn't stir when I place her in the crib, swaddled and warm. I touch her cheek before I grab my boots and coat. Brennus stands by the crib. Morhenna gets up to follow me.

"Be sure to bring that journal of yours, too," Guennéan tells me. "I'm eager to read what you've written about the titan."

GUENNÉAN LEADS ME THROUGH THE SNOWY VILLAGE OF LÒCHRAN, her nose pressed close to the pages of my journal. Morhenna waddles after me, determined to not be left behind. The air's alive with the presence of bloodgifted. I never thought a place like this could possibly exist. The titan's bones are stacked behind the buildings, forming a wall. The winding roads cut snake around stone houses hidden in the heart of this towering forest. What takes my breath away is the sight of houses built *into* the larger trees, connecting upward with wooden stairways. With all the bloodgifted here, I wonder what they've been doing to keep the Failinis from finding this place.

Guennéan tells me the names of different people we pass while they wave to her. Everyone we walk by stares at me. A few older bloodgifted and children follow us as we pass the Great Hall surrounded by shops and tents. I pull my cloak closer and try not to look away. Without Percy to draw part of the attention away from me, I feel more exposed. Everyone here is hiding from the Failinis, but it's hard for me to walk around and not feel guarded all the time.

"They've been talking about you," Guennéan says and looks up from reading to make sure I'm keeping up. "It's not every day someone awakens a titan. You've become quite famous around here."

I clench my hands and force myself to make eye contact with the villagers, managing a weak smile. Percy would already know everyone's names and be talking with them like he was an old friend. A hammer hitting metal rings out from a smithy adjacent to a tavern and splits the calm. A woman blacksmith brings the hammer down as she shapes a sword. Her neck and arms course with orange light. She reminds me of Leith.

"The Council will be excited to read this. I don't think even the Acadamaidh has anything like it," Guennéan goes on. "I'm surprised that you didn't write at least several books' worth. An ancient probably has a whole library's worth of memories to record."

I used up all the space in that journal to write down what I could comprehend. "There was a lot to sift through...but I couldn't fully understand everything I was seeing," I reply. It's like there's an eternity of memories still coursing through me, and what I wrote only released a fraction of it. Still, the titan seems satisfied with the price I paid.

The road goes deeper through the trees, and the houses of Lòchran thin. I wonder how far back into the woods the village goes. I don't want to go too far from my baby. I resist the urge to glance back in the direction of the healing house.

"Wait!" I turn to see the man who was outside the healing house after I gave birth running up to us.

"Seems Louarn's finally found you," Guennéan mutters.

"I wanted to talk with you," the man, Louarn, says, grinning. He stands too close with wide blue eyes rimmed with purple. He's a bit younger than me, and like Guennéan and Anstice, his gift thrums against me with the familiar coolness of a boneweaver. At his side bounds a cat... completely made of bones.

"Me?" I ask.

"Yes! You're the one who raised the titan." He shakes my gloved hand. Morhenna eyes the skeletal cat as it rubs against Louarn's leg. Glowing magic twines around its limbs and spine, burning in its eye sockets. "I'm Louarn. I'm a boneweaver too. How did you raise an ancient? Have you always been able to do that? What did it feel like—"

"One question at a time, Louarn," Guennéan tells him.

He releases my hand. His breath plumes around him like

smoke from a chimney. "Och, sorry! Brennus says I talk too much. I'm just so excited to meet you! Everyone's been talking about what you did."

"I haven't done anything like this before...except raising a barrow. The most I raised before that was five, so this is all new to me," I mumble, my cheeks warming under his stare. I'm talking with two boneweavers. I wonder how many others are here in the village.

Louarn's eyes widen. "Gods' bones! You raised a whole barrow? I've never raised more than ten people at a time. How many was that? I bet it was hundreds. You're like Guennéan. She could raise hundreds when she was younger."

Guennéan raises an eyebrow. "You make it sound like I'm old and feeble now," she says, the journal still open in her hands. "You've forgotten who trained you."

"Didnae mean any offense. You're as spry as a spring chicken," he tells her.

She sniffs and continues walking. "Flattery won't save you, boy. I'll remember this, so you better watch yourself."

"Sometimes she can get so stern. Habits from when she was a general in the Regency's army," Louarn whispers as we follow.

I take in the hunched woman ahead of us. A general? They had to have known she was a boneweaver, so why was she allowed to live? And why would a boneweaver ever serve the Regency when they hate us?

"So, what's with the chicken?" Louarn continues, looking down at Morhenna as she keeps her distance from the undead cat. Snowflakes land on her speckled feathers.

"She's been with Percy and me since we left Àitesìol," I tell him.

"Morhenna?" he replies, head tilted.

"Percy thought it was cute. We had another one named Siobhen, and two others, Fergus and Fiona. Morhenna only used to like Percy, but I guess now"—I almost say that he's gone before I stop myself—"she's lonely and has put aside her disdain toward me for now."

Louarn chuckles. "I wasn't aware chickens were capable of disdain."

"This one is," I mutter, and my eyes go to the cat. "What's with the cat?"

"Oh, Alw?" Louarn bends down to scratch the skeleton beneath its bony jaw. "He was my first cat. I kept him and use his bones to build my stamina for sustaining my bloodgift."

I've never seen anyone keep a body reanimated for long. It almost acts like a real cat, but that must be because Louarn is making it behave that way. If Morhenna died, I bet her bones would dislike me, too.

"So, what was it like raising the titan?" Louarn's expectant gaze shifts back to me. "How did you do it?"

"I don't know. We were fighting the Failinis—my husband and I...Then I felt it, and it answered me. I only held it for a few minutes before I blacked out." I remember the warmth of my blood seeping out of my eyes, nose, and mouth. If I had kept going...

"It was like you were full of power and being sucked dry at the same time," Guennéan says, heaviness weighing down her words. "I've seen many bloodgifted overuse their gift."

Louarn falls silent as we approach a church made of twisted trees and stone. Its branches extend above the steeple and creates a covering. A rootsower must have shaped the church out of living plants around the existing foundation.

Behind it sits the titan's lupine-shaped skull, its dark sockets peering down over the roof while ravens perch on its broken horns. Its teeth are larger than me, the power flowing from it making my blood hum. How many people did it take to haul this here?

"What were its memories like?" Louarn asks quietly as we cross the church's threshold.

"It was hard to understand because I didn't know what it was saying. I saw it creating things with the gods and fighting the morrigans," I tell him, our voices echoing off the vaulted ceiling.

His eyes go to the dark veins still visible along my neck. "I have to draw the dead as my price. In the beginning, they looked like shite, but I got really good over the years, if I do say so."

Hundreds of candles flicker throughout the room and are clustered on the altar at the front of the church. A comforting warmth embraces me. Light flickers across the paintings of the gods in their human and heavenly forms on the walls. Offerings of food, dried flowers, and baubles are left by the fanes for each god. Morhenna struts around under the eyes of the gods without any concern for this holy place.

I stop by a painting of Arianrhod standing with her four wings extended, smiling down at me. Black hair spills down her head, and inky feathers cover most of her pale body. There are clay tablets with poems carved on them around her shrine. There are bits of bone inside them. Between Arianrhod's cupped hands is a human skull dipped in gold sitting on a shelf carved into the stone. I'm pulled toward it, the voice speaking in flashes of crows and a sea of skeletons.

Arianrhod's face appears in illuminated brilliance for a moment, and tears fall down my cheeks.

"Boudica was one of the first boneweavers Arianrhod blessed to help raise the gods. She was someone that kings and people came to because she could reveal the secrets of the dead," Guennéan says beside me. "When the other bloodgifted turned against the boneweavers, she fled from the Mainland with others and came to Errigal."

"How...how is this here?" I ask, sucking in a breath.

Guennéan touches the mural before sitting on the bench. Louarn bows his head, hand going to the pendant he wears. "Most likely, some of her followers passed her bones down to others to keep the stories alive. We only have her skull, and how it came here is a mystery."

Arianrhod's four eyes remain on me as Beathag stands on her left. The god's heavenly form bears lupine features with the ears, tail, and fur of a rabbit. Two of her eyes are round, while the other two are slitted. At her feet are images of babies, flowering plants, and animals. Bright colors surround her human form and spiral over her fur cloak as she nurses a child and heals another. Her clawed fingers and soft face embody serenity and cruelty. The child she holds reminds me of mine now, and I ache to get back to her.

"Do you ever think that the gods have abandoned us?" I ask, drying my face. "We're hated by everyone even though we have the blood of the gods. Why do we have these gifts if we're just hunted down?"

The old woman pats the space next to her. I sit, knees creaking from the cold. "Terrible things happen, but that doesn't mean the gods are silent. I look at memories like those of Boudica and see the wonders the gods did, which gives me faith that they'll do such things again. Sorrow may exist for today, but it doesn't last forever. I don't need to read your bones to know you carry much sorrow with you. You'll have to decide if what you've endured is greater than the gods' ability to bring about something good from it."

I've faced dark days before, but Percy was always beside me as a steady presence I could hold onto even when he cried in my arms alongside me. I don't feel nearly as strong without him. I need to find him. I'm not ready to be alone again or raise our daughter by myself.

"If the gods can die, what hope is there for us?" I whisper.

Guennéan looks at me. "Some of them may be dead for now, but their spirits are still alive. Their power still exists in the world. We are Arianrhod's children, and we carry her gift in our veins. Bloodgifted exist to carry out the purpose of the gods—to use our gifts to serve others and restore balance to the world. Raising the titan is a sign that things are changing."

My head snaps to her. "What do you mean? What I did was an accident, and it nearly killed me. I can't raise the gods."

"No one boneweaver was meant to bring the gods back on their own. Arianrhod gave the power to all boneweavers so they could work together. Our gifts are always growing and changing. Yours could be doing the same, unlocking abilities our kind hasn't had access to for centuries. You can read as much into it as you'd like, but you can't deny that you've done something extraordinary," Guennéan tells me. "Louarn certainly looks like he believes you might be a savior."

Pink rises in Louarn's cheeks. "I do not! It could be happening, though—the return of the gods. Maybe the other boneweavers here could learn from you," he says to me and holds his cat in his arms.

"I'm nothing special. Not a savior or anything like that," I tell him.

"Who knows why you were able to do what you did, Morana, but I wouldn't call yourself nothing special," Guennéan says.

I flex my fingers, the aches cracking the numbness. The first time that Percy called me amazing, I didn't believe him. I take in Guennéan's wrinkled face as she stares at the golden skull. Was she ever ashamed of being a boneweaver?

"You fought with the Regency even though you're a boneweaver," I say, my voice echoing in the quiet. "How's that possible? Don't the Failinis kill the boneweavers they find?"

Guennéan sighs. "Not always," she mutters without looking away from Arianrhod. "As much as they like to despise us, they still want to use our power. It's when it becomes something they can't control that they deem us dangerous. After the Darkening, boneweavers were used to create armies of the dead. Nowadays, if the Failinis find boneweavers, then the Regency takes them and forces them to fight."

Guennéan stands and picks up one of the tablets. Sadness shadows her features. The poem etched into the clay is about a windsinger who died escaping from the Failinis. His voice seeps through the carved words. Parts of his bones are mixed in with the clay.

"I was taken from my family when I was young. The Failinis were raiding smaller towns in Tìr Dhè to find fresh soldiers for the army. They said I could die or fight, and I chose the latter because I was afraid that they would kill my family. I did many things I wasn't proud of, used too many of my friends who fell in battle to make sure I survived. It took me many years before I finally escaped.

"I served on the frontlines for twenty years. I lost count of how many dead I raised, how many poems I wrote," she tells me. "The years changed, but the wars were always the same. Conquest, border disputes, feuds between neighboring countries. Only boneweavers seem to be able to remember how many have paid the price for these conflicts. It used to be that all bloodgifted were encouraged to join the army, but now, if the Failinis find a strong enough bloodgifted, they force them to join."

The chill in the air burrows beneath my layers. Could that be why the Failinis were in Àitesìol that day, looking for bloodgifted they could take? If they capture me, would I be forced to raise something like a titan until it kills me? Whatever wars the Regency wage remains across the sea seemed so distant from Errigal's shores. I'm learning how little I know about the world beyond Errigal. It's hard to care about the wider world when your own is being threatened.

The pouch at Guennéan's side is full of fragmented echoes from several voices. "Whose bones are in that bag?" I ask.

Guennéan puts the tablet down. "Friends I couldn't leave behind, others I found and eventually lost. We always carry the dead with us. In the past, some boneweavers kept pouches filled with bone fragments of their village's dead to preserve the memories. They were keepers of the dead, and people came to them to hear the stories of their deceased loved ones. They also were important in recording bloodgifted's skills to pass down."

She gestures to the church around us.

"We don't only learn from the living. No matter how much of our history is removed from stories or books, we will always have the bones to pass on their memories to us. Our libraries are in the barrows and graves, knowledge the Failinis nor the Regency can take from us."

Her words stir up something inside me. It's a sense of pride I haven't felt about my bloodgift before. When I was with Anstice, I had that sense of belonging I craved. Now, I'm sitting with two boneweavers, and a village full of others.

"Will you fight the Failinis after what they've done to you?" I ask.

"You can't fight prejudice with weapons. It's only defeated by the truth, but only by those who listen to it. And truth can't be shouted at a mob that's been deafened by their own noise. They are bloodgifted like us, but their duty to protect has become misguided by fear," Guennéan says, her face lined like tree bark. "Whatever you decide to do with your new abilities will be up to you, Morana."

As much as I want to learn from Guennéan and meet other boneweavers, I can't stop thinking about Percy. "I can't stay here," I say, standing.

"The Failinis can't find you here. This place is safe," Louarn tells me with the cat curled in his arm.

"I don't care about the Failinis finding me. All I want is news about where Percy is and how I can get him back. I won't leave him to be tortured or killed. "

A sad look crosses Guennéan's face as she stares at me. "We had scouts following the Failinis that attacked you who haven't returned," she says. "There's been a snowstorm hovering in the lower part of the mountain that the windsingers and waterdancers have been keeping away from the village, but I don't know anything else I think it's ill-advised for you to go after him, especially in your state. Going alone is a death sentence."

"Is there anything I can do to make the Council help me go find Percy?" I ask. Since she's on the Council, she's the only one who can vouch for me.

"Lòchran's a sanctuary, not a prison, but you need to understand the risks both to yourself, your child, and to us. If you're caught and tortured, the Failinis could find out about this place. If you choose to take a risk, it will be your decision. Our priority is to anyone who comes here seeking refuge, but we also must make sure the whole community is safe."

My hands clench as anger surges through my chest. "So, if you manage to find out where Percy is, I'll be on my own."

"I can talk with the other members, but going after one person isn't something we usually do."

"Even if they say no, I'll go with you," Louarn says. "We can find others to help." The optimism in his voice reminds me so much of Percy, and I'm moved by his willingness to help even though I haven't known him for very long.

"Don't go over the Council's heads," Guennéan says.

"Percy's alive, and I'm going to find him. I have to do whatever I can to get my family back!" I snap.

All the bones in this church vibrate, a swirl of whispers dancing among the candle flames as my power builds in my veins. The titan's voice is clearer, and while still all-consuming, I could reach for it and maybe hold it long enough so that the Failinis wouldn't be able to stop me.

Louarn's wide eyes dart between us. Guennéan places a hand on my arm, and I tense. Her words are soft, and the candlelight shimmers as my eyes water. “Percy’s alive. I can feel it. His ring...I can find him,” I tell her.

Guennéan’s gaze drops to my ring finger. “If the Failinis are keeping your husband alive, they’ll be taking him to Auchendrain. And if he’s a skilled enough bloodgifted, they’ll probably send him to the front. And if they learn that you’re alive, they’ll come for you. They’ll want to use your power in the Regency’s wars. Or you’ll be killed.”

The anger drains from me, and I lean against one of the pillars. Louarn moves closer, worry resting on his face. Are the Failinis really going to force Percy to serve in the army? Being on the run has already forced him to go against his oath as a healer. The thought of such a caring man being turned into a soldier and forced to kill makes me sick.

“Percy’s a healer, not a fighter,” I say as a shiver crawls up my spine.

“Fleshmenders can do more than heal,” Guennéan says, her voice heavy. “I’ve seen some pull blood from a person without touching them. Rootsowers that can create thorns sharp enough to spear a person and plants so poisonous they kill on contact. A bloodgifted’s abilities are meant to help and protect, but they can easily be turned into a weapon. People are quick to fear us because we’re close with death. Your husband may have little choice in how he’s forced to use his power, especially if they threaten the people he loves.”

The rip in my heart grows. “I can’t let that happen. I have to get him back,” I tell her as my voice cracks. My fingers tighten around my ring, desperate for any sign that Percy is alright. “I’m not going to let them break him.”

“Your love for your husband is strong, but don’t forget to focus on your child and regain your strength. I’m sure you have more wounds to heal than the ones Brennus can see. For now, rest and be with your daughter," she tells me. "You can stay here and start a new life for you and your daughter. When you're both strong enough to travel, we can help you get to Tearmann."

My eyes go to Arianrhod again. Is it selfish to want to go after Percy even though our child is so young and finding him is dangerous? I wouldn't forgive myself if anything happened to her, but abandoning Percy is also unforgivable. I won't let Percy die without meeting our daughter.

Morhenna eyes me as she flies onto the bench. At least I know she'd be by my side if I went after him, and she'd put up a good fight. I hear the echo of Percy's voice telling me I'm being selfish. I unclench my hands. My daughter needs me.

"If you're up for it, I can teach you how to hone your bloodgift and about boneweaver history," the old boneweaver says, and my eyes widen. "I can't teach you how to wake a titan, but I have my own tricks. I'm confident you'll pick them up quickly."

THE BONE POWDER SIFTS THROUGH MY FINGERS AS I SIT IN THE church with Louarn, Guennéan, and Brennus. The bench digs into my backside, adding to the tightness in my back. My daughter sleeps against my chest in her sling under my shawl. The particles whisper with broken voices I can't piece together. There are ribs and finger bones mixed in with an ulna, spine vertebrae, and a tibia. Their voices are tiny droplets against my senses that move too quickly for me to grasp. Guennéan can move them with ease and form different objects, but I can't pull out one whole bone.

She gave me the pouch to practice with while she tells me about the history of the boneweavers. This and meeting other boneweavers Louarn has introduced me to and villagers in Lòchran helps keep my mind off things these past week, but I wrestle with worry and nightmares that keep me up. Every day I ask Guennéan about finding Percy, I get the same response: they have no idea where he is.

Guennéan's green eyes watch me as she sips from a flask, the purple light of my bloodgift reflected in her irises. "There were boneweavers that could pull memories from living bones," she says, beginning another story. "Some boneweavers were soothsayers. People brought them the bones of those who had been killed to find out how they died and who their family was. They were valued for their abilities to discern the truth. The Regency even used some to extract the truth from dead spies and enemies." The old boneweavers voice is soothing, and the bone shards seem drawn to her.

"How can a boneweaver pull memories from living bones?" I ask.

"They have to separate it from the body," Louarn says as he sits on one of the church's steps, the candlelight turning his hair coppery. He's eating a piece of bread, and Morhenna goes for the crumbs he drops.

The chicken eyes the other bloodgifted cleaning the church as she waits for more crumbs to drop. The bone cat, Alw, lounges at his feet, its yellowed skull resting on dainty paws. Brennus leans against a pillar next to Louarn and reads through Percy's journal. Other than us, the church is quiet except for the voices of the dead hanging in the air.

"Do you want to tell these stories, Louarn?" Guennéan asks, her gaze going to him. "I had to tell them to you several times because you never listened."

"I listened. It sometimes takes longer for things to sink in," he replies with a sheepish grin and touches the piece of titan bone hanging from his neck. "So, the soothsayers required a piece of bone to read a person's past and uncover lost memories. They used those memories to give a prediction for their future. Those who wanted that kind of information needed to bring a piece of their own bone to be read. When the Failinis began hunting boneweavers, they'd look for people who were missing parts of their fingers and toes to determine if there was a boneweaver among them." He looks back at Guennéan. "How did I do?"

"Eh, decent. But you're a better singer than you are a storyteller," she tells him and takes another sip from her flask.

"What's the craziest story you've written about a person?" Louarn asks me, and I lose the bits of bone I started piecing together. I sigh, shoulders slumping.

I've collected so many stories over the years. Sifting through them is like flipping through a thick tome. Names and voices whisper together as I gloss over sections until I find the one of a man named Somerled who had died near Taibhse.

"There was this man named Somerled who kept a herd of cows and wandered with them for years. Being alone for that long made him a bit daft," I tell him. "He wore clothes made from their hair and a pair of their horns on his head. He thought he was seeing loireags in the highlands, so he'd chase after them. One winter night, he thought he saw a loireag and chased after it on the back of one of his cows, naked. He died from the cold."

Louarn tilts his head, looking up at the ceiling of living branches. "Wonder if he did it because he was in love with them," he mutters.

I focus on the bone powder again as it wiggles under my fingers. A few voices are clearer, coming together like a woven design on a blanket. If I can master this, could I move all the bone fragments buried in the ground? Guennéan must be extremely powerful if she can call something so small. I raised a titan, yet I can't do this.

"What's Percy like?"

My head snaps up at Louarn's question. The little movement in the pouch stops, and I lose my hold on the dust. The ring is tight around my swollen finger. How can I begin to tell him about the man who means everything to me and whose absence is like a severed limb?

"Percy's..." His name catches in my throat. "Percy's the first person outside my family who called my gift beautiful. He cares for people at the cost of his own self and isn't afraid to cry, yet always sees the bright side of things." I sniff, and a cracked laugh escapes. "Percy likes to tell plant puns. They're bad, but now I miss them. I miss him."

Tears land in the bone powder. The tightening knot of worry sits heavy in my stomach. How can I be patient when all I can think about are the horrible things the Failinis might be doing to him? Captain MacAdoh's rage burns more intensely with each encounter. Percy wounded him, and he won't forget that. They know he's doublegifted. If he ends up in a cell in Auchendrain, I may never see him again.

"I told you that you ask too many questions, Louarn," Brennus tells him, his voice sharp.

Louarn sits up straighter. "I'm sorry. I shouldn't have asked."

"It's fine," I croak.

The dust from the pouch swirls over my head, glittering with purple light before darting toward Guennéan. Her eyes are like glowing amethysts while the light pulses around her skull. The bone powder twists around her arm, and with a flick of her finger, they reform into different shapes. For a moment, I can imagine her on a battlefield, a powerful boneweaver moving armies of the dead.

Guennéan brings the bone fragments back to the pouch on the bench. "You struggle to move the fragments because you're focusing too much on the flashes of memories we usually feel from intact ones," she says. "That's what gives our power the opening to answer their call. At this size, you must find a different way to connect to them."

"I'm trying. It's like trying to grab water." Irritation laces my words. My baby fusses, and I set the pouch down and open my blouse to let her latch. I peek at her under the shawl, her small face calming me.

"Focus on the fragments of emotions. Connect with them as you did with the titan and coax them to rejoin their other pieces. We understand what makes up a bone, but with the smaller pieces, we need to dig in deeper than the marrow and minerals to pull out its true essence."

When my baby finishes eating, I cradle her near my shoulder and pat her back until she burps. Ever since giving birth, my emotions have been difficult to control. They shift so quickly and plunge into deep sadness more than they did while I was pregnant. It's hard to rein them in and not be knocked back by them. Brushes of sadness and pain are embedded in the bones, and it'd be easy to sink into, but I fear I might not be able to swim back to the surface.

The doors of the church open, and wind blows snow inside. I wrap the shawl over my baby as the candles flicker. A tall woman with short black hair steps inside. I recognize her from a few days ago. A shadowcatcher named Tegan, whose husband Abello is a boneweaver.

"The Council is meeting now, Guennéan. They want to see Morana and Brennus," she says.

My heart leaps into my throat. Do they have news about Percy? Brennus' face reveals no indication of what this meeting is about as he closes the journal. Louarn told me that Brennus was taken in by the fleshmender council member, Iseabail, when he first came to Lòchran. She's practically his mother, so he knows some of what goes on in their meetings, but is tight-lipped about those things.

Guennéan retrieves the bag of bone powder and ties it to her belt. "Seems our lesson will have to wait," she says, and the purple light fades from her eyes.

Louarn jumps up. The light dies from the skeleton, and the bones move to his belt where he affixes the skull. "Can I come too?" he asks, his voice carrying across the church. Brennus goes over to Louarn and brushes crumbs from the boneweaver's tunic.

"Only if you can keep your questions to yourself until the end," Guennéan tells him.

I put my baby back in her sling, and she cries against my chest as I follow Guennéan. Morhenna's claws tap against the floor behind me. Snowfall brushes against my cheeks, thick clumps falling from gray skies.

Tegan takes us to the Great Hall with a rounded roof decorated with detailed knotwork. Thick curved wooden beams are carved with all eleven symbols of the gods. Inside, the main space is empty but warm. There's a circular chamber in the back where ten other bloodgifted sit around a glowing brazier.

The eyes of the Council are on me. My skin prickles, my heart ready to jump out of my mouth. Two other people stand off to the side—a heavyset, one-armed woman with braided blonde hair and a man with a dark beard. I met them the other day, but their names escape me. Guennéan is the oldest council member as she takes the empty seat next to the dark-skinned woman I recognize as Iseabail, the fleshmender, and a pale woman with snow-white hair and violet eyes I heard Louarn call Beitris.

Iseabail stands, the furs around her reminding me of the image of Beathag in the church. Her pleated hair hangs down to her shoulders. "Morana Bracken," she says in a voice like wind through the trees. I stiffen and try to quiet my baby as her cries grow louder. "We've heard your petition to leave Lòchran and search for your husband. Brennus has spoken on your behalf, as has Guennéan."

"So many Failinis close to the village is worrying," Teutas, a short man with brass loops in his beard, adds. "And they now know about the titan's bones on the mountain."

"I'm sure Guennéan has told you that going after one person puts the village at risk. Lòchran has survived by remaining hidden from the Failinis. Many have crossed through her over the years, but they've not had a reason to linger here until now," Iseabail goes on.

My stomach sinks as my gaze darts to the shadowed faces. Louarn stands close to me, his hand resting on my arm. Their words don't sit well with me.

"We do respect you for raising the titan. The bones have been a boon for the village," a shadowcaster named Vortigern says.

"Why am I here if you're only going to tell me there's nothing that can be done?" I ask, fighting tears as I bounce my daughter until her cries stop.

The council members shift. I only hear the crackling flames from the brazier. Iseabail clears her throat. "The scouts that followed the Failinis chasing you have been captured and taken to Dunathol near Loch Auchendrain. Only one managed to make it back before the storm hit. Normally, prisoners would be taken to the capital, but the storm has kept them at the fort. Your husband is among them."

My heartbeat fills my throat. He's alive. I see the map of the eastern part of Errigal in my mind, with Auchendrain on the far end of the island. From here, and if they're following the mountains, it'd take the Failinis weeks to reach the capital, longer if the weather has been bad. For the first time in weeks, hope grows a little bit brighter. Percy might not be at Auchendrain yet. There's a chance to rescue him. The tension I've been holding for weeks loosens, making my legs weak.

"This provides us with a short window to strike the fort and get our scouts and your husband back," Iseabail tells me. "Our windsingers have been keeping the storm around the fort, but we'll need to move soon. Our scouts being captured puts the village at risk. Dunathol, like most Failinis forts, has titan bones embedded in the exterior wall to prevent bloodgifted from attacking it directly.

"The only way to get into the fort is to remove the bones from the walls or go through the main gate. Our boneweavers have tried before, but none have been able to move the bones. You're the only one who has been able to do this. If we're to get our people back and your husband, you'll need to go to the fort." Her gaze softens as she goes to my child. "I know you want to find your husband, and you have a child, so this request is a great one to ask of you."

While my elation grows, I remember what happened when I used my power on the titan. It nearly killed me. Would I be able to do it again? And if something happens to me...I look down at my baby, her tiny hands curled near her face.

"I don't know how I awakened the titan before," I tell them. "I could only hold onto it for a few minutes."

"We'll be sending twenty bloodgifted with you to ambush the fort once the walls come down. As you know, the titan's bone offers them protection, but it also makes it difficult for bloodgifted to sense each other. Brennus and another fleshmender will be there to make sure you dinnae over-exert yourself. And Louarn has been considered to go as well. Better to have two boneweavers than one."

Louarn's face lights up, a wide grin plastered on his face. "Gods' bones!" he gasps, his voice rising.

"Best calm down before they change their minds and take you off the mission," Brennus tells him, arms crossed.

"This attack will draw the Failinis' attention to the mountain, and no doubt they'll be searching for the village. If they haven't gotten Lòchran's location from the scouts, then we'll be safe," Teutas adds. "They can't be allowed to follow you back here."

"If you were able to call the titan's bones, you can do it again," Guennéan tells me and warms her hands near the flames.

"And my child?" I ask. She's stronger, but still helpless. I don't know how long I'd be away from her. Going after Percy means leaving my child behind. If neither of us returns...Our daughter would be taken care of, nameless but loved. I don't know how to choose between Percy and my child without feeling like I'm being torn in two.

"Rowenna would watch her. She'd be in good hands," Brennus tells me. "I'd advise you to stay here, but that seems pointless."

Percy's smile burns in my mind, making my chest ache. I could see him again. I can almost smell the calendula soap on his skin. "I want to bring my husband back," I tell the Council. "I'll go to the fort."

"A group will be gathered in the next few days," Iseabail says. "Lyall and Magnus"—she gestures to the other two bloodgifted in the room—"will be leading this mission. You'll receive more information in the days to come."

Beitris' violet eyes sparkle in the firelight. "Guennéan mentioned that your ring is connected to your husband's and that you can tell that he's still alive through it," the rootsower says. "How ingenious. I've heard of rootsowers sending messages through plants."

My fingertip presses against the carved primroses. "My husband's idea," I say.

"I look forward to meeting him," Beitris replies. "I want to study this bloodleaf more, and his insight will be beneficial."

I meet Guennéan's gaze. I know she played a part in persuading the Council to infiltrate the fort, and I am forever grateful. Her smile is crinkled, but there's sadness in her green eyes. I'm afraid of facing MacAdoh again, but this time I won't be alone.

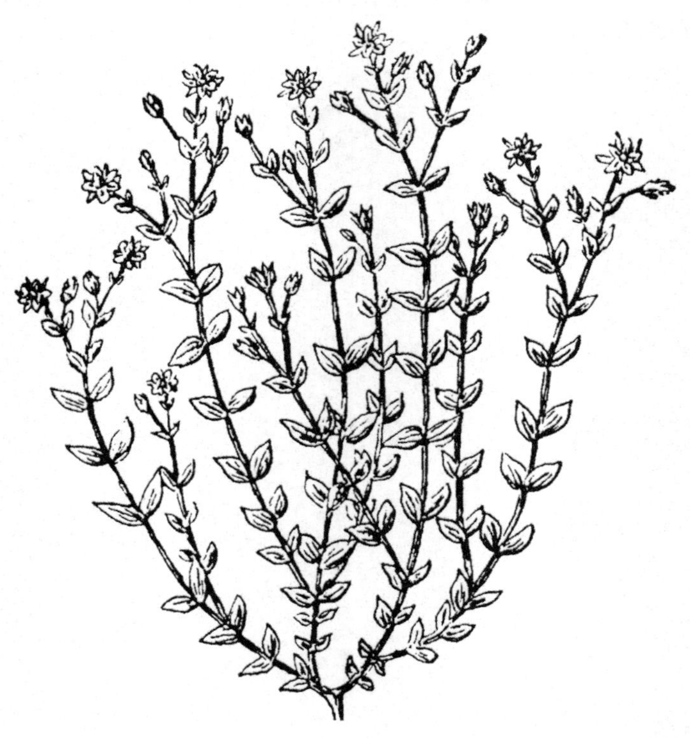

XXII
Thyme
Thymus Serpyllum

Bravery · Swift movement · Love

I slip into my boots and throw a heavy cloak over my wool-lined coat. Da's pendant rests against my chest, a heavy weight against my sternum as I think about what lies ahead. My thumb brushes against my daughter's cheek as she sleeps with a belly full of milk. Her crib has been moved to the upstairs room in Rowenna's house, where her two other children sleep.

"Remember to put ice or a warm compress on your breasts if they become painful. Keep massaging them when they become full," Rowenna says as she puts tea and ointments in my pack. "These will help with your aches."

"Do you think I left enough milk for her? I know Innogen doesn't mind feeding her, but she has her own child," I say and adjust the blanket Ma made around my baby. How much will she grow by the time we return? Will she know I'm gone?

"It'll be enough. She'll be well-fed while you're gone. You'll be surprised how much she'll have grown when you return. And I'll make sure no one eats your chicken."

"If anything happens to me," I start, swallowing the lump in my throat.

"I will take care of her like she's my own." Rowenna

places a hand on my shoulder. "But I believe you'll return with your husband."

"Thank you, Rowenna." I kiss my baby's forehead, breathing in the smell of powder, milk, and what I can only describe as her scent. "I wish I was leaving you with a name, mo chridhe, but nothing's come to me yet. I'm going to rescue your da, and I'm sure he'll have a name for you," I say to her. "He'll be excited to meet you."

The door to the room opens, and Guennéan steps in, silver hair tied back. The whispers of the bones she carries fill the room. "Lyall and Magnus are almost ready to leave," she says. There's a wrapped bundle under her arm, and the familiar ancient voice seeps through the fabric.

I tear myself away from my baby and grab my pack. Four bone knives hang from my belt. To carry bones so openly and not have to hide my bloodgift comforts me. I've been practicing on fragments of the titan's bone Guennéan gave me, and the power flows easier, but it's still like wading through a rushing river and trying not to get swept away.

"Remember what I taught you. The titan's bone is the same as any other. It's made up of emotions," the old boneweaver tells me and holds the bundle out. "I had the blacksmith make this. Hopefully, this will serve you well."

Under the oilskin is an axe about the same size as my old one with a sharpened head and a handle made of the titan's bone with ravens carved along it. Power thrums through me, and my palms warm as I pick it up.

"Thank you," I say. Those words are too flimsy compared to what she's given me. I loop the axe through my belt and bend down to hug her. Guennéan's body is so frail in my arms, but I feel the muscles beneath her furs.

"Don't snap me in half," she says, laughing.

She places something over my head. I look down as I pull away at the pendant with Arianrhod's symbol carved from another piece of the titan's bone. It pulses against my chest in time with my heartbeat.

"Anytime one of Arianrhod's kin comes into their power, the world is a better place. Don't let the Failinis or anyone else tell you otherwise." Guennéan gives me a sad look as she takes my hands, gripping my fingers. "May the gods, both living and dead, guide your path and bring you back safely," she says, her voice carrying the heavy weight of someone who has seen too many people leave who have never returned.

CLUARAN'S KNOBBY, SNOW-COVERED SPINE MAKES TRAVELING TO Dunathol difficult, even with the windsingers carving a path through the snowstorm. The swirling gray and white around us makes it impossible to tell what time of day it is or what's beyond the groaning trees and mountains. Without my child, I'm even more untethered, like I'm missing two chunks of myself instead of one. Six days feels like a year, and I keep pushing myself harder, frustrated by every ache, snowdrift, and blocked path that keeps me separated from Percy.

Brennus, Louarn, and I are huddled with three others, our breaths curling in gauzy tendrils as the winds beat against us and snow freezes to our clothes. The veins around Brennus' eyes glow pink as he uses his powers to command nearby animals to scout out the area, his gaze slightly unfocused as he sees through their eyes. Here on a ridge overlooking the fort, I hear the call of ancient bones. All of us have a piece of the titan to hide our presence. The group of twenty has split into three teams and is spread out through the surrounding forest until it's time to move in. The storm has kept the Failinis inside, and only a few scouts have been seen.

Lyall's left hand glows with a tawny light as she creates a dirt replica of the fort from the ground. "Magnus' group should be in position on the other ridge," the earthcarver says, pointing to the southeastern side of Dunathol. "And the rear group will be air and ground support once the walls come down. Our aim is to free the prisoners and escape before the Failinis can rally. The initial element of surprise will catch them off guard, and we'll use the storm to disorient and hide our numbers since they will outnumber us."

Doran, a lightcaster, directs an orb of light toward the middle of the fort. He's a former Failinis who deserted many years ago before ending up in Lòchran. "There's only one entrance, and there are usually thirty Failinis within the fort, probably more now until the storm abates. Prisoners are kept in the middle," he says with ice in his dark beard. "Barracks sit behind the prison, and usually, there are at least eleven guards on the walls. Alarm bells are located by the gate. In this weather, they'll have flamekindlers, windsingers, and waterdancers on the wall because they can weather the storm easier than other bloodgifted."

"See anything?" Louarn asks Brennus. His face is nearly hidden in his hood, and the scarf is wrapped up to his chin.

Brennus blinks, looking at something past us. "Comhachag and the other two owls see only eight on the walls," he says. "Dozen or so moving about outside. The rest must be in the barracks or in the prison."

"Morana." I stiffen as all eyes turn to me. "Head to the gate with Brennus and Doran once I get word from Magnus that his group is in place," Lyall tells me. "You won't have long to bring down the walls before the Failinis realize what's happening. Once the bones are removed, send up the signal for us to move in. Doran's illusion should hide you, but if they start to attack you, withdraw. Remember, this could be a trap, but we'll use the element of surprise as long as we can."

I nod and flex my stiff fingers. The axe is a familiar, comforting weight at my hip. Somehow despite the cold, my hands are sweaty. So much relies on me. Can Percy sense I'm near through his ring? Seeing his smile again and the look he'll have when he sees our daughter keeps me from being paralyzed by the fear pounding through my chest. I clutch at my pendant, sending up a silent prayer to Arianrhod. No matter what happens, I'm not leaving without Percy.

DUNATHOL'S DARK SHAPE LOOMS THROUGH THE SNOW AS BRENNUS, Doran, and I step out of the treeline. My thighs burn from walking through the snowdrifts, but my blood hums being so close to the fort. The bones along its walls sound like they belong to a titan, but it's only a fraction of its body. Eight long pieces surround the fort, parts of a femur and a finger. White light glows along Doran's veins on his face as he holds an illusion in front of us woven together by lightcaster magic. If we remain near him, we won't be seen. With the pieces of bone from the pendant and the axe, my bloodgift is overflowing in my veins.

This is the most powerful I've ever felt, yet I'm still afraid.

I stare up at the wide gate of the fort, where two bones

run through the wood and iron. I stop several yards from the gate, the words of the titan almost palpable against my skin. Its voice carries a similar rage and loss as the other one did. I take a deep breath, the cold air settling in my lungs while snowflakes melt on my tongue.

Brennus' boots crunch in the snow as he stands beside me. "Dinnae try to hold onto your power if breathing becomes too difficult or if you're experiencing intense pain," he tells me.

Swallowing, I let my bloodgift flow out to connect with the bones. Its memories slam into me like a shock of boiling water, and I struggle to keep my grip on the voice. They're infused to the wood, and the sensation holds me in an iron grasp, trying to crush me. Wood groans over the howling winds cutting my face as I strain against the heat of memories. Fire spewing from the cracked earth, the ground shuddering as morrigans clash with hulking beings made of diamonds and stars. It wrestles with creatures armed with talons and gaping jaws as they hurtle into a fiery chasm. Its rage is feeding off me, and I dig beneath it until I find the pulsing core in its marrow—its loss and sorrow.

Tears freeze on my cheeks as I sink to a knee, barely aware of Brennus clutching my arm. A warm trickle runs down my nose, and I don't know how long my veins can contain the magic before they burst. I let the pain of the bones crash into me, letting it find my own until they're woven together. I let the pain of losing my first child, the years of isolation and fear, the bothy going up in flames, Anstice, and Percy's scream as he's dragged away bleed out until it drips down my cheeks. Although my grief and loss are tiny drops compared to the titan's ocean of memories, the heat of its rage gives way to the cool ashen taste of death. Purple light glows along the bones on the fort's walls, cutting through the snowstorm.

With a yell, I wrench the bones free, and they spear the ground. Doran and Brennus curse, and I sink to my knees. Part of Dunathol's wall groans and falls. Shouts go up as wood breaks against the ground. Red droplets fall into the white snow, and for a moment, I think I'm back on the mountain before Percy was taken, the ringing returning to my ears. The ancient memories press down on my skull as they flood my mind. Its name is like swirling fire and glitters with the light refracted off diamonds.

"Morana!" Brennus' voice reaches me, and I stare up at him. "Can you move?"

"Aye," I manage to get out, my body heavy and weightless at the same time as he hauls me up.

"Doran, send up the signal," Brennus shouts.

The lightcaster lifts his hand skyward, and a bolt of blinding light shoots out before exploding overhead. Warmth needles through my limbs and soothes the pain beneath the humming power coursing through me. The bones jutting out of the ground are about twenty feet long and as thick as caber logs. The purple veins of my gift are still tethered to them, and I draw them into the air, joints creaking under their weight. I hurl them at the gate, bone spearing metal and wood until the gate is slammed off its hinges. The desire to tear the fort apart surfaces, but I need to find Percy.

The winds churn faster, and a cyclone slithers down from the sky, crashing into the middle of the fort. I put my hand up to shield my face as icy snow clouds blast against us. Fresh deaths pull at me. When the haze clears, I see dark shapes with different colored glows moving across the courtyard of the fort. Lyall's shout rings out, and the ground shakes. Bursts of flame light up the fort, and the smell of smoke makes my heart race. I grab the axe, and I stagger through the destroyed gate. My ring pulses, and the energy tugs me forward.

Failinis and Lòchran villagers fight among the scattered sections of the broken wall. A body is sprawled across the ground, blood staining the churned snow. Magnus rushes through the fray and strikes a waterdancer charging at him. A Failinis comes out of the building in the center—the prison—and spots me. His green cloak snaps behind him as he gathers shadows to form giant beasts, magic glowing black along his exposed skin. I raise my axe to fend off the shadow creatures coming for me. The blade slams into the side of one and slices through it. An owl screeches, and Comhachag dives for the shadowcatcher, talons digging into his eyes. The shadow creatures dissolve with the man's scream.

A knife flies through the air and strikes the Failinis in the throat. His death sloughs away from his crumpling body, fresh memories flashing across my eyes as he struggles to comprehend the separation from life.

"Morana!" I whirl around to see Louarn running through the smoke and snow with a lightningstriker, Eiric, his bone knives drawn. The purple light of Louarn's magic outlines his skull, his hazel eyes wide. "Are you alright?"

I touch my nose, blood frozen on my gloves. "Aye. It's nothing," I reply and try to wipe away the blood.

Brennus looks Louarn over, worry knotting his brow before it releases. "Where are Lyall and the others?" he asks as his owl circles overhead.

"She's holding off the Failinis by the barracks and sent us to find you," Louarn tells him.

"Percy's near," I say, struggling to catch my breath. A few more deaths brush against me. My eyes dart around, looking for any sign of MacAdoh.

I look to the prison as two other Failinis rush out, one shooting shards of ice at us. Louarn raises the nearby corpse to take the impact of the attack before Eiric gathers her bloodgift. The air crackles, and lightning streaks from her fingertips through the waterdancer. The owl circles back and swipes at the arm of an earthcarver tearing apart the ground, throwing him off balance. Brennus charges at the Failinis and slams a yellow glowing fist into his chest. The earthcarver drops to the ground unconscious.

"Louarn and Doran, watch the entrance," Brennus says through his billowing breaths and steps into the prison.

The damp smell hits me as my eyes adjust to the dimness. A few torches burn from sconces. Four cells take up half of the room across from a table where the guards had been playing cards. Brennus grabs the keys hanging on a hook. In the shadowy corners, there are a few prisoners huddled under threadbare blankets, their hollow eyes watching us. The smell of stale sweat, tallow, and piss hits me through the smoke and blood hanging in the wind. I don't see Percy, but the ring pulses with each beat of my heart.

Gripping the axe, I go for the stairs leading to the lower level of the prison. Heavy and rattling breaths come from the rows of cells, and human shapes are visible in the dim. Keys jangle as Brennus begins unlocking cells, light dancing across the walls from a ball of lightning crackling in Eiric's hand. The sounds of fighting outside are muffled underground, dust falling from the ceiling as the ground shakes.

"Some of these people aren't our scouts," Eiric says.

"Might as well free them all," Brennus replies.

"Percy?" I call, peering through the bars. Brennus and Eiric come down the stairs behind me. My ring feels like it's ready to fly off my finger to seek him out. I go to call out again, but the sound dies as it leaves my lips.

Beyond the bars of the last cell, a man sits huddled against the wall, shivering. His hair is greasy, his chained hands bloody and caked in dirt. My lungs can't take in enough air as I recognize Percy's battered face. He's always been like a sunflower that bends but never breaks. To see him broken takes away what little strength I have left. His brown overcoat is torn and stained with dark splotches.

"Percy! Percy!" I grip the bars, willing them to break. "Brennus! He's here!"

Brennus jams the key into the lock. Each second is agonizing until I hear the metallic click. I push the door open and stumble in, falling to my knees. I shake Percy's thin shoulders. His heart is still beating, but his eyes are closed. The pulse in my ring has calmed down, finally reunited with the other.

"Percy, can you hear me?"

His eyelids flutter, and the familiar brown eyes so full of life stare blankly at me. His glasses are gone. A dark gash cuts across his right cheek. Percy's eyebrows crease as he squints, and a shaky breath spills from my lips. He presses himself against the cell wall. His hands are clutched to his chest and are ice cold.

"Morana? What's happening?" His raspy voice scrapes my insides raw. The shackles around his wrists rattle as Brennus unlocks them, and they clatter to the ground. "No...This can't be real. I saw the avalanche. The giant."

"I'm here, mo ghràdh. We're going to get you out," I whisper and hold his stubbly face, my thumb brushing over a dark cut on his chin. "There's a group of bloodgifted out there fighting the Failinis. They're holding them off until we can get you and the prisoners out."

Percy flinches but touches my cheek. "Your face...Are you hurt?" A sob frees itself from my chest, warm droplets hitting my arms. The last two fingers on his right hand are gone, now red, cauterized stumps.

"It's nothing. I used too much of my bloodgift," I tell him. My sorrow and anger writhe into a thorny bush that crawls up my throat. Sadness and relief seep from the bruises on his face as tears cut through the grime.

"Our baby...?" His broken words tumble out, and he looks at my stomach, which isn't as round as it had been. Panic creases his face. "What happened?"

I brush some of the dirt from his face. "She came early but is a bonnie lass as perfect as can be. She's waiting to meet you," I tell him, voice cracking.

He bows his head. I grip his hands, the bones too close to his skin. I kiss him and feel the dried scabs along his lips. His skin is feverish and sweat dampens his temples despite the cold room. In all the years I've known Percy, I've never seen him get sick. The Failinis have weakened him so much that he can't even heal himself.

Brennus looks Percy over, mouth pursed. He touches Percy's neck, and yellow light spills down his fingertips, but it stops against Percy's skin. "Something's wrong," Brennus says. "I can't use my bloodgift on him."

"What do you mean? Why not?" I ask.

"They did something," Percy pants, shaking. "They fed me

—fed all of us—something that stops us from using our gifts. It was the same color as the brollachan's ichor."

Did Captain MacAdoh manage to collect the black ooze during the fight? If they managed to kill the brollachan, what will that mean for the bloodgifted they capture in the future? Being separated from one's power is an empty feeling, and my heart breaks for Percy even more, knowing he's endured this for weeks.

"Gods. I heard the Failinis used something to stop bloodgifted," Brennus hisses. The feeling of helplessness returns. "I willnae be able to heal him until this passes from his system."

"It wears off after a day," Percy rasps. "They gave us the mixture this morning."

Brennus' jaw tightens. "We dinnae have time to linger here. Eiric, take the others, and signal to Lyall or Magnus that we have our people." The lightningstriker takes the keys and finishes unlocking the remaining cells.

I help Percy stand. He sags against me with a grimace, and I hold him close. I take off my gloves and coat and put them on him. They're too big on Percy, but they'll keep him warm.

"You should've stayed where you were. Stayed safe with our child," Percy mutters as I lead him to the stairs. "I never wanted you to put yourself in danger..."

Percy's face is drawn, his hand clutching his side. His eyes are like over-steeped tea, the depths too dark to see through. Percy's never sunk into despair for long, but I fear that the Failinis have broken his spirit.

"I wasn't going to leave you behind, Percy," I tell him. "You have to meet your daughter."

Percy's head sags against his chest, ragged inhales

making his shoulders quiver. A cough forces him to stop. His legs are shaking as we take the steps slowly. I pick him up in my arms. His added weight makes my knees and joints ache, but that pain is nothing I can't bear.

"Morana! I can walk," he says, gripping my arms.

"You're in no state to walk," I reply. "I raised a titan while pregnant, so let me carry you as far as I can."

A ghostly smile hovers on his lips, his arms wrapped around my neck. I see the flicker of light return to his eyes. "I guess I can't tell you no, Mor."

Louarn looks at us as we reach the door. The Failinis' corpse stands beside him with ice spears still embedded in his chest, eyes glowing purple. The smell of smoke is thicker, and flames burn in the distance. "Doran and Mhairi have taken some of the freed bloodgifted toward the forest. Lyall's making sure our people make it out. Magnus has been telling those who can to retreat," he says. "Is this your husband? I've heard so much about you—"

"Not now, Louarn," Brennus tells him and ushers the remaining prisoners outside. "Morana, head for the woods. Louarn, go with them. Eiric and I will bring up the rear."

I hold Percy tighter and head toward the gaping hole in the fort's wall. Dead and wounded litter the ground. We're almost there. We're almost free. We're going to see our daughter again.

A keening sound sails overhead, and a ball of fire explodes in front of us, cutting off our escape. Louarn skids to a halt, Brennus cursing behind me. Flames erupt in the gap, catching two prisoners trying to flee. Their screams mix with the howling winds. The inferno blasts against my face while the smell of burning flesh clogs my nose. My throat tightens as their deaths find me in the flakes of falling ash, the desire to reach for their bones clashing with the horror burning my throat.

From the smoke and flames, Captain MacAdoh emerges, and I step back. "So, you *are* alive," he says, his blade-like grin making me shudder. "Now I can pay you back for bringing the mountain down on us."

Once again, he stands between us and freedom, of a chance of safety. My fear screams at me to run, but my legs won't move. Behind us, a serpentine form bursts from the snow and encircles us. The fog and snow are blasted away to reveal a waterdancer standing on a still-standing section of the wall. Louarn readies his weapons, and purple light burns brighter around his skull as he reaches for the animal bones buried underground. The titan's bones are several yards away, but it might kill me if I try calling them.

Percy slips from my arms and stands beside me. His legs shake, barely able to support his weight, and the fear on his hollow face spreads to me. I hand Percy the axe. I don't know how much good that it'll do, but it'll give him a fighting chance.

"Morana," Percy says. The tremble in his voice makes my heart twist. "I—"

"I'm not going to lose you again. We're going to make it out and see our child," I say. The purple outline of my skull reflects in Percy's eyes as I let my bloodgift flood my veins.

Captain MacAdoh ignites his hands and advances while the snow serpent prepares to attack. "We'll draw their attacks and create an opening so you can escape," Brennus whispers, his eyes darting around. "Louarn, stay with them as best you can. And don't get killed."

"I'll try not to," Louarn tells him.

Louarn and I bring skeletal horses, bears, wolves, and whatever else we can raise up through the frozen ground. The rattling whispers overlap with the titan's. The ground churns and snaps the frozen serpent in half. Lyall sprints toward us with a few remaining bloodgifted. Eiric shoots a bolt of lightning at the waterdancer, knocking them back before they can reform the construct.

Heat melts the snow as MacAdoh rushes at me. Louarn and I throw up a wall of bones and send sharpened antlers shooting at him. The flames blacken the bones and stings my skin as a blast surges for us. I try to keep the barrier up, but I feel it snapping. Captain MacAdoh braces against the skeletal wall, smoke rising as the bones crack. His teeth are gritted, sweat slick across his twisted face. Fire bursts around our bone shield like orange claws.

"Morana!" Percy yanks me back.

The flames blacken the spot where we had been. Louarn shouts as he rolls away, putting out the parts of his clothes that are on fire. My power wavers, nearly slipping out of my fingers. Sections of brittle bone fall away under MacAdoh's relentless blast. No matter how many bones Louarn and I add. It's not enough. The three of us press closer together as the fire entraps us in a writhing inferno. The air grows thin, and I can smell my clothes starting to singe. Brennus yells for Louarn on the other side of the flames.

Rolling to his feet, Louarn hurls three of his bone knives toward the Captain as he readies another attack. The flames shift and burn up two of the blades, but one manages to slice through his arm, causing the fire around us to die down for a moment. I send chunks of blackened bone flying at the Failinis, but he recovers and turns them to ash.

The future slips through my glowing fingers. I stare at Percy as he coughs against the smoke, drenched in sweat. I'll protect him with my last breath. This can't be the end.

A mound of earth slams MacAdoh back into the broken fort wall. Lyall and Eiric are holding off the waterdancer as three more Failinis rush to attack. "Go!" the earthcarver screams.

"I'll cover your escape," Louarn tells us.

"What about you all?" I ask.

Louarn flashes a smile despite the soot and small burn marks on his face. "We'll be fine."

Looking around the ruined inside of the fort, I realize that the six of us are the only ones left. Everyone else has escaped, and four lie dead. The remaining Failinis have us outnumbered. A loud cawing sound fills the air as a swarm of black crows swoop down from the sky. Brennus' bloodgift rolls off him as he sends birds at the other Failinis. I grab Percy's hand and turn toward the gate where the titan's bones are.

Orange fills the corner of my eye as Captain MacAdoh readies a blast of fire. It streaks toward us, and I reach for one of the titan's bones. I hurl it through the ball of flames at MacAdoh while Louarn blocks the rest of the fire with several corpses and bone shields. I stumble as blood flows from my nose, and the bone crashes to the ground. Louarn moves to strike the Captain as he dodges my attack, but the Failinis sweeps his leg, and flames shoot out toward the boneweaver, pushing him back. He tries to land a blow, but the Captain is stronger and more skilled than him.

I lick the blood from my cracked lips. The ancient's voice wrapping around my skeleton like a vice. It's desperate to be written down, stealing my strength to sustain itself. My body is heavy, but we have to keep moving.

Percy's hands go to my face, staring at his fingers as if hoping his magic would be back, but his veins remain unlit, and frustration darkens his face. "You can't use your power anymore. It could kill you," he says, trying to keep me steady.

The howling of wolves grows closer, and the sounds of fighting continue around us. "I..." I rasp, my eyes going to the gate.

Percy's hands are yanked away from my face. His scream makes me whirl around as he's dragged back by a whip of flames wrapped around his ankle. "No!" I grab his arm again, heels digging into the hard ground.

My muscles strain, and Percy's face contorts with pain as the flames eat away at his trouser leg. I drag up a boar skeleton and wrap its bones around the flamekindler's whip until it snaps.

"Just go!" Percy shouts, struggling to stand.

I kick snow over the devouring tongues eating away at his skin and clothes until they die with a hiss. "I'm not leaving you!" I say.

More bones gather around us, each new voice making my body heavier until my body is ready to come undone at the seams. My veins burn, and I taste blood. I have to get Percy out of here. Bones crack, and the scent of char thickens as Captain MacAdoh steps through the crumbling shield in a swirl of ash and snow. Heat radiates off him, and icy fear rushes down my spine. I can't see Louarn through the smoke stinging my eyes.

"Did you really think you could get away?" MacAdoh sneers, advancing toward us.

I grab the fallen axe, standing in front of Percy. There's nowhere else left to run. Each breath is like inhaling ice shards. More whispers crawl into my mind. The dead latch onto me, and if I keep calling them, there won't be anything of myself left to give them.

"You could have left us alone!" I shout. "I wasn't hurting anyone!"

"Boneweavers always end up hurting someone. The barrow. The titan. Your existence is a stain," the Failinis says. "Your kind is only good dead or serving the Regency."

The Captain's blue eyes melt into orange disks as he rushes at me, fire shooting from his hands. I scream, and four skeletons slash through the flames while yellowed jaws clamp around the Captain's ankles. As the fire weakens, I charge at him with the axe raised and anger tearing from my throat in a yell. I hurl loose bones at him, my veins filling with icy heat as I channel more of my gift.

MacAdoh's eyes widen as he burns the skulls at his feet to blackened husks. He throws his hands up, and the bones stop. The axe freezes mid-swing, my knuckles white around the handle. The Failinis struggles to keep them from his face, the purple outline of his skull visible. Beneath the hot rage of his gift, there's the cool thread that connects with my own power.

"You're...a boneweaver?" I breathe. That's why his blood felt familiar and how he could sense what I was. He's doublegifted, but his boneweaver nature has been stifled so much by his flamekindler side that it barely nudges my senses.

Captain MacAdoh's face twists as the two magics flicker behind his eyes. "I gave up that part of myself long ago," he seethes and gathers another burst of flame in his other hand.

I slam the bones into him as he lets the flames loose, the edges burning my arm. Sharp pieces pierce his sides and arms. Before he hits the ground, a large hand of bones breaks through the earth and grabs his legs. I feel his femurs fracturing as he screams. It rams him into the earth, and he gasps, thrashing against the restraints of skulls, ulnas, and ribs. I stagger to him, ready to bring my axe down into his chest, unable to hear anything beyond the chattering of the bones and the titan's roar. I can end it all here, and his death will be one I long to hear. With him gone, Percy and I have a chance to be safe with our child.

Beneath the burning rage, I see the wounded man's fear breaking through. The blade stops inches from his heart. I know that fear because it's the same one I've felt for months—for years. For all the misery he brought us, he's a boneweaver.

I step back, lowering the axe. "How can you do this to your own kind?" I pant. "You kill and imprison people just like you."

"I'm not like you!" he shouts, spittle and blood landing in his beard. He lets out a guttural cry as he cauterizes his wounds with a glowing hand, smoke rising from the seared flesh.

My anger cools to pity. I don't know what led him to join those who hunt down our kind, but he chose to kill that part of him. I'm sure it was a lonely life, having no other choice but to hate his other bloodgift and be twisted by the Regency. He's no longer a wolf who terrifies me—he's just a broken man. Killing him would make me no better than him.

"No matter how much you tried to hide from your boneweaver nature, you can't hide from what's in your blood. You'll always be one," I mutter.

I move the bones around the Captain to form a cage. Skeletal remains hold him in place. He may be a boneweaver, but he's left his gift to wither and doesn't have the power to get free. He's no longer a threat to my family.

"I'll kill you!" MacAdoh screams, flames spewing from his mouth as he tries to get to his feet, but his injuries make him fall. "I'll find you and tear you apart! There will be nowhere left for you to go!"

I turn away, his curses getting lost in the chaos of swirling winds, the cawing crows, and the snarling wolves lunging at the remaining Failinis. The ashen taste of death draws closer with each raspy breath the Captain takes. I go to Percy as he tries to get to his feet. A sob breaks free, and I haul him up, holding him close.

"Are you hurt?" Percy asks.

"I'm fine," I reply through the fiery pain biting into my arm. "Can you walk?"

"I'll manage. You don't need to carry me," he says.

"Morana!" Louarn rushes over, red burns visible through the ripped fabric on his arms. "Thank the gods you're alive! I blacked out and couldn't find anyone." Drying blood runs down his temple. He looks at MacAdoh, still thrashing against the bones, and goes for a knife.

"Leave him," I tell him. I know the Failinis can sense death approaching. "Where are the others—?"

Brennus breaks through the smoke with Lyall and Eiric

close behind, wide eyes landing on us. Comhachag is a dark spot against the sky as he soars over the trees. He rushes to Louarn, gripping the back of his neck as he takes in his state.

"Gods, I thought they got you," Brennus says.

"I'm alright. I asked them a bunch of questions until they couldn't stand it," Louarn says with a laugh. Brennus lets out a heavy exhale as he presses his forehead against Louarn's.

"We need to move before the Failinis regroup. There are still at least twenty remaining," Lyall says.

Brennus and Louarn take Percy's arms and help him through the broken gate. I cough, tasting iron in my mouth, and my vision starts to blur. Eiric catches me as I stumble. Lyall's power surges through the air, and her hand slams into the ground. Giant cracks break the courtyard, and jagged rocks block the Failinis from following us. I spare one last look over my shoulder as Captain MacAdoh strains against the bone cage. We leave the fighting behind and run to the woods. The rest of the bloodgifted are at the top of the slope.

The snowstorm has died down, but there's a new sound on the wind, a rumbling roar. Churning white cascades down the mountainside toward Dunathol. The avalanche slams into the fort and covers it in thick clouds. Trees groan around us as strong winds rip through them. Tears roll down my face, and I feel several deaths spreading beneath the snow. One crackles with a cold familiarity like a flame being snuffed out, filled with howling rage and sorrow.

XXIII
Elderflower

Sambucus

Rebirth ❦ Transformation ❦ Endings

Steam rises from the cup of tea in my hands, my face a broken reflection across the dark amber surface. I don't know how long I've been staring into the depths or when Percy brought it to me. My eyelids crack as I blink and focus on the scattered papers and dusty wood shavings on the top of the desk. Small reminders keep appearing around the bothy, tucked into corners and forgotten where they were left before I lost my baby.

My neck creaks as I look out the window. The gray rain melts the garden behind the glass. The months have slipped past me in a soupy mess I struggle to wade through. Most days I don't feel like I know who I am, like I'm living in the body of a stranger. Somewhere past the garden walls, a tiny dream is buried beneath a willow tree far beyond where I can sense the bones.

Through the hazy drizzle, a purple teardrop catches my eye. It stands out against the white snow melting on the ground. My knees pop as I shuffle to the back door and pull my brown tonnag closer. Cool air hits my face, the warmth of the stove at my back. The fresh air fills my lungs. The wind helps to blow away the heavy cobwebs cluttering my mind. I'd forgotten the smell of the garden.

Icy rain hits my face as I step outside. The chickens cluck at me in their coop, and Siobhen peers through the slats.

Poking up through the snow is a cluster of purple crocuses with yellow centers. I bend down despite the soreness in my legs and run a finger along the purple petals. Arianrhod is the god of death, but she's also the god of cycles and rebirth. From death comes life, she and Beathag turning the seasons between each other. Even though the rain is still falling, and the hollow ache inside hasn't shrunk, I feel the clouds parting. The thought of tomorrow doesn't fill me with dread as much as it did yesterday.

"Morana, what are you doing out here in the rain?"

I turn and find Percy standing behind me, raindrops rolling down his glasses. "Just looking at the flowers," I say. "Spring's coming."

Percy gives me a small smile, something like relief swelling in his brown eyes. I haven't been able to see their color in a while through my tears and downcast gaze. "So it is," he says, taking my hand. "Let's go back inside before we catch colds."

Droplets hit my face as I look up. I stand, and we walk back to the bothy. I remove my shawl and hang it by the stove to dry. Water drips from my skirts onto the floor, and I shiver.

"What are you thinking about?" Percy asks, taking off his coat.

"I was thinking that it'll be time to clear the leaves from the walkway soon and that the desk needs to be cleaned up," I tell him.

He tugs on his earlobe. "I've let things get dusty, haven't I? It's been hard to keep up with the little things."

"I'm sorry, Percy," I mutter as my dress clings to me. "You've done everything for me for months while I..."

Percy brushes locks of wet hair out of my face. "You were grieving—you still are. This hasn't been easy for either of us. We've both been trying to survive this sorrow as best we can..."

"But I wasn't there for you," I tell him. "I was too wrapped up with how much I was hurting that I didn't help you. I wanted to grieve alone and shut you out."

His palms are warm against my cheeks. "All I wanted was for you to remain here. It was hard not being able to help you. And it hurt that you didn't seem to want me close, but I kept praying that you'd come back to me and here you are."

My shoulders slump. I think about crawling back into bed and burying myself under the covers until my shame fades. I'd often hear Percy crying in the other room while I sat in the bedroom, knowing that he blamed himself for losing our child as much as I did, but I couldn't muster the strength to go to him. I had no soothing words for him.

"Do you remember those days when you did get up, and you'd make supper without saying a word?" he goes on. "I know that was difficult for you, but you did it, and it was usually my favorite foods. There were some nights I'd come in here and find that you had left hot water for me or a cup of tea. You were trying in your own way to be there for me."

I have a few hazy recollections of cooking or setting out tea, but I hardly spoke to him, and I should have even when I couldn't find the words. I wrap my arms around him like he's done for me for so many months even when I couldn't stand to be touched. His head rests against my chest, his breath warm against my wet clothes.

"What do we do now?" I ask, listening to the rain tapping against the window.

"I don't know. Probably get out of these wet clothes, eat something, and think about tomorrow," he replies with a sigh and holds onto me.

"I think I'll make some shortbread." It seems like such a small thing, but it's something. We'll rebuild, piece by piece. It probably

won't look like the life we imagined. But whatever tomorrow looks like, I hope I'll face it with Percy.

PERCY LAYS ON THE COT IN THE HEALING HOUSE, HIS SKIN PALE AND the sweat still a sheen across his forehead. Shadows dance across his bruised face. I've been sitting at his bedside for hours, nursing our daughter and writing to quiet the voices in my head. My body aches, and my veins are hollowed out from overusing my bloodgift, but I'm whole for the first time in weeks with my family around me.

Once the brollachan ichor left Percy's system, Brennus was able to start healing the burns and his fever. The stub of his fingers is the only wound he can't fix. We traveled back to the village looking over our shoulders for the Failinis that never appeared and mourning the four bloodgifted who died in the battle. Percy hardly said anything the entire journey. Even when we got to the village, and he held our daughter for the first time, all he did was cry. The hollowness in his eyes makes me afraid that the Failinis took more from him than his fingers.

Ula moves on the other side of the curtain dividing Percy from a man named Robert, one of the scouts rescued. In the light of the crackling fire, I can see that my daughter and Percy have the same face when they sleep—a brow that always seems creased in thought and the same round lips. Percy was eager to see her despite being so feverish and exhausted. Seeing him holding her pushed all my emotions into my ribcage to the point where it was hard to breathe.

The door opens, and the cold wind seeps Guennéan in. Morhenna is tucked under her arm. "Still up, I see," she says quietly as she comes over. Her eyes go to the new journal in my lap, and she sets Morhenna down. "I thought you might want your chicken to keep you company."

"I'm almost done and will move on to the others," I tell her, leaning back against the wall. "I wanted to be here when Percy wakes up again."

Morhenna comes over and tucks herself beside Percy's head. She doesn't cluck at me for being so close to him. Seems we've reached an agreement for now.

"You should get some rest, too, after all you've done."

Even despite my exhaustion from our return yesterday, I dreamed about Dunathol's broken walls, MacAdoh's fearful face, and the avalanche burying the fort and the Failinis. People were lost rescuing Percy and the others, and I worry about how destroying the fort will affect the village.

"Do you think the Failinis will come and find this place once others find out what happens?" I ask.

"It's a possibility, but we knew the risks when we allowed you all to go," she tells me. "If they come for us, we'll be ready. We aren't the only sanctuary for bloodgifted that exists."

"Thank you...for everything," I tell her. "Without you all, I wouldn't have gotten Percy back. Our family wouldn't be here."

"I'm happy you both are reunited and that you all made it back safely." Guennéan cracks a smile. "What will you do now?"

"I'm not sure. Percy still needs rest, and our child is still too young to travel during the winter. We owe you all much, but I don't think Errigal is safe for us at the moment."

"There's no need to decide anything today." The boneweaver peers down at my child. "Have you finally thought of a name?"

I close my blouse as my baby finishes nursing, her eyes opening as she wriggles. She starts to fuss, and I set the journal aside to rest her against my shoulder. "I think I have one," I say, glancing up as Brennus' hulking frame appears from the kitchen.

The fleshmender checks on Percy again, crouching down and touching a glowing finger to his wrist. Soft yellow light seeps beneath Percy's skin and returns more color to his face. There are bags under Brennus' eyes, and I've seen the same ones under Percy's eyes before when he's used too much of his gift to heal people. The healing house is filled with the freed prisoners and the injured villagers Ula and Rowenna have been helping to treat.

Brennus stands. "I'll be back in a few hours to check on him," he says.

"Thank you, Brennus," I tell him. "I know you thought going to rescue Percy was a risk, but I'm forever grateful for what you did for us—what you've done for Percy."

He nods, his gaze dropping to the floor. "It was nothing. Louarn would have never let me hear the end of it if I didnae go," he mutters.

Guennéan slips her arm through Brennus'. "I told you—face of a bear but a soft heart." Brennus frowns as she winks at him. "Help me prepare a cup of tea. The cold's settled in my bones."

The two of them head back into the kitchen, leaving me with Percy's breathing. It's surreal to have him back, and I'm afraid I'll wake from this dream at a moment. I take Percy's uninjured hand, soaking in the warmth of his palm.

He stirs, unfocused eyes opening. "I didn't mean to wake you," I whisper.

"I feel like I've been sleeping for years," he says, shifting onto his side to face me. "I had the strangest dream that I saw you raise a dead titan, that I was captured, and then we escaped, along with some unpleasant things." He touches our daughter's head, eyes growing misty.

I push the hair out of his face and scoot closer. "It happened, but you're here now. We're safe from the Failinis. They won't find us here."

Percy's eyes drift around, and his head bumps Morhenna, who doesn't budge. "With Henna keeping guard, I don't doubt it." The chicken warbles as he strokes her speckled chest. "How are you feeling?"

"Tired and sore, but that's nothing new," I tell him.

His fingers tighten around my hand as he looks at the darkened veins. "You should get some sleep, Mor."

Setting the journal aside, I set our daughter next to him. He moves to make room for me on the cot, and I slip under the blanket, pressing against him while our child lays nestled between us. Even though he's thinner now, his shape still fits against me. Percy stares at our daughter as her small fingers flex, feet kicking the blanket swaddling her. Her fingers wrap around his thumb, and his crooked smile appears.

"She's perfect. I think she has your nose," he whispers. A tear escapes and falls on his pillow.

"Really? She looks like you when you sleep," I reply and run my fingers through his hair.

"I'm sure you must have been scared doing this on your own. I'm sorry I wasn't here..."

I kiss Percy's forehead as his voice cracks. "I was, but Brennus and Rowenna made sure everything went well. She was so tiny I didn't think she was real."

Our conversation quiets as we stare at our child. When she falls asleep, Percy doesn't look away from her. Sadness and happiness swirl around in his eyes. He shifts and holds his injured hand close to his chest.

"Does it hurt?" I ask and look at his missing fingers.

"Not anymore. My body remembers what was there even though I know the fingers are gone," Percy murmurs. "I worked with patients at the Acadamaidh who could still feel their missing limbs. I can use this opportunity to continue my studies about limb regeneration."

"Please don't experiment on yourself. I don't want you to lose any more fingers," I tell him.

"I won't. I want to have at least most of a hand for our daughter to hold."

There's pain under his words, a silent struggle. The Failinis took so much from us and have now left behind something even more painful than a scar—something only time will be able to heal.

I take his right hand and kiss his knuckles. "We're together again," I say. "That should give you some *peas* of mind."

Percy stares at me, eyes widening. "Did you, my wife, make a *pun*?" he asks.

The corners of my mouth lift. "It's only another dream, mo ghràdh."

"If that's the case, then this is one I don't want to wake from."

His mouth finds mine, tender with traces of chamomile tea and honey. I cup his cheek, not wanting him to pull away.

"I finally know what to name our baby," I tell him. "Heather Anstice Bracken."

"I think that's a perfect name," he says. "You even chose a plant name."

"It suited her."

The words settle over her like a prayer. I watch Percy until he slips back into sleep. Even though this isn't where I imagined we'd be, huddled on a cot in a village hidden in the mountains, I cling to this moment, letting it warm every part of me.

THE BONFIRES BLAZE AGAINST THE NIGHT, ORANGE SHADOWS dancing across the snow. People twist around the sparks and move with the sound of bagpipes and the fiddles through the center of the village. Meat roasts on spits, and a waterdancer stirs a cauldron of soup that smells like cream and spices.

The Festival of Arianrhod happens at the beginning of the new year to celebrate the ending and beginning of another cycle. Here in Lòchran, the boneweavers join in the celebrations by creating a winged sculpture of the goddess made of bones draped in feathers and bolts of purple fabric. They also tell stories of the dead around the fires.

I sip the hot cider on a bench at the edge of the celebrations, stomach full and Heather bundled against my chest. This is her first festival, and her eyes swim with the lights dancing through the air. She's grown so much, and two months have flown by faster than I'd like them to. By the time I go to write Ma another letter, my daughter might be walking. I tried to tell her everything that's happened since we left Teaghlach, but I worried it'd be too heavy for the messenger ravens to carry.

Percy talks with Iseabail and Beitris by a large tree with colored ropes hanging from its branches. Morhenna huddles close to his leg. He's slipped right into the fabric of this place like he's been here for years even though it's only been a few months. When he was well enough, he started working with the council members and some other rootsowers to regrow the bloodleaf and study its effects. Brennus even lets him work at the healing house. Watching excitement return to his eyes and seeing him smile again makes my heart swell.

Guennéan sits next to me, bundled up in thick furs with her silver hair pinned up in braids. Her eyes drift over the laughing villagers. "Too much excitement?" she asks. "Or are your knees giving you trouble again?"

"Knees. And feet. And hips. Mostly everything today," I say as I shift on the bench. The cold makes my arthritis worse despite Percy's efforts to dull the pain.

She lets out a raspy laugh. "That's another thing you and I have in common."

My gaze goes to Louarn and Brennus getting food on the other side of the bonfires. Outside of Teaghlach, I couldn't imagine finding another place to call home, to be somewhere I don't have to hide. And Tearmann will hopefully be that place too, someday.

"The Festival of Arianrhod on Tearmann is a beautiful

sight. The different towns there get together and throw a massive celebration in the capital city," Guennéan tells me. "I've been lucky enough to visit it a few times to make sure the boneweavers who made it there were settling in well, and every time it's something to behold. Seeing so many of our kin using their bloodgifts freely...It's a feeling unlike any other."

"Are the towns there like Lòchran?" I ask and fix the cap on Heather's head.

"Some are similar. The island is run by a council like Lòchran is," Guennéan says. "Someday, with more sanctuaries like this, the world will be able to see that boneweavers aren't dangerous and that peace is achievable when all bloodgifted are allowed to live together without fear."

Here, I can believe such a dream is possible. How long will it take for the rest of Errigal and the Regency to accept boneweavers? I touch the pendant of Arianrhod, the titan's bone filling me with warm power. Captain MacAdoh's defeated face no longer fills me with fear, only pity for the man he became. In the end, he couldn't escape being a boneweaver, no matter how much he tried to burn that part of himself away.

Percy breaks away from the council members and comes over to us. His nose is red, and despite his smile, I can tell he's shivering beneath all the layers of clothing. I open my arms and let him under my shawl, rubbing his shoulders. He nestles close to me and kisses Heather's nose. She giggles and has a gummy smile on her face. Morhenna doesn't attack me when she sees us so close together, but I can tell by her beady-eyed stare that she's not happy with it.

"Is there any way to convince the flamekindlers to make the fires hotter?" Percy asks.

"I suppose there's always whisky," I tell him. "Or we can go back to the tavern where it's warmer."

Percy's grin widens. "I never thought you'd be so forward and ask me back to your room, Morana."

I roll my eyes and finish the rest of my cider. "Glad to see your sense of humor is still intact."

"The Failinis weren't able to take that from me," he says with a dry laugh.

Most of the physical injuries from our fight with MacAdoh are gone, but the shadows of his ordeal remain. His smile's hidden more, his eyes darker as he stares off in the distance. The two missing fingers are permanent reminders. His nighttime mutterings are broken nightmares, and all I can do is hold him until he calms.

Even though we could make a home here, Tearmann will offer us a place to heal from the memories that scar us. Too much hurt lingers in Errigal and even though MacAdoh is dead, his shadow haunts my dreams. Once the mountain passes are clear, we'll leave to start a new life. It's an exciting and saddening thought, and a piece of me longs to stay.

Guennéan gets up and takes my empty flagon from me. "Young love. Such a beautiful thing," she says, green eyes glittering as she winks. "I'll get you a refill, Morana."

Her boots crunch through the snow as she goes to the tavern. "You look excited about something," I say to Percy.

He pushes up his glasses and holds the pouch of bloodleaf that's now not as full. "I've figured it out. Well, Beitris and her rootsowers also helped. We figured out how to replicate the bloodleaf and grew some seeds. With the hothouses they have here, I'm sure they'll be able to get it to grow."

My eyes widen. "That's exciting!"

"It is. They still want to keep this quiet as much as possible, but if they can grow it here, then this could help so many bloodgifted that are trying to escape the Failinis. With further study, it could even be used as a medicine." The baby pulls on the drawstring. "These seeds will be for us. I want to grow some when we get to Tearmann."

I brush away snowflakes that gather in Percy's hair. "Are they worried about the Failinis discovering its existence?"

"Yes, but if we can uncover its secrets, we might be able to come up with an antidote to its effects," he says, and his breath clouds around my face. "Iseabail and Beitris have sent word ahead to Tearmann, so I can begin healing again once we get settled. They gave me a list of people to talk to on the island who can help me with my research."

I take his hand, and we head toward the tavern. People wave as we pass, raising their drinks to us. Eiric is sitting around a bonfire with Lyall and Magnus, her laugh booming.

"Iseabail was telling me about the plants they have there and this part of the island where rootsowers have gathered almost every plant from Errigal and Tìr Dhè," Percy goes on while keeping a section of my shawl wrapped around himself. "That alone will be worth the trip."

"It's good to see you so excited again, but isn't making a new life for your family enough of a reason to go?" I say.

He leans up to kiss my jaw. "You know what I meant, mo ghràdh. Anything on the island won't compare to your smile or our daughter."

Louarn spots us and drags Brennus away from one of the

bonfires. "Morana! Percy!" he shouts, stumbling through the snow. His cheeks are red. "Are you leavin'?"

"It's getting late, and unfortunately, it's only going to get colder," Percy says.

The smell of whisky rolls off the boneweaver. "I'm goin' to miss you so much," Louarn says and wraps his arms around us, careful not to crush Heather. "I'm happy, but sad. Do you know if there's a word for that? Why aren't you in here, Brennus?"

Louarn grabs Brennus' arm and pulls him close so that he bumps against me. "Why are you trying to say goodbye now?" Brennus asks, steadying Louarn. "You're going with them to the Chaill Harbor in a few weeks."

"I know...but I want them to know how much I'll miss them." Louarn tightens his embrace.

Brennus sighs, giving me an apologetic look as he untangles Louarn from us. The boneweaver is humming a song. "He had one too many drinks. He'll be fine in the morning," he tells us. "When he says his real goodbye, dinnae be surprised if he breaks down crying."

We follow the trail of sunken footprints in the snow toward the tavern where Guennéan is talking with another council member. Thoughts of the weeks to come and all the goodbyes we'll have to make don't rest so heavily on my shoulders, and there's a lightness in my bones that surpasses all my aches, and the wounds still left on my heart. I squeeze Percy's hand, his missing fingers a reminder of what's been lost and the healing ahead of us.

The boat cuts through the waters of Loch Sùil, a speck in Errigal's left eye. Louarn rows the boat and the older waterdancer, Omaos, parting the icy waters. Brennus and Guennéan sit across from me and Percy. They made the last five days of traveling less painful—especially Brennus, who hadn't planned on coming with us until Louarn convinced him to. I pull my shawl closer against the cold spring air, looking for signs of kelpies or the green and yellow scales of another oillipheist beneath the gray waters. The serpents prefer fish, but the one I saw gliding under the boat the other day was larger than a tree. It's hard to be comfortable around something that could easily capsize us.

Percy rubs the stubs on his hand as the boat slices through the water, holding Heather in his arms. Morhenna is tucked between our legs. His gaze rests on our baby, but it's unfocused. The last few days, he's been strangely quiet.

Percy catches me staring and smiles. "Did you ever think we'd get to this point, Mor?" he asks.

"I didn't. I certainly didn't think Morhenna would survive," I reply, shifting against the hull digging into my back. The chicken lifts her head at the sound of her name before preening her wing. "Maybe she has some divine protection after all."

"I thought if anyone was going to survive, it'd be Henna." Percy wipes away a spit bubble from Heather's mouth. "This all will be an interesting story to look back on. Percival the Healer and Morana the Titan Raiser."

I tilt my head. "Where did you hear that? No one's called me that." At least not to my face.

"I think it has a nice ring to it. Don't you think so, Louarn?"

The shaggy-haired boneweaver looks up. "I've heard a few people call you that," he tells us.

"Did you tell them to call me that?" I ask, cheeks warming. "Don't you dare make up a song about me. I didn't do anything worth singing about."

"It might be good to have some new songs about boneweavers," Guennéan says with a grin. "Ones that sing our praises rather than spread fear."

"I think there are worse things than being immortalized in song, mo ghràdh," Percy says as water mists the outside of his dark coat.

Fog shifts, and the mountains ahead of us shimmer to reveal four massive slitted eye sockets. An illusion put up by lightcasters. It's only part of a round skull resting between the mountains, its lower jaw missing, but its sheer size blots out the weak sun. My blood's humming even though we're miles away.

"Amazing, isn't it?' Louarn says, grinning as we all stare at the skull. "Liùsaidh's skull, one of the few remains of the gods in Errigal. It hides the harbor from anyone who isnae a lightcaster or a boneweaver."

A bone of the gods. The skull speaks in a similar voice as the titan, but with a tone much older—the flashes of memories much more brilliant. Stars are sprinkled into the sky, and daylight is unraveled as four shimmering wings brush the heavens. Liùsaidh's echoes are too much to bear compared to the titans. The skull's shadow swallows us as we near the harbor of the Chaill Firth. The fog stops at the stone gates surrounding the mouth of the loch. Light streams through a hole punched through the bone, turning the waters blue. Houses are built along the inside of the skull with swaying bridges connecting them.

"The Failinis don't come this way because there are so few settlements. As far as they know, this is the edge of the world, and nothing exists beyond the Wailing Sea. Perfect place for a hidden port," Guennéan says.

Omaos brings the boat in. The waters reflect in his blue-gray eyes, his white hair like the foamy waves that crest in the distance. People on the docks toss ropes to him and Louarn. The bobbing waters make it hard to stand. Brennus helps Guennéan climb out, and I follow Percy and Morhenna. Beneath our feet, the docks creak, and the damp tang of the salty air fills my nose. People move around us, carrying cargo and scurrying to other boats. Through the thrum of the bloodgifted filling this harbor, I sense a few cool threads belonging to boneweavers. This place almost rivals Auchendrain's sprawl—and all of it hidden from the eyes of the Failinis.

I look back at the inlet we sailed through as the highlands sleep against the horizon under a blanket of snow. The rest of Errigal is barely visible through the mists, but I can see Teaghlach and Ma's house, Neòinean with Anstice's bakery, and Àitesìol where our garden used to be. Every rolling hill, heather field, and river is imprinted on me. All the months and miles we traveled led to this moment, and I can't shake the sadness beneath the excitement, feeling like that scared fifteen-year-old girl who left home on her own so many years ago.

"The ship's this way," Louarn says. He and Brennus grab our packs from the boat. Morhenna lands on the dock and ruffles her speckled feathers.

Percy takes my hand, and we follow Louarn. The churning waves knock against the ships anchored in the harbor. I've never seen the ocean before or been on a ship. I lick salty droplets from my lips, taking in a deep breath as tears mix with the sea air. Somewhere out there is Tearmann Island. Once we get there, I can add it to the map Percy gave me.

Louarn takes us to the end of the harbor where a dark ship with a carved kelpie affixed to its bow is anchored. Its sails flap in the wind, and I crane my neck back to take in its tall masts. At least twenty other people wait by the gangplank while the crew moves across the deck. I've only seen ships in books but have never been on one. From here, it'll be a four-day journey. I've been warned to expect choppy seas and constant swaying.

When Louarn turns back to us with Brennus and Guennéan beside him, there are tears in his eyes. That's all it takes for my throat to tighten. The time for goodbyes has come. I'm glad he came with us, despite all the questions he asked along the way. Louarn sniffs as he hugs me.

"I'm going to miss you," Louarn says. "I wish you were staying in Errigal, but I know you'll love Tearmann. I know I talk a lot and ask a lot of questions, but you're like one of my sisters, Morana." He looks at Heather. "I'm sure she'll be just like you."

I pat Louarn's back. "We won't be gone forever," I tell him. "You'll always be welcome to visit us."

"You took such care of Morana while I was gone and risked your life for us. You'll always have a seat at our table—same with Guennéan and Brennus," Percy says with a smile.

The younger boneweaver claps Percy on the back. "Write

when you can. I'll visit once you find a house—and bring Brennus along too."

"Take care of yourself," I say to Louarn.

"Brennus will make sure I dinnae get into trouble," he replies, giving me another hug. Louarn wipes his eyes and straightens as he pulls away. Brennus places a hand on his shoulder.

Guennéan approaches, the bones on her necklace and in the pouch at her side wrapping me in comforting whispers. Her hands hold mine in a strong grip that belies her age. "In all my years, I never dreamed I'd meet a boneweaver like you. Seeing what you've been capable of gives me hope for the future of our kin," she tells me, and her face is blurry through my tears.

"I feel like I haven't done much compared to what you've given me," I reply. "Saying thank you doesn't seem like it's enough."

"It's our duty to pass on our knowledge. I'm grateful for the chance to pass on some of my knowledge to you. And if your child is a boneweaver, I hope you will do the same." She gestures for me to stoop down. Her breath warms my cheeks as she kisses my face. "Whatever Arianrhod has planned for you, I wish you both the best on the next part of your journey. Live well, Morana, and may the gods bring you safety."

I hear Anstice's voice behind Guennéan's raspy words. "I had a friend who said something similar to me," I tell her.

"Ironic, isn't it? It was a saying boneweavers would tell each other in the olden days. It's meant to remind us that a life well-lived leaves behind the best stories in the bones."

Guennéan swipes at her eyes, sniffling. "Brennus, you've

come all this way just to stand there silently. Best say something before we're all greeting mess."

Brennus shifts on the dock, arms crossed. He releases a sigh. "Morana, when I first met you, I thought your stubbornness would be the death of you. I think you'll be a great mother, and Lòchran willnae be nearly as great without you," he says. "And Percy, you're a skilled healer. It's been an honor to work alongside you these past few months. Tearmann will be lucky to have you."

It's hard to read Brennus' stony features and what he's really thinking, but there's the wisp of a smile beneath his beard. He's a man of few words, but the ones he's chosen to share bring fresh tears to my eyes. Who would have thought Brennus' goodbye would be the one that'd undo me the most? Percy lifts his glasses to dry his eyes.

Brennus gives us a nod and moves closer to Louarn. There's still so much left to say, but I fear if anything else comes out of my mouth, I won't be able to move from the dock. Louarn manages a smile that helps cover the pain of parting.

I imagine for a moment that Anstice stands behind him with her gap-toothed grin. Ma, my brothers, Glenna, Tréasa, and their children would fill most of the crowd. Da is with them, and I can hear him telling me how proud he is.

"Best board your ship before it leaves without you," Guennéan tells us. "Haste ye back."

I taste salt on my smile as I take Percy's hand, taking in one last look at those we're leaving behind. "Ready?" Percy asks me. I nod and dry my face with the sleeve of my coat. "I haven't known Brennus that long, but that goodbye almost made me cry."

As we head for the gangplank, Percy hands Heather to me and picks Morhenna up. Heather smiles up at me. I don't know what future the gods have for us, but I pray it's one with more smiles than tears. One day Heather will know the story of her name, all the sorrow and joy that brought us here. She'll know our love for her and grow up laughing at her father's puns. And if she's a boneweaver like me, I hope she'll see that there can be beauty in death as there is in life.

Epilogue

The yellowed pages of the journal close. A wrinkled hand glides over the etched heather flowers on the wooden cover. Night presses against the window of the cottage.

"That's all for tonight, wee bairns," the old woman says, leaning back in her rocking chair. The last words of the story hum on her lips.

The five children sitting on the cowhide rug by the fire groan. "But what about Great-Nana and Papa making it to Tearmann?" a girl with dark hair asks.

"What about Great-Auntie Anstice? How did she and Great-Nana find each other again after the Failinis got her?" the older boy says and sits up.

A chorus of pleas rises as the children move closer to their grandmother. "You can't stop there, Gran. Please tell us a little more."

She smiles. "All the best stories leave you wanting more, Louarn," she tells her oldest grandson. "I'll tell you the rest tomorrow."

An old man with a beard crouches by the fire to add in another peatbrick. "You all should head home before the sídhe come out and try to nibble on your toes," he says and wiggles his fingers at the youngest children.

They giggle as he scoops up two of the girls. The front door opens, and a woman with chestnut-colored hair steps in with the warm night air. Louarn looks at his mother, sighing and grabbing his shoes from by the hearth. The old man sets down his granddaughters and kisses their heads.

Holding the journal close, the old woman stands, her back cracking. "I was just sending them home, Blair," she tells her daughter.

"What story were you telling them tonight, Ma?" Blair asks, running her fingers through her son's blond hair.

"The one about my parents going to Tearmann."

Blair smiles as the rest of the children hug their grandparents goodbye. "That's one of my favorites," she says.

"She didn't tell us how it ends," Louarn tells her from the doorway.

"She did the same thing when I was a child. The ending is worth it, but you and your cousins need to get to bed, mo chridhe. Tomorrow's a busy day with the Festival of Erroll happening," his mother replies.

Blair waves the children out, and they run down the moonlit path to their house down the hill. The fire flickers and throws orange shadows across the walls of the cottage. She kisses her parents on the cheeks before leaving.

The old woman puts the journal on the table, glancing at the support beam in the middle of the room. She traces the names carved into the wood with the heights of her and her siblings through the years, stopping by markers for her three children. The memories running through her blood flash with familiar images like the well-read pages of a book. Tearmann had been home for seven years until she came back to Errigal, wandering the hills with her grandmother, aunts, uncles, cousins, and herds of cows. Tears collect at the edges of her eyes. The five years since her parents' passing hadn't lessened the ache of loss.

She goes to the front window, pulled by the call of the bones of the barrow past the towering elder tree. Her grandmother's house is a white tooth against the night. Smoke rises from the chimney toward the rest of Teaghlach. She hears her mother's voice telling her about the hills where she walked with the cows, the festivals, and her father telling her about the elder tree marker for the house. The stories she heard growing up lived in her veins, told to her by the voices of the dead.

Her husband, Ramsay, comes up behind her, head resting against hers. "Are you going to sit with them again, Heather?" he asks.

Heather touches the titan bone pendant hanging from her neck. The call buzzes through her fingers as she follows the grooves of Arianrhod's symbol. "Not tonight. Ma would tell me to spend as much time with the living as I can," she replies, taking Ramsay's roughened hand.

Heather kept the memories of her parents close when her grief became too painful. She kept their deaths close as only a boneweaver could, continuing to tell the story of their legacy and love. She passed them on to her children and then to their children to show them the love that still existed even long after death. With each story so told to anyone who would listen, she tried to remove the dark stain hovering over boneweavers.

"Percy and Morana would be proud of you."

"I know. Their bones told me."

"You sound like your mother when you say that," Ramsay

tells her and kisses her cheek, his silver beard tricking her face.

Heather gives him a smile as she looks up at him. “Ma always said that we never truly bury the dead. We always carry a part of them with us.”

The End

Glossary

The Bloodgifted

Beastcharmer: those who can speak with and control animals.
Boneweaver: those who can reanimate the dead.
Earthcarver: those who can move and shape the earth.
Flamekindler: those who can create and manipulate fire.
Fleshmender: those who can heal and create flesh.
Lightcaster: those who can create light.
Lightningstriker: those who can summon and direct lightning.
Rootsower: those who can grow and manipulate plants.
Shadowcatcher: those who can move and create shadows.
Waterdancer: those who can create and manipulate water.
Windsinger: those who can summon and shape the air.

The Gods

Artair (ar•ter): the god of animals and beasts. He takes the form of a huge bear with antlers and moss growing along his fur. He created the beastcharmers.
Arianrhod (ar•i•an•rhod): the goddess of death and omens. She has messengers that go out into the world with her Eyes

to watch and give warning. She guides souls to the Forests of Cadal. She takes the form of a raven with four wings and four eyes. She created the boneweavers.

Beathag (beh•ak): the goddess of life and rebirth. She and Arianrhod balance the world and are the eldest of the pantheon. She takes the form of a rabbit-wolf creature with four eyes. She created the fleshmenders.

Caorthannach (queer•hawn•nock): the goddess of fire. She tends to the fires beneath the earth and keeps its core molten. She created volcanos when she needed to make her way to the surface to cool off. She takes the form of a wingless orange and blue dragon. She created the flamekindlers.

Ciardha (cia•rd•ha): the goddess of shadows and darkness. She brings about the night. She takes the form of a giant cat made of living shadows with four glowing eyes and a tail that is always tethered to darkness. She created the shadowcatchers.

Deòrsa (der•sah): the god of the earth. He shaped the foundations of the earth and raised the mountains. He burrows through the earth to create valleys and caves and to avoid Sorcha's wrath. He takes the form of a badger with four eyes and precious gems encrusted in his fur. He created the earthcarvers.

Erroll (er•roll): the god of the wind. He directs the wind and is constantly weaving its paths through the world. He takes the form of a serpent falcon with eight long tail feathers and four wings. He created the windsingers.

Kester (kehs•ter): god of plants and growth. He brought all plants into being. He and Arianrhod created the Forests of Cadal. He takes the form of a six-legged elk covered in flowers and moss with four sets of antlers that intertwine. He created the rootsowers.

Liùsaidh (lwee•sah): the goddess of light and guidance. She created the sun and stars with Caorthannach and measures out the daylight. She takes the form of a moth with four eyes and glowing constellations on her wings. She created the lightcasters.

Muiredach (mur•dock): the god of the waters and the rains. He controls the waters of the rivers and seas. He takes the form of a horse with white spikes along its spine. He created the waterdancers.

Sorcha (sor•kuh): the goddess of lightning and storms. She controls lightning and can create storms when she fights with Muiredach and Erroll. She and Deòrsa are constantly at odds, and she tries to strike him from the skies. She takes the form of a four-winged serpent. She created the lightningstrikers.

Creatures

Bean nighe (ben nee'•nyeh): a type of female ban-sìth that haunts streams and washes the clothing of those about to die.

Brollachan (brol•lachan): a shapeless darkness that craves bodily form that are said to be the spirits of the morrigans after they lost their bodies.

Cat-sìth (cat•shee): a slender, black spectral cat about the size of a dog with a small white spot on either its belly or near its neck.

Cu-sìth (ku•shee): a spectral hound that roams the highlands.

Kelpies (kel•peez): a shape-shifting spirit that usually takes the form of a horse and inhabits lochs and rivers.

Loireag (lor•yack): a fairy responsible for overseeing the making of cloth through all its stages.
Morrigans: creatures that rebelled against the gods and caused the Darkening by killing some of them.
Oilliphéist (oll•eh•péist): a sea serpent-like monster that inhabits lakes and rivers.
Selkie (sel•kee): a shapeshifter able to change from seal to human by shedding their skin.
Sídhe (shee): fairies.
Titans: ancient beings that were the guardians of the world for the gods until they were killed by the morrigans.
Will-o'-wisps: glowing specters that said to lead people to their deaths if followed.

Foods

Bannock: a flatbread made from grains.
Black bun: a type of fruit cake covered with pastry that typically contains raisins, currants, almonds, citrus peel, allspice, ginger, cinnamon. and black pepper.
Caboc: a type if cheese made with double cream and formed into a log shape and rolled in toasted pinhead oatmeal.
Clapshot: made by the combined mashing of turnips, potatoes, chives, butter or dripping, salt and pepper, and served with haggis, oatcakes, mince, sausages or cold meat.
Cranachan: a dessert with cream and fresh seasonal raspberries, oats, and whisky.
Cock-a-leekie: a soup consisting of leeks and peppered chicken stock, often thickened with rice or sometimes barley.
Damson: a plum-like fruit.

Hairst bree: a harvest soup traditionally made with summer vegetables
Tablet: a confection made from sugar, cream, and butter.
Tattie drottle: a soup made with potatoes that are boiled in milk with leeks or onions.
Tattie scones: a flat bread made from mashed potatoes.

Other

Bairn (behrn): children.
Bampot: idiot.
Barrow: a burial mound.
Blootered: drunk.
Brae: a steep hill or slope.
Bunnet: a flat, brimless hat.
Burn: a small stream.
Byre: a barn, especially one used for keeping cattle in.
Caber: a roughly trimmed tree trunk.
Cairn (kehrn): a mound of rough stones built as a memorial or landmark.
Cèilidh (kay·lee): a social event with music and dancing.
Crabbit: grumpy or agitated.
Croft: a small rented farm comprising a plot of farmable land attached to a house.
Dinnae fash: don't worry.
Failinis (faw·ihn·ish): the organization that hunts boneweavers and enforces the laws of the bloodgifted.
Fàilte (fahl·cheh): welcome.
Fane: a temple or shrine.
Feileadh mòr/fèilidhean mòra (fell·ugh more): a blanket-

like piece of fabric wrapped around the body with the material loosely gathered and secured at the waist by a belt.

Greeting: cry/crying.

Mo chridhe (mo chree·yuh): my heart.

Mo ghràdh (moi rah): my darling.

Quaich (kwayk): a special kind of shallow two-handled drinking cup or bowl

Scran: food.

Sgian dubh (skee·an doo): a dagger.

Skelf: a sliver of wood or a very thin person.

Tonnag (tuh·nuhj): a type of shawl, usually a tartan.

Triskele: a symbol with three connecting spiraling parts.

Triquetra: a triangular figure composed of three interlaced arcs.

Acknowledgments

This was a book that came out of nowhere. Literally. I should have been working on the sequel to my trilogy, but instead I had a random thought about a necromancer woman and her husband and their chicken being on the run. Thus, *Hills of Heather and Bone was born*. This story was my love letter to cottagecore with a dash of dark, but it eventually also became a story about anxiety, grief, and loss. I wrote this book during a season of sorrow and difficulties, which made it mean so much more to me. So, it truly means a lot that you've taken the time to read this book.

There are so many people who helped this book become the thing you hold in your hands. My writers' group (Sara, Shannan, and Tori) helped brainstorm so many things in this book and were some of the first eyes to see it. Their feedback and encouragement meant so much. Also, a special thanks to my Aunt Loureen who has always championed my stories and was one of my first beta readers. A huge thank you goes to my other beta readers: Ember, Tessa, Amber, Emmy, Tori Tecken, Marylin, and Lana.

Once again, Jade Mae Yee has done amazing work bringing this cover to life. I couldn't have imagined Morana and Percy any other way and so thankful to have gotten another beautiful cover from Jade.

A huge shoutout to my copyeditor and proofreader

Maddy, who helped make sure that book was as perfectly edited as it could be (and being another fan of Morhenna).

I also want to thank one of the best Discords around: the Indie Accords. Without them, this novel would have been written much quicker. But seriously, the Discord is full of wonderful people who love Indie books and were so helpful with answering questions and cheering me on.

And of course, a huge thanks to you, reader. Without you, this book would be just an idea on a Word Document. I don't want to write for an audience, but I write in the hopes that this book will find the right person when they need it, even if it's just one person.

WANT TO KNOW WHAT KIND OF BLOODGIFTED YOU ARE?

Take this short quiz to find out what bloodgifted you are.

https://www.buzzfeed.com/redheadwriter95/what-kind-of-bloodgifted-are-you-6i7gtyhh9h?utm_source=dynamic&utm_campaign=bfsharecopy

About the Author

K.E.Andrews has always been an avid reader, which sparked her passion for writing at an early age. Her love of traveling has taken her to different places around the world, reminding her that there are always more stories to tell. She is often found at her desk, attempting to write, binging Netflix, or trying to complete a craft project. She currently lives in Powder Springs, Georgia.

BOOKS BY K.E.ANDREWS

Let the Hurt Girl Speak

The Assassin of Grins and Secrets

Sonder and Morii

Let the Hurt Girl Heal

Priestess of Moonlight

Instagram: @k.e.andrews

Website: www.keandrews.org

Goodreads: K.E.Andrews

Facebook: @k.e.andrewsnovels

Don't forget to leave a review. You can also sign up for my newsletter to learn more about new projects, upcoming books, and more.